Black Fog

Black Fog

V.J. Mack

Edited by Stan St. Clair

StCP

ISBN 978-1-935786-16-0

Printed in the United States of America by
St. Clair Publications
P. O. Box 726
McMinnville, TN 37111-0726
http://stan.stclair.net

Dedication

I would like to dedicate this book to Charlene Freudenthaler; without her, it would not have been written. When I told her all about my dreams for the book she said, "Vivian, honey, don't tell me about it, write it." She is gone now, but I know she is proud of me.

Acknowledgements

I wish to thank Haywood Smith and Catherine Coulter, who both encouraged me to read and write. THANK YOU SO MUCH. I did, and it has finally paid off.

Most of all, I want to thank my children for standing by me all these years of writing. There are no adequate words to say thank you. I love all three of you very much. Linda, Judy, Kay. Thanks again.

Author's Note

As a Child I sat at my Grandfather's knee and listened to his stories about the past, like where the family came from in Scotland. I always dreamed about the family and the old homeland.

Now I can write all about the stories I was told and put myself there in Scotland.

I hope you enjoy reading this book, as I have enjoyed writing it.

Watch for my newest novel about Kimberly and her adventures in China leading up to the surprising ending.

Chapter 1

Sam O'Brian, Editor-in-Chief of the Albany Daily Tribune, was anticipating his forthcoming fishing trip. It would be the first time in years that the sixty-three year old man would be able to loosen the stringent control he held over this newspaper factory. With his thoughts on this expected pleasure, the ash on his fat, black cigar grew steadily longer.

Not paying any attention nor hearing the sounds of the spring raindrops hitting the window, Sam was in his own little world. He smiled to himself thinking back to the time he was an eager reporter working his way through the dog-eat-dog world of newspaper reporting to where he was today, editor-in-chief.

Sam lost his smile at the thought of the wife and child who had been lost to him on a winter's night when they were driving into town to pick him up at the paper. That was the night that Albany had the worst snowstorm ever.

Peggy, Sam's wife, was blinded by the snow. She had not seen the drunken driver coming right at them. Sam wiped away the tear that had started down his cheek. He could still see his little girl, Kathleen, with her red curls and crystal-green eyes. She had looked just like her mother ... his beautiful Peggy. Maybe that is why he felt so close to the young reporter he had hired from Marshall, North Carolina.

He felt like this young woman could be his daughter, if she had lived. He had been around twenty-five when he started with the paper, and now, shaking his head, he was almost sixty-three.

A big smile came over his face as he remembered how they had met.

It was at a big reporters' awards ceremony around 1943 in Albany at the Convention Center. There she was a young reporter from Ashville, North Carolina; he remembered at one time it was also known as Little Chicago. A lot was going on in that town back in the thirties. But that was then, this was now. Sam could see how nervous this young woman was.

Sam thought to himself, *that's Marie Dotson. The best private eye in the business, wonder what she is doing up there?*

Sam made his way through the crowd to where Marie was standing next to a captivating redhead with hypnotic golden-green eyes.

"Hello, Marie. What in the world are you doing here?"

"Hello, Sam. This is my friend Deirdre. Deirdre, I would like for you to meet the best newsman in the country, Sam O'Brian.

After the introductions, they didn't have any opportunity to talk shop as the ceremony was beginning.

"Ladies and gentlemen, may I have your attention please, the awards presentation is about to begin. Our speaker for the evening will be Mr. Joleno L. Donovan son of our late Wild Bill Donovan."

Cheers rang out all through the large convention hall. Mr. Joleno Donavan stood up behind the podium. He looked very much like his father standing there. He put his hands in the air to quite down the large crowd. When they finally grew quiet he spoke, "It is an honor to be here tonight. First, it is a great privilege to be up here with these two remarkable ladies — Miss Deirdre MacDarroch and Miss Marie Dotson."

Sam came back to reality, when his office door burst open. The expletive died on his lips as he recognized who was barging into the office without knocking.

His eyes fell upon a very tall redhead, in a skin-tight black leather jumpsuit, who was soaked to the skin from the rain. She rapidly approached his paper-cluttered desk.

Deirdre MacDarroch, was beautiful, intelligent, and one of his best reporters. She was a five-foot eleven-inch tall pain in the ass with a figure that required second and third looks.

But now she was apparently terrified. Deirdre's large, gold-speckled, green eyes looked panic-stricken. "Sam!" she said between gasps, "I'm in some deep shit here. You've got to give me a leave of absence!" She started pacing the floor, pausing just long enough to wring water out of the long red braid that hung over her shoulder.

"Now, what the hell have you gotten into?" he demanded as he clamped down his now long-dead cigar.

The balance of the ashes dropped onto O'Brian's portly stomach and drifted down to the already ash-covered carpet.

She perched on the corner of his desk and said with a nervous chuckle, "Just doing my job, that's all. Just doing my job."

"What do you mean *your* job?"

"Well, maybe I dug a little too deep this time!"

Sam shoved back from his desk, walked around the desk and grabbed her shoulders. "My Lord, Deirdre! What have you uncovered? Nothing ever frightens you, but, by God, you are frightened now, aren't you?"

"You're damn right, I am! Look Sam, I have pictures and have written my column. Please, I need to get out of town in a hurry. They're after me."

"Who and what are you talking about, lady?"

"Damn, who do you think, Sam? Who have I been tracking for the past six months? The Campbell brothers. I have pictures of them robbing the museum. Sam, Byron was even there and I have him in the pictures." With shaky hands she handed him the roll of film.

As he took the film he noticed the roll was very damp. "Good Lord, Deirdre! You mean Byron Campbell? The big guy? The head of the United Kingdom's mob? Here in New York? You know that you have just signed your death warrant, don't you?"

"Yes, yes, yes, I know." As she took a deep breath, she wiped her forehead. "Sam, I have to leave and I need money to get out of town. Can you help me? I can't go to the bank now, it's too risky."

"How much do you need, and where will you go?"

"I know where I'm going, but for your own safety, I can't tell you. I have Duke and Major and they will be going with me. You remember my two black dobies, don't you?"

"Oh yeah, I remember them. What about your car? I'm sure they know your car."

"Sam, I am not that big a fool."

"No, but you're very stubborn." He smiled at her. "Babe, watch your back, even when you get where you're going." Sam went over to the safe and took out a wad of bills that would have choked a horse and handed them to her.

Tears stung Deirdre's eyes. "Sam, what can I say?"

"Dedicate your next book to me. Now get the hell out of here."

"You got it. The next book is yours. I'm stopping by my locker before I leave. I have a wig and other stuff for a disguise, just for occasions like this."

"Smart girl. Now what about your car?"

"Thanks to Marie, who knows everybody, I've got a new ride. There's a little reception waiting for me out front, I'm sure."

"Marie? Marie Dotson, the private investigator?"

"That's the one! You knew from the very start Marie and I felt like twins. Oh man, the cases we uncovered together! We worked out some great stories for the newspaper, didn't we?"

Sam gave Deirdre a hug and a fatherly pat on her derriere. "That you did. Thanks to you and that private eye friend of yours the newspaper got some great headliners. Maybe one day we'll meet again." He tried hard not to show his emotion, but he couldn't help but let a tear escape. It was like losing his little girl all over again.

"I pray so, dear friend. Sam, you know you have always been like a father to me, but most of all, a dear, dear friend." She couldn't and didn't look back as she walked out the door.

Deirdre hurried to her locker where she got out an old black wig and a pair of bibbed overalls, and headed for the ladies lounge to change.

After changing, she took one last look into the mirror to make sure her long red hair was all tucked under the wig. She opened the lounge door and looked up and down the corridor to make sure all was clear. She saw that it was, then hurried very fast to her office just down the hall. As she entered, she looked around smiling and thought to herself, *I have really enjoyed working at the paper. I'm going to miss it... and Sam.*

Deirdre walked to the window overlooking the street out front. Scanning the area, she noticed a dark blue sedan slowly cruising down the street. Quickly, she jerked back and took one last look around her office. "OK, lady, let's get the hell out of here," she muttered as she ran to the elevator. She pressed the button for the first floor and stepped inside. Deirdre hurried through the back doors which led into the pressroom and out to the newspaper parking lot. She glanced over her shoulder as she jumped into the driver's side of the waiting van.

"Everything OK, girlfriend?" asked Marie.

"Yeah, so far. Where in the world did you get the sign on the side of this old crate?"

"Over there, off Sam's car." She pointed her finger. "It just slid right off." Marie laughed so hard it brought tears to her eyes.

Deirdre looked over at Sam's car. Yes, indeed, it had been relieved of its newspaper sign. Deirdre smiled as she nodded her head, "Sam would know who did this job."

"Let's go. I'll drop you off at your apartment. Then be on my way."

"No kid, how about *your* apartment? That way I can check on things for you."

"You're right, Marie, I know I left some food and staples that you could use."

"I'll just take them to my place."

"That's great. But how will you get home?"

Marie smiled, "Silly, I'll just call a cab. Come on, let's get your stuff out of the apartment and get going. Deirdre, you know you're not safe out here."

Little did Deirdre know that in Marie's large handbag she carried a bottle of bleach and red hair dye, also had her SIG Sauer P230 pistol. Just in case those bastards were still after her dear friend.

"Did Sam come through?"

"Oh, yes, and then some," Deirdre smiled to herself.

Byron Campbell was not a man who usually paced. Today was an exception. His mouth was strained with angry tension and worry lines creased his forehead. As he waited, Byron sat down with a smug look on his face . . . he would have her soon. No one knew that Byron Campbell had followed Deirdre into the Black Fog. When he came into the future, he had started his own mob. They had helped him look for Deirdre, among other things — like making his mark in the underworld.

He smiled as he thought of the ancient contract that was put out on Deirdre.

It had all happened during a raid on Jura. Laird Robert Campbell was in on that raid, matter of fact he was the head of it. He hated the MacDarrochs so bad it ate at him like a cancer. It all started one month before Deirdre's birthday when she would have been fifteen. Deirdre was not only a warrior but a bodyguard who had been trained in China. She had always been tall and very strong for her age. She had been lifting heavy objects, such as boulders and oars on her father's ship since she was seven.

This day of the raid Byron was told that she rode like a champion, twirling her sword around her. Riding hard as she knocked Campbells off their horses headless, shouting the war cry of the MacDarrochs.

During the raid she had turned to her far left to see Laird Robert Campbell being thrown from his horse, hitting his head on a rock, knocking him unconscious. *I'll leave him something to always remember me by.* She smiled to herself.

Deirdre had ridden up and stopped just short of her victim, jumping from her horse to beside Laird Robert's body. She had turned at that moment to see if anyone was watching her. Deirdre couldn't help but laugh to herself as she took her sharp dirk from her boot, and proceeded to carve a "D" on his cheek.

Laird Robert almost died of the infection, but recovered, leaving a big red "D" on his cheek. He swore that he would get Deirdre one day. All he could think of was he would watch her die . . . very, very slowly.

Suddenly Byron was brought out of his daydream when his office door burst open; he wheeled around to face the intruder. "Well, did you get the bitch?"

"Sorry, boss. She got away," Carl answered, wiping the sweat his brow.

Sparks shot from Byron's eyes as if he'd like to kill the bearer of bad news. "How? You stupid son-of-a-bitch!" Campbell spat through clenched teeth.

"Well, she went into the newspaper building. Charlie and Nick rode around while Pete and I stayed in the car out front. She didn't come out." Sweat popped out on his forehead. "Honest, boss, she didn't come out!"

"Are you sure?" Byron shouted out through clenched teeth.

"Yeah, we are boss." Carl's dry throat made it harder and harder for him to speak.

Bryon pounded his fist on his desk, "Did you see anyone leave the damn building?"

"Yeah, of course." Carl's voice quivered. "Lots of people, but no redhead."

Byron Campbell hoped beyond all hope that he would capture Deirdre, then all the Campbells could be a peace. Their revenge would have been complete and not all would be lost.

He was in such deep thought he didn't hear the hall doors slamming and men's raised voices coming towards his door. The next thing that Campbell knew, agents from the FBI burst into his office

"Hands up, NOW! You must be Byron Campbell, the exaggerated Big Boss. Well, Big Boss, you are now the houseguest of the United States Government, for crimes committed. When we are through with you, the United Kingdom wants your butt."

Byron Campbell stared hard at the large muscular man as he was fitted with handcuffs. "What's your name, sonny?" he sneered.

"That, I feel, is none of your business." William glared at Byron with hot hate in his eyes.

"I would just like to know the name of the man who captured me and how you found us?"

"Let's just say a concerned citizen. By the way, big shot, my name is Agent William Ledbetter, on loan to the FBI from Scotland Yard, if it's that important to you."

"Oh yes, it is." Forgetting that he was in cuffs, he tried to put his large hands on his hips. With fire in his eyes he asked, "Where the hell is your proof of anything illegal?" Byron's smile turned into a sneer.

Agent William answered, "That's where you're dead in the water, my friend. We have your number," as he led Byron Campbell and his men outside to the patrol wagon that was waiting for them in front of the building. A crowd had gathered on the other side of the street to see what all the excitement was about. Suddenly, out of nowhere, came a large shiny black car, with darkened tinted windows. As Campbell looked up to see the commotion, the sneer that he carried so well became a look of glazed amazement.

The car blocked off the view of the crowd. When Byron saw the car, he recognized it. He became pale, panic-stricken with beads of sweat popping out on his brow. His nostrils flared with fright. William saw what was about to happen and shouted to his men to get down. Just as they were about to draw their guns, it happened. The car slowed down; one could see the windows slightly open and a machine gun barrel was brought within view. The machine gun rat-a-tat-tatted without warning. Byron Campbell fell to the ground, with holes etching his chest. Some of his men died, while some barely survived. That, in itself, really astonished Big William. It was evident that someone did not want them fueling the fire of damnation for the Campbells.

Not far from all the commotion, a police car had just rounded the corner. Patrolman Davis heard people screaming and sounds of a machine gun going off. He drove like mad down the street where he had heard the noise.

What he saw was like a war zone — people running, some had even lain down so as not to be hit by stray bullets.

Patrolman Tom Davis had joined the police force five years ago. In all of his five years, he had never seen such a bloody slaughter.

"My God, it looks like a scene my father told me about on the beaches of Normandy during World War II." Tom got out of his car when he saw a very large man pull himself up from the steps.

Tom shouted, "Are you alright?"

"Yes, I think so, who are you?"

"I'm Patrolman Tom Davis. I came on the run when I heard all the noise."

"Patrolman Davis, could you please get all these people out of here? It's bloody enough where I'm standing, much less where the citizens are. Oh! By the way, I'm Agent William Ledbetter."

"I'll check to see if any are hurt. Glad to meet you, Agent Ledbetter."

"Thank you so much, I'll see how things are up here."

While Patrolman Davis was checking the crowd, Agent William looked over and saw to his men.

His men picked themselves up off the steps. They looked out at the dead and the wounded. He breathed a sigh of relief to see that none of his men were among them. He said to himself, *Man alive, look at the mess, blood everywhere.*

Agent William's aid, Dan, spoke up, "Wonder who they were Chief? That was too damn close. We had Byron Campbell and his men surrounded on all sides." William looked unbelievably surprised as Dan spoke.

"Damned if I know, Dan. Come on, boys. Let's see who's left to sing."

Looking over the mess, he saw a pool of blood around Byron Campbell's head. Byron's men were bleeding to death. William heard the ambulance siren. "Only just barely in the nick of time I'd say," he said to himself, aloud. When he looked over to where Byron Campbell lay, he noticed he was trying to take a breath.

"Wait a minute; the big man is still breathing." Bending down close to Campbell's ear he whispered, "We got you. Thought you would like to know my real name, it's Sir William MacDarroch."

Shock with disbelief flashed in Byron's eyes as he died, knowing who his captor was. All the rest of Byron's men would sing. Sang their hearts out, they did. Told the courts all they needed to know.

Chapter 2

Deirdre drove like mad to get home to North Carolina. She stopped over each state line to fill up with gas and to let the Dobermans run and also to give them water.

She took the route from New York down through New Jersey. In Cape May, she pulled over into a rest area to try to get some much-needed sleep in the back of the van with the dogs. The next morning she had to hurry to get to the ferry before it left. *I can get some hot tea later*, she thought to herself as she drove through the ticket booth.

Deirdre moved slowly up the New Jersey ferry ramp into place. She patted Duke and Major on the head and told them to be good. The well-trained dogs always did what she told them to do.

On the ferry she had a breakfast of hot tea and a sweet roll, and then she went back down to the van to stand in the fresh air.

Once on the Delaware side, Deirdre drove off the ferry, down the ramp, and across to the Chesapeake Bay Bridge. She was wondering about her sisters, and thought she should call them. *I'll contact them later, in Rocky Mount.* Savoring the thought, she heard a weak snort out of her boys.

She drove into Rocky Mount many hours later. Deirdre looked down at the gas gauge and thought to herself, *Hmm ... better get some fuel, and take care of the boys' needs. Then I'll call the girls.* As she stopped the van at the hi-test pump, the attendant came out of the building. Seeing him she said, "Excuse me, can I use your phone?"

"Are you calling local or long distance?" he asked.

"Long distance, but no problem I'm reversing the charges," Deirdre said with a smile on her face.

"The phone's in the office on the left," the young man said, with a gleam in his eye, as he watched her walk into the station. He thought to himself, *She may have overalls on, but man she knows how to wear them!*

Monica heard the phone ringing and went to answer it just as Kimberly entered the room. "Now, wait a minute, baby sister, I'm expecting a phone call, and I'll answer it."

"Really, Kimberly, goodness sake, what are you afraid of? I'll hear a man's voice on the other end?" Laughing, Monica moved over to the sofa.

Kimberly told the operator that she would accept the charges. "Deirdre, are you alright?"

"Yes, thanks for accepting the call, Kimberly. Look honey, I'm in Rocky Mount and will be in Marshall just as soon as I can. Have everything ready for us, but for heaven sake, don't forget the Scotch."

The previous day's excitement and the long drive were catching up with her. Exhausted and pitiful whines from Duke and Major had her looking for the next rest stop. The tired dogs whined once more. "I know, guys. You need water, food, and a good run."

Just as the words came out of her mouth, a sign came up: REST AREA. "Look over there. It's a place to play. Time for a break and a good run, guys."

Deirdre stopped the van and straightened her wig while reaching for the leashes for her boys. They really showed their appreciation at being released by romping and playing together. People started to move frantically to their vehicles for protection. The two large dogs jumped and played with their master, but she could control them with just a few words and a whistle. They watched in amazement as Deirdre, needing a little exercise herself, joined in. They rolled in the grass together loosening up their stiffness. Everyone seemed amazed at the size of the dogs and how she was able to handle them.

After awhile, she got up and brushed herself off. She whistled for the lads, and retrieved their water bowl for some cool water. After they emptied it, she filled it a second time and put the boys in the van while she went to relieve herself.

After a few minutes, Deirdre returned to her van and started to get in when a man stuck his head out of his truck window and yelled, "How much do they weigh?"

Deirdre shut the door and yelled out of the window, "Duke, the largest one, is around a hundred and thirty-five pounds, the smaller one, Major, is close to a hundred and twenty-five pounds, give or take a pound or two."

His wife yelled, "My word, young lady, how do you handle them and where did they come from? I mean, where were they born? Not in this country anywhere."

"I handle them with lots of tender loving care, and they came from a breeder friend of mine in Germany." Saying this, she drove away. "All right, my boys, we're off to Marshall and the old home place." She thought to herself, *Wonder what we'll find there?*

Deirdre looked around as she drove down the highway to Asheville. "This has grown into a nice city," she thought aloud.

On the other side of Asheville, Deirdre searched for the Weaverville sign. She came to the Beaver Lake exit, which would lead her to Weaverville, then into Jupiter. Now she needed old Highway 25, which ran parallel to the French Broad River.

Deirdre was simply delighted to see the beautiful foliage from the willow trees over the softly flowing water of the river. She smiled to herself, remembering the times she and Grandfather George went fishing. "It's beautiful, isn't it, boys?" She always talked to the boys as if they would answer. "I remember how Grandfather George called the French Broad River 'Frenchie'. He said it reminded him of a French lass he once knew, who couldn't make up her mind, always going here and there."

There were trees lining both sides of the highway as she looked out of a bug-covered windshield. Every now and then she could smell the fresh tang of pine in the air. Someone was cooking out; she could also smell hickory burning.

A little further down the road she smelled the mixed fragrances of roses, honeysuckle, and lilac making a hardy perfume. She savored all these fresh country aromas. It brought to mind memories of the town where she spent her late teen years.

"Goodness, how long has it been since I've been home, I guess it must have been when Great-Grandfather passed away."

Deirdre remembered the hurt in her heart. It brought tears to her eyes. She dearly loved the old man who had raised them.

She heard the dogs whine, then bang their pans against the side of the old van. "OK, OK, lads. Big Jake's Café should be just before we get into town. How would you like a large steak?" Their loud and excited barks were all the answer she needed, "Alright, alright, I get the message. Hold it down a bit."

She tugged at the irritating wig again, deciding it was time to get rid of the damn thing before it drove her crazy. She took it off and tossed it to the floor and used her fingers to comb out her long ginger-red hair. "Boy that feels good. Where is that café? Close, I hope!"

The rumble of her insides interrupted her nostalgic thoughts. "There's Big Jake's! Now, where is the turn off that goes over the railroad tracks? Ha ha! There it is. Hallelujah! We made it!"

Big Jake's looked the same. *But wait one minute, it's not the same. It's larger and he has added tables outside.* Deirdre thought to herself as she looked at the family's favorite café.

It's still a white box of a place. There were a few stools at the counter and about eight booths inside. Behind the counter was a big old coffee pot. Jake and his Dad had owned the place as long as she could remember. His burgers were the biggest and the best around. His secret for steaks was what put them on the map. Tender, juicy, and succulent were terms that came to mind when asked to describe the food.

She drove over the tracks, and parked in front of the café. Deirdre looked around and then down. She smiled to herself at how she looked. All of a sudden, she felt very much at home in the overalls she was wearing.

The bell jingled as she went inside. As she looked around, Jake came from the kitchen. He asked as he approached the counter, "Well, hello lovely lady. What can I get for you?"

Deirdre turned and smiled and said, "Take it easy, big boy. Do you remember when we were younger and I gave you a bloody nose?"

"Well, I'll be a monkey's uncle, if it's not Deirdre MacDarroch." He held his arms out and she rushed into them. Those big bear arms felt so good.

"Hey, why the tears, friend?"

"Oh! You. It's just good to be back home."

Jake stood six-foot five and looked like the big, black bear he had killed many years ago. All the hunters brought their wild game for Jake and his father to cook because they were the best around. He always had a big warm heart and was a wonderful person. For that reason, everyone loved him, as they had loved his father before.

"I see you still have all the black and white seats, but you have a lot more chrome now than you had before. I like the idea of tables outside." She smiled at him.

"Yep, sure do. They work me to death. Say gal, what are you doing back here? Aren't you working for one of those big newspapers in New York?"

She pulled away with a frightened look on her face, "Why?"

"Well, on the television, some mobster by the name of Byron Campbell was shot down in front of an office building close to where your newspaper office was.   Seems he was being arrested by the FBI."

"Jake, do you think it's in the paper here?"

"Yep, I think so. Let me go look." He paused, then turned and asked, "Why, Deirdre, did you know the guy?"

"Please Jake, just get me the paper."

"OK, be back in a minute."

Deirdre plopped down on one of the chrome counter stool like a lead ball. She was lost in thought. The barking of Duke and Major brought her back from her deep anxiety. Shouting as if the lads could hear her, "Sorry lads," Deirdre moved straight back to the kitchen to find her boys some food. That's where Jake found her looking for meat.

"What are you looking for?"

She jumped and turned, poised to fight. Then she saw who had spoken. "Gee! Jake, you scared me half to death."

"Sorry. Here's the paper. You go on out front and I'll fix you a steak."

"Huh? Jake, I'm so sorry but I have my two dogs out in the van. Could you fix three big T-bones for us? One for me with two eggs over easy.   Make it a really thick one," she said, and measured about an inch and a half with her fingers, "Medium rare, please — the others the same, medium rare."

Deirdre walked out of the kitchen as Jake watched, "How can she hold all that? She's so skinny." But after a quick study he decided, "No, no everything is just perfect with her."

While Jake was cooking, Deirdre read the paper. It was all about the shooting in New York. She turned the page and screamed, "Oh! Dear Lord, No! It's not true!"

Hearing the scream and trying to balance two plates and coffee cups, Jake came out on a run. "What's wrong?" he asked looking at Deirdre's pale face.

"They have me listed as dead. Oh, no, it had to be Marie, a dear friend of mine." She looked at Jake. "Would you please make a phone call for me?" she asked, with tears in her eyes.

"You bet. Who do you want me to call?" he asked as he placed the steak and eggs in front of her.

Deirdre gave him the number and the questions to ask. As Jake was dialing the number, in walked Kimberly and Monica, her sisters. Kimberly was a tall, slender blonde with green eyes; Monica was shorter, with black hair and deep brown eyes, with a great body. It was hard to believe they were sisters.

Kimberly saw Deirdre as she walked into the café and exclaimed, "Deirdre, what in the world are you doing here? We thought you would be at home after your long trip." Kimberly looked closer and saw the tears running down her sister's face. She went over and put her arms around her as she slid next to Deirdre. Monica got into the booth on the other side across from her sisters.

Deirdre looked up in surprise. "I stopped in to get the lads something to eat. What in the world are you two doing here?" She wiped the tears from her face.

"Just the lads?" asked Monica smiling as she looked at the steak and eggs in front of Deirdre.

"We stopped in to get a cup of Jake's wonderful coffee before going home. Why are you upset and crying?" Kimberly asked again.

"It's a long story, honey. Here's the paper. Read it first, then maybe it will give you an idea. I'm terribly worried about something. I am afraid Marie has been killed. The killers must have thought she was me! You see, I dropped her off at my apartment. She wanted to take home what was left in the refrigerator, or so she said."

"What in the world brought all this on?" asked Monica.

"Please, sisters," Deirdre said in a choked voice with tears running down her face, "give me a moment to get it together." Deirdre wiped her eyes and taking a deep breath, drew back her shoulders. She pulled herself together, and then started telling them what had gone on, how she gotten the pictures of the heist the Campbells had pulled — just everything. Kimberly picked up the newspaper that Deirdre had handed her to read.

After drinking in the article, Kimberly handed the paper to Monica, then looked over at Jake and asked, "Who are you calling?" Jake told her what Deirdre had asked him to do.

When she had laid the newspaper down, she said, out of the blue, "My Lord! It had to be your friend you told us about, Marie. You mentioned that she was the same height as you and had the same build. Do you think it's possible she dyed her hair or maybe she used a wig, because her hair was so dark she couldn't have gotten it done in time! Yes, it had have been a wig. But what time did you drop her off? Sister, would she have had time to have dyed her hair?"

"Well, knowing Marie, she would have bleached and dyed her hair, then done away with all the evidence. Then just sat and waited. The paper said she had a Bible in her hand. Yes, it was my Bible, Monica," Deirdre said very softly in reverence.

"I bet she did that to throw them off of your trail! Big sister, it would be just like her to do something like that."

"Deirdre, it broke our hearts when you told us she had incurable cancer!"

"Yeah, Goldie." (An endearing term used by the sisters when talking to Kimberly.) "I remember. Maybe this is the way she wanted to go out, helping you, Deirdre," replied Monica.

"Perhaps" said Deirdre. "But right now I need to check with Jake on the phone call."

"Hello, may I speak to Sam O'Brian, the Editor-in-chief?" asked Jake.

A soft, sexy female voice asked, "Who's calling, please?"

"My name is Jake Mull. I'm calling on behalf of Deirdre MacDarroch's sisters."

"Oh yes! Just one moment. The FBI agents are here and Mr. O'Brian is in conference with them. Please hold."

Turning to Deirdre, Jake whispered, "The FBI's there."

"That's just fine," Kimberly said with a huff in her voice, "hand me the phone, Jake. I'll take it from here." She was as mad as a hornet.

"Hello. Hello, this is Sam O'Brian. Who is this?"

"Sam? This is Kimberly, Deirdre's sister."

"Kimberly, hello. Honey, I'm so sorry about Deirdre, but you called at a very inconvenient time."

Sounding teary and choked up, Kimberly asked, "Sam, can you please arrange to have Deirdre's body shipped home, or do I need to come there to claim her body? By the way, were you the one who identified her?"

At that moment, a strange voice came on the line, "Miss MacDarroch, before we can release her body, you will need to come here and identify it."

"Well, sir, if I may ask, just who the hell are you?"

"My name is Agent William Ledbetter. I'm on loan to the FBI from Scotland Yard."

"It's because of you that my sister is dead."

"No, I'm afraid you're wrong there, little lady."

"I don't think so. May I speak to Sam, please?"

The line went silent and then Sam was back on. Kimberly knew the FBI was listening, "Sam, can you please meet me at the airport? I want to bring Deirdre home. Please?" The emotion in her voice was very real.

"Yes, honey. Kimberly, I'm the one who identified her. I'll make the plane reservation, then call you right back."

"No, our phone isn't hooked up yet. Just make it for early morning and meet me at the airport."

"All right, honey. You know, Deirdre was one of my best reporters. I'm really going to miss her. Take care and remember you can call on me at any time."

Softly, "Thanks, Sam," and she hung up.

"You were great, Kimberly. Especially about the phone," Deirdre said with tears running down her face.

Kimberly attempted a smile as she spoke, "I just did not want them tracing the phone call. As you know, they will."

"Deirdre, I think we should get you home. Come on, honey. You've had a long, hard day. Do you feel up to driving?" asked Monica.

"Yeah, I'll be fine," she replied as she walked over to Jake.

"Thanks for everything, dear friend."

"Don't you worry, honey. Big Jake will take care of things if they call or drop in."

"Jake, could you call about the plane in about an hour and call us at home?" Kimberly asked as she handed him a number and kissed him on the cheek.

"I'll be glad to, Kimberly. And don't you worry, Deirdre," Jake told them as he opened the door. "I'll call you in one hour." He handed Deirdre the steaks for the dobies.

All of them drove out of town, Deirdre in her old van and Kimberly with Monica in her new silver Buick, looking for the Bull Creek sign. Monica was very distressed at what had happened inside Jake's. They were very down at the news of

Marie's death, so she tried very hard to change the subject as she smiled and said, "Kimberly, I love your new car."

"Thank you, I do too. Don't you just love the silky, silver look?"

"Yes,-I do. It suits you. Goes great with your blonde hair," Monica said to her with a giggle in her voice.

Kimberly wasn't really paying attention to what her sister was saying. She was more concerned with Deirdre. "Monica, I'm very worried about Deirdre."

"Why? She's always been able to take care of herself."

"Good grief, Monica. Didn't you notice her? How thin she's gotten. How pale she is. How hollow her cheeks are? Damn, baby sister, she looks like death warmed over."

"You know, you're right. It's this whole thing about that Campbell story she's been chasing these last few months; now it's Marie and the way she was murdered. They were so close, like sisters. It's a shame Marie developed cancer and found out there was no cure. What's so sad is that it had already spread throughout her whole body before it was even diagnosed. You have to still wonder why they killed her.

"It wasn't Marie they were after, silly. It was Deirdre."

"Are you sure? Why? We need to ask her later, that's for sure. Kimberly, remember when Marie had her detective agency? She and Deirdre solved so many cases together."

"Right you are. Deirdre would turn around and get a hell of a story out of it. Marie was like a twin sister to Deirdre. Kind of like her other half. Funny, it's like she said once a long time ago. She felt like a part of her was missing, remember?"

"Yes, I remember."

"You know, Marie was the same built as Deirdre, but her hair was jet-black like yours."

"By golly, you're right. But we talked about that back at Jake's. With her standing in the doorway with the light behind her anyone could have mistaken her for Deirdre.

Deirdre pulled out onto the highway. Driving straight through town, she decided it hadn't changed much; the river on the left, the old movie house, and then Morgan's drug store. They were all still there. "Good grief! They have a large chain grocery store now. OK, that's good. But it's still the same wonderful little town I remember. The town is on the right side of the tracks and the river on the left."

"We really need to get away for some R and R, especially Deirdre." I'm glad we're taking that vacation to Scotland".

Kimberly squinted her eyes. "She needs it, but I wonder if she'll be safe! Now where is Bull Creek Road? It's almost dusk and I can't see anything."

"Stop the car and let Deirdre lead the way in. Did you call the caretakers, Mr. and Mrs. D.?" asked Monica.

"Sure did. I asked Mrs. D. to stock the place with food. But I brought the Scotch."

"Good show, Kimberly."

Kimberly stopped the car and Deirdre pulled up right beside her. "I'll lead the way in, Kimberly. I see you have forgotten the way."

"No, Deirdre. I haven't forgotten. It's just getting dusk and you know I have night blindness. Plus it's hard for me to read the signs. I told Mrs. D. to put in supplies, but I brought the Scotch."

"Good girl, Kimberly, I'll need it. Now, you girls follow me."

The sounds of munching and crunching that came from the back of the van brought a warm and tender smile to Deirdre's lips as she listened to the lads finishing their dinner.

"There it is, Bull Creek Road." Deirdre took the turn onto the side road, and then drove another five miles. Along the right side of the road was a big bank filled with bushes of gooseberries. They were still just under-ripe, but soon they would be swollen and sweet. *Yummy.* The thought of pies and the sweetness of the berries made her mouth water.

Just past the big gooseberry bank was a private road on the left side with a sign reading, "Private—Keep Out." Below it, a second sign read, "Enter at your own risk."

I don't remember that last sign, Deirdre thought to herself.

As she moved closer to the house, she noticed how clean the fields were. Someone must have cut all the weeds down. *Wonder who it was? They even did a lot of trimming on the grounds.* The smell of wild honeysuckle mixed with rambling roses was intoxicating.

Deirdre stopped the van and just sat there. She rolled the windows down further and breathed deeply. She jumped when she heard a car horn blow behind her, and a voice just outside her range of vision asked, "Are you just going to sit here all night?"

"Woops. Sorry, must have been wool gathering. Who are the caretakers here? I forgot their names."

"It's Dan and Ruth Douglas. Mrs. D. takes care of the inside and Mr. D., the outside. Deirdre, you should remember, you're the one who hired them," Kimberly reminded her as she splashed through the small creek to Deirdre's side of the van.

"I did? Oh yes, now I remember, how thoughtless of me."

"OK! Can we move out of the creek now? My feet are wet."

"Goodness, Goldie. I'm so sorry," Deirdre said with a smile as she started the van.

"Thank you so much," replied Kimberly in a piqued voice.

Kimberly got back into the car with a big sigh and shook her head, "I don't know about that girl."

"What do you mean?" asked Monica.

"Baby sister, she didn't remember Mr. and Mrs. D.'s name and she's the one who hired them!"

"You've got to be kidding."

"No, I'm not."

After crossing the stream, they drove up a small hill. As the house came into view she could see it was still the same. The wide covered porch ran all the way around the house. It was built of log and river rock. Deirdre remembered an old root cellar under the house where she used to hide and eat the carrots, apples, and even raw turnips. What wonderful memories she had of the place. Thank God, nothing was changed.

By the time they arrived at the old home place the moon was just coming out. It was full and bright as day. She could even see the tin roof that had been painted green — Great-grandfather's favorite color. Deirdre could make out the hollyhocks beside the corner of the house, remembering how she and her sisters used to make dolls out of them.

Great-aunt Judith planted a small lilac bush that had grown into a tree and was in full bloom. The warm evening air combined with the smells of fresh-cut grass and the floral fragrances almost overwhelmed the senses.

The old barn, where they used to jump out of the hayloft, had been home to Great-grandfather Oliver's two mules, Old Maude and Jack. There were two more stalls for Big Red and Gray, his horses. Of course, he had about five good milking cows. *Boy, do I remember having to clean out that barn,* Deirdre thought, smiling to herself.

She drove down to the old barn where she parked her van between its two large doors. Kimberly pulled in behind the old beat-up van.

"Deirdre, remember when we had to clean out this old place?" asked Monica.

"What did you say? Being the baby, all you did was nothing. It was Goldie and I who got stuck with that job."

Deirdre turned around and saw a light in the windows. "Girls, do you see the light?"

"Maybe Mrs. D. left the lights on," Monica said.

"Most likely she wanted it to be cozy when we arrived," Kimberly added.

Low growls and raised hackles greeted Deirdre when she slid open the van's side door. Duke and Major jumped out and began sniffing and growling their way up to the house.

The three sisters looked at one another. "Deirdre, I have a bad feeling about this."

"Now Monica, don't let your imagination run away with you," Deirdre warned, as she called to Major and Duke.

"But Kimberly, don't you remember? This mountain has Great-great-grandfather Donald's spirit floating about as well as Great-grandfather's," Monica reminded her.

"No, I never forget. Deirdre, you do remember the stories don't you?" asked Kimberly, walking back to the car to open the trunk.

"Well, yes, I do," she answered, looking around with a smile like the cat that swallowed the canary. She knew something no one else was aware of. "But, come on, let's get unpacked and fix a bite to eat. Then we can talk."

"You're right. We'll eat on the porch," Kimberly said, as she took her suitcases out of the back of her new silver Buick.

"Eat!" exclaimed Monica. "Deirdre, you just had a huge meal."

"That's all right, Monica. I just need a little snack and a Scotch or two or three."

"Need any help with your luggage?"

"No thanks, Goldie. I think I have it all, but thanks, anyway. I'm going to let the lads run and stretch their legs some more. It's really strange the way they took off and then came back so easily. Do you have everything, Monica?"

"Sure do."

Deirdre looked up at the house as she took the last piece of luggage out of the back of the van. She saw smoke coming from the chimney. Before she could tell the girls about it, they were already on the front porch.

"Oh! Brave Warrior, Deirdre. Hurry up, slow poke. You have the key, remember?"

"Try the door; I bet it's open."

It was. "Well, I'll be," remarked Monica.

Deirdre came up on the porch, put her hand on the screen door and pushed. She smiled as she spoke, "It's good to be home, Papa Oliver. Yes, very good."

"Why in the world are you shouting? Kimberly asked.

"Was I?"

"Yes, Deirdre, you were," Monica pointed out.

"Sorry. Just wanted the Great One to hear me," she said as she put her black alligator luggage into the bedroom Great-grandfather had occupied when she was growing up.

Deirdre sat on the large spindle featherbed he had slept in. The walls were painted pink because Mama Sara loved pink. He hated it, but that was what Mama Sara wanted. Therefore, to make her happy, he painted it pink.

On the windows were the old lace curtains she hung when he finished adding to the house. When he first built the house, it had been just a single room cabin with a loft. All Mama Sara had to do was ask him to build her a larger one and that's when he added rooms to the cabin.

If you looked real hard, you could see where she had mended the lace curtains through the years. She had been very good at lace making. As you looked around the house, you would find her handiwork everywhere.

On the old dresser were Mama Sarah's silver brush and comb. She brought them over with her from Jura, Scotland. It was told that she had them in her hands when the Black Fog brought her over. She too was lost and Papa Oliver found her when he was hunting. Looking closely, Deirdre found a hand mirror framed in silver.

She began to brush her long, red hair with the brush, smiling to herself at how Mama Sara used to brush her hair and braid it when she first came here.

Deirdre had tears in her eyes at the thought of her. How frightened they were when Great-grandfather brought them down from the mountain. She began smiling because she had wonderful memories of Papa Oliver and Grandfather George, who was born in this very room.

Wiping tears from her eyes, she called, "Girls, did you find your rooms?"

"Sure did. We're going to unpack. How about you?"

"Just about to do that, Monica."

Kimberly came down the hall from her room, and peeked around the door where Deirdre would be sleeping. "Then we can talk. Let's see what Mrs. D. has made for dinner. We can eat on the porch," she said disappearing again.

When they gathered in the kitchen, each of the girls was lost in their own memories. They filled their plates with southern fried chicken, nicely golden brown, corn on the cob with lots of butter, a nice big garden salad, hard rolls, and cold glasses of iced tea.

They wandered out to the porch, and as they looked down the hill where the big persimmon tree grew, each remembered the wonderful sweet taste of fully-ripened fruit and the mouth-drawing twang of one that was not quite ripe.

"What memories I have of sitting out here," remarked Monica.

Kimberly smiled, "Oh boy, me too. Remember the peddler man that came around once a month with all kinds of goodies? Mama Sara bought cloth to make our dresses, and Grandpa George always bought us some candy. One time Grandfather George was chewing tobacco and Deirdre had a square of licorice with an apple stamped on top. You made out that it was your chewing tobacco so you could see how far you could spit.

"Yeah, and Grandfather George told you to move and you didn't. Then you looked up at him and he spit in your eye." Monica and Kimberly laughed so hard they were crying.

"Boy, do I. Every time I think about that, my eye burns." Deirdre laughed just as hard as her sisters did.

"Remember when we were young and sat under the persimmon tree? And how good a cold drink of water from the spring would be when we were hot?" asked Kimberly.

"You bet I do," Monica answered.

"Remember, Monica, when you tried to catch the crawfish?" asked Deirdre.

"I did catch one in the old drinking gourd. You know, the one that always stayed on the hook by the spring," smiled Monica.

"Deirdre, Papa Oliver told us that the crawfish would keep it clean," Kimberly said with a puzzled look on her face.

"Kimberly, you couldn't understand how they could do that, remember? Papa didn't know either. But what grand memories we have," Deirdre said with melancholy in her voice.

"Those were the good old days."

"Oh yes, I remember. Oh, how I have missed this old covered porch. This place and all the good times we had growing up here."

"What say we take in the dishes and come back to sit on our porch," Kimberly said quietly.

Monica spoke aloud, "You know, I remember that we were never this nice to each other on Jura. Why now?"

"Silly," answered Kimberly, "We were home then. We felt safe there, so we spoke our minds. There we knew where we stood with one another, but not here. We were afraid here, didn't know what to expect."

"Do you remember our sword fights? Hey, what warriors we were. Kimberly, you took care of the sick, and were always out looking for healing herbs, so you could discuss your healing powers with the other healers," Deirdre remarked with a broad smile on her face.

"Yes, I do. I really miss home," Kimberly spoke with tears running down her cheeks.

"I remember too. Dad took me aboard his ship and taught me how to navigate the lead ship. When are we going home?" asked Monica.

"You both know that it was the Black Fog that brought us here. I really think it messes up our systems in some way. We only had one another. We were only, let's see, I was fifteen when I married Tommy, and you, Kimberly, were just nineteen months younger, that would make you about thirteen and a half. And Monica, that would have make you close to ten. So you see, we had to look out for each other. Now I'm not saying that it hasn't been fun, but sometimes I would just love to whack the two of you. And I'm sure you both wanted to do the same with me. But I tell you here and now, when we get home, LOOK OUT!" smiled Deirdre as she spoke.

Everyone got up and helped put the dishes away in the old-fashioned kitchen. Despite the antique appearance, every-thing was completely modern. The old icebox was electric, as was the stove, which looked like an old wood burner. Bright, yellow-checked curtains hung at the window above the sink with its old hand pump.

Deirdre gazed around the room and smiled. The rectangular table was covered with a bright, yellow-print cloth. Ladder-back chairs had cushions to match the curtains. What memories played across her mind. Winter days spent playing on the polished wooden floor with whatever stray animal happened to be in residence at the time. The summers spent helping to preserve the crops of corn, beans, apples or grapes that came from the arbor.

Going back onto the porch, the girls found their favorite step again. Simultaneously, a deep sigh of nostalgia crossed each woman's lips as they settled a little more comfortably and watched the night grow still. Fireflies twinkled like bright little lanterns across the yard and around the lilac bushes. The soft murmur of the little creek they crossed was comforting after such a long tension-strung day. A slight breeze came whispering through the leaves in the trees.

Deirdre shivered, "My goodness, I feel a chill in the air. What say we go in and light a fire? Don't forget your drinks; don't want the Scotch going to waste."

"But it's the first of June!" exclaimed Kimberly.

"That's alright. It sounds like fun and we can pop corn in the old, long-handled popper the Great One had when we were, as he always called us, "small." Remember, Deirdre? The Great One; isn't that what the Cherokee called Papa Oliver?"

The girls got up and one went one way to get the popcorn and the other to look for the popper. Deirdre went back into the great room to light the fire. She was not surprised to see it already burning. The firelight reflected off the walls that were as highly polished as the floor with its old, bearskin rug. There was an old pump organ in one corner and Papa Oliver's rocker was in the other. *Funny, looks like a mist is in that corner.* Deirdre thought to herself.

In the middle sat the old, puffed couch. Sit on it and you would almost sink to the floor. Large pillows were thrown everywhere. It was a happy room.

"Gee, that was fast," said Monica, as she and Kimberly joined Deirdre. "Look how hot it is," she continued while placing butter and salt on the table next to the fireplace.

"But I didn't light it," Deirdre protested. "It was already burning when we got here."

"You're kidding me," Kimberly said in a high, strained voice.

"No, I'm not. I saw the smoke as we came from the barn. I have a strong feeling The Great One is here with us. But, well, let's start popping the corn and we'll see."

They moved the large cushions and placed them on the floor in front of the fireplace. As the corn started to pop, each sister returned to her individual thoughts.

When he was alive, Papa Oliver, who was a big man, standing over six-foot four-inches tall, could stand in the middle of the fireplace. An oven, built in the side, allowed for baking bread and cakes. Iron hangers were for cooking in heavy, black iron pots that were now stacked on and around the old raised hearth.

Deirdre looked around the room, "I've always loved this room. By the way, I forgot to ask, what did you do about your businesses?"

"I sold my chain of Health Food Stores, and put my money into the old bank in Asheville. Just like you said to. Deirdre, you said the Birds had been running that trading post since the first Scot came to these mountains," remarked Kimberly.

"How about you, Monica? What about your fishing fleet?"

"I sold them to a man who had retired and had nothing to do. He was bored with retirement. I put the money in the same bank."

"That's good. I'm proud of you both."

"What about you?" asked Kimberly?

"I've used that bank for years. The royalties from my books are in there, as well as most of my paychecks from the newspaper."

"Why that bank? It's not like we'll be back, now is it?" asked Monica.

Smiling at both of them Deirdre made the remark, "Well, you never know now, do you?"

"Remember Great-aunt Judith playing that old pump organ over there in the corner? I'm so glad you kept it, Deirdre."

"Me too, Kimberly. I also remember that she played while I pumped. Then Great-uncle Jim would play his fiddle and Great-uncle Byron would play his banjo. They would play and sing the old Scottish songs."

Monica broke in, "We would all sing and dance while Papa Oliver sat in his rocking chair smiling as he patted his foot, smoking his pipe."

"I remember his pipe. It was white with a long stem and he kept it right there on the mantle." They looked up to the white oak mantle, not at all surprised to see his pipe laying there, still a little warm.

Kimberly got up with a very strange look on her face. Monica stood along with her, having the same look. They both turned to gaze at Deirdre.

Chapter 3

While the girls were waiting for Deirdre to say something — anything, the sound of the phone ringing brought all three up short. They all jumped, startled. Kimberly finally said, "I'll get it."

She looked at Deirdre as she got up, "Are you all right, Deirdre?"

With tears shining in her eyes, Deirdre looked at her and nodded yes. All at once her shoulders started to shake and tears overflowed like a dam bursting.

Going over, Monica took her in her arms, holding her very tight, rocking her like a small child while Kimberly answered the phone.

"Hello."

Hearing crying in the background, Jake asked, "What's wrong, Kimberly? Are you girls OK? Who's crying?"

"Yes, Jake. All this has really hit Deirdre hard — us too. We've been doing a lot of talking about Great-grandfather and Marie and other things."

"Oh, yeah. I understand the shock and all. Look, your tickets are at the airport. They are for day after tomorrow. Anything else I can do?"

"Wait one minute." Looking down at Deirdre, she asked, "Deirdre, do you want Jake to do anything else, honey?"

Tears seemed to be choking her, "Here, give me the phone please, Kimberly."

"Are you sure?"

"Yes, please."

Deirdre took the phone. "Hello, Jake. Please excuse me for not sounding myself."

Jake remarked, "That's OK, kid, just take it easy."

"OK, buddy. Look, I know you have never been around my lads, I mean, dobies, but could you come over and meet them? If the three of you click, would you stay here while we're gone?"

"You know good and well I will. Look, you get some rest tonight and I'll see you girls tomorrow."

"Yes, you sweet man. Thank you so much. How about one thirty in the afternoon?"

"That would be just fine with me. I'll get my helper to come in early and see you around that time."

Jake came the next afternoon and met with the lads. Duke liked him immediately but Major was a little standoffish. But, seeing how Duke liked Jake, Major finally came around. All three were good friends by the time Jake started to leave.

"Thank you, Jake."

"But, Deirdre, do you really think you should go? What I mean is, after what has happened. I'm very concerned for your safety."

"I have to, Jake. I have to find out who did this to Marie. You do understand, don't you? I have to get the mad dog who did this; and I will, you wait and see!"

"OK, OK, don't get upset. But gal, you be careful."

"Thanks for worrying about me, Jake. I'll be careful. Thanks again," Deirdre said, waving to Jake as he was getting into his car.

"Thanks from me too, Jake. I'm going to see if I can get Monica and Deirdre a ticket on the same plane."

"You don't have to Kimberly," he called from the car. "That is what I thought was weird. There were already three tickets."

"What?"

"You heard me, Kimberly, three tickets."

"Thanks. The key will be in the arm of the old green rocker on the porch. It's the one with round arms; all you have to do is twist the right arm off. The key will be in the hollow end, in case we forgot to tell you."

"OK, you girls be careful now."

"We will." Kimberly yelled as Jake drove off. She turned, then looked at Deirdre. "Lassies, there are three tickets at the airport. Can you believe it?"

"Yes, we heard." Deirdre shook her head in disbelief and suddenly smiled. "Good old Sam. He knew. I don't know how, but he knew. Better go and wash my black wig. I think I have a dowdy summer suit and shoes with low heels. That should do it."

"How about an old hat with a veil to cover part of your face."

"That's real good, Kimberly, real good."

The next morning, all three were at the airport going through the line when the bell went off in Deirdre's lane.

"Oops. I am so sorry I still have my keys in my pocket, silly me," she apologized, while thinking to herself, *I wish I had brought a weapon of some sort; don't know what we'll come up against.*

No one seemed to notice the glint in her eyes as they boarded the plane. *You'll get yours, Campbell, whoever you are. Oh yes, you'll get yours.*

You'll get.... Deirdre leaned back in her seat, closed her eyes and smiled to herself. She thought how clever Sam was to put the ticket in Marie's name. Crazier still, she had even found Marie's driver's license in the van's glove compartment to identify herself when she picked up the ticket. It worked. *God is good, yes, and he'll be with me as I take care of the Campbells,* she thought as she fell asleep.

Deirdre felt the wheels touchdown and her eyes flew open. She straightened up, adjusted her hat, put on her gloves, and smiled at her sisters. "Are we ready to go, girls?"

"Yes! Are you?" They both asked as they looked straight at her; then Kimberly said, "What are you up to?"

"The less you know the better off you both will be. I'll let you know as much as I can."

"Now, you just listen, dear sister. Don't go and do anything stupid. We know how stubborn you can be," remarked Monica.

They put Deirdre between them and held on to her arms until they got to the baggage claim. Deirdre felt like she was being watched. Kimberly saw the look on her face. "What's wrong?" she asked.

"Don't you girls feel it? Someone is watching us."

"You're right, Deirdre, I feel it too. Look over to the left. Could it be that large man?"

"Monica, it could be the FBI."

"Kimberly, want me to go see?"

"No, Monica, leave it alone!"

"Why?"

"Because, they'll show their hand sooner or later and we don't want to draw any more attention to us than is necessary."

"Right, Deirdre."

"Watch the name," she warned speaking in a whisper.

"Sorry, it won't happen again."

"One slip and we could be dead meat," whispered Deirdre.

"Are we ready to go, Marie? I want both of you with me when I identify Deirdre. Then we can go home," Kimberly stated in a choked voice.

Putting her arm around Kimberly, Deirdre said, "Honey, now don't you go all to pieces on us."

They left the airport in a taxi heading to the River Bend Hotel, where they could change clothes. As they got off the elevator and the bellboy opened the door to their room, Monica asked, "Marie, why is this hotel called the River Bend?"

Before Deirdre could answer, Kimberly spoke up, "Look out the window, Monica." As she moved over to the window, Kimberly pointed outside their hotel room. "See, there is a river and the hotel is built on the bend of it. Now you see why, little sister?"

"You don't have to talk to me like I'm a child, Kimberly. Besides, I didn't ask you. It was Deirdre, I mean Marie I was addressing, so hush."

Deirdre smiled. "Girls, please. All this is bad enough and we don't know who is following us, or why."

As they were leaving the hotel, Deirdre noticed a big, dark blue sedan parked on the other side of the street. Kimberly hailed a taxi for them. After they got into the taxi, Deirdre whispered "The dark blue car that was across the street; I recognized it from before."

"What do you mean?" Monica asked

"When I left the newspaper building, it was out in front."

"Marie, do you think it's you-know-who? Damn, I wish I had my weapons."

"I don't know, Kimberly."

"Is it following us?" asked Monica.

The driver spoke up. "Yes, it is."

"Who the devil are you?" Monica asked.

"I'm a friend of Sam's, young lady. He had a feeling this was not over."

"But what is your name?" Kimberly asked.

"Miss MacDarroch, my name is Tom MacGee."

"Well, Tom MacGee, where is Sam?"

"Your name is Kimberly, isn't it? Well, miss, Sam said he'll meet you at the morgue. Big William Ledbetter of the FBI and Scotland Yard will be there."

Deirdre was listening to the conversation and smiled to herself.

"Tom, why do they call Mr. Ledbetter, Big William?"

"Well, Monica, is it?"

"Yes."

"He is six feet five inches tall. He's not fat, but boy does he have a lot of muscle. He was born in Scotland and his family goes generations back on the Isle of Jura."

"But, Ledbetter? That's not Scottish, is it?"

"I heard he changed it for other reasons."

"You mean he has a deep, dark secret of some sort?"

"Could be, Miss Kimberly, could be."

Deirdre, after hearing this conversation, was wondering just what Big William Ledbetter was hiding.

"Here you are, ladies, the city morgue. I'll be here waiting on you if plans don't change. Be careful."

As the girls walked in, Deirdre saw Sam talking to a very large man who just had to be Big William Ledbetter.

Seeing the girls, Sam excused himself. With tears in their eyes, they went over to hug Sam. "Now girls, you know Deirdre would not want all the tears and carrying on."

Deirdre moved over, putting her arms around him and whispered, "Thanks, dear friend." As the tears were running down her cheeks, she asked, "How did you know it wasn't me?"

Hugging her, he whispered, "You girls had better go back home, pack and leave for Scotland as soon as you can. She didn't have your strawberry birthmark on her backside."

"How did you know about my birthmark?" Deirdre whispered.

Sam smiled and patted her hand. "Remember on your job application, the section about identifying marks or scars? Unfortunately, this is one of the reasons we ask."

"Sam, thank you for everything. We'll take the body home, tonight," spoke Kimberly in a little choked voice.

Before the girls left the morgue, Sam called the Gray Funeral Home. They sent a hearse to transport the body to the airport. It had been suggested by Sam and William that they ride in front with William's driver.

"You girls be careful and I'll see you later," remarked Agent William. They just nodded and left.

The three sisters watched as they loaded 'Deirdre's' body onto the airplane. After settling into their seats, it hit all three at one time. "What did he mean, he would see us later? He even smiled," remarked Monica.

"Deirdre! I have the funniest feeling about that man! I have seen him somewhere before, but for the life of me, I can't remember where," Kimberly spoke with a puzzled look on her face.

"You're so right. I have the same strong feeling."

"Me too," Monica remarked, wrinkling her nose.

"But where, Deirdre? Where?"

"Kimberly, please honey, go to sleep. It will come to us, I promise."

"OK, I'll hold you to that."

"Me too," Monica replied with a big yawn.

The next thing they knew, the girls felt the wheels touch down once again, but this time at the Asheville-Hendersonville Airport.

Deirdre thought to herself, *Thank God we were able to get a straight through flight from Albany to home.*

As the girls watched and waited, the plane stopped on the side of the airfield instead of going to a gate. Puzzled, they joined the other passengers and walked out the airplane door and down the steps. There to meet them was a black hearse with the name "North" on the side.

The girls watched as the body was unloaded. They started walking toward the terminal just as the driver got out of the hearse. "Ladies, if you will ride with me, please."

"Who says so?" demanded Kimberly.

Looking right at Deirdre, he replied. "I believe you know, being the oldest, Miss Deirdre MacDarroch."

"Yes, I get your meaning Mr...."

"Mr. Hugh MacLean, in Agent William's service," he said with a smile.

"Holy Cow!" Monica's shout was stifled when Kimberly clamped her hand over her mouth.

The girls looked around and sure enough there was the Big Man himself and he had no intentions of leaving them alone.

The service for Marie was short but touching. Her ashes were taken to the top of MacDarroch Mountain and laid to rest. After that labor of love was completed, the girls sat down under the huge old oak.

Deirdre jumped back up. "My word, I forgot to go back to Marie's apartment to look for a letter Marie said years ago she would hide there for me in case anything happened to her."

"Is this what you are looking for?" asked William as he came from behind the oak tree, handing Deirdre a letter.

"How in the world did you know?" asked Deirdre, looking up into his eyes.

"I guess I was just lucky. Maybe I had a guiding spirit." William smiled at her.

Kimberly spoke up with a determined look on her face. "Now wait just one cotton-picking minute. It's your turn to answer some questions."

"Shoot," he said, smiling. "Just a figure of speech, of course."

"First, I for one, would like to know who the devil you are?"

"Kimber, right?"

"Yes, but it is Kimberly, thank you."

"Well, number one, I was hired to make sure that you lassies got to Islay and Jura, Scotland, safely."

"And who, may I ask, hired you?" said Monica.

"Do you lassies really want to know?"

"Yes, otherwise I would not have asked."

"All right then. It was really your Great-grandfather Oliver."

The girls just looked at him with their mouths wide open. Deirdre asked, "But how? Where? When?"

"Well, number one, I received a letter from his barrister, Angus Gordon, the old Laird's letter."

"Now wait just one moment."

"Miss Deirdre, please, let's go back down to the house, and then we can sit and talk."

Dusk was spreading its shadowy blanket as they started down the mountain trail. An old and familiar sound made them all freeze in mid-step and look to the top of the mountain.

There, outlined against the sky's rapidly fading light, stood the figure of a man in full Scottish dress, playing his song of Scotland on the pipes. He stood there, straight and tall, beside Marie's marker. It was as though he was playing the song in her memory.

The song of the pipes faded along with the mysterious piper. The sisters looked at one another, then at William. They were all rubbing their arms as if from a chill.

Chapter 4

Deirdre asked as they entered the house, "Mr. Ledbetter, would you please talk to us?"

Monica looked William in the eye when she spoke, "You know, you look very much like someone I used to know."

"Really? People say I have that kind of face. But you know, you lassies need to leave no later than day after tomorrow for Scotland."

With a very serious look on her face, Deirdre asked, "Who are you, really?" A vision started to come back to her. Scenes that she had pushed way back in her memory all these years.

"I feel you already know that answer, lassie."

The other two just looked on in amazement, and then Kimberly blurted out, "There is something about us you do not know, sir. Each of us was born with a veil over our eyes, so we were told. Unusual, they say, for three sisters in one family. But we can't see what is pertaining to ourselves. Like I can't see what will happen to me, but Deirdre and Monica can. And I can see what happens to them."

"Yes, it's true, Golden One. But there be one more."

Kimberly, looking frightened, moved closer to Deirdre, as though she would protect her. Deirdre took her hand and then asked, "How did you know her nickname? And who is the other?"

"Sorry to have frightened you, lassie, I didn't mean to. It was your mother, of course."

No one had noticed when Monica slipped out of the room and returned with her dagger, which was now firmly pressed against the big man's back, just over his kidney. Monica spoke with anger in her voice, "All right, mister, who the heck are you to know so much about us? Tell us, or so help me God, you'll draw your last breath."

Startled, William spoke very quietly, "Now wait one minute, lass. I don't mean you any harm. I was sent here to take you back to Mr. Angus Gordon, like the letter says."

Deirdre looked as though she had just come out of a dream. "My word. I completely forgot about the letters. These letters should tell us something."

Kimberly looked into Deirdre's eyes. "Sister, did you see something?"

"Later, Kimberly, later. Let's get this out of the way first. I'll read Marie's first, here goes. It says,

Dear Deirdre,

I know this will come as a great surprise to you, as to what I'm about to say, but here goes. From the very start, when I first met you, I knew you were different. What I mean is the way you always took action and were not afraid of anything or anybody. You remember the time I took a trip and not even you knew where? Well, my friend, I went to Islay, Scotland. I remembered all the stories you had told me about Islay. I went to the museum there and I was certainly surprised. A whole section was devoted to your family. I read the story about what happened to you and your sisters. See, I told you a long time ago that I was like a big bulldog and when anything bothered me I ran it down. That is why I was a damn good detective. When you get this I will be dead. I loved you and your sisters, all of you were my own family.

Love to you,
Marie

They all lowered their heads and each said a quiet prayer. Monica raised her head then spoke up. "OK, read the other letter, Deirdre. Will you please read it out loud?"

"OK, Monica, here goes," she said as she opened the second letter. It held instructions on what to do about going to see Angus Gordon. Deirdre unfolded the letter that was once white paper but now had turned yellow with age. The letter read:

My darling lassies. This is to inform ye of things ye must do. First ye go and see Mr. Angus Gordon. He and his family have been our legal advisors for many centuries now. He also has many things to ask ye.

Now in the other letter it will tell ye things that only ye will know. All things will come back to ye, so ye will keep them to ye self. I will be with ye *always. Don't forget the name Sea Oaks. 'Tis your home.'*

God Speed
Your Loving Great-grandfather Oliver.

With that read, Deirdre's hands were shaking. She looked up to see tears in William's eyes. Wanting to ask why, but thought better of it. Now was not the time. The time would soon come.

Deirdre took a deep breath as she opened the other letter. Simultaneously, she was seeing something out of her past. She didn't even realize the others were in the room and watching her very closely. She looked up as though in a trance, and then mumbled, "Uncle William, take us home." Deirdre shook her head and came up with a smile.

"Are you alright?" asked Monica.

"Yes, I am. Now to the next letter."

"What did you see?" Kimberly asked.

"Later, Kimberly, later."

"That's what you said a little while ago."

"I know, Kimberly, and I will when the time is right."

"And when will that be, may I ask?"

Looking up at Kimberly with fire in her eyes, Deirdre snapped, "When I am damn good and ready, or maybe not at all, with your accursed attitude. Now sit down if you wish to hear this."

Not once since they came here could Kimberly remember Deirdre ever speaking to her in that manner. Pouting, she went over and sat down next to William and Monica.

Deirdre opened the third letter, glancing at it before she read it aloud.

"Well, what in God's name are you waiting for?" Monica asked in anger.

Deirdre ignored her, and kept on reading. When she finished, she folded the letter back up, and put it in her pants pocket. Without a word, she ran out of the room, with tears in her eyes. As she went out onto the porch and up the mountain trail to the top, she was wiping tears all the way.

As Deirdre climbed the hill, she thought of their life back in sixteen eighty-two before they got pulled to the twentieth century and wondered, *What will we find when we go home?*

William looked at each of the girls. "Is she always like this? I mean the anger. I know she's stubborn, but..."

Kimberly interrupted. "No. It must have been something in that last letter that she didn't want to tell us about."

Monica turned and looked at the big man, "She has never, since we came here, spoken to us that way. Do you know why?"

"Lassies, I believe I do. If you will excuse me, I'll see if I'm right."

William stood in the front yard and looked up to heaven. "Well, you did it good this time, didn't you? Well, Grandfather Oliver, you're the great-grandfather of all these lassies, and I thank you for taking care of them. I know, you did guide them and I bet you got them ready for anything.

"You couldn't find the way back home. Maybe it was not meant to be. Is all that in the letter? The lassies were brought here when the Black Fog came again to Scotland. Now, I need to help Deirdre figure this out if I can. Old man, you did it this time."

As Big William walked up the path to where he thought Deirdre would be, he heard crying. "Lassie love, don't you cry now." Going over to where she was sitting, he spoke softly, "Now, now." Putting his arms around her, "Well go ahead and cry if you must, will do you good."

"You are our Uncle William from Jura and brother to our dad, Laird John MacDarroch. You are here to take us home, are you not?" Deirdre sniffled.

"Yes, lassie, that I am. Also, to see that no harm will befall you from the Campbells. You know, lass, I lost my wife in that cursed fog. Not only was I looking for you but also her," he said with his head bowed and tears in his eyes.

"What's her name?" asked Deirdre, wiping tears from her eyes.

"Sue. Her eyes were blue as the heavens, hair down to her knees. Looked like a golden strawberry patch, when the sun shone on it. God, I miss her. I love her so much, she's my life. I want to keep on looking for her. But enough of that now. Back to the letter."

"Wait just one minute, Uncle William, Sue sounds like someone I know. But we'll wait and see."

"Now lassie, please, back to the letter."

Deirdre smiled at him, and then spoke, "Now the letter said a lot of things, like we should go to the museum to really see about our history or part of it. It also said that I should not tell the girls anything about our mysterious family. But we three have known about our family and the mysterious goings on in it for years now. Like why our rings never came off and how they grew to fit the finger as we grew and how the blue-green stone turns more green than blue when I think about Jura. Then the small fresh-water pearls are warm to the touch. My sisters' do the same. How we sense things."

"I know, My Lady, I know."

Deirdre started to get up, but sat back down. "What did you call me?"

"My Lady, and one day you'll be Laird."

"But I can't be. It's the male first-born only who can be Laird of a clan."

"That I know, lass. I have a story to tell you and you must listen and not speak until I finish, alright?"

Nodding her head, Deirdre agreed.

"Alright now, have you ever felt like there should be two of you?"

"Yes, that I have."

"Well, love, you had a twin brother who was born five minutes before you. His name was David. A fine young man, he was. But very hot-headed, and much like you in some ways. You both would fight, taking the same training, but he would let his anger get to him, where you would bide your time, then go for the kill."

"I remember now. One day I hid in the bushes and watched Mother and Father sword practice on the playing field. Oh! Uncle William, the moves she made. I always wondered why I could not learn to use a sword."

"I, too, remember that day. Your Uncle Jamie found you and brought you to us on the field."

"Yes, and that is when Mother said it was time for me to start learning."

"You remember your brother, David, went wild at the thought of you learning. But your mother won out on the matter and you started. Love, remember your Grandfather Kirk and your mother taught you."

"David didn't like it one bit. But he loved ye and was always afraid of something happening to ye."

"What happened to him?" she asked with tears running down her face.

"After you were taken from us, in the Black Fog; there was a raid by the Campbells. David fought like a madman, blaming them for your disappearance, as well as Tommy MacDonald, your husband. It was he who put the ring on your finger. I would say you're about twenty five now. Tommy would be about twenty eight."

"Have you by any chance found Tommy and his brothers?"

"No lass, I have not. Thank Dhia, you were found on MacDarroch Mountain.

"You mean, thank God," correcting her Uncle William.

"That's what I just said. "Thank God. What's happened to you lassie? Have you forgotten your own Scottish tongue?"

"I must have, but I'm sure it will come back to me."

Deirdre sat in silence for a minute, and then asked, "I wonder how Tommy MacDonald feels now?"

"I don't know. Do you remember anything about him at all, lass? For it was like I told you, he was lost the same as you. Have you seen him?"

"No, I have not. But I do remember what he looked like. I was fifteen and we were married. I knew him all my life and loved him, and still do. I remember his black hair and those wonderful blue-violet eyes. Oh, Uncle William, I do hope he hasn't forgotten me."

Laughing, he asked, "May I ask you if you have had another man?"

"It's really none of your business, but there have been a few men in my life, none that I would have been physical with. I've been too busy, being a reporter and a writer."

"And I know you're a damn good one, too."

"Yes, I am a damn good one."

"Uncle, will you tell the others, or shall I let them read the letter? And that Sea Oaks is really our home?"

"Yes, yes, and yes to the last one. You know, when I think about it, Tommy and his brothers came home before I left to find you lassies?"

"How would we know?" Just at that moment Deirdre heard voices coming up the mountain; she recognized the voices as being Kimberly and Monica. She looked up to see them staring down at her. Throwing open her arms, she said, "I am so sorry that I spoke to you both so sharply. I guess it was reading the letters."

"We knew something had to be wrong. You have never, since we came here, spoken to us that way," Kimberly said, as she went into Deirdre's arms, crying as well.

Monica ran to Deirdre and threw her arms around her neck. Being brave about the whole thing she asked, "Are we allowed to read the second letter?"

"Tomorrow. Let's all go down and try to get some sleep. This has been one hell of a day, wouldn't you say?"

With a large smile, Kimberly answered. "You had better believe it, sis."

Monica looked up into William's face then said, "Especially when you find out that your Uncle has come so far to collect you and take you back home."

"How in the world did you ever guess, lass?" Laughing, Uncle William hugged Monica to him.

"Told you that you looked like someone I once knew. You used to ride me on your shoulders when I was small, a long time ago. Remember, Kimberly?"

"Yes, I do, and how Uncle William used to go with me to get wild berries and herbs. Most of all when we went to pick apples and he would eat the green ones, even when I told him they would give him great pains in the lower parts of his body."

"And boy, did they." They all laughed and it seemed they were all more at ease by the time they reached the house.

Duke and Major were on the porch to greet them with wagging tails and barks of joy. They spotted their master, and jumped up on Deirdre, sniffing her to make sure she was all right, as they always had done since they were pups.

"Oh dear! What am I going to do about my lads? I can't take them with me."

"What about the caretakers, Deirdre? The lads love them. They've gone over to their house every day. Mr. and Mrs. D. love them as well, so you know they would take good care of them.

"Good idea, Kimberly. I'll call them tomorrow."

The next morning while Kimberly and Monica were reading the letters, Deirdre called Mr. and Mrs. Douglas about the lads. They were more than happy to keep them. Deirdre told them that she would give them all the papers on the dogs and a letter stating that they belonged to the Douglas'.

"Are you really going to give them to us? What about when you come back?" asked Mr. Douglas?

"I feel very strongly that I may not be coming back, not in this lifetime, at least. They are yours because," she choked some on the tears she was trying to hold back, "I know that you will take good care of them and love them."

"Now don't you go and worry yourself, Ms. Deirdre. They will be like our children."

With goodbyes out of the way, Deirdre hung up the phone and wiped tears from her eyes. "Well... that's done, we need to pack and get ready to leave tomorrow morning. Mr. and Mrs. D. will be over to clean up and get Duke and Major. Man alive, girls, the time is here. Where in the world has it gone? When we got here it was the first of June, and now, it is almost the end of July."

"The letter said we need to be back on your birthday Deirdre, the 27th of July. That's when we were planning on going, anyway. And can you believe it is here already?" asked Kimberly.

Deirdre smiled as she spoke, "Yes, I know. Time has just flown by, but look at all that has happened. Funny, isn't it?"

"No, Deirdre, it isn't. He planted it in our heads."

"Who, Monica?"

"Who else but Papa Oliver? That's who."

"My goodness, Monica, we planned this trip two years ago."

"Yes, we did, but who suggested it first? Now think about it," asked Monica.

"She's right, Deirdre. He sat right there in his rocker and said it would be a good trip," Kimberly spoke with a giggle.

"You're right!   Oh, what the heck.   We were going anyway." smiled Deirdre.

"Yes, that you are, Deirdre. You will be there in time for the Black Fog again, but you will get there in time to find out about yourselves," laughed their uncle.

"Girls, did you know that Uncle William's wife was also taken by the Black Fog at the same time we were?" asked Deirdre.

Both girls looked at their Uncle and he nodded his head.

Deirdre explained to her sisters that she thought it might be Sue, who was an airline flight attendant friend of hers.

Kimberly and Monica dropped their jaws as they looked at each other. "What next?" asked Monica?

They did not notice that in Great-grandfather's rocker, a small mist seemed to be smiling, smoking a pipe, and Papa Oliver chuckling and saying, "Now the trip really begins."

Chapter 5

The next morning, Mr. and Mrs. D. came over. Mrs. D was cleaning the kitchen when Deirdre popped her head in the door and said, "Sorry that we left things in such a mess, Mrs. D., but our uncle had to have his hot tea this morning and insisted on making scones."

Mrs. D. smiled. "Why, that's alright, honey. Men always make a mess in the kitchen when they cook. I'm used to it after all these years. Now you run along and finish packing before Mr. D. gets back with the lads."

"Thank you again for taking them, Mrs. D. I can leave knowing that they will be well cared for."

Deirdre left the kitchen and went to her bedroom to finish packing.

She was thinking about Duke and Major, and how they always knew when she was going away. When they saw her packing her suitcases, they would get very nervous and start to pace. So, on this day, Mr. D. took the dogs for a ride in his old blue Ford truck. Of course, he never let them ride in the back. It was always in the front seat with him. Deirdre could see the love that he had for them written all over his face.

Kimberly called the airport to make certain the limousine would pick them up in time to catch their plane. She left the living room saying to Deirdre, "Think I'll walk up the mountain for a little while."

"That sounds like a good idea," replied Deirdre, as she heard the screen door close.

As Kimberly walked around the corner of the house that led up the path to the mountain, the phone rang. Deirdre picked it up, and then remembered too late.

"Hello?" she asked hesitantly.

"Hello, this is Sue Gordon a friend... God, is that you? Deirdre?"

"Sue, please keep this under your hat. It could mean my life."

"You know I will. But I just got back into the country; saw your picture in the newspaper saying you were killed. Please explain to me what happened. No, wait one minute. I need a drink first."

"So do I. You hold on, too."

Deirdre, with perspiration popping out on her face, looked at the phone, then picked it up and prayed, "God please let her keep quiet."

"Hello, are you back?" came a question over the phone.

"Yes, I'm here," answered Deirdre.

"Now, girlfriend, what happened?"

Deirdre told Sue the whole story. "Marie Dotson? That name sounds so familiar. Wait a minute, I do know her. We were brought up in the same orphanage together. It was St. Mary's on Staten Island, New York."

"You're kidding me, Sue. You knew her? How old was she when she was left at the orphanage?"

"Let's see, Deirdre. The old nun, Frances, told me she was about nine years old."

"How old were you, Sue?"

"Mother Superior told me that I was in shock when they found me. When I came to they said that I told them I was ten and six summers. In other words, I was sixteen years old. You know, Deirdre, I had a ring on my finger, a heavy silver band with love knots all around it. To this day it will not come off."

"What did you say?"

Sue started to speak, but Deirdre cut her off. "Which hand?" asked Deirdre.

"The left hand, on my ring finger. You know something else, they had a doctor give me an examination to see if I was still a virgin."

"What did they find?"

Laughing aloud, she managed, "That I was not one." Sue stopped laughing, and the tone of her voice turned serious. "You know, Deirdre, I still dream of the man I belong to. He is not of this time. I have often wondered what it means. Maybe that is why I have not had any success with men. Not even my husband."

"Sue, I need to go now. All of this has really taken the wind out of my sails."

"I understand. Deirdre, don't worry. I'll not say a word."

"I know you won't, Sue. We scattered Marie's ashes on the MacDarroch Mountain. She's at peace now."

"That I know, Deirdre; that I know. Have a safe trip," Sue said as she hung up.

Deirdre stood in silence, still holding on to the phone. *How did she know I was going on a trip?* she thought to herself.

Kimberly came into the room and saw Deirdre standing there with the phone in her hand. "My God, Deirdre, you know better than to call anyone," she said as she crossed over to her with concern shadowing her face.

"I didn't. It rang just after you left and it was just a reflex to pick it up."

"Who was it?" she asked with tightness in her voice as though her throat was very dry.

"It was Sue Gordon, the airline stewardess. She thought she was talking to you at first, and then figured out it was me. She knew Marie. They came from the same orphanage; it was St. Mary's on Staten Island, New York. She knew all about her," Deirdre finished with a vacant look in her eyes.

"Deirdre, what's wrong?" asked Monica as she came into the living room.

"Quiet, Monica, she's having a vision; I'm sure of it. Let's just leave her alone for a while." Kimberly took Monica by the arm and they quietly left the room.

Deirdre was seeing a vision of the wedding of her Uncle William and Sue many centuries ago. She just knew they would be reunited soon.

The trip to the airport was exiting, anxious, and sad. Deirdre tried to think of what was ahead. She was not only a reporter, but she wrote historical romance books. It was her way of living in that other time and place that she loved so much. She had sent her last two manuscripts to her agent, Peter Armstrong, right before they left.

William had packed their weapons in a long, wooden box that was sealed and marked with his name and address. As added security, he placed the FBI seal on it as well as the one for Scotland Yard.

The limo pulled into the Asheville airport, right up to the Delta Airways entrance outside the ticket desk. Kimberly and Monica checked in, but Deirdre hung back.

"Deirdre, you had better check in," suggested Kimberly.

"Wha, what?"

"I said you had better check in. Are you feeling alright?" asked Kimberly.

"Yes, Kimberly, I was just looking around for the last time."

"Now, you don't know that for sure," remarked Monica, shaking her head.

"Come on, Monica; let's go get something to read."

"Right with you, Kimberly. See you on board the plane, Deirdre."

"OK, but I do know, Monica, I do!" Deirdre shouted after the girls. Deirdre started walking to the gate when she heard a voice she knew.

"Hey wait up, you red-headed person! Where do you think you're going, lady?"

Deirdre looked around and saw Sue. *Could she really be Uncle William's wife?* she wondered to herself. They had known one another for years. Sue had been an attendant on just about every flight Deirdre had taken on her book-signing tours.

"Well, hell, Sue, how are things? I'm waiting on my sisters, Kimberly and Monica. They went to get gum and something to read. Have you by any chance seen them?" Leaning closer to Sue, Deirdre whispered, "Thanks for everything, Sue."

"No, but they have about another twenty minutes yet. Don't worry, they'll make it." Looking around, she spoke softly, "Deirdre, you know I would not do anything to jeopardize your life, you feel like a sister to me."

"Thank you, Sue."

Deirdre boarded the plane, and Sue found her a seat in the first-class section. As Deirdre started to get into her seat, she gave her head a hard whack on the overhead rack.

"Deirdre, are you alright? Did you hurt your hard head?" Sue asked, smiling at Deirdre. "You know, I remember you doing that a few times before," she said, laughing as she looked around.

That was when she noticed William coming aboard. "Oh, now say, what do you think about that big hunk-of-a-man getting on the plane?"

"He's my uncle," Deirdre said, holding her head.

"What a man. Is he married?"

"Yes, he is handsome and no, he's not married, he used to be. But you are."

"Not any more, honey. I'm as free as a bird." Sue left to get Deirdre something for her head, which she knew had begun to hurt like the devil.

Coming back to Deirdre's seat, she handed the aspirin and a glass of water to Deirdre, and then said, "Here, is something for your head. Really need to go and do my job. How did you like living in the mountains?"

"Oh, Sue, it's like living in heaven. By the way, what are you doing on this flight?"

"Going to New York, silly."

Deirdre smiled at her and then said, "Sorry, Sue that was a silly question."

"I'll be back to let you in on something a little later," Sue said as she walked toward the front of the plane. She was looking at William with his red hair and beard, but most of all, his bright blue eyes. Big William was just that, big, not fat, but all muscles with a broad chest, flat stomach and long legs. He was often heard to say he was just very well-built, in all departments.

Deirdre smiled to herself at the way those two looked at each other. *Funny, it's like they know one another. Sue may be the one.*

"Boy, we just made it," remarked an out-of-breath Monica as they boarded the plane.

"Here I am, girls. Your seats are here with me."

"OK! Wasn't that Sue?" asked Kimberly.

"Yes, it was, why?"

"Just thought it looked like her. Come on, Monica, slide through to the middle seat. I'll sit on the aisle."

"And just why must I sit in the middle seat, might I ask?"

"Just because your legs are shorter than ours," answered Kimberly.

Deirdre knew right then that Monica was just a little irritated at Kimberly. "Monica, we can change seats later on to give each other the freedom of not feeling cooped up in one spot. Will that suit you?"

"Yes, thank you, Deirdre, it would. Now why didn't you think of that, Kimberly?"

Deirdre watched the girls get settled. She looked up to see Sue, welcoming the other passengers aboard. Deirdre turned to see Uncle William watching her, smiling to himself when he saw Sue as she greeted the other passengers. But when she smiled at him, he stopped, and then started reading his paper.

Silly man, thought Deirdre, *He knows her and thinks no one can see it. I feel for sure he was the one who put the ring on her hand. By*

George, look at him blush. He is taking her left hand and looking at it. Yep, that's her alright; the man has tears in his eyes and so does she.

Deirdre just grinned as everyone fastened their seat belts when the light went on to get ready for takeoff. The plane taxied down the runway and in a heartbeat they were airborne. Deirdre looked over and saw Kimberly's hand turn white from the grip she had on the arm of the seat. Then the lights went out.

"Ladies and gentlemen, this is your captain speaking. We'll be arriving in New York in about three and a half hours. So please, sit back and enjoy your flight. The flight attendants will be around to take your drink orders momentarily. Thank you for flying Delta Airlines."

Deirdre took her seat belt off, and looked around to see who was interesting on the flight. No one of interest.

She still couldn't shake this mystic apprehensive feeling. Maybe it was all the things Great-grandfather had told them about the mystery that had surrounded their home, Jura. He would say something about the castle named Sea Oaks, and that our clan dated back as far as the year six hundred and one.

"Deirdre," Monica said, as she shook her a little.

"What is it, baby sister?"

"I still can't believe that we are going. And please stop calling me that. I'm grown now."

"Yes, honey, we are going. Sorry, but you'll always be little sister to me."

Just at that moment, Sue came up and leaned on the seat in front of them. "Well, I have good news for you. At least I hope it will be."

Deirdre looked up and saw Sue's smile, "OK, woman, give."

"Guess what? I'm going to be on your flight to Glasgow, Scotland. Now, what do you think of that?"

"Sue, that's just great! How did all this come about?"

"Deirdre, I got the assignment not more than ten minutes before we took off. It was like something out of the blue."

Deirdre asked, "Look, we have a long layover in New York, right?"

"No."

"How long do we have then?"

"We just have a three hour layover."

"OK, then. Could we go for a drink and a sandwich?"

"We sure can. Will your uncle be joining us, I hope?"

"Yes, of course he will. How does that sound to everyone?" Deirdre looked at her sisters with a smile.

"Fine with us, you know that," they answered.

"Oh! By the way, are you still writing?" asked Sue.

"Why yes. Why do you ask?"

"That's great. You see, I just bought your latest in the gift shop at the airport. Would you please autograph it for me?" she asked, laughing.

"You know damn good and well, I will. You just bring it to me and I'll do it. I just sent my very last two manuscripts to my agent. You'll have to read them when they come out. They're better than all the rest."

The next thing Deirdre knew, Sue was handing her the book to sign. A young passenger was looking on. "See, I told you it was her and you wouldn't believe me," she was saying as she looked at her mother.

Deirdre smiled at the young woman when she, too, pulled her copy of the book out of her bag. "Will you please sign mine, too?"

"Yes, I'll be glad to. Hope you enjoy it," Deirdre said as she asked for her name.

"I have read all of your books and loved every one of them. Oh! My name is Betty English."

"Well, Betty English, enjoy your trip and the book. We have," Kimberly spoke up, to everyone's surprise.

The young woman walked off with a big grin on her face.

They all three laid their heads back and closed their tired eyes.

All of the great stories Great-grandfather Oliver had ever told Deirdre came to mind. There was something he would say and then giggle. "Now what was it? Oh, well, maybe it will come to me later."

Suddenly, her hands and feet got icy cold. Seeing Sue, she motioned for her to come over. As she came closer, Deirdre asked, "Sorry, Sue, but could I have a blanket and a pillow? It seems all of a sudden I've developed a chill."

"Sure." Sue opened the storage compartment overhead; Kimberly and Monica asked for a blanket and a pillow, too.

"Now if you girls need me, ring."

"Thanks Sue. We'll do just that." Deirdre spoke turning to her sisters, "Now tell me, why did you need a blanket and pillow when I did?"

"I got a chill and then my feet and hands got very cold," answered Kimberly.

As Monica looked at each of them, her face grew pale. "So did I. By the way, how is your head feeling? Did the aspirin Sue gave you do the trick?"

"How did you know?" asked Deirdre.

"Oh, you know," remarked Monica.

"I bumped my head on the upper rack as I was getting into my seat, that's all, and I have a little headache."

They looked over at Deirdre with a smirk on their faces. "You do that quite often, don't you?" They laughed.

"Oh!! Go to sleep, both of you," Deirdre said smiling.

They fell asleep with unanswered questions filling their minds. The next thing Deirdre knew, Sue was shaking her. "We are about to land at Kennedy in about five minutes. I'll wake your uncle," she said as she left with a big smile.

Deirdre watched Sue wake up her Uncle William with a gentle shake. Uncle William smiled up at her and said, "Thank you." Deirdre saw his lips move as he pulled Sue down and whispered something into her ear. He then took her hand and kissed it. They smiled at each other, and then Sue went back to work.

"Monica, sister, wake up. We're landing at Kennedy."

"What? Are we there already?"

Laughing, Kimberly answered. "We must have slept the whole way. One more leg and we're home."

"Deirdre, are you awake?"

"Yes, Kimberly. Let's get our things together. We're going to meet Sue at a cocktail lounge named Martini's for a drink and sandwich." Looking at the girls, Deirdre gasped. "You took your hair down just like I did."

"Yes, we did. Feels a lot better, doesn't it?"

"You bet, Monica. It sure does. Now we have to get Uncle William," she said, looking around for him.

"Deirdre! He's not here," Kimberly said, as panic touched her voice.

"Take it easy, Kimberly. He's most likely out looking around to see if it's safe."

Trying to catch up, Monica asked, "Deirdre, when does our plane leave for Scotland?"

"In three hours. Wow! Can you believe it? Sue is going all the way with us."

"You're kidding," replied Kimberly, her very large eyes, trying to check everyone out.

"My goodness, Kimberly. Didn't you hear her when she was telling Deirdre? Where in the world were you, in never-never-land?" asked Monica.

Deirdre smiled at her two sisters as she spoke. "Ladies, please, let's go." She started down the aisle to get off the plane, "Come on. Let's go have a drink. I think a big tall Scotch sounds nice, don't you?"

"You bet. I could sure use one. How about you, Monica?" asked Kimberly.

"Exactly, with a nice big sandwich, with lots and lots of dill pickles."

Seeing Sue, Deirdre called out. "We're right behind you, Sue. Just lead and we'll follow."

"Isn't your uncle coming?" asked Sue, looking around to see if she could see him.

"I'm sure we'll see him. He never turns down a meal with a beautiful woman," Deirdre said, smiling at Sue, just like a fat mouse that swallowed a big chunk of cheese.

Smiling and turning a little pink, Sue asked, "When did you girls take your hair down from the long braids? I bet it feels good to have it free and out of the dang tight braid. Wish I could," she said, touching her big bun at the nap of her neck. "Look, people are stopping and looking at you. Bet the men would love to run their toes through it." Laughing, she led them down to the cocktail lounge.

As they entered the lounge door, it was quite dim and hard to see. But all heads turned to stare as four lovely ladies came in the door with light from the hall shining through. Sue found them seats in a booth and, giggling like school girls, they chatted as they each enjoyed their tall Scotch on the rocks. The bartender saw them as they came in and just couldn't keep his mind on what he should have been doing. As his gaze went from one to the other, customers began to complain about their orders.

"We had better order our sandwiches. If you want to talk to your sisters in private, this corner is the best. Oh look, there's your uncle."

"You're right, Sue," Deirdre said as she got up and went over to the bartender. "Could you fix some of those turkey and ham club sandwiches that you're so famous for?"

"I sure can, good-looking. By the way, my name is Harry."

"Thanks so much, Harry."

Sue smiled at Deirdre then said, "You still got it. Scotland had better look out. By the way, that black leather jump suit doesn't hurt either. I love your boots. Hey, I just noticed they are up to your knees. All of you are wearing the same thing."

"Thanks for the compliment, Sue, but it's not black. It's the darkest green ever. They are so comfortable to travel in."

They were all laughing as if they had good sense when Monica remarked, "I'm starving."

"We all are." Just then, the bartender came over with the biggest club sandwiches they had ever seen, with lots of pickles and chips. Looking over at Big William, they all smiled. He had two clubs. When he saw Sue looking at him, he winked.

"Alright, does everyone know how to eat this big baby?" Deirdre looked at the bartender and said, "Thanks, Harry."

"I'll have a hot tea if I can get one," answered Sue. "Do you girls mind if I go over and sit with your uncle?"

"Well, of course not. Go ahead," smiled Kimberly.

"How about the rest?" Deirdre asked, "What do you want to drink?"

"Let me think. You go ahead, Deirdre. I can't make up my mind," started Kimberly, looking out of the corner of her eye at her Uncle William and Sue laughing at something Uncle William had just said.

"I can't either, right now. But Uncle William sure has. He knows what he wants and I bet he gets it too," remarked Monica.

"Well, while you two are trying to make up your minds, and watching things that are none of your business, I'll have a hot tea, please," stated Deirdre with a little admonition in her voice.

"I'll have the same as Deirdre. Come on, Kimberly, we're waiting for you, don't take all night."

"Alright. I'll have the same, hot tea. I hope you're happy now, Monica?"

The bartender smiled and said, "We have a very good lemon pie too, if you would like it later?"

"Thank you, Harry, we'll think about it," Deirdre answered with a wink.

Conversation came to a halt when they started eating. Sandwiches and chips were wolfed down with ease.

"Boy is this good," Kimberly said out loud. "No telling when we'll eat like this again. Maybe not for a long time, I'm thinking."

After they finished, Sue came back all smiles. "Guess I had better go and see to everything. See you gals on board." She turned, blew a kiss to Uncle William, and left singing to herself.

"So long," called Monica. Then she looked at Deirdre.

"OK, let's hear what you have to tell us, Deirdre."

"Come on, Monica, let her finish her sandwich. Just because we wolfed ours down, that's no sign she has to."

"OK, OK, Kimberly."

As Deirdre was finishing up, she wiped her mouth. "Think I'll have a large piece of lemon pie."

"What?" both girls said at one time. "Where in the world do you put it in that scrawny body of yours?"

"Must be my metabolism," Deirdre answered with a big smile on her face, "and I am not scrawny, it's all muscles, the same as yours. Well now, I received a phone call from a Mr. Angus Gordon right before we left. I was about to call my agent; when I picked up the phone to dial, there he was on the phone. It didn't even ring."

"So that's why we didn't hear the phone," remarked Monica, unasked questions shining in her eyes.

"What did he want?" asked Kimberly.

"Get this. Great-grandfather told him to call on the day we left—that very day. He has already made arrangements for us to stay at one of the local hotels."

"But, how, Deirdre?" asked Monica.

"Beats me, honey, beats me."

"Well, go on and finish telling us," urged Monica.

"That's all, honey. We'll find out the rest when we get there. Except, I feel our Sue is Uncle William's wife, Sue."

"What?" asked Monica.

"So, that's it. I'm glad for him, but let's get back to this Mr. Gordon. Are you sure about it? How did he know about us and when to call?" asked Kimberly.

"Kimberly, all I know is he said that he was told to call us on the day we left. But now I'm wondering how he got our phone number. Anyway, we have to be there on my birthday, which falls on the lunar waxing. It is very important, he said.

Because the moon would be waxing, and has every ten to fifteen years, and this is the tenth year — it would be the fullest."

"What is waxing? What does it mean, Deirdre?" asked Monica.

"Monica, waxing of the moon is like a window or portals opening between the past and present. It's like a doorway or a window opening or maybe a rip in the veil of time."

"Yes, also waxing means increasing in size, and time increased in length," Kimberly said, smiling at Monica.

"But also we need to consider the magnetic variations; lunar, solar, stellar, and terrestrial. When, at times, the moon is the fullest, the door closes, until the new moon every few years gets larger than all those before." Deirdre smiled as she finished the question of the waxing of the moon for Monica.

"So, Deirdre, what do you suppose is ahead of us?"

"Kimberly, I really don't know. But we have to be ready for anything. And I'm sure that we are. In any case, we have Uncle William."

"Well, I sure hope I'm ready," remarked Monica.

"Monica, you are as ready as we are. We are ready for anything that comes our way," Deirdre said with a smile on her lips.

Kimberly hugged Monica. "Sis, we are ready."

Looking around, Monica remarked, "Well, he's gone again."

"Who?" asked Kimberly.

"Uncle William, of course," answered Deirdre.

All of a sudden they heard their names over the sound system. "Would the MacDarroch sisters and their uncle come to gate nineteen? We are about ready to board."

They were hurrying to the gate, when they looked to the side. Uncle William and his FBI friends had captured a man who looked at Deirdre with so much hate in his soul that it burned from his eyes and made cold chills run through her body.

The agents took him away and Uncle William came over. "Hurry, get on the plane. He's a Campbell. Hurry now, let's go. I'm sitting with you on the plane. I asked your friend Sue to arrange it."

"Your wife," said Deirdre; then, swallowing hard, she put her arm through his. "They know now that I'm not dead."

"They do, lass, you must be on guard."

"Do we have to tell Kimberly and Monica?"

"Yes, we do, it's only fair that they know what to expect and be on guard for their safety as well as yours, lassie." Smiling really big now he said, "Yes, I found my darling, Sue."

Chapter 6

"Uncle William, you're right." Smiling, Deirdre ran with Uncle William along side. "We had better hurry, can't afford to miss the plane."

"You had better believe that," Kimberly puffed as she ran up alongside of Deirdre, almost out of breath.

Monica ran past them. Deirdre laughingly called, "Monica, why are you in such a hurry?"

"I don't know, but it seems important to me for some reason."

Out of breath, they got to the gate and laughed together. Sue was waiting for them with a smile. "You guys just made it. What happened to you?"

"We got to talking and the time just ran away with us. Sorry to be late, Sue." Deirdre answered, out of breath.

Sue looked at Kimberly. "Kimberly, the seating arrangements have been changed at the request of your uncle."

The girls looked down at Uncle William who was already in the seat beside Deirdre. "Why?" asked Kimberly.

Uncle William got up from his seat to go and sit by Kimberly. Monica headed for the ladies room. "Love, we caught a Campbell; they know that Deirdre is not dead. Here, take this," he said, slipping Kimberly a small derringer that fit into the palm of her hand. "Put this in your pocket; keep it close. Here is one for Monica, give it to her as soon as you can. Explain things to her. Be careful, love, remember you have one shot only, so make it a good one." He leaned over and kissed Kimberly on the cheek, got up, and went to sit down by Deirdre again.

Deirdre and Kimberly had settled in their seats by the time Monica came back from the ladies' room. Monica leaned over her seat and looked at Deirdre, then smiled. "Deirdre, you have such a glow about you! You seem so happy, why?" Deirdre knew Monica was trying to keep the conversation light. Kimberly had already explained to her about the guns.

"I guess it's because we are finally going where we belong. I know there are a lot of things that we don't understand, but I feel that Angus Gordon will help us find some of the answers that we are seeking." Deirdre smiled at Monica as she answered her question.

"Uncle William, tell us how long you have been looking for us? And did you come in a Black Fog?" asked Monica.

Uncle William smiled, "let's see now, I have been looking for you for about ten years. As for the rest, that's a long story."

"Well, we are not going anywhere, are we?" replied Kimberly.

"No, lass, I don't think so. Alright then, get comfy, here we go." Uncle William smiled at his nieces. "After you were taken in the awful fog, your mother happened to remember the saying from the old seers, who got it from the Queen of the Fairies, that there was another way to get what she called 'the window opening'."

Before he could finish Monica interrupted, "What window?"

"If you'll just listen, Monica, he'll explain. Now try and be quiet, please!"

"Oh... alright, Kimberly. You go right ahead, Uncle, and I'm sorry, I'll not say anything else until you are finished."

Uncle William smiled at her and said, "It's alright, love."

"See, he's not mad."

"Monica, please, for goodness sake, if you don't hush we'll be home before he's finished." Kimberly spoke in anger.

Monica bowed her head. "Sorry."

Deirdre reached over and patted her hand. "I know you have a lot of questions and I understand; but, honey, we need to know everything, OK?"

"Yes, you go right ahead, Uncle William." Monica spoke with a smile on her face.

"Now, where was I?" Asking, he patted Monica's hand and gave her a big hug. "Oh! I remember now. The window, or as she, the Queen, said, 'a rip in the veil that covers the future,' well, you could even call it a doorway. It's like an opening between two worlds."

"Like the past and future?"

"That's right, Deirdre, lass."

"But, tell us how you got here," Kimberly said.

"Kimberly, I was shown a place that had been forgotten for many centuries. Only the old seers and the Fairy Queen knew. Your mother took me there. The place was among a thicket of trees and muck. A place, I was told, that had been there since the year six hundred and one. The stones were very large, leaning upon one another.

Strange, most were buried in the muck, but, lassies, one, through all the years, stood tall, with another leaning against it. Your mother said that if you hear a loud buzzing sound that felt like it would make you deaf; that would be the time. It happens only once a year on All Hallows Eve. That's how I 'came through the doorway,' as your mother called it."

"Wow." Monica let out her breath that she didn't know she was even holding. Kimberly just stared off into space, while Deirdre was in a thinking mode.

"My girls, something else happened to me as I was coming through. It was like I passed someone coming back through to the past, as I was coming to the future."

"Strange." Deirdre commented with a very puzzled look on her face.

"On Jura, can you find this place even now, in this time?" asked Deirdre.

"Yes, you can if you know where to look; only the old seers know this place."

"Is that the way we'll go to get home?" asked Monica.

"No, child. I'll go back another secret way; you'll learn it one day. But you'll have to go by the way of the Black Fog this time — and its time is close."

"Well, I guess we'll find out soon enough. Monica, why do you have such a strange look on your face?" asked Kimberly.

Looking back at Kimberly, then at Deirdre, she spoke. "Deirdre, something has been bothering me since you talked to us back at Martini's, so here goes. How did you get that scar on the inside of your left knee?"

"I was told that I was trying to whittle a stick with Great-grandfather's knife, why?"

"I don't think so. It was caused by something else, but I can't put my finger on it just now; but when I do, I'll let you know."

"That's kind of you." Deirdre smiled at Monica. "Lassies, we had better get some sleep. Hold on. Do you feel it?"

"You mean like slow motion?" they asked together.

"Yes, I do. I have had that feeling ever since we started planning this trip," answered Deirdre.

"And it will not go away," smiled Uncle William, looking up from his magazine and joining their conversation.

"Do you know what we're saying?" asked Monica.

"That I do, lass," he answered, looking at them with a big smile on his face.

"You know what we must face, don't you, Uncle?" asked Kimberly.

"Yes, lassie, that I do." He closed his eyes, and tried to get some rest. "Now, let's get some sleep, lassie." Patting Deirdre's arm, Uncle William spoke quietly, "There is a lot ahead of you. Get as much sleep as you can."

Seeing Sue, Deirdre motioned for her to come to their seats. As Sue stood over her, she whispered, "Sue, we all could use a pillow and a blanket, please. I think we can sleep now."

Reaching up over their heads, Sue handed each of them a blanket and pillow. "I'll wake you when we are about to land," she said as she patted Uncle William's arm.

"Suits us," remarked Monica.

"Thank you, Sue, for your thoughtfulness," Kimberly said with a smile.

"Thanks, Sue, for everything. Goodnight," Deirdre said squeezing her hand.

"Goodnight, Deirdre, all of you enjoy your trip."

"Sue, love."

"Yes, William, what can I do for you?"

Whispering, "Would you have the Captain get in touch with Scotland Yard for me? I need to speak with someone; it's a very important matter. It's a matter of life and death."

"I'll speak to the Captain," Sue said, speaking with sweetness in her voice.

"Thank you, my sweet lass." Uncle William said with a kiss on Sue's cheek.

Sue jerked back in amazement. She was blushing as she entered the pilot's cabin. Sue told the captain of the request. The captain asked for William to come forward.

She nodded, and turned to go out the cabin door. As she opened the door, she fell into Uncle William's arms. When he finished kissing her hard, he murmured, "Thank you, love."

Sue sat down, feeling quite weak. *Why did he do that? Not that I didn't like it*, then she touched her ring. *I wonder, is it really him?* She turned pink all over again, smiling to herself.

After things settled down again, the girls went back to sleep. Each would say it was like moving through fog and in slow motion. All of a sudden, Deirdre felt Kimberly's hand squeeze her arm. Looking over at Deirdre, she whispered, "I'm sorry. Hope you don't mind, but when Uncle William went up front I moved up here to be beside you."

"It's alright." Taking her hand in her own, she held it tight, and they both drifted off. Deirdre woke up with a start. *Must be just a little turbulence.* The blanket had fallen off, and Monica was holding Kimberly's hand. Deirdre smiled to herself, then fell back to sleep.

After being in the plane's cabin all night, Uncle William went back to his seat but whispered in Deirdre's ear, so softly Kimberly and Monica could not hear him. "I just got through talking to Scotland Yard. They will send some good men that I requested by name to meet the plane in Glasgow."

"That's good, so they know what to do?" Deirdre asked.

"Deirdre, you must be prepared for anything," Uncle William said as he patted her arm.

"We are, Uncle. Don't worry about us. We are ready for anything."

"Deirdre, you're speaking a little of the Scottish."

"Aye, I know. We are ready, are we not, sisters?"

Everybody was now fully awake and nodded their heads in agreement. Monica looked over at Uncle William and punched Kimberly. "What put that dreamy look on Uncle William's face, I wonder?" Then she laughed.

The rest of them watched as Uncle William blushed a deep red. Then they looked up at Sue and saw her blushing as well. Kimberly interrupted the teasing. "Look, I can see the airport, we're here."

Deirdre thought to herself. *It's like a dream. Time to fasten our seat belts. One more thump and we'll be on the good old ground once again. Then just a short flight and we're home.*

After getting off the plane, they headed for the shuttle that would take them to Islay. Monica looked around and saw Sue with Uncle William. Even from where she stood she could see Sue glowing and the shine in her eyes. *What's going on here?* Monica wondered to herself. *Love is certainly in the air.*

"Slow down, Deirdre, you're running like you are in a hurry now." Kimberly called, darting after her.

Did you see that?"

"See what, Monica?" asked Kimberly.

"Uncle William with Sue!"

"My word," was all Deirdre could get out. "She is his wife, so what's the matter with that?" Just at that moment, five men from Scotland Yard came over and surrounded the girls. Startled, Deirdre looked to see if Uncle William was anywhere near. He was looking at her and nodded with a smile. She then knew everything would be all right.

They were standing in line to get on the shuttle for Islay, when Uncle William came over. "Lassies, you will be alright now so, I must leave you."

"But, why? You are just going to leave your wife, Sue? What do you intend to do with her and does she know where you come from?" asked Deirdre.

"Yes, yes, she does. We are to marry again, when we get home. She'll be coming with you, so you had better be looking after my darling.

Deirdre looked at her Uncle William with a puzzled look on her face, "Something has been bothering me, Uncle."

"Well, ask it, lass."

"How did you know where to find us?"

"Why, I read your newspaper column, love. Then I called the paper, using my FBI connection, and they told me where to find you," he replied, smiling at her.

"I'm glad—oh, so glad. Come on, Sue, we need to get going."

Sue hurried over; as she and Deirdre were walking, she whispered, "Deirdre, do you think I will fit in again?"

"Of course, you will be fine. You are from there, remember. Sue, lass, are you sure? Life is not easy there. You know you cannot come back."

"Yes, I know, but I love him more than my life. I knew and he felt it—that we were married sometime before."

"Sue.... he not only felt it, he knew it. He told me that he not only was looking for us, but also for you, his wife."

Monica looked at Sue with a big smile. "Sisters, have you not noticed she is starting to act like us." Everyone had a big smile and began to laugh with Sue and Uncle William. "I feel funny calling you Auntie Sue," stated Monica.

The shuttle had arrived and the boxes Uncle William had put his name on were being loaded. The sisters watched them very closely in case, when they landed, they would need their weapons fast. Still dressed in their leather and with their long hair flowing down their backs, they got all types of frowns, stares, and gawks from the crowd moving around them. Even Sue let her hair down and it flowed down to her knees. Laughing together, they didn't care who looked at them or how they appeared to others.

Deirdre hooked her arm through Sue's, with Kimberly and Monica on the other. The four walked up to the gate and boarded the plane to Islay. Their hearts were pounding loud and hard and the "almost home" feeling washed warmly over them.

Landing on Islay, a short time later, the women fairly jumped out of the shuttle. Seeing that all the baggage was on a cart, they went to match their numbers and pick up what was theirs. The large wooden box was there with Sue's name clearly printed on it this time. Deirdre looked at Sue. "How? How did it change? Uncle William's name was on there first."

"By the way, Sue, did you just up and quit your job?" Deirdre asked.

"The answer to your first question is, I really don't know," replied Sue. "The answer to your second question is, yes, I just quit."

After getting their suitcases and boxes that had the weapons in them, they hailed a cab which was in front of the airport. When the cabbie stopped in front of them, his eyes fairly bugged out of his head. His excitement showed clearly when he spoke. "I would know you anywhere, My Lady, you and your sisters. Why, my word, you are Sir William's wife, aren't you? We have been waiting all these years for you to return home."

Kimberly looked at Deirdre, then the others. "Do you mean to tell me that the whole Isle has been waiting, too?" asked Kimberly.

"Yes, that they have!"

The cabbie was so excited he drove off and left them just standing there. When he came back around the corner, he found them all laughing. Laughing with them as he opened the door for them to get in.

The cabbie never stopped talking. "I'll be going home in a few days, before the Solar Waxing which is to come on the twenty seventh of July. I'll see you then, my ladies."

Deirdre sat back in the cab. The confusion showed when she asked, "My good man, how in the world do you know us and how do the people know?"

"My Lady, we know and grew up with the stories and legends. Besides, we have a museum with everything in it you need to know. The legends say that you will come back one day and everything will change. But we'll see, won't we, My Lady?"

"Yes, we will see," Deirdre answered with a puzzled look on her face as she looked at her sisters and Sue. Puzzlement showed on their faces as well.

"Deirdre, did you hear what he called us?"

"Yes, I did, Kimberly, that I did. But love, we always have been.

"Monica, did you understand what he called us?"

"Yes, I did, Kimberly, and we are that. I just wish our brother, David, was here," she gulped with tears in her eyes.

Deirdre spoke to the cabbie. "Sir, could you please take our bags and boxes to Barrister Angus Gordon's office? And tell him, please, we'll be at the museum. That we were told to go there first."

"I will, My Lady, I can do that for you."

Riding along and looking at the shops, Sue was entranced with what she was seeing. Kimberly and Monica had their noses pressed against the window, looking. All Deirdre could think about was what she would find at the museum.

She looked around at the small, wonderful town with all its little shops. They were all white-washed with colorful wooden shutters at the windows. A cobbler shop had its sign in the shape of a shoe. There was a quaint dress and kilt shop. In its window was an old-fashioned dress that looked like it would be perfect for Sue.

There were older shops with their dusty windows displaying a variety of antiques and junk. "Look, there is the pub and inn. I wonder if we'll be staying there," Monica pointed out.

"Monica, we'll get there soon enough."

"My Lady, Deirdre, you're right. I will have to get use to calling you that," remarked Sue, grinning.

"You know we are going to have to go shopping. What do you think? And get a nice dress for Sue," Deirdre said, smiling.

"You got that right. I'm glad we came early, aren't you?" Sue smiled as she asked the question.

"Yes, oh yes!" answered Monica and Kimberly.

The cabbie came to a stop. "Here you are, My Lady. I'll go straight away to the office of Angus Gordon and leave your things. But I should warn you, he will go through everything you have in your bags and boxes."

"Thank you for the warning but we were told that a long time back. What he will be really looking for I have here in my pocket."

Laughing, the cabbie drove off. Deirdre looked at her sisters and friend. "OK! Let's go and see what we can find in here."

People stared at them as they entered the door into the museum. Looking around, the women noticed the clerk behind the counter was speaking to another group of visitors.

They had their backs to her, so she couldn't see their faces. "You go right ahead and look. If you need the history on any of the families and clans, there are books in the same section as the pictures."

"Thank you very much. Don't worry about us, we'll find our way," Deirdre spoke in a soft voice.

"What?" asked the lady behind the counter? "Oh! Alright, go and find what you need. Any questions, just ask."

"Thank you," replied Kimberly.

As Sue turned the first corner with Kimberly, she gasped. "Deirdre, come quick and see," Kimberly whispered and motioned. Following them around the corner, Deirdre looked up to where they were pointing. It was a portrait of Uncle William with a beautiful woman beside him. That woman was Sue. "How?" She asked with tears in her eyes. "How?"

"Look, maybe this book will tell us." Deirdre opened the book and began to read. When she finished, she looked at each of the women. "You were lost in the Black Fog. It seems a lot of people were."

"I do belong to him!" Sue said with joy and the tears running down her face. "He knew, but didn't say anything. You know I felt it when I saw him. I just knew I belonged to him. I dreamed of belonging to someone all the time I was in the orphanage."

"Deirdre, look." Monica called from around the corner of another room. There, on the wall, was a portrait of Deirdre holding the reins of a big, black stallion. At her feet lay a very large lynx with long limbs and a short tail. The largest they had ever seen. Under it the plaque read, "DEIRDRE MACDARROCH BORN IN THE YEAR OF OUR LORD 1666. LOST IN THE BLACK FOG, IN YEAR OF OUR LORD 1681. WIFE OF SIR THOMAS EDWARD MACDONALD.

Beside Deirdre's portrait was another. A very beautiful man on his horse. The inscription read: SIR DAVID MACDARROCH. TWIN BROTHER OF DEIRDRE MAC DARROCH. SIR DAVID DIED IN BATTLE WITH THE CAMPBELLS AFTER HIS SISTER WAS LOST. HE BLAMED THE CAMPBELLS FOR THE LOSS OF HIS TWIN.

Crying, Deirdre placed her fingers on the portrait saying, "My brother. Why were you so hot-headed? I remember you now, my dear, I love you. I'll make you proud."

The other girls saw him and started to cry also. Both said together as they looked up, "We love you and miss you, big brother."

After seeing the portrait of their brother they went in search of their own portraits.

Kimberly and Monica found their portraits. Their excitement built when they found Mother and Father, Laird John and Mary Kate MacDarroch. In another, next to it, was their Uncle Jamie, and yet another was of their Grandfather Kirk, their mother's father. He was a Viking Chief and Laird.

After they looked at all the portraits and read the books, they had a better idea of what to expect from their clan.

Monica shouted, "Deirdre, Kimberly, Sue, come here quick!"

They rounded the corner and stopped abruptly. There on the wall was the Laird Glen MacDonald's family. Thomas Edward, better known as Tommy, was husband to Deirdre MacDarroch. It was written on the plaque beside the portrait. The same with his brothers. The MacDonalds were lost the same year, 1681, on Tommy's wedding day to Lady Deirdre MacDarroch. The brothers, Hugh and Richard, were betrothed to Kimberly and Monica MacDarroch.

As they started to leave, it was Sue they could not find. "I'll go and see if she went back to the room where Uncle William's portrait is," Deirdre told them.

"Wait a moment, Deirdre. We all need to go back to the MacDonald room."

"Why, Kimberly?"

"Because I thought I saw our ring, or one similar to ours, on their swords."

"Let's go, lassies, I would like to see this too. We must hurry before Angus Gordon's office closes."

"At least he'll have plenty of time to go through our things," laughed Monica.

They had just rounded the corner when they heard crying that sounded like Sue. They found her with her hand on Uncle William's chest. Looking up, she spoke in a choked voice. "I was never happy with anyone, I have always loved him, and he, me."

"Now, Sue, we know that. Don't make yourself sick. You will see him very soon, I promise," soothed Deirdre.

"Do you think he still loves me, Deirdre?"

"Yes, lass, I do."

The women left the MacDarroch room and went to the MacDonald room. Looking up, Deirdre saw the same stone in Tommy's sword that was in her ring.

They just stood there in amazement, looking at them. "Do you think that the stones on their swords get warm and change colors like ours do?" Kimberly asked as she touched the stone on Hugh's sword.

"Maybe, but I can't be sure. We must go to Mr. Angus Gordon now. Come on, let's go," Deirdre urged as she started to the front of the museum.

With the girls following her up to the front the lady at the counter looked up. "My word, the comparison of the MacDarroch lassie's and you are remarkable. Even the other lassie looks like the one in the picture with Sir William MacDarroch. But funny, she too, disappeared. May I ask what your names are?"

Smiling at one another, "I'm as of today Lady Deirdre MacDarroch MacDonald. I had a twin, David MacDarroch, was his name. These are my sisters Kimberly, and Monica. Sue is my Uncle William's wife. Your name, please?"

Just as Deirdre finished asking her question, the lady behind the counter, Janet MacLean, fainted dead away. The ladies smiled, walked out the front door, and headed for Angus Gordon.

"Sure hope that poor woman is OK."

Chapter 7

The women hurried down the street to reach the office of Mr. Angus Gordon, Barrister. Deirdre started to say something to Sue, but saw her slip into the little dress shop across the street.

Just at that time, Kimberly tugged on Deirdre's arm.

"What's the problem?!"

"Look," Kimberly spoke softly.

Deirdre looked in the direction Kimberly was pointing. Deirdre saw a man who looked rather fragile, coming out of a residential library doorway. He was slightly bent at the shoulders, but still tall. His thinning white hair was tied back with a black leather string. The black suit and white shirt were clean and neat, but looked old and frayed around the collar and cuffs.

"Excuse me, sir. My name is Deirdre MacDarroch and these are my sisters, Kimberly and Monica, and this is Sue... Sue?" Looking around, she realized Sue had not returned yet.

"Well, now, you're finally here," he said, smiling at the three sisters. He shook Deirdre's offered hand and then gave it a little fatherly pat.

"Yes, Mr. Gordon; that we are. You have our luggage and two boxes?" Deirdre asked.

"Yes, I have all of it," he replied, still smiling at them.

"Did you find anything of interest, Mister Gordon?" asked Kimberly with a mischievous grin.

Laughing aloud, he answered her. "Yes, I did, lass, that I did." Mr. Gordon unlocked his office, and then stepped aside to let them in. "Come, lassies, sit down."

They entered into a small, dim office that smelled quite musty, with books piled high. The whole place was in need of a good dusting. The bright sun barely shone through the dingy front window.

Deirdre wondered, 'How could he see anything, let alone find anything in all this?'

"You will have to move some of my ledgers out of the way before ye can sit down."

Looking up at that moment, she saw that Sue just made it before Mr. Gordon closed the door. "Mr. Gordon, this is Sue, a dear friend of ours, and wife of Sir William, our uncle.

He nodded his head toward Sue to acknowledge her as she came in and sat down with the others.

Leaning over, Deirdre had the letter in her hand. "Sir, we have a letter that is addressed to you from our great-grandfather, Oliver MacDarroch."

Barrister Gordon reached out his hand, which was shaking just a little as Deirdre placed the letter into it. Smiling, as he held the letter to his heart, he asked, "My word is the old goat still living?"

"No Sir, he passed away two years ago. He had just had his one hundred and fifth birthday."

Laughing so hard tears ran down his cheeks, he told them, "The old goat said he would live to be past a hundred."

Then he turned and really took a good look in Sue's direction. "Glory be, it *is* you, Sue lass. How in the world did they find you? I know William MacDarroch will be a happy man," he told her, wiping his eyes.

Going over, Sue put her arms around Mr. Gordon. "I wondered if you would notice it was me, Uncle Angus. He was and is a happy man, Uncle."

Angus Gordon pulled back from Sue. "Was? Is? Then he made it. Hallelujah. Praise be to our Lord." Looking at Deirdre, Kimberly, and Monica, he continued, "He found you too, did he not, lassies?" Angus started dancing a little jig all around the office, he was so happy.

Deirdre spoke, smiling at the little man. "You're happy, Mr. Angus Gordon? Can you let us in on it?"

"Oh, My Lady, I would be happy, too. You see, your mother had a friend who was a seer; you know too, your mother was a seer as well."

"Yes, we do, Mr. Gordon, as well as are we. That is what makes our family so mysterious, you see; no one knows this but the family. We each see things different from one another. We see things that can help someone else, but can not see about ourselves. But would you mind getting on with it; we would love to go home to Sea Oaks, please."

Dancing again, Angus Gordon started singing. "Glory, glory be; it is the true ones."

Deirdre looked at her sisters and Sue. They just shook their heads. "You're telling us that there were others?"

"That there were! But none knew the name of their home, nor did they wear your rings. But most of all, they didn't know about your gifts. So, your mother kept having her dreams. Then the next thing we knew, your Uncle William disappeared. Bless be, he found all of you. How?"

"Dear Mr. Gordon," Deirdre looked at him and smiled. He looked like a young lad, he was so happy with joy.

"I know, we'll all talk later. Now I must read this letter from my old departed friend. Excuse me, please."

Deirdre, with her sisters and Sue, watched him very closely as he read. They saw the expressions on his face change from time to time, and then he would smile real big and laugh out loud.

When Angus Gordon put his letter down, he just looked at the lasses. All he could say was, "Glory be."

"Mr. Gordon, It's getting late. Could you show us how to get to the inn?"

"Yes, yes of course, but I thought you would like to spend the night at a small cottage on Jura, down close to the beach."

Kimberly looked at him with a big smile on her face as she looked at the others. "That would be just grand, wouldn't it sisters?"

"Yes!" was the reply from them all.

"But what if the fog comes while we are there?" Monica asked.

"Oh! Come on, Monica, get a grip. If it does, it does," remarked Deirdre.

"You'll need a boat to get to the other side. Can you row, lassies?"

"You bet we can, sir."

"Come then. Follow me." Looking at his watch, "Oh no, it's too late, the darkness will set in shortly. You will have to sleep at the inn. Have something nice and hot to eat, and get a good night's sleep. You can start out in the morn."

"If you think that is best." Deirdre was smiling at him as she spoke, "Mr. Gordon, one other thing please?"

"What would that be, lass?"

"The man who drove the cab told us some things that are a puzzle to us. He said that he knew we were coming and so did the whole island. Now, how did he know?"

Angus Gordon smiled. "Well, now, he most likely knows the legend that has been handed down for many a year. We don't know how it will come about, but things will change. But don't you worry about it."

Deirdre remembered what Uncle William said, "Like a doorway from the future to the past."

"We're not. Just good to be home. Mr. Gordon, we are ready for anything, so don't *you* worry."

"I'm not, lass," he answered her with a smile for them all.

The next morning after a good night's sleep at the inn, Deirdre woke to find the boxes and luggage in their room. "Come on, sleepy heads. It is way past time for you to get up. Get ready to go."

All she heard were moans and groans. "What time is it?" Kimberly asked as she stretched like a cat.

Deirdre looked out the window then back at Kimberly. "It's almost eleven in the morning. Come on, I feel we need to get on the move."

"So do I, lassies," Sue was saying as she splashed water on her face.

"Please, get up. I'm going to change clothes and get ready to go. I'll go with or without you," Deirdre said firmly.

"Well! What's gotten into her?" Monica asked.

Sue smiled. "I feel she is more anxious to go home than you."

"I don't think so!" cried Monica, getting up in a hurry.

Kimberly was watching her sister, Deirdre, very closely, smiling to herself. "I see you're wearing your other dark green leather with your sword down your back. You have your Chakram on your belt, but where do you have your dirk?"

"Why, in my boot, of course. Are you all going to stand around here all day just gawking at me or are you going to get ready?"

Monica asked, "Deirdre, do you have proof that you're Lady Deirdre MacDarroch?"

"As for proof, little sister, I feel I am proof enough."

Laughing, Kimberly asked, "Why in the world are you in such an all-fired hurry?"

"I think I know. Deirdre, like me, is wanting to get home," Sue answered.

Everyone was ready to leave when someone knocked on the door.

"Who is it?" asked Monica.

"It's Angus Gordon, lassies. Are you decent?"

"Yes, we are, come on in," Kimberly answered.

Mr. Gordon opened the door, but just stood there looking at the lassies. "My, my, don't ye look just grand now. But you forgot a little something, I'm thinking. You look just grand in your green leather and boots to match, up to your knees yet." Scratching his chin and turning his head sideways, "Yep, you need something. Oh! Now I know what it is."

Deirdre asked with a smile, "And pray tell what could that be, may we ask?"

"Well lass, you can't go without your tartans, now can you?"

Laughing, the lassies answered, "No, of course we can't."

"Well now, here you are," Angus Gordon said as he chuckled to himself, pulling things out of a carpet bag.

Deirdre put her tartan around her and hooked it on with her belt that had her Chakram on it. She had her sword down in its sheath between her shoulders.

Her sisters watched all of this, and they did the same. Monica spoke up, "What about your buckle? Are you going to leave it off?" she said, smiling really big.

"Oh! You're right, where is my head?" Deirdre asked. As she finished speaking, Angus handed her the buckle with its pearls, emeralds and sapphires on it to show that she was the true Lady MacDarroch MacDonald.

Sue had a worried look on her face when Deirdre spoke to her.

"Now Sue love, you need not worry about anything. We'll watch over you."

"Thank you, Deirdre," Sue spoke as she wiped tears from her cheeks.

"Now you know good and well we'll all look after you. You need never worry. If we don't, Uncle William will kill us for sure," remarked Kimberly.

"Alright now, are we all ready?" asked Mr. Gordon with a big smile.

"Sir, we wish to thank you for having the boxes brought here last night with all our things."

"It was a pleasure lassie; now here is a basket of food for you to take along. Remember, don't be afraid of anything. Take things in stride and you'll know what to do. God bless you all and don't forget, I'll see you soon." Giving all four a big hug and with a smile on his face, he was gone.

The girls boarded the small ferry that would take them over the Isle of Jura. As Deirdre looked out over the water; she didn't know what was ahead for them. But, she did know that they could face anything and handle it—as long as they were together.

When the ferry landed, the girls walked into a glen and then had to walk up a long, steep hill. "Boy, will I be glad when we get to where we are going," Monica remarked.

"We are almost there, I'm thinking."

"How do you know, Deirdre?"

"Oh! Just a feeling I have."

"My word, will you look at that tree up on the hill."

"Kimberly honey, we are there."

"Deirdre, how do you know this?"

"Kimberly and Monica, don't you remember it?"

"Deirdre, I do. We used to climb it as children," remarked Sue.

"You're right, it was — or is, I mean — the old apricot tree. You remember how we used to climb it and eat the apricots, and then get sick. Man, the stuff Mother would give us to take for an upset stomach!"

"Did you have to remind us of that?" Monica said with a funny look on her face and then smiled.

They all settled under the big tree and started to get the food out of the basket when Sue looked up and saw Deirdre going over to the top of the cliff. She smiled to herself as she watched Deirdre, not realizing this was the very spot where it all happened.

Deirdre looked out over the ocean; then turned to scan the land. It was breathtaking. It was like a fairyland with its beaches, and wildlife. There were flags which dotted the hillside. Mixed in with all of the white and purple heather was iris, as they were called back in North Carolina. There were the bright yellow, white, different shades of purple iris, along with the gold with purple throats. What a sight to behold!

Deirdre looked at her sisters and Sue, eating their cheese, pork and black bread, as she stood on the top of the cliff. Eating in the same spot where she and her sisters had disappeared many years ago.

"Deirdre, come back and eat something. It's very good," shouted Sue, knowing Deirdre was close to the ocean and it was hard to hear.

"Is it not grand here?" Kimberly asked with a big smile.

"Just look at everything around us," Monica answered.

Sue was just staring out into space with a dreamy smile on her face. Deirdre smiled as did the other lassies watching her.

"Now I wonder what she is dreaming about," Monica asked.

"Oh! Go on with you now. You know what I'm thinking," Sue answered, blushing.

Deirdre stood on top of the cliff. Thinking to herself, *It was here, in this very spot, where it happened many years ago, and here I stand again.*

Kimberly looked up, "Deirdre, come back here right now, please."

"Now look here, Deirdre MacDarroch, you heard Kimberly. It's me speaking now. Get your butt back here this minute," demanded Monica, wringing her hands together.

"Please, Deirdre, please come back over here," pleaded Sue.

"Now don't worry, it's alright. It's so beautiful here," Deirdre said, turning toward them with a big smile.

"My God, look!" Pointing out to the sea, Monica ran up to Deirdre. There, out of the blue ocean, came the deepest, blackest fog they had ever seen. It was rolling in very fast. Deirdre reached out to her sisters and Sue. They grabbed at Deirdre, but not fast enough. They stood there with a terrified look on their faces. Deirdre had fallen onto a small ledge below.

"Deirdre! Deirdre, where are you? Can you hear us?" shouted Monica.

There was not a sound of anything to be heard, just the dampness of the fog, with the roar of the sea. Kimberly shouted at the top of her lungs, "Deirdre, do you hear us. Oh! God in heaven, please don't take her from us again!" they all shouted with tears running down their faces.

The girls shouted again and again. Hearing the running of horse's hooves pounding hard on the path, they turn toward them.

The fog was as black as velvet, wet, and the smell of sulfur was almost too much to bear.

Scotland 1692

While the lassies were crying for help, on the other side of this deep black fog, the sun was beginning to set. There was a celebration going on at Sea Oaks Castle, of old friends meeting after a long time. Laird John MacDarroch, with wife Mary Kate, was welcoming Laird Glen MacDonald and his sons who had been away.

"They have John. But they came back about some time ago."

"Really now!"

"They have been in Her Majesty's Service on their return."

"You do mean Queen Alice, daughter of James, who fled to France?"

"Well then, as you know, we all love her, but the king is another matter all together."

"You're so right, John. We feel the same way."

It was during all the joy making that William, brother of Laird John, came bursting in the door shouting. "Raid! Raid, brother, it's the Campbells, they are burning, killing, stealing cattle, sheep!"

"Brother, you're back! Where?" looking around to see if the lassies were with William.

"I'll explain later, now there is no time to waste. We must hurry."

"John, old friend, we'll help you. They are our enemy too."

"No, Glen, you stay and enjoy the homecoming of your sons."

"My Laird, sorry to disobey your orders, but we are ready for a good fight." Tommy MacDonald smiled at Laird John, turned, and looked at his brothers. "Lads, let's ride."

Mary Kate had a sad smile on her face as she looked at her husband. "I feel much sadness will come from this."

"No wife, It is joy you will be feeling," he said, kissing her on the top of her head.

Mary Kate, with Molly at her side, readied all the things they would need to tend to the wounded.

Hours passed, but to Mary Kate it seemed like days when all of a sudden the door opened. Clan members, with William and his brother, Jamie carried Laird John in with a bad wound in his side. "Bring him into our bed chamber."

"Mary Kate! Mary Kate!" Laird John was putting pressure on his side, trying to hold the blood back that was gushing from his wound.

"John, don't speak, you will be fine. Lads, now lay him gently on the bed. William, have Molly bring lots of hot water with garlic in it and some linen."

"Of course, sister, that I will."

"Mary Kate, wife, William told me, love, he found them. He found them!" John passed out with a smile on his face.

"Now ye be quiet while I try and stop the bleeding," Mary Kate said, even though she knew her husband had passed out.

Lady Mary Kate had a smile on her face as well as tears running down her cheeks. She wiped them away as she looked out the window. The sun was just beginning to rise.

Much later, the Captain of the guard came to the door of the bedchamber with Timmy, Molly's young son, by his side. The boy, with a big smile on his face, said, "My Lady, our lads have run them off. We had a few wounded but the Campbells suffered more deaths and wounded than we did."

Chapter 8

"Kimberly, listen. I hear horses coming on the path toward us," observed Monica nervously.

Sue, in the meantime, lay down and was looking over the edge of the cliff. The fog had lifted a little and the rising sun created an eerie, surreal atmosphere as lighter patches of fog drifted and swirled before disappearing. *We have come to the other side; it is almost morn,* thought Sue. She could see a darker shadow that had to be Deirdre, lying on a small ledge. Looking up with a start, she saw three young men riding toward them. As they drew near and were coming to a halt, Kimberly took a few steps forward to meet them.

"Please sirs, our sister went over the cliff, I know she is on the ledge below." Kimberly looked up with tears running down her cheeks.

The three men just sat there, looking at her in stony silence. "There is no ledge here," sneered the one on her right.

Kimberly's eyes narrowed as she scrutinized the three. The speaker on her right was glaring at her with dark brown eyes that snapped, daring her to contradict him. His equally dark brown hair was pulled back and fastened at the nape of his neck. His broad shoulders were tensed and his hand rested on the hilt of his sword. She gasped as she recognized the plaid of his kilt and tartan. "MacDonald," she whispered to herself.

"Oh! Please, sir, I did see her. Please look over for us," beseeched Monica, coming to stand in front of the big red stallion.

Its rider was a chilly-looking young man with honey-blond hair and green eyes that were so hard and frosty, Monica found herself rubbing her arms as though she had caught a chill. As her eyes traveled from his ruggedly handsome face to his wide shoulders and defiantly-crossed arms, her eyes grew wide and round as his clothing registered. Looking back at his face, the word she uttered was hardly more than a breath that would have been a question. "Richard?"

"May I ask why we should?" he demanded.

Sue, hearing all this, got to her feet and turned. Kimberly and Monica were staring rapidly at the two men before them. It was, however, the third one that caught her attention. He was several inches taller than the others. He sat in his saddle in a relaxed manner. He only had enough grip on the reins to maintain control of his mount. His was a dangerously handsome face framed by hair as black a raven's wing. From what Sue could tell, his eyes were a strange violet blue that seemed to take in everything, but reveal nothing. *God, help me and William. My love, come quick. I'm about to stir this pot.*

Putting her hands on her hips and striding defiantly to stand directly in front of the black-headed man, she began to speak with confidence and authority. "Now you knuckle heads, do you know to whom you are speaking?"

The two outside riders shook their heads no, but there was no response from the other, except for a small twitch at the corner of his mouth. *He's laughing at me,* Sue fumed to herself. Having also recognized the MacDonald tartan, she figured it would be safe enough to continue. "I didn't think so, but I'll try to explain it to you, so you'll understand. The one on the ledge is Lady Deirdre MacDarroch MacDonald. These are her sisters, Lady Kimberly and Lady Monica MacDarroch. I'm the wife of Sir William MacDarroch. Now we know that Deirdre is down there.

If you don't help us, it will look really bad for you later. I can assure you of that." Looking around to Kimberly and Monica, she smiled and said, "That's more than I have said on this whole trip."

"Yep, it would be funny, Sue, if I wasn't worried about Deirdre," Kimberly spoke with anger. She shook her long blonde hair away from her face. Blue fire flashed from her eyes as she looked at the man with brown hair. "I know you, Hugh MacDonald, sitting there on your big white horse with not a thought to ladies in need. Your father would be fair ashamed of you this day." He looked at her as if he were in a dream.

"Well, are ye just going to scoot there on your great red horse, Richard, ye big brave man, or are ye going to help? Oh, why am I talking to you, you're no good." Monica stomped away from them.

Hearing the sound of hooves pounding on the path, the three women looked in that direction. There was a most wonderful sight. It was Uncle William.

Monica rejoined Sue and Kimberly when she heard a shout. "Lassies, what is wrong?" Uncle William came riding at a gallop. His horse reared as he pulled to a hard stop. Dismounting his horse, he took Sue in his arms and swung her around, and he kissed her hard and deep, then slapped her on the rear. Turning her loose, he asked, "Where is Deirdre, lassies?"

Sue and Kimberly started talking at the same time. "These big brave men. . ."

William interrupted. "Lassies, one at a time, please."

"Alright, Sue, you tell him."

"Thank you. Well, this is how it was, William my darling. These brave men, whoever they may be, wouldn't go down to get her."

Getting red in the face, he exploded. "WHAT DO YE MEAN, GET HER!"

"Uncle William," Monica broke in, "Deirdre fell and is on the narrow ledge over the cliff. I believe she is unconscious because she'll not answer."

"Move over you brave laddies," he growled at them. Going over to the top of the cliff, he shouted, "Deirdre, lass, can you hear me?" Turning with concern and fury on his face, he stormed at them, "If she is badly hurt, my lads, you will rue the day."

All at once they heard, "HELP, anyone up there?" Deirdre put her hand up to rub her head. "Damn, my head hurts."

"Deirdre, love, are you alright?" called Kimberly.

"Yes, I am. What's all the commotion about up there?"

"Never you mind, be ready, I'm lowering down a rope."

"Who is it?" shouted Deirdre.

"It's your Uncle William. You're home, lass."

"Yahoo, hallelujah, we're home! Oh! Hell, my head hurts. Hurry up there."

Hugh and Richard seemed to come to their senses. "William, I'll go and get her," the third man finally spoke.

126

"Tommy MacDonald, she has a name. Lady Deirdre MacDarroch MacDonald, twin sister of David MacDarroch. She is the eldest daughter of Laird John MacDarroch and my niece, as well as your wife. Now you can take that with you. Now tell me, do you think you can handle that?"

Tommy looked around as a flush covered his face. Then he looked at his brothers. Hugh was ogling Kimberly and Richard stared at Monica. Both had goofy smiles on their faces.

Shouting came from the ledge. "Uncle William, if you throw me the rope, I can tie it around me. Then you can just pull me up."

"Deirdre, lass, are you sure?"

"Yes, I am, I have not broken anything, it's just my head that hurts. Come on, let's move it, please."

William tied the rope to the saddle horn of his horse, Trojan. Going back over to the edge, he started lowering the rope. Tommy appeared at his side to help lift Deirdre up. "Change of heart, Tommy, boy?"

"No, just want to see. I'll pull. You know that there have been a lot of false ones, William."

"Yes, but this one is not."

"We'll see," Tommy replied, looking doubtful.

"That's fine. Now are you ready, Deirdre?"

"Yes, I am."

"Here we go then, Trojan, back boy, back."

With Trojan pulling and the two men guiding the rope, Deirdre came to the top. Her wobbly knees gave out; as the rope was untied she fell to the ground on her knees.

Tommy finally allowed himself to look down. What he saw took his breath away. Her red hair had fallen over her face and with the bright morning sun shining through it, it looked like fire. Brushing it away from her face as she sat up, he saw sparkling green eyes with golden flecks smiling at him. Was this really his Kitten? as he remembered his nickname for Deirdre.

Deirdre, from her sitting position, looked up and saw nothing but broad shoulders that fairly blocked out the sun shining down behind him. The rays of light played around him, giving him an invincible, magical appearance. He was by no means magical. He was only a man. A rugged, handsome warrior. As he squatted to lend her a hand, the plaid he wore opened on the side revealing a bulge of hard muscle.

It wasn't proper for Deirdre to look or to stare at such a private area; she knew that. Twentieth century habits would be hard to break. She sighed and turned her gaze back to his face. His expression didn't indicate he had noticed her taking a little peek at his thigh. She let out a sigh over that blessing. But she saw a hard darkness in his eyes.

Standing up on her feet, her legs were still just a little wobbly. Deirdre pushed her hair back from her face.

Tommy looked at her in her curve-clinging leather. "You need to cover yourself, My Lady."

Looking down at herself, Deirdre smiled up at him. "You're right, My Laird. My tartan is still down on the ledge. Could you be so kind and get it for me?"

"Yes, I can."

Deirdre noticed that he was splattered with blood. He tied the rope around his waist and with William's help lowered himself down to the cliff's ledge.

He quickly reached the ledge and immediately spotted Deirdre's tartan with the MacDarroch buckle on it. The emblem on the buckle shone bright with the stones on it. Then a flash went through his mind. He had seen the ring on her left hand. He had put an identical one on his Kitten's hand. But he had to be sure it was really her.

Tommy climbed back up the cliff and walked over to Deirdre. "I believe this is yours, My Lady," he told her with a slight bow.

Deirdre smiled up at Tommy, "Thank you so much, husband."

"Husband?" Tommy smiled.

"Yes, that you are, Tommy Boy. Your Kitten is home."

"Are you now? And who said you were?" he asked as he came closer to her with a smile on his face.

"Yes, I am, and I said so. I'll have you know that I'm not one of those who just claimed to be. It's the real me. So there."

"Well now, let's see. The others didn't have her mark. Guess you'll have to show me. That is, if you want to prove it to me."

"Why you black hearted bastard, I'll do no such thing."

"Well then, I guess you're just as phony as they were."

Deirdre had had enough. She stood on her tip toes and gave him a kiss. Not a long one, mind you, but enough to bring back memories of sweet kisses that turned hot and long. She stood back and smiled at him. To her surprise, he grabbed her and held her close and he whispered in her ear, "Did you like what you were looking at?"

Deirdre pulled away, saying as she looked up at him, "Why you, you ..." That was all she got out before he kissed her again.

"Yes?" was all he could say as warmth and hope began to seep into his chilled soul.

"Love, come back later after you clean up. I need to go and see my father and mother."

"Go, Kitten, I'll see you later." Tommy gave her another kiss and squeeze. *Is it this easy? Slow down lad; don't go in to fast,* he thought, smiling to himself. *But, I'll have fun in the meantime!*

Hugh and Richard also left with smiles on their faces, for they too had gotten their greeting.

William put his arm around Sue, thanked the MacDonalds, and turned left to go up to Sea Oaks. William stopped, turned, and shouted, "Tommy lad, you and your brothers look out for the Campbells, and they are out for your blood. As you know, Robert is out to get those three for killing his brothers."

"Thank you, William, we'll watch out for ourselves." Waving goodbye, they left, riding out of sight.

Deirdre, with her sisters, looked up. The sight they saw was breathtaking. There it stood, like it had for hundreds of years. It was magnificent, half facing the hills; another part, a roaring sea, then on the other side was the loch, or lake. What a wondrous sight. The towers had the MacDarroch and MacDonald flags flying high. There were guards on the walk that surrounded Sea Oaks. They looked to the left and there they saw a beautiful garden of roses.

Monica broke the silence as they stood there, taking in all the beauty. "Deirdre, how did Jura get its name?"

"Monica, love, don't you remember? Jura comes from the Norse word meaning Deer Island. As you know, we have plenty of red deer and other wild game. I had forgotten that you were so young when the fog took us. You were only ten, at that time."

"Thank you, I forgot for a bit there, it's so grand, is it not?"

"Yes, it is, little sister," answered Deirdre, smiling at Monica, knowing she didn't like the words little sister. Looking back up to the castle, she marveled at its magnificence.

The lassies ran, at a high speed, up to the large oak door, bursting through it. Running hard, they ran right into Elias, the captain, and Connie, the housekeeper. As soon as they got into the great hall it looked warm and inviting — so homey. Monica's nose went up into the air as if she smelled something. "Well I'll be. I smell Grace's scones freshly baked." Off she went on a run, shouting at the top of her lungs, "Grace, love, we're home."

Grace, hearing all the commotion, came out of the kitchen, "Glory be, you're back. Praise be — and safe," she said, wiping the tears from her eyes.

"Dear Grace, don't cry. We're home, safe and sound." Deirdre put her arms around Grace and kissed her cheek.

"Lady Deirdre, you and your sisters were soulfully missed. Have you seen your mother and father yet?"

"No, but as soon as we have one of your scones, we'll be on our way." Kimberly smiled right along with Monica and Deirdre.

The ladies backtracked, hugged and kissed Elias and Connie again, leaving them laughing and shaking their heads. "They're home," smiled Elias.

The girls ran up the stairs shouting, "Father, Mother, we're home."

They got to the top of the stairs, turned to the left and headed toward the family tower. It was like they had always known where to go. The door opened from their parents' chamber just as they were going down the hall. Out came the most beautiful woman the lassies had ever seen. Her hair was jet black and hung down to the back of her knees.

You could feel and see her bright green eyes going through you when she looked at you, like they did when they were small. Mary Kate looked up toward the noise. She couldn't believe it was her lassies running towards her.

Holding her opened arms wide, she said, "It cannot be, it cannot?" As they got to her to give her a big hug, they fussed over who got the first kiss. So Deirdre let her sisters go first. "Mother," Deirdre said softly, as she looked at her.

"Is it really you, my darlings?"

"Yes, Mother, it is us."

After hugging her, they heard a voice from the bed-chamber. "Who the devil is making all that noise? You know Angus and I are at work here on all my important papers."

The three lassies went through the door first. "'It is us, Father, we're home," Deirdre spoke.

"Now, how many more of you phony lassies are coming, pretending you're my loves? Get out of here now! Mary Kate, get them out of my sight."

Deirdre looked at her sisters and at her father, and then said, "Before we leave, may we show you something first?"

"What is it?"

Looking first at Kimberly, then at Monica, Deirdre said, "Would you know the truth if you saw it? And did the others have these?" Deirdre turned her back and dropped her jumpsuit down around her knees. The sisters followed suit.

"Now, you can't do that!! You're grown women," John shouted. "Angus, close your eyes."

"Sure, I will, John," he said with laughter in his voice.

"You saw us when we were your babies; you saw my bottom. Look, here is the strawberry on my ass. How I got it, you ask? Well, I'll tell you. Mother told me she was picking wild strawberries, slipped and fell bottom side down and marked me. I was born on your birthday, July 27th. Now how about them apples?"

John sat there with his eyes full of tears, knowing all the time William had found them, but didn't let on. He wanted to see what they would do.   Kimberly followed with, "Mother likes berry pies. She dropped some on her thigh and that's how I got mine, you silly old man."

Monica spoke up, "I got the paw on my ass when Mother's Irish Wolfhound jumped on her backside and left a paw on mine. Now Father, what do you think of that?"

"Mary Kate, love, it is really them.   Lord above, we have been waiting so long."   Crying, he held out his arms. All three ran into his open arms, crying even harder.

Mary Kate wiped her eyes, and then said, "Now, now, your Father has had a bad time. He must know!"

"Mary Kate, love, our lassies are home, really home."

"I know, husband, they need rest and a bath."

"You're right, Mother, where is that Maude, love?" Deirdre darted out of the chamber, leaving John laughing out loud.

"Sara, I'm home . . . where are you?" Kimberly shouted.

"Sue, Sue, I am home," yelled Monica at the top of her voice.

"Wife, they're home, they are truly home."

Just at that moment, the lassies stopped, turned around and went back into the bedchamber of their parents. "Angus Gordon, we were told to give you these, so you would know we are who we say we are." She handed him the letters and legal papers with the deed, then handed her father his letter. They walked out, leaving him with his mouth open.

"What is it, Angus?"

"Now, now, husband, calm down. You might pop the stitches." Mary Kate spoke softly to John as she touched his arm.

Angus Gordon read the legal papers, and looked at John MacDarroch, unbelief on his face. "You will not believe this but it's the same legal papers we have just drawn up. And the letters were written by Oliver MacDarroch, your grandfather."

"What are you saying, Angus?"

"What I am saying, John, is that the lassies went into the future with one of your relatives, one that went on earlier. As you have always known, John, a lot of strange things happen when the black fog comes. They had these papers that you just signed before me, just now. It must have been handed down to him, and he, too, will return. He gave these to your lassies to prove to you, and everyone that they are the true ones. Go on and read your letter. But I'm wondering how they got them."

"Angus, are ye sure? You know my Grandfather Oliver got lost to us the same way as my Great-grandfather Donald did—in the black fog. As you know, it was the same way we lost the lassies. Angus, I feel it's some kind of curse."

"Glory be, John, do you think they will come back too? Maybe they are already here somewhere."

John MacDarroch read his letter, which told him everything that had happened; how they couldn't come back. They had no way, but knew he had gone to find Mother and Father. Maybe they had to stay for some reason. And this was it, to help his great-granddaughters to get home. "Angus, they have always loved us. The good news is he is trying to come home, but he doesn't know when."

With tears running down his face, he looked up at his wife, Mary Kate. "My darling, my grandfather is trying to come home."

Mary Kate went to John and put her arms around her husband. "I know, darling, I know."

"Do you, my love?"

"Yes, I do, you see, he has not gotten permission from the Council to come back; they felt your father, Isaac, should stay to guard his home where the lassies lived, your grandfather's home."

"Wife! What are you saying? Is it that they will need to go back at some time? The lassies, I mean."

"Yes, John, now don't you get upset. But to meet your grandfather!"

"I'm not upset, Mary Kate, love. It will be just grand when and if I can."

"Are ye sure, John?"

"That I am." Looking at Angus, "Now, Angus, don't you get upset either."

"I'm not upset, John. My, my, wouldn't that be wonderful," he remarked, leaning back on the back of his chair with a big smile on his face.

"Angus, it would be a wondrous thing to see my grandfather. I loved him very much; so many memories."

"It would indeed, John."

The door burst open, and William ran into the chamber. "John, the MacDonald lads have been captured by Robert Campbell. They were beaten up so badly that they were unconscious and bloody when they were taken away!"

"What are you babbling about, man?"

"You heard me, John! We have to tell the lassies. What Deirdre will do is another thing."

"William, get in touch with Jamie, he'll know how to tell them."

"No, John, I'll tell them." William walked out the door and down the hall to Deirdre's bedchamber.

Deirdre felt like something was wrong, so before she went to her chambers, she stopped by the salon to collect her thoughts. That's where Uncle William found her. He knocked on the door.

"Come in," replied Deirdre.

Uncle William came through the door with a grim look on his face.

"Uncle William, what's wrong?"

"Now, lass, what makes you think something is wrong?"

"I just have a feeling in my gut, you might say."

"Deirdre, love, there is. You see, I went on patrol to just check to see if any more of the Campbells were anywhere around."

"And?"

"There were. Now, honey, I want you to stay calm. But Robert Campbell and his men beat up Tommy, Hugh and Richard very bad. They were bleeding like slaughtered pigs. Now I want you to stay here and try to stay calm," he said, putting his arms around Deirdre. She nodded yes as tears were running down her face.

Deirdre spoke very softly, "What about Kimberly and Monica?" She was looking up into her Uncle William's eyes.

"I'll tell them, honey, and then bring them down here."

Deirdre heard the door close. She went to her knees in prayer, asking the good Lord for guidance.

The door opened and Kimberly entered with Monica following. Seeing Deirdre on her knees in prayer, they fell on theirs.

Afterwards, Monica and Kimberly looked to Deirdre. "What now, Deirdre? How can we help them?" asked Kimberly, choking on her tears.

"We'll get them out. But, first we'll get in touch with Grandfather Kirk, you know, Mother's father."

"We'll get Father, with Uncle William, Uncle Jamie and Uncle Ira from the church. We need to talk to Grandfather first, I think."

"But what if we can't?" Monica asked.

"Well, we'll just wait until we see him; now let's go to our chambers, get a bath, eat, but most of all, rest. This has been very hard on all of us."

"You're right, that it has!" replied Kimberly. "I just had a grand idea. Let's say you and Tommy were married again. You found one another while you were gone and got remarried."

"Do you think it will work?"

"Yes, I do, Deirdre. Kimberly is right, it will work," smiled Monica.

"Alright then, I'll go along."

Deirdre entered her bedchamber. Maude was wiping her eyes. She had not changed one bit, to Deirdre's way of thinking. Maude was still short and round, gray white hair; her brown eyes could see right through you, with that bonnet cap on her head that Deirdre hated so much. She turned toward Deirdre saying, "Well now, where in the world have you been? No, no, don't tell me. Your water is ready for your bath. Now enough of this silly business; take off your clothes. Get ready for your bath."

"I'll not do that until I have a hug first! Why, a person might think that you were not glad to see me," Deirdre said, holding out her arms for Maude with a pouty look on her mouth.

"Goodness!! You are something, love; that you are." Going into Deirdre's arms, Maude started to cry again. "It is so good to have you home."

"There, my, Maude love, the pain in your ass is back." Deirdre looked around and asked, "Where is MacTavish?"

Deirdre heard a loud yawn. Out from under the bed came her big lynx. He was the biggest lynx her clansmen had ever seen in all the Isles and Highlands.

Holding out her arms, "Come here, my big lad. My, my, you have gotten bigger." MacTavish went into Deirdre's arms, licking her face all over. "Now, my big lad, go and find something to get into."

Deirdre got undressed and climbed into the steamy tub of hot water, with oil of rose and heather that Maud had added. It was a great feeling just being home. She didn't hear Maude come back in until she said, "Here are your clothes, lass. Then you are to go straight away to see your father. He wants to talk to you."

"Will do, sweet Maude, will do." Sitting up in the bath, Deirdre said, "Maude is the old apricot tree still in the garden?"

"Yes, it is, why?"

"I just wondered," she said, as she lay back in the tub with a smile on her face.

"I see you're thinking about Tommy lad. Well you can't help him now, love."

"Why not?"

"Because he and his brothers are in Laird Robert Campbell's stronghold, deep down in the prison. The lower floor, they call it The Belly," shaking her head. "Beaten, they were, bad. Bloody, they were, all of them. Why, I bet anything that they never cleaned them up at all."

Deirdre got out of the tub with anger in her voice, "I'll get them out and the Campbells will wish they were never born. You'll see, you'll see, sweet Maude."

"Don't let your mother and father hear the way you're talking."

"And why not, pray tell?"

"It will upset them, you know it will."

Deirdre lifted her head as she looked at Maude who was smiling, "You know that you will have the support of the whole clan. Here now, put on your robe instead of standing there in all that you were born in," Maude was laughing out loud.

"Maude, now you have to keep this under that bonnet of yours, love."

"What are you saying, lass? Keep what under my bonnet?"

"Maude, we have a traitor in our clan. So will you help me start a rumor? It was Kimberly's idea."

"Are you sure about the traitor?"

"Yes, that I know, and for sure. Let everyone know that Tommy and I are married—that we met while we were gone. Alright?"

Looking startled, Maude answered Deirdre. "How did you know that they had vanished the same time as you lassies did? Why they just came back the same day your Uncle William left to go and find you. Also, they were here on the same day of the raid. It was a big celebration your father had for them. That is why they were here. Besides, you can't say that you don't remember that you were married before you left us, but of course it wasn't consummated."

"Maude, what are you saying?"

"You heard me right."

Deirdre was standing butt naked with the robe still in her hand when the door burst open. Kimberly entered with Monica right behind her. "Did you know that the lads disappeared when we did?" asked Kimberly.

"Yes, Kimberly. Don't you remember how we were pulled apart from them in the black fog? Do you remember me telling you as he went into the other funnel, I heard him cry out that he would love me forever?"

"Deirdre, what does this mean? Did we meet them, do you know? Were they misplaced persons like we were?" asked Monica.

"You are kidding us?" Kimberly asked.

"No." Staring out into open space, Deirdre changed the subject. "You know we can just say in the rumor that we got married again, but not any wee ones."

Maude reminded Deirdre to put on her robe. Then Deirdre started walking around the chamber as she tied the robe around her. She stopped by the window to look out. There she saw the garden below. "Maude love, are those roses blooming in the garden?"

"Yes."

"Did Father or Mother plant them?"

"Darling, don't you remember? Tommy planted them, when he first told you that you were his now and forever. You know when he came home from court that year, he asked you to be his? That's the first place he went; picked the red one then went out to the place where you disappeared. He threw it over the cliff into the sea."

With tears running down her face, Deirdre turned around. "I'll get him out; you will all see!"

"Now, Deirdre honey. Wipe your eyes and tell us how."

"Kimberly, Monica, I don't know right at this moment."

Shaking her head, Monica looked at Deirdre with a worried look on her face. "Maybe you'll find out more when you talk to Father."

Very softly, Kimberly spoke, "Deirdre, Monica, don't talk so loud. I feel someone is listening to us." She pointed to the door. They all three were like their mother. They, too, had the sight. Seers, they were called. Four in the same family was quite unusual.

Deirdre whispered softly and told her sisters that she was going to put on an act for the traitor. They nodded their heads yes, and so did Maude.

"You're right, lassies; you know that Tommy and I were wed again after we found one another. Let's see, it was about a year now. We were going to celebrate our one year being together. Now I find out he is in prison at Robert Campbell's stronghold." Deirdre spoke loudly. She took the dress that Maude handed to her to put on.

"Deirdre, take it easy, just calm yourself down."

"Kimberly, I know we have a traitor in our midst."

"Deirdre, quiet please, they could hear you."

"Let them," Deirdre shouted with tears in her voice. But smiled at her sisters. "What am I going to do without him?"

Monica, Kimberly and Maude smiled at Deirdre, when, at that moment, they heard a soft knock at the door.

"Come."

There stood a very thin lass with three little ones; two hanging on to her skirt, and one on her hip. They looked half-starved. Their little arms were as thin as bird's legs. Looking hard at the young lass, Deidre asked, "Are you not my cousin? Your name is Annie, isn't it?"

"Yes, My Lady," Annie answered with trembling in her voice as she looked into Deirdre's face.

"Annie, what is it?" Deirdre looked at Maude, hoping she would understand about taking the little ones down to the kitchen and feeding them.

Maude, bless her, she did understand Deirdre's look. "Now you little loves, come with old Maude and we'll get you some milk with hot buttered scones. Would you like that?"

They looked up at their mother. "Go, my darlings, it's alright," she said, giving them a hug.

Maude took the baby in her arms; the others followed her as she left the chamber. Closing the door after them, Deirdre asked, "Now Annie, what's bothering you so?"

"My Lady, I pray you find it in your heart to forgive me."

"My word, lass, what have you done?" Deirdre looked in Annie's eyes as she asked the question.

Kimberly and Monica looked on with sympathy in their eyes and hearts. Touching Deirdre's arm, Kimberly then whispered in her ear, "She is the one! Be easy with her please, Deirdre."

Deirdre looked Kimberly in the eye, then at Monica, and back at Annie. "Annie, sit down. Monica, hand her some cheese with bread. Would you like something to wash it down with, Annie?"

"Thank you. First, please, My Lady, I'll need to tell you why I am here. But I ask if you would take care of my babies, they had nothing to do with all this."

"You have my word, Annie, don't worry. Now tell me."

"It happened after you were taken from us. I fell in love with a man of another clan."

"Go on. Take your time."

"Thank you," she managed, as she nervously twisted the hem of her blouse which had come out of her skirt.

"The man was a bitter enemy of our clan. But he treated me with tenderness. He loved me very much, was a good father to his children. He fed us well, treated me royally and bought me lovely dresses.   But later on, he didn't like what his laird was doing and stood up to him about it. The laird of that clan had him killed after our third baby was born. Then he told me if I didn't help him he would kill my babies."

Looking up at Deirdre with tears in her eyes, she continued, "So, I spied on my own for him to save my little ones, My Lady. When I saw my chance to run with my babies, I came back here only to find out that my father and mother died when our cottage was burned in the raid. My Lady, do what you will with me, but please don't make my babies pay for my treason against the clan." Annie put her hands up to her face and cried until it seemed she couldn't stop.

Deirdre didn't know what to say. She just turned and walked out the door, leaving everyone in shock. Finding herself in front of her mother and father's bedchamber, she knocked.

"Come in." It was Mary Kate. "Deirdre, what is it, honey? Why are you crying?"

"Mother, I'm sorry. Where is Father?"

"I'm here, lass. What is wrong?" she heard him say as he came out from behind the bath screen in his robe. "I was just finishing up my bath. Now, love, what is it? Why are you crying?" He was holding out his arms to Deirdre.

Deirdre ran into his arms, "Father, I have a very big decision to make. It is really a tough one. So, I came here to tell both of you about it. Well now, before I start, don't say anything until I finish, please, Father?"

Laird John MacDarroch looked at his wife, then back at Deirdre. "I will not say anything until you are through."

"Thank you very much, Father." She told them what had transpired a short while earlier. Deirdre watched her father's face. He looked like he would explode, but all of a sudden he had tears in his eyes. "Bring the lass to me."

"I will, Father, but I'm going to stay, you hear? I'm staying!" Deirdre shouted at him, and then stormed out of the room. Before she closed the door, she heard her father say, "Mary Kate, love, she is just like me, is she not?" John was laughing. "So, you old fox, that's the way of it." Deirdre smiled to herself as she walked to her chambers. She started to open the door when she heard Monica and Kimberly tell Annie not to worry — that she had nothing to fret about.

Deirdre thought to herself that they didn't want this to happen again, so they should make her an example. Opening the door, everyone looked up. To see the look on Deirdre's face shocked them. "Annie, I'm sorry, but my father wishes to talk to you and he is not a happy man."

Annie slowly got up, her legs weak as water. Monica tried to help her, but she pushed her hands away. "I thank you, but I have to go this alone. Thank you, Lady Deirdre."

"Don't worry about your babies. They will be taken care of as though they were my own. Just like I told you."

Annie, with Maude, followed Deirdre, Kimberly, and Monica up to the family tower. Maude had left the little lad and lassies in the kitchen with Grace, eating her wonderful cooking.

When they got to the door, Deirdre knocked. "Come in." John was sitting in his chair, with Mary Kate beside him. The look on his face was very stern. Annie came in; she was very quiet. Maude guided her in with the rest following.

"Maude, I wish you to stay. The rest will not say one word; if you do, you will be put out. Anything that is said in this chamber this day stays. Whoever lets it leak out, I will deal with them severely, is that understood?"

"Yes, sir," they all answered.

"My Laird, I'll tell you the truth of it, like I told Lady Deirdre, do with me what you will, but I beg you to take care of my babies or I'll not tell you anything. I have nothing to lose. My husband is dead; he was a good man to me and his children. So I want your promise, My Laird." Annie looked at John MacDarroch straight in the eye.

"Glory be, lass, you have guts, yes you have, I promise. You're like your mother, that's why your father, my brother loved her so."

"I know, My Laird." Then Annie told him exactly what she had said to Deirdre.

Laird John asked, "What do you know of the raid that put the MacDonald lads in prison at Robert Campbell's stronghold?"

Annie turned as white as a sheet. "I don't know anything, My Laird."

"Now Annie, you do know, now tell me, because the look on your face tells me you do."

"Oh! My Laird, if he finds out, someway, somehow, he'll find me."

"Now, now, Annie child, don't be frightened. I know how you feel. Often times I feel the same way. Now, come lassie, tell me. Your father, my brother, and your sweet dear mother, loved you very much. You know that they were in that fire. You know your family loves you so you have nothing to worry about."

Annie looked around at all of them with her face wet with tears. Deirdre went over to her, put her arms around Annie and drew her close. "It's alright, love, go ahead."

Drawing her shoulders back, she looked John in the eye and the rest of them in the face. "It was Laird Robert Campbell. He killed my husband, Roy Harris because Roy would no longer bow down to him. Then he started threatening me with taking me wee ones. Laird John, I tried to go to you, but he locked me in an old tower. I tied the wee ones all together with a rope I found in an old chest where we were being kept. I lowered the babies down to the courtyard. The oldest one untied them, and I pulled the rope back up and then I climbed down.

"We slowly made our way to the stable where I found a cart and horse all ready. It must have belonged to a farmer that always brought things from his garden to the cook. I put the babies in it, and then led the horse quietly out and down close to the water so not to be heard.

"I knew where one of Roy's friends lived next to the steam. He is a fisherman, so I took his little boat. I laid the babies down in the bottom where they fell asleep. When we landed we walked into your woods, but it was too late to save anyone. But I know how you can get Tommy and his brothers out."

Deirdre looked at the others, then at her father. Smiling at Annie, "Oh, love, can you help?"

"That I can."

Chapter 9

Annie told Deirdre that there were only a few guards during the day. They doubled up at night when they figured that there would be more escapes tried than any other time. "You're right. Now we'll call Uncle William, Uncle Jamie, also Uncle Ira, I mean Father Ira."

"Yes, he is... now what are you thinking, lass?" asked Maude.

"They will not be expecting anything to happen in the daylight hours, so that is when we'll strike. But right now I need to talk to my uncles."

"I'll go and get them." Monica said as she stood up.

"No, not now. You go and get Father and Mother."

"I can do that. I can't wait to show the Campbells and that so-called King William a lesson. They don't know who they are dealing with!" screamed Monica as she ran out the door.

Kimberly smiled. "They had better watch their steps around Deirdre."

"You better believe that," Annie said with a smile.

Deirdre was smiling to herself as she listened to the girls talk. "Annie, can you sew?"

"I can, My Lady. I have been told that I do a mighty fine stitch."

"Well then, you can help with the sewing."

With tears running down her cheeks, Annie choked out the words very softly. "Thank you so, God bless you, My Lady." She went over to Deirdre and kissed her on the hand.

"Now Annie lass, please... you are very welcome, but you will work hard. But most of all, Annie, remember, we are your family. We want you to be safe."

"Oh! I will, and thank you again."

Just then the door opened. In walked her father, mother, Uncle William, who was tall and big as an ox, and Uncle Jamie, who was also a big man, around six-foot seven inches tall. Both of Deirdre's uncles were big men with deep red hair and bright blue eyes like their brother, Laird John MacDarroch.

"How did all of you come to know?"

"Deirdre darling, we were with your father and mother discussing things over," Uncle William said, going over to sit down.

"I see. Where is Monica?" Deirdre asked as she looked around for her. "Uncle William, where is Aunt Sue?"

"The lass went to get your Uncle Ira. As for me, darling, she is home baking. Now, tell me what's going on, lass?" asked Uncle William.

"I'll wait to tell you when we're all together. Pray God is looking over us this day.""

"Deirdre, what are you up to?" asked Mary Kate with a smile on her face, because she knew that it had to do with the MacDonald lads.

"I'll tell you all about it, Mother, when Uncle Ira and Monica get here."

Uncle Ira came through the door just at that time. "What in the world is going on now? This lass just ran into the middle of my prayers shouting, Uncle Ira, hurry, come with me it's very important, hurry!" Sitting down and wiping his brow, "But land sakes, it's good to have them home." Hugging Kimberly and Monica, he looked at Deirdre, saying, "And you, our wildcat warrior. Give us a hug."

Deirdre went over with her arms open, hugging him and giving him a big kiss.

"Alright now, listen up. We are going to get the lads out of Robert Campbell's prison and we need your help, but first we want word sent to Laird MacDonald."

"Lass, have you lost your mind?" John MacDarroch asked, with a worried look on his face.

Deirdre looked around the room at everyone, tears running down her face. "No, I have not; now if ye don't want to help, we'll do this alone."

Kimberly, with Monica, stood beside her, all three together. Kimberly spoke in a very quite tone. "Now it's not necessary for any of you to go or do anything."

"Kimberly is right. We don't need you and I feel like I speak for Deirdre and Kimberly; we can do this ourselves. So you can leave now, we need to make our plans."

Everyone in the chamber sat there with their mouths open. "What are you saying, child? You don't want our help?" asked John MacDarroch.

"No, Father," Deirdre spoke up. "We would love to have your help, but if you or anyone else is going into this with the attitude that it can't be done, then we don't need it; this is going to take a lot of togetherness, not pulling apart."

"Niece, we would like to hold a meeting down in the library to talk things over. We will send for Laird MacDonald," stated Uncle Jamie.

"You will not have a meeting without me, Jamie," remarked Mary Kate.

"Now, now, wife, this is man's business."

"And most likely muck it up like the last time, husband."

John and the men had a shocked look on their faces when Mary Kate left the chamber saying, "Well, come on; let's get to the heart of things. Well!! Are you going to just stand there and waste the day away?" Mary Kate stood at the chamber door patting her foot.

They all followed her like lambs to the slaughter. The lassies could not help but laugh as soon as the door closed. "My word, did you see the look on their faces, lassies?" laughed Maude.

"Bet they will get a tongue lashing from Aunt Mary Kate," Annie stated as she wiped the tears from her eyes from laughing so hard.

"Poor men, they are in for it now." Monica was also laughing.

"You got that right." Kimberly was laughing so hard she fell off the stool that she was sitting on.

"Alright, alright now let's stop this," Deirdre said, trying not to laugh herself.

It was about an hour later that they really got calmed down. Hearing a knock on the door, "Come in," Deirdre called out.

Elias came in. "My Lady, your father would like for you to come down to the library."

"We're on our way, Elias, thank you. Come on, lassies; that means you too, Maude, my darling." Deirdre laughed, going out the door.

Running down the stairs, up to the library door, Deirdre knocked. "Come in." The voice was that of her mother who was standing behind the desk, and seemed to have all the attention from the men.

As they all got seated, Mary Kate looked at her lassies then said, "We have sent word to Glen MacDonald about coming here. Now all we have to do is wait. But Deirdre, if you have anything to say then do."

"Thank you, Mother, but I would rather wait until Godfather Glen gets here."

"Then Deirdre, will you make your plans, while we wait for Glen to get here."

"Yes, I will, Mother." When they got up to leave, the men were muttering something under their breath. The lassies could not help but laugh as they left the room with Mary Kate following behind them.

"Let's all go up to my chambers so we may discuss our plans. Coming, Mother?"

When they settled down in Deirdre's chambers, Maude went down to get them something to eat and drink. They all had a strong feeling this would take a long time.

"Annie?" Deirdre asked after they had all gotten settled down. "Now tell us what you know about the stronghold of Robert Campbell."

"Well, as I said, it's well guarded, but I got to thinking, Roy, my husband, once told me about an old tunnel that goes from the church; they called it a priest hold, I think."

"It is," Mary Kate said as she sat down in front of the fire. "It's under the Holy Water Bowl in the entrance hall. It's made of stone, and *very* heavy. They hide there when there is great danger or put all the altar cups, crosses of jewels and gold in so as not to be stolen."

"But this one is said to have an old tunnel going from the hole up to the lower part of the dungeon where the MacDonald lads are; but mind you, the tunnel is old and may have fallen in."

"Oh! Annie, thank you so. With Uncle Ira's help and the others we will get them out. Now, Kimberly you and Monica, with Molly's help, get the old cave ready; you know the one! The one we used to go to."

"We'll see about the hole in the top, to make sure it draws out the smoke. They will need to keep warm." Kimberly smiled with tears running down her cheeks.

"Right... I'll see all about the food while Kimberly and Molly will see to the herbs and things for the heating the water," Monica remarked, while she danced from one foot to the other.

"What in the world is the matter with you, Monica?" asked Kimberly.

"Well, I'll tell you. I don't like not being able to go along, that's all."

"Love, I know, but I need you here to help get things ready. You know, when the lads are discovered gone, this will be the first place the Campbells will look."

"I know you're right. Deirdre, I'll do as you say, but all of you remember this, I'll take care of my Richard."

"We will remember. But you also have to remember, you'll be needed in the great hall when the Campbells come here. First we have to make our plans on how to get to the Campbells' stronghold."

"Deirdre? I bet Grandfather Kirk would help. Don't you think he may have a ship we could use?"

"You're right, Kimberly; we'll wait until he gets here."

"Why don't you dress like a monk, Deirdre; then you can go in as well?"

"Good idea, Mother, I could do that. Let's see." Walking about, Deirdre stopped, and turned to Annie, "We'll need a cart with straw and very, very large wine barrels — about three or four. Where would they be, so we could lay our hands on them?"

"Why, I believe the barrels would be right behind the altar, in a room where the priest dresses for weddings and such. You know there should be at least three there, waiting for the ship to come, and it's due soon. Where to get the cart, I don't know. What would you need a cart for, Deirdre?" asked Annie.

"We'll put the lads in the barrels then move them to the ship, of course."

"Deirdre! That is a good idea, now Annie do you know what day the ship is due?" asked Mary Kate.

"No, but it won't be long, it's a French ship. It always brings Laird Campbell wine. I believe it's around the middle of the month."

"Deirdre, wouldn't Uncle Ira know?" asked Monica with a smile.

"Maybe he would, just maybe. You know Grandfather would have to get a ship that looks like a French one."

"I bet he has one! To my way of thinking," remarked Deirdre.

While they were waiting, Deirdre sat down thinking about when she was small. Grandfather taught her how to fight, along with her mother. Mary Kate has always been proud of her father. Grandfather had no sons, but two beautiful daughters, her mother and Aunt Ellen, who also married a Scotsman. But she was widowed now. Aunt Ellen was light like grandfather and mother dark like her mother was.

There came a knock at the door. "Come in," called Deirdre.

A whole lot of the men came in, including Laird Glen MacDonald. "We're here, lassies, what's the plan?"

Deirdre went over to give Laird MacDonald a hug. "I'm so glad we're home." She then turned to give the others a hug.

There in the doorway stood Grandfather Kirk, smiling all over himself. "Give us a kiss," he said, holding out his arms to them.

Chief Kirk had just gotten settled down when Deirdre asked him a question. "Grandfather, how long will it take from here to the Campbells' stronghold? Then by cart from the time we get off the ship?"

"It shouldn't take long, why? What's going on in those pretty heads of you lassies?"

Deirdre filled him in on their plans, as she looked around at each of their faces. "Well! What do you think?"

Uncle Ira smiled. "You have a good one there, lass. I know the priest at the Campbell stronghold. You know, I had forgotten about that old tunnel. It has not been used in many a year; could be dangerous, but with God's help, we'll make it."

"Thank you, Uncle Ira, what say the rest of you?" asked Deirdre.

Grandfather looked around at the rest then spoke, "You're, right, my mighty warrior, I have captured a French ship, let's see... not too long ago, and love, I'm with you all the way. How about the rest of you?" Chief Kirk spoke, stroking his beard. "Are you afraid to go? If so, we'll let you stay here with the women folk."

158

Grandfather Kirk was a Viking from Norway, but he stayed both at Sea Oaks and at a stronghold, still in Norway, his homeland.

"Now, now, you listen here, Kirk, you may be my wife's father, but you'll not talk to me that way."

"Now, John, I don't mean any disrespect to you."

"I'm sorry, Kirk, but you are right. Lassies, you tell us what you want us to do and we'll do it," John MacDarroch said while looking at his brothers. Every one nodded their heads yes; they too would do what was asked of them.

"Deirdre, love, you must remember that Patrick Campbell has always had his eye on you ever since you were a young lassie. He called you his enchantress."

"Oh! Grandfather, you are incorrigible. You know there has been no one in my life but Tommy MacDonald. He has my heart for now and forever."

"I know, but it still worries me about that man. He is very tricky and can't be trusted," remarked Grandfather.

Deirdre smiled then spoke, "I promise I'll be careful, now don't worry." She reached up and gave him a big hug and kiss.

"When do you think we should get started?" asked Uncle William.

"As soon as Grandfather gets the ship and Uncle Ira has the robes. Right, Deirdre?" answered Kimberly.

"You are right, Kimberly."

"Well, in that case we'll start on the early tide, day after tomorrow." Grandfather left on that, with a big smile on his face.

"Mary Kate, I'll say good night, and you lassies sleep well for you have a big day soon. Rest as much as you can. I'll have a cart with horse on board for you. Now don't worry about the wine and extra barrels, I'll have them," Uncle Ira said as he and the rest gave the lassies a kiss good night, then left.

Going over to the door behind her mother, Deirdre spoke in soft tones, "Mother, will you say prayers for us while we are gone?"

"Why, Deirdre, you know that I will and things will come along just fine. Don't you worry." Mary Kate kissed them all good night and left to go to her chambers.

Godfather Glen was still there. "Deirdre, lassies, do ye realize how much I love you? You're risking your lives to save my lads."

"Yes, we do, and do ye realize how much we love your laddies? You know we were promised to them many years ago. Matter of fact, Deirdre was married to Tommy and we were promised to Hugh and Richard before we were taken from them. Why, Godfather, our lives are not worth anything without them," Kimberly said as Deirdre and Monica all gave him a hug.

"That I do, you see, lassies; the lads were taken away in the black fog when you were. When they came back to me, the first thing they asked was if you were home. When we said no, they cried like babies. They have been looking for you all these years. But I must warn you, they will not believe it's you. I know that all of you have your own secrets and that alone will help convince them. Now I will say goodnight and Godspeed."

Glen MacDonald gave them a hug and a kiss with tears in his eyes. "I'll play your game with the Campbells, and so will everyone else. God be with you, lassies."

"Don't worry about us, darling. I know what to do, Godfather," Deirdre spoke softly to Laird Glen MacDonald.

Laird Glen turned to leave; when he got to the door he turned. "No, lassies, I will not, for I know you will do the right thing." Passing John MacDarroch at the door, Glen reached out and gave John a hug. "We have brave lassies, John." He left wiping tears from his eyes.

"Now ... what did you say to Glen to make him cry like that?"

"Father, we don't know, you were standing there," remarked Monica.

He patted Monica on her cheek, "Deirdre, lass." John went over to her then gave her a big hug. "Now, what did *you* say?"

"I didn't say anything — only that we loved his sons."

"That's what I like to hear, as I'm sure he did. Kimberly, Monica, you know that your work is the most important, getting the lads well and strong."

"We know, Father, but that isn't going to be easy."

"I know, Monica; they will be hard to convince that you are who you say you are. That will not be easy, lassies. I'll say goodnight now." Their Father left them to retire.

"Did you see the tears in Fathers eyes?"

"Yes, I did, Monica," answered Kimberly, looking at Deirdre, then at Monica. "What is the matter, Deirdre?"

Deirdre wiped the tears from her eyes. "You know, it's just so good to see everyone helping out."

"What did Laird Glen mean when he said we would have a hard time convincing the lads who we were? Deirdre, you remember when Tommy helped you up from the ledge and he kissed you? As did our lads welcome us with a kiss. Why did they say it will be hard for them to believe who we are?" asked Kimberly.

"I don't know. Maybe they were just testing us," Monica spoke with sadness in her voice.

Deirdre spoke with a choking tone, "Please, don't say that."

"But we have to think on it, Deirdre. You know there have been others."

"But thinking of him making love to them drives me crazy. Don't you feel the same?"

"Believe me, it does," cried Kimberly.

"And me also," Monica spoke with tears in her voice. She turned and headed for the door. "Let's go to bed. Maybe things won't be as bad as we think. The morning will be a bright new day, and maybe the sadness can be put behind us"

They all went to their beds exhausted; knowing things would be very tense for everyone the next few days.

The next morning the girls came running into Deirdre's chamber, eagerly shouting, "Deirdre!! Molly and I are going to the cave and see what shape it's in."

"Wait, Kimberly, I have a better idea; let's all go, I mean you, Molly, Annie, Monica and me. We can take things as we go, it will be like a picnic if anyone is watching. We'll do it this morning."

All but Deirdre went to the kitchen to gather the things they would need for a picnic plus supplies to leave in the cave. Grace was going into the kitchen. She was a tall, thin woman, with dark hair that had streaks of gray. She always wore it in a bun at the nap of her neck. Grace had been with the family for a great number of years.

Smiling at them, she handed Monica a very large basket of food. She then handed the other one, which was filled with herbs and bandages, to Kimberly. "Now, do you have something to boil water in?" asked Grace.

"No, we don't," answered Molly with her brown eyes just shining. Molly was about Kimberly's height; her hair was one long honey-blonde braid; slim, full breast, small waist, and full hips. But her best feature was her big smile. Molly had been left a widow with a young lad named Timmy, who worked very hard in the stables with the horses. He had always loved working with the horses.

They all gathered where Deirdre was waiting on the lassies to get the things together. She thought back; it was Uncle Jamie who took Timmy with him to hunt and fish. The way they would laugh and talk together brought a smile to her face.

"Molly, is Uncle Jamie still taking Timmy hunting and fishing with him?"

Molly blushed as she answered, "Yes, he is."

"And how do you feel about my Uncle Jamie?"

"Well, I'm sorry to say, My Lady, but I feel that he doesn't like me. He just won't ever speak to me when he picks up Timmy; he just grunts."

"Wasn't Uncle Jamie good friends with your husband?"

"Yes, he was, and the woman your Uncle Jamie loved died when we had a very bad winter. She died with influenza, and she was a very good friend of mine as well."

"Molly, do you think he feels guilty because of his feelings for you? Maybe because he and your husband had been such good friends?"

"You know, My Lady, you just might be right."

"Well, time will tell, Molly."

"It will, My Lady; that it will."

"Molly, besides healing, can you sew?"

"Yes, I can; I'm very good at it."

"Then you move within the walls. Annie, my cousin, is also moving into one of the two small cottages. Annie also sews, so you can help with the dressmaking."

"Are you sure, My Lady?"

"I'm sure. Now, let's get on with fixing up the cave."

They left Sea Oaks on horseback. They went into the mountains behind the castle, where the trail led to the cave. "Deirdre, I have a strong feeling we are being watched," Monica made the statement as she rode up beside Deirdre.

"I feel it too, but let's start singing."

"Annie, Molly, Kimberly, do all of you remember this one?" Deirdre started to sing an old song of the highlands and the others chimed in.

Looking behind her, Deirdre saw men on horses. She stopped and turned, putting her hand on her sword, when one of them spoke, "Now.... lass what do you think you're doing?"

The voice was of Patrick Campbell. Deirdre faced the Campbells—Earl and Patrick. "Well what are you doing on my land; you know you're not welcome here."

"I know, but I heard you were back, and I had a loving feeling to see you. Just thought I should come and welcome you home, my way."

Deirdre started getting steamed up. She drew her sword as she started getting off Thunder, thought better of it, and got back on. Deirdre's sisters, with Molly and Annie, came up behind her and moved to Deirdre's side.

"Now, what were you saying about giving me a welcome, you bloody bastard? You and yours get off my land or I'll bury you under it!" she snapped as she wielded her sword.

"I intend to marry you, Deirdre MacDarroch." Patrick said with a smirk on his face.

"You low-life, how can that be? She is married to Sir Tommy MacDonald." Annie spoke up with pride in her voice.

"That's right, they have been remarried a year now," Molly spoke up in a loud voice.

Patrick's face was all red. "Is this true, Deirdre?" He was trying not to lose control of his temper, but it looked like he had steam coming out his ears.

Trying not to laugh, Deirdre answered him, "Yes, it is. Why?"

"Well, where is this beloved man of yours?" he said, smiling, knowing all along where Tommy was.

Deirdre looked him in the eye as best as she could, also knowing full well where the lads were. "You see, Patrick, he came back before I did, then with the raid and all, you remember the raid? You know how things are put on hold?"

"Well now, is that so? I know all about that. So, Deirdre, are you going to have your father's birthday party after all that has happened?"

"I am, if it is any of your business."

"Just wondering if King William is invited?"

"No, not that I know of."

"Well, how about that, the king will not like that. But are we invited to have a bite to eat with you?" asked Earl Campbell, smiling at Kimberly.

"No and no! Now I think you should go; you have been here long enough."

"My father will not like that."

"Well Patrick, I really don't care what your father likes." Deirdre spoke with anger in her voice.

"We will be leaving, Deirdre. Oh! When will Tommy be back from his trip?"

"Look here, Patrick Campbell, how should I know, we understand that it may take some time in dealing with the Chinese Emperor about spices and silks. But I know I'll get more loving from him when he does return. You know, Patrick, he is the best lover, and he makes me shout with joy."

"You have not yet had me, lass."

"Never in your lifetime! By the way, Patrick and Earl, why are you way down there? Are you afraid to come closer to us?"

"Ni, it's just we have heard what happens on this mountain. It belongs to the fairies. It's a fairyland; you had better watch out for the Fairy Queen, she is very evil."

"Well then, I'll just have to have a meeting with her, won't I?"

"We'll see." Laughing hard, Patrick turned away, leading the others back down the mountain. She could hear his wicked echo of laughter all the way down.

Chapter 10

Little did anyone know that Queen Megotta was listening with a big smile on her face. "We will work together, Lady Deirdre."

"We will not go to the cave this way. I feel they are still watching every move we make."

"I feel it too, Deirdre. Look!! Is there not another way to the cave? Like by the waterway?"

"You know, Kimberly, I think so."

"Why can't we go to the beach this evening? Then we can see if it is under the dock?" asked Monica.

"You're right, Monica, that's where all the silkies stay. I know it will smell, but that is the beauty of it. Remember, they used to guard the front entrance, but way in the back the stream starts. We'll need torches so we can see our way."

"Yes, Kimberly, we have been around them all our lives. Matter of fact, we raised some of them from pups until they were fully grown."

"Deirdre, do you remember when we all had two pups each and Father had a fit about it."

"Oh yes, Monica, I do remember that." Smiling to herself, Deirdre started to remember many other things. "Wait a moment... I just thought of something; it's not the beach opening, but that's good to remember, just to throw off our enemies."

"Now what have you got in mind?" asked Monica.

"You must not say a word to anyone."

"We understand. What is it?" asked Kimberly.

"I'll not tell you until we reach home. On to Sea Oaks; let's hurry." Giving their horses their head, they rode hard at a high gallop.

There were Campbell spies all over Sea Oats, watching them. But Annie, being very alert, rode up beside Deirdre. "Don't look now, My Lady, but there are quite a few Campbell spies around us. Can you see them?"

"I guess they think I don't know my own men. We must be very careful, lassies. Let's laugh and say awful things about Patrick Campbell."

"That we will," each agreed, laughing.

"The nerve of that Patrick Campbell — coming up to me this day and saying those things to me."

"I know; it was a disgrace and you carrying Tommy's baby," spoke Molly, trying not to grin, let alone laugh.

"But he doesn't know, Molly." Deirdre spoke with a quiver in her voice.

"You don't mean that Laird Tommy doesn't know?" asked Annie.

"No, he doesn't," answered Deirdre.

"Now, you will take it easy, you must rest when we go inside," Kimberly requested as she helped Deirdre down from her horse.

They walked up to the Campbells that were dressed in the MacDarroch colors. Having gotten a good look at them, the lassies smiled.

Seeing Uncle William, Deirdre shouted at him to wait up so they could go with him. He smiled at Deirdre as she came up and gave him a big hug. Deirdre gave him the details of what had happened on the mountain and about the Campbells at Sea Oaks. Uncle William left laughing.

Seeing Uncle Jamie out on the practice field, Deirdre went over to tell him. As the lassies left and went inside, Uncle William slapped his brother, Jamie, on the back, telling him what the lassies had told him. They both started laughing while going back to the courtyard from the practice field.

Monica went straight to tell their father about what was going on while Deirdre went with Kimberly, Annie, and Molly to their chambers.

"Now what is more important than getting out there and taking care of those Campbells?" Molly asked.

Going over to her wardrobe, Deirdre pushed all the clothes aside and mashed a lever, which had a round knob that Grandfather had put in a long time ago. Deirdre turned to watch their faces. The whole wall shifted open behind the back of the wardrobe.

"My goodness, Deirdre, how did you find it?" asked Kimberly.

"Kimberly, don't you remember it? It's the other way into our secret cave. Now I'm going in to see what shape it's in; but all of you, stay here."

"I don't think so. We're going with you," Molly spoke up as the rest shook their heads yes.

Just then, Monica came in startling them. "Father and the others are rounding up the Campbells; he is putting them in the deep dungeon. Lord help us, you found it! Oh, Deirdre you found it! Now let's find our lads." Smiling, she gave Deirdre a hug. "You remember, we used to hide in there from the lads when we were children."

"But now let's light up the torches to see and get going."

"Deirdre, do you expect to find anything blocking it up?" asked Annie.

"I could not say, Annie. It's been a very long time and there is a stream running down into the loch. I pray we have no cave-ins of any sort."

"Amen." The others spoke like a prayer.

The good Lord was kind to them at least half of the way, then all of a sudden, right in front of them was a very large rock slide that blocked the way.

"Oh! Damn, now what?" asked Monica.

"Number one, little sister, watch your mouth. Second, we'll start moving the rocks."

"You're right, Deirdre, let's get started," agreed Kimberly.

They all pitched in and before they knew it, they were through and could continue on. "Do you hear that? It sounds like a new underground spring that I have never heard before. Wonder if it's a fresh one. Now watch your step." Holding their torches high, what Deirdre saw took her breath away. She stopped all of a sudden. "It's an artesian spring." Deirdre spoke in a far off voice — in a faint whisper.

"A what? What do you see?" asked Monica as she slipped down to where Deirdre was standing in shock. "My word, what a wondrous sight to behold."

The others crowded around Monica and Deirdre. All she could hear from them was, "Oh, my word."

"It's like a fairyland. Look at the flowers, the ferns, moss, and the flowery bushes," Deirdre said in shock.

"But, how? Wouldn't there have to be light coming from somewhere?" remarked Annie.

Kimberly looked around Deirdre and pointed to the top. It was like a big hole from above. You could see all the roots from a huge tree and it looked like the only way it could live was that the roots were down into the spring. "Oh my, would you look at that." Molly crossed herself. She seemed to be very frightened, just as the rest of them.

"Now, look and listen. We have to go on, how far I don't know, but we have too. Our time is running out," announced Deirdre.

They took each other's hand and made a human rope. Staying on the side, they found themselves in front of a large waterfall. What they saw as they went under the waterfall were rooms cut on the inside of the cave. "This is it!! Here is where you can fix their places to sleep; even the old pallet covers are here—the ones that we used, do you remember? You can light a fire with the newness that has been made; anyone would think it was the mist rising from the new spring. Do you think you can get back down here by yourselves?"

"Sure, you bet we can," was Kimberly's answer, looking at the others.

Molly reached down and tasted the water, smiling. "It's cool, fresh water."

"Wonderful, I'm going back and have fresh straw brought to my room. Kimberly, you and Molly start getting the pallets cleaned up and then we'll stuff them with the fresh straw."

"Deirdre, we'll need lots of garlic and something to store it in," remarked Kimberly.

"You'll have everything you will need, dear sister, so don't worry about it. I'll talk to Grace about some of the things."

Deirdre ran up from the fairyland, through the wardrobe. She almost knocked Maude off her feet. "Whoa, watch where you are going, lass."

"Maude love, we need your help; get Sue and Sara, you will not believe what we have found. Never in a million years!"

"Oh...you mean the underground tunnel that leads to the fairyland?"

"How in the world did you know about that?"

"You may not believe this, but the fairy, Queen Megotta, was here in your chamber, looking for you for years, Me Lady. When you were a wee baby she looked after you, the same as I did, lassie. I know she will be so glad you're home."

"You're so right, Maude," a voice came from behind Deirdre. The room held a bright glow in it. "You're home now, My Lady."

Bowing, Deirdre took the queen's hand and kissed it, out of respect to her. "Yes, Your Highness, I am."

"To stay? No, I don't think so this time."

"Why do you say that, Your Highness?"

"My dear, it's too early to tell as of yet. Now you be very careful in your quest to help the MacDonald lads. Don't trust the priest that will be there. He's not the regular priest. Tell your Uncle Ira, also, to be careful. Send the crew from your grandfather's ship first and let them handle him."

"Bu...but Queen Megotta, my grandfather and his crew don't speak French!!"

"But they do. You ask him. I must go now; don't worry about your lad, in time he will know who you are and he'll find his joy as well as you."

The next thing Deirdre knew she was gone. She turned to look at Maude, "Maude did you know that Grandfather could speak French?"

"He always did, you do too, and you and your sisters speak a lot of different languages. Your Uncle Ira and the monks, as well as the nuns, taught you well."

Just then Kimberly, Monica, Molly, and Annie came up smiling really big. "We got it done. It's all clean, food stored, herbs for healing and we even have pots to cook and fix the herbs. Did ye know there was an old table down there?" Looking at them, "Deirdre, Maude what's wrong?" asked Monica.

"Monica, when you were on the boat and around Grandfather, did you speak with each other in another language?"

"Yes, we did, but we spoke French more than any other, why?"

"I just wondered. Kimberly, how did you get all of the things you needed? I haven't spoken with Grace."

"She just brought them down for us. Didn't you see her?" asked Kimberly.

"No, I didn't. I need to speak with Father Ira." She left the chamber with a shocked look on her face as the others looked at her in wonderment.

"I wonder what's on her mind," Annie said as Deirdre left.

Finding her Uncle Ira in the chapel, Deirdre knelt down to pray. Father Ira saw Deirdre as she was getting ready to leave the chapel. "My child, what are you doing here?"

He saw her face with the tears running down. "I need to talk with you. Oh... Father Ira, I was warned that there is a new priest at the Campbells' and he is not to be trusted."

Deirdre's Uncle Ira, seeing how distraught she was, said softly; "Don't you worry your sweet head about it, love. Your old Uncle Ira will take care of everything. Now you go back up to the castle and you get some rest. Tomorrow will be a hard day on you; now be off with you. Your other uncles and I, with the Great Chief, Captain Kirk Harrkon, have things to do; you'll have to do as we say, lassie, is that clear?"

Wiping her eyes with the back of her hand, she looked up into a beautiful smiling face. "Uncle, I promise you that I'll do as I'm told this time. I'll not fight any of you. I just want my Tommy free and safe; my sisters want their men safe, also. We are ready for them, but for now, I'll go rest."

Uncle Ira gave Deirdre a big hug as she left the chapel. Smiling and shaking his head, he spoke aloud, "I pray she will do as she promised; she will have to be strong. Tomorrow will take all her strength." Bowing his head, he prayed, "Dear Father in Heaven, be with us on the morrow. Help us to get the lads out safe; bring them home, and let things go well. If it be your will, Father, Amen."

Early the next morning they were on board the ship and ready to sail. Father Ira asked that they all bow their heads for a word of prayer. "Gentle Jesus, with faith in Your healing powers and confidence in Your constant compassion, we ask that You take heed of our suffering spirits. May our souls find rest in Your comforting love and relief from sorrow and anguish. Relying on Your love, we especially ask Your help in getting the MacDonald brothers out safely. We place our trust in Your power to heal our spirits from the feeling of hopelessness, unrest and despair. Amen."

They all got dressed in their robes, so they would look like monks. Grandfather and his crew all dressed as French sailors. Uncle Ira had the large wine barrels up on deck so everyone could see. He had also gotten a horse and cart. With the French flag flying, they sailed up the sound of Jura into the sound of Gogh then Loch Fine. There they saw Laird Robert Campbell's stronghold in which they knew he had the MacDonald brothers. Robert Campbell had three other strongholds, but the main one was called Glen Yon.

Grandfather helped Deirdre get into a very large wine barrel. He left the top open just a slant so she could get air.

All of a sudden Deirdre heard Grandfather tell Father Ira he was putting on a monk's robe and to have the lads start singing in French. It was beautiful the way the lads' voices blended together.

Father Ira was standing at the rails so he could be seen. It seemed as if he was blessing everyone on shore as well as the wine.

Boy, would they be surprised to see what was in one of the barrels, Deirdre thought as they neared Robert Campbell's stronghold. Father Ira came by the barrel that she was in and spoke very softly. "Love, be very quiet."

Feeling the ship dock, Deirdre became just a little unsettled, wondering what would happen next. The barrel she was in was being lifted up; put into a cart with straw piled up around the barrel.

Father Ira, the priest, as everyone called him but for Deirdre, walked around and blessed the people there at the Campbell stronghold.

Suddenly they stopped and Deirdre felt herself being lifted up again. She heard Father Ira being greeted by the priest from the chapel. "Bless you and all, and where in the world would be

Father Fred this fine day. He'll be missing the blessing of this fine wine."

"He was called away all of a sudden, but I'll be glad to help you, Father."

"Well now, I'm known as Father Ira, and who might ye be?"

"Father Peter, at your service, Father Ira."

"It's grand to meet you, Father Peter. Shall we go in now, and then we can have the lads put the wine barrels in the back room?"

"Maybe we can have a wee bit of the grape, Father Ira?"

"Well, who is to say we can't? Wouldn't want it to be a bad lot, would we? Laird Robert wouldn't like that, would he?"

Laughing, Father Peter led the way. Deirdre was the last barrel to go in. The lads stopped at the entrance of the church next to the Holy Water Bowl stand just long enough to lift Deirdre out of the barrel.

She could hear all the laughter going on in the back room. She, Grandfather Kirk, and Uncle William, with the help of two more of the men, slid the post back. Then they jumped into the opening under the Holy Water stand and closed it back, so no one would suspect what was going on.

They moved very slowly at first because it was a little tight and quite dark. As they moved along, they came across some torches on the wall. After lighting them, they moved a lot faster, when they abruptly came to a dead end.

Looking around, Uncle William looked and pushed all over the rock wall until he found a loose rock. As he removed it, a stone door started to creak as it slid back. It revealed a cavern of slaughter and decay as if a huge carnivorous scavenger had used it as its dwelling.

The odor of fungal meat-eating flora gave Deirdre a feeling of stepping into a festering, weeping wound and her saliva taste of a pustule jungle rot.

Her driving force was to get the lads out in a hurry, before the smell alone would kill them. Turning to her grandfather and uncle she said, "Cover your nose and mouth with your tartan, both of you, the smell is unbelievable. You could expire from the stench alone."

"We know what you mean; Lord above, how can the lads stand it?" asked Uncle William.

"I don't know, but let's get them out of here and home."

"Deirdre lass, be careful," spoke Grandfather as he entered the tomb of death.

In a soft voice, "I feel this is a trap; watch where you walk and what you touch, lass," remarked Uncle William.

"A what?" asked Deirdre as she felt shivers run all through her body.

"William lad, I feel you are right about it being a trap. I, too, feel something is not right here. Deirdre lass, you be extra careful."

"I will, Grandfather, now you two please watch your step." Deirdre had always been very protective of her family and that would certainly not stop now.

She went in slowly and very, very careful as not to make any noise, with her sword drawn. There was not a sound that could be heard. They moved in just a little bit more until she heard voices. "Tommy, answer us, are you awake? Man alive, Richard, he hasn't answered us since they threw us into this God-forsaken hell hole."

Deirdre slipped up very quietly. "Don't speak; we are here to take you home."

"Who? Who is there?"

"Shhh, Uncle William, have you or Grandfather found the keys?"

"Here they are," Uncle William said as he handed her keys to the cell doors.

"Who in God's name are you?"

"Don't ask questions, lad. Come on now, let's get you and your brothers out of here and home. You'll have to be very quiet, as quiet as a church mouse."

"Who are you? I have asked you for the last time!"

"Hugh, I'm Chief Kirk, grandfather of Kimberly, Monica and Lady Deirdre."

Looking into the eyes of Grandfather, he said, "She is home? Was it really and truly her we saw?"

"Yes, laddie that she is, and they are the true ones."

With tears running down Hugh's cheeks he turned to his brother Richard, "You heard?"

"That I did!" Richard answered. He, too, was crying. "Monica?"

"Yes, she too, now come on, we must hurry. We have a long way to go. Deirdre lass, are you ready?"

"As soon as I can get Tommy to move. Oh, Uncle William, Grandfather, they have beaten him so; all of his body is so bloody. Can you help me, Uncle?" she asked, knocking a large rat out of the way.

"OK, lass, let's try. William lad, you take Richard and help Hugh. It looks like they took all their hate out on Tommy." He picked Tommy up in his arms and carried him out like a baby.

Just as they had gotten out of the secret door, they heard the guards coming down the stairs. "You go ahead with the lads; I'll take care of them."

"Not alone you won't, lass," Grandfather Kirk replied.

"I can take them, now go!"

"You will do no such thing. Remember your promise to your Uncle Ira."

Uncle William left Tommy along with Hugh and Richard in the secret passageway, and the door almost closed.

"Charlie, my lad, let's see how the MacDonalds are doing."

"You know, Edward, that Tommy looked half dead the last time I saw him. Patrick really beat him bad."

"You know why, don't you, Charlie?"

"It's because Patrick is mad with jealously, for the want of Deirdre."

"That you are right, but he'll never have her."

"You got that right, my buckaroo. Now just stand there like good little lads, and I may just let you live."

Startled at her presence, the lads responded, "Now, Lady Deirdre, we were just following orders."

"Charlie—that's your name, is it not?"

"Yes."

"Are you the one who helped beat the MacDonald lad, Tommy?"

"No, Lady Deirdre, it was Patrick, My Laird Robert's oldest son."

"I see, thank you for the information. Now if you will just follow me." They thought they could get away, until they felt another sword in their back.

"Now, lads, follow her." They heard another voice from the shadows. Charlie was shaking as well as Edward, for fear of not knowing what was ahead. Deirdre pushed Charlie into a cell. Edward was pushed into another one by Grandfather Kirk.

Deirdre heard a thud. She knew the guard had met with a fatal blow by the hand and sword of her grandfather.

"Let's go, lass. We're finished here."

"Be right behind you," As she brought up her sword and lifted off the head of the guard. She locked the doors and left.

They had just gotten to the entrance opening when it opened up all the way. "We must hurry now," Uncle Ira spoke in a soft tone.

"Where is the priest, Uncle Ira?"

"Why... My Lady, he is sleeping like a baby," he said, smiling at them.

Chapter 11

Uncle William, with Grandfather, put Hugh, Richard, and Tommy in the wine barrels, while Deirdre put on a monk's robe. Then they left.

Donald, one of the crew, lifted the barrel that Tommy was in, almost dropping it, but he caught it just in time.

Everyone got on board the ship and put the barrels below so they could get the lads out of sight and cleaned up. The stench of their bodies was unbelievable, it would make you vomit. After the first mate, Donald, and Deirdre bathed the lads in garlic water, they smelled better, only like garlic.

Donald put them in their clean bunks, and fed the lads barley water, because they had not eaten in only God knows how long. The crew prayed that the food would stay down. Tommy's brothers seemed to be doing fine, but Tommy was the one that worried Deirdre. She was going to take care of cleaning and feeding her Tommy, personally.

She put her arm around his neck to clean all the old blood off his face. He stirred somewhat, mumbled something that you could not understand, then quieted down.

As Deirdre finished washing Tommy, she tried to feed him the barley water. Tommy rose up on his elbows, and looked her right in the eye. "Who the bloody hell are you? And take that shit away from me. I'll not eat it. I know you're trying to get rid of me, but I'll not die; you will not have her. My Kitten is mine, and only mine, forever. Do you hear me, all of you damn Campbells?"

He fell back — back into darkness. Deirdre just sat there crying, not knowing what else to do.

Hugh spoke in a soft tone, "Don't worry, Deirdre, he'll be fine with your care."

They were getting closer to home when Grandfather came below. "How is the lad, love?"

"I just don't know!" she said, getting up and going into his arms.

"Now, now, the lad has a lot of fight in him, my darling. Don't you worry; he'll be fine when we get him home."

After getting them home, everyone helped get the lads into the secret cave. Annie and Molly were left with them after getting everything settled. Maude came running into the cave shouting that the Campbells were riding up the road to Sea Oaks. Kimberly, Monica and Deirdre were asked to come as fast as they could to get dressed and go to the great room for the evening meal.

The three of them went to the castle where they entered through the secret door. They dressed properly and quickly and made sure to close everything up so as not to be seen. Even Grandfather came back with his men after hiding the French ship.

They were all eating, laughing, listening to the music and watching the dancers when loud banging was heard at the door. "Elias, please answer the door."

"I will, My Lady." He left to open the great door, only to be pushed out of the way. Patrick Campbell and his men stormed their way in. Deirdre spoke up, "What right have you to break in here this way?"

"We are looking for escapees from our dungeon."

Standing up because the clan was getting upset, she shouted, "Now tell me who they were and I'll be glad to help you find them, Patrick." Then Deirdre motioned for the clan to sit down.

"Well, I can't say," remarked Patrick Campbell.

"My, my, you can't tell us who? Now, why is that, pray tell?"

"Laird John MacDarroch!" shouted Patrick.

"Patrick Campbell, you are talking to Lady Deirdre, next in line to be Laird of our clan when I decide to step down. Now tell her; I command it," Laird John said, standing next to his daughter.

"She... what?"

"You heard me! Now if you will not tell our Lady who the ones are that you are looking for, you will have to take your men and leave our land—and don't come back. Now if you do that, you will have a war on your hands! Are you going to tell us who you are looking for or not?"

Patrick gave Deirdre a hard look, turned with his men, left the hall and stomped out the door very mad.

Later the people told them Patrick and his men left the Islands by boat, very angrily shouting he would be back.

Little did anyone know that Queen Megotta was listening to what Patrick was saying as he left with his men.

"Deirdre!!"

"Yes, Father."

"Do you feel that we have not heard the end of this?"

"I think we all feel it, Father, this is just the beginning." As she looked around, everyone in the hall was nodding their heads.

Kimberly looked at the door and saw Queen Megotta standing there. "Deirdre, we have a royal guest."

Deirdre looked over to the door where the queen stood with a large smile on her face. "You handled that just fine. Patrick was so mad; you should have heard him. My people will help you all we can, Lady Deirdre." Like a twinkle of an eye, she was gone.

"If you will excuse us please, we have some important things to do."

As she was leaving the hall the whole clan stood up, held their cups high, and shouted, "Long live our Lady Warrior, Deirdre."

Kimberly stuck her head through the door of the armoire, and asked Deirdre, "What in the world are you looking for?"

"I'm trying to find my wedding ring to go with this other one. It doesn't come off, but the wedding ring just slipped right off. Here it is, thank goodness. Let's go."

"You know the dress you have on is the one Tommy loved on you. The green makes your eyes bright."

"Thank you, Kimberly. I had almost forgotten." As they came closer to the opening of the cave, they heard a loud crash, with words behind it that would make Father Ira blush.

"Damn it to hell, you leave me alone; I don't need your help. My God!! If you lads believe they are who they say they are, then you are damn fools."

It was Tommy's voice she heard, thinking to herself, *Well they didn't say it would be easy.* But here goes. "Well, well, if the big man isn't back with us. How are you feeling? From the way you were shouting, I would think you were well."

Tommy looked at Deirdre in hard silence, "And may I ask who the hell are you supposed to be?" leaning back with beads of hot sweat on his forehead from the high fever that wracked his body.

"Oh! It's a game you're wanting to play. Well, I'm the true Lady Deirdre MacDarroch MacDonald. I married you on my father's birthday. I was taken away the same evening as you, when a heavy thick Black Fog rolled in. Now if that isn't enough, I have more stories to tell you."

"And stories are all they are."

"Really, now?"

"Yes," he said. He tried to get up, but still weak, he fell back on the pallet. Deirdre went over to him. "Leave me be," he shouted.

"I will not, you are still weak!"

Kimberly handed her a pail of cool water. Thanking Kimberly, Deirdre started to wipe Tommy's brow, and he shoved her hand away.

"Now we are going to get one thing straight, I'm going to wash you down; your fever is coming back."

"Leave me be! She is gone and I'm tired. I want to be with her."

"I'm here and you had better get used to it, I'm here to stay; is that understood, little man?"

Everyone looked at her as if she were an ogre. "Well what are you looking at? Go and do what you need to do; I'll see after him." They all left with huge smiles on their faces.

Whipping around, she could now see a faint smile forming on Tommy's lips. "So that's the way it's going to be. The water looks so inviting; think I'll take a swim while he sleeps."

While Deirdre stripped off all her clothes, she looked back at Tommy and saw he was asleep, but restless. Diving in the cool water, she thought about their swimming at their secret pool in the forest. The water was so great; she just didn't want to get out, but thought she had better, to see how he was doing.

Getting out of the water, Deirdre saw that he was rolling and very restless. Feeling his forehead, he was burning up with fever, indeed. Deirdre was still wet, her body very cool; she got in beside him, and held his hot body to her cool one.

Tommy looked at her; she saw how glassy his eyes were from the fever as he looked at her. Dark dreams came upon him. He cried as he held her so tight it was hard for her to breathe.

Then he got on top of her with his hands roaming all over her body, kissing her neck then worked his way down. When Tommy heard her moan, he smiled. "You're mine; I knew you would not leave me. Oh!! Kitten, I'll never let you go, you're mine forever."

He kept on, not stopping. He started kneading her buttock. Tommy's arousal lay heavy against her thigh, the heat of it making Deirdre squirm. "Never," he whispered.

He chuckled, as he clipped her wrists with one big hand above her head. He thrust his knee between her thighs, rubbing, spreading her, trapping her with his leg to the pallet and leaving her vulnerable to his touch. His callused hand molded her flesh, diving to stroke her belly, and hip; she wanted more and nearly shouted for him to touch lower.

"Aah," came a choke, as his tongue circled and flicked her nipples between his lips. He drew deeply again on the delicate peak.

Deirdre started arching into him, jerking on his hold; he released her wrists and moved lower, licking her ribs and parting her flesh which was damp with the aching. Deirdre gripped his shoulder, her body slicking.

He moved his weight; he quickly spread her thighs and covered her softness with his mouth. She cried out loudly, and he chuckled, parting her flesh, probing the dewy fold with his velvet tongue.

Deirdre squirmed, trying to bend her leg and ease the throbbing. They used to play this game of "Say my name." She would say "No," which she did this night. Tommy fell back on his haunches, looking at her with the fever in his eyes, yanked her to her feet, loving the way Deirdre swayed, unsteady on her feet.

Before she could pull away, he caught her hips in his broad hands, tipping her up to the heat of his mouth.

He licked. Then he drew her long leg over his broad shoulder. His tongue snaked, flicking the core of her being. Deirdre's knees felt as though they would buckle out from under her.

Her hips rocked. Tommy smiled, soothing his hands up her thighs and dipping his fingers between. Tasting her still, he parted her vee, plunging two fingers inside.

"Oh!! Sweet mercy!" The heat of her desire throbbed through her, purring like a cat against his touch, her flesh quivering with the coming peak.

Deirdre rocked. Tommy moaned encouragement, he withdrew and plunged deeper.

"Who am I?"

"My Laird," Deirdre gasped, grinding up to him, shameless, unbridled in pleasure.

Deirdre accepted it, let it shower like hot rain, her body was reaching for undiscovered rapture just on the edge. Tommy always seemed to love to torment her. He was demanding to hear his name on her lips.

She refused when his tongue circled the bud of her desire over and over. She cried out in Gaelic. Cursing him, one long moan, and still Tommy mastered her body.

Even as feverish as he was, he still tasted her desire. Her passion-slick muscles clamped and pulsed, Tommy lifted his gaze, watching her climax spread through her. Her head tipped back, her fingers deep in his hair. Deirdre's lips parted in breathless pants, her eyes closed against the tension trying to escape.

They drank in each other's ecstasy, feeling it rip through both of them with a ruthlessness that unmanned both of them, and fractured them as Tommy entered her. Then he lost control, which made him spill his seed. They both went over the edge and sank boneless into one another. Tommy gathered her up in his arms. Their bodies both soaked with the heat of the moment. She touched a trembling finger to his cheek, then jaw, then to his fevered lips.

Deirdre looked at him; he seemed to be resting very peacefully. It was early in the morning just before dawn that she got dressed, ready to leave, when she felt a hand on the hem of her dress.

"Please, don't leave me."

Kneeling down, "How are you feeling?" She touched his forehead to see if he still had a fever.

"Who are you? I can't see you in the dark?"

"It will be light soon and you can see. Who am I? Someone who loves you very, very much."

"But who? If you know me, you know I have but one love."

"I know, now you must get some rest. Your brothers are here; I'll get them." She looked down and saw he had fallen back to sleep.

Before she left, Deirdre asked Hugh and Richard to look in on Tommy. Hugh smiled at her when she asked him to see about

Tommy. "You know we will. Did you have a good time last night, sister?" he asked with a wide grin.

Feeling her face grow red, Deirdre smiled, turned, and left. As she went out from the falls, there stood Queen Megotta. "Don't worry, I'll see to him. Rest now, you'll need your rest for what's to come."

Deirdre entered her bedchamber; she was very tired. She went to the window. The sun was very bright this morning. It was just too much having Tommy not believing who she was. Deirdre, feeling herself drained, her energy gone, yelled and screamed at the sky as she looked out of her window threatening anything, promising everything if they would just send him back to her. "You have to come back to me Tommy; you just can't leave me like this." Deirdre cried herself into fretful sleep.

While Deirdre was sleeping, little did she know that it was night once again. No one had bothered to wake her because they knew that she was very tired and needed the rest.

What she didn't know was that Tommy had slipped out of the cave, gotten on a horse, and rode off. "Deirdre, Deirdre, wake up, honey, please."

Rubbing her eyes, and stretching, "What's wrong, Kimberly?" she said.

"Tommy is gone!!"

"What? Where? How?"

"He slipped out during the night."

Getting up, she felt as if she had been drugged, "How long have I been asleep?"

"One night and a day."

"My word."

"Deirdre, do you know where Tommy might have gone?"

"I believe I do." Deirdre got out of bed and put some clothes on. She started for the door, taking Kimberly's arm and patting it. "Kimberly I'm going to our secret place to see if he is there. Don't worry, Tommy will be alright,"

"It really isn't Tommy I'm worried about. It's you."

"Well, don't worry about me, I'll be fine," picking up her sword and chakram, she left the chamber with Kimberly right behind her. Deirdre headed for the kitchen then out through the back door.

"Deirdre, please be careful..."

"I will, Kimberly, see you soon."

Walking toward the stable where Thunder was kept, she was thinking to herself, *You're at our secret pond, Tommy lad, I know that is where you will be.*

Deirdre rode through the meadow and up to the deep forest, traveling very quietly as she approached their secret pool. She looked hard and there he was with his head bowed low.

"So this is where you are love. Had a feeling you would be here at our secret pool," she said, smiling as she got off of Thunder.

"How did you know of this place? You couldn't have, unless my Kitten told you before you killed her."

"What in the world are you saying, Tommy?"

"What I'm saying is you must have tortured Deirdre, and then took her place. To try and fool all who loved her."

"Have you gone absolutely crazy man? It's me."

"Oh no you're not!"

Deirdre was mad, madder than she had been in many weeks. "Well, I tell you what then, I'll release you of your vows of marriage."

"You can't do that, because we were not wed."

"No, well here goes." Deirdre took her wedding ring off her finger then said the words as she turned three times in a circle, "I, Lady Deirdre MacDarroch MacDonald do hereby relieve Sir Thomas Edward MacDonald from his vows, I put him aside." She went over before she left and put the ring in his hand. "Forever is no more, it's dead." As she climbed on Thunder to leave, Tommy stood with his mouth open. He took two long strides and grabbed her arm, "How did you get her ring?"

"Oh! You fool. Yes, you are a fool, Tommy MacDonald! I'll tell everyone up at Sea Oaks what I did here and then it will be legal," jerking her arm out of his grasp. "We are finished from this day on. I have no husband!"

Tommy just stood there with his mouth wide open. As he turned, he saw Queen Megotta standing by the pool. "She is right, Sir Tommy, you are a big fool. You see, she is the true one.

But now it will be a long sad day before she'll ever come back to you." Then she vanished.

Not hearing Hugh ride up, he heard Hugh's remark, "Tommy, you are truly mad *or* a fool, whichever comes first."

"Hugh, tell me, do you believe she is the true one?" Tommy asked.

"Yes, I do, and so does Richard."

"I don't, but she has a very bad temper like me Kitten. Here look, see she put her wedding band in my hand."

Hugh looked at it then looked Tommy in the eye, "Did you read what is in the ring?"

"I remember it says, forever. That was what she said as she put it in my hand. My Lord, Hugh, it is her. She doesn't want me and I don't blame her. I have got to go to her, out of my way man. Thank you, Hugh."

Chapter 12

Tommy rode like the devil himself was after him. He had to get back up to the castle in a hurry. He jumped off his horse just as the great doors opened for him. Tommy looked at the guards; they were shaking their heads. Dashing through the doors into the great room, "Deirdre, you can't do it, Kitten!"

Everyone in the great hall did not know what was going on. They were just looking on with wonder of what was going to happen.

Deirdre turned and looked him straight in the eyes. "I can't, you say? Well, let me tell you something, Sir Thomas Edward MacDonald, I can do as I choose."

"I know now who you are; no one would have ever had the courage to say what you did, but my Kitten."

"So, it's Kitten now, is it? Well I'll not have anyone call me a liar and get away with it!" Deirdre shouted so loud everyone in the whole castle heard her.

"I'm sorry. I know now that you are the true one. No one would ever face me the way you did, Kitten. You didn't set me aside, did you? I couldn't stand it if you did. I wouldn't want to live without you, my Kitten."

Deirdre looked at him and saw tears running down his face. All of a sudden, he was shaking, and then down on his knees he dropped, crying hard.

She couldn't stand it. This big man in front of her was crying like a baby. She went over, knelt down in front of him, put her hand under his chin and turned it up, "No, my darling I didn't." Smiling at him, she also had tears running down her face, "No, my 'mo chiedhe', my heart."

Everyone understood what was going on, and started shouting. "To the MacDarrochs and MacDonalds forever, together!"

"Ever one, enjoy yourself." Tommy picked Deirdre up and ran to the door, taking two steps at a time to her bedchamber. He went straight over to the bed and dropped her in the middle.

"Tommy, do ye really believe it is truly I?"

"Yes, Kitten, I do because, as I told you downstairs, no one would have the guts to talk to me like you did. They would never live to get away with it."

After a wonderful night of lovemaking, Deirdre was sleeping like a wee baby. She must have been more tired than she thought with all that had been going on.

Tommy had slipped out of bed without her knowing. Looking down and thinking to himself, *If you really are who you say you are, then you won't mind me seeing that little mark on your backside.* He just had to see for himself.

Deirdre had always slept naked and he knew it. She always hated nightwear. Sleeping with her left leg out from under the covers and laying on her right side, left leg thrown over the right. Tommy got down, and to his surprise; there it was, right before his eyes, the patch of strawberries. "Praise be; it *is* you, my love, it is really you."

After he had his cry, Tommy crawled back in beside her. He put his arm around her and snuggled down, holding on as if he would never let her go.

The door opened very quietly and Maude slipped in. She looked over at the bed and saw Tommy cuddled up beside Deirdre and just smiled with tears in her eyes. Maude backed out, softly closing the chamber door.

Deirdre didn't realize the whole family had been in her chamber at some point that morning. They were planning a big celebration of their reunion. Laird John sent word to Glen MacDonald to let him know what had transpired.

When Deirdre finally woke, she felt a large arm over her body. Turning over and seeing Tommy's face, she just smiled; leaning over, she kissed his soft lips.

Deirdre was slipping out of the bed when a large hand grabbed her and pulled her back into it. Laughing, Tommy rolled on top of her and started kissing her all over. "Kitten, do you have any idea how happy I am? No, of course not; you couldn't." He remembered where her spot was that made her laugh, which was behind her knees.

They were playing and rolling over one another when the door opened. Maude came in, and so did the footman, bringing a very large tub and lots of hot water. "Maude, my darling, for me?" Deirdre was trying to cover herself while Tommy just stood there in his magnificent naked body.

"I don't think so, my Sir Tommy; it's for the both of you. Now there will be a big celebration going on down in the great hall soon, if you think you can tear yourselves away from one another."

"Thank you, Maude, we'll be ready."

"Now Kitten, speak for yourself. No telling what will happen when I get you in the tub." Tommy smiled at Maude, then winked his eye. It made Maude turn as red as a beet.

"Oh no you don't! We have duties to perform and we will do them."

"Of course we will."

"Now you can go and jump into the loch if you want to," smiling as she got into the tub, sinking down into the warm water.

"Wouldn't that just be great? Would you come with me, my darling?"

"Don't think so. Here, help me wash my hair."

He smiled as he got into the tub with her. After he helped wash her hair, she washed his. They both loved to wash each other, like the days when they were young, in their secret pool.

"Tommy, do you remember when we first found the pool? We always were there when anything went wrong. We always knew where the other one was."

"Like the time I came and found you there. You knew that I had to go to the king's court for the training to be a knight."

"That's when I begged you not to go. I was afraid that you would like the lassies in court. It was very hard on me to let you go, even though we were young."

"But I came back and found you all grown up and oh, so beautiful! You were laying on the big rock with nothing on. Your long red hair was the only thing that covered you up."

"Only, when I saw you looking at me I stood up so you could get your eyes full. They almost fell right out of your head."

"You were a brazen wench then. I stripped, jumped in, and we met in the middle of the pond. I knew then, you were really mine for ever. I took you then and there."

"That you did. I have been yours from the time we were wee babies. There has never been anyone else but you."

"I know that, Kitten, because when you left the cave I looked down and saw where I was bloody and a spot on the pallet. But how could it be? I ask myself. But that is when Queen Megotta explained to me about when a female goes without a man for many years, she is like a virgin."

"Oh, really? She told you that, did she?"

"Yes, she did, and she laughed at me; said that I turned very red in the face. Hugh and Richard heard also."

"Oh... I see." She was smiling at him as she got out of the tub, holding a large linen towel to dry off with.

"Kitten, you know I just had you and I want you again; does the feeling ever go away? Do you think I could have you again?"

"Yes, my darling, you can. You have every right, you know, you're my husband," she said, smiling as she spoke.

They stepped back into the tub; they made love again, washed each other, got out and dried each other off and started getting dressed. He laced her up and helped with everything but her hair. That's when he called Maude. As Maude was fixing her hair he asked, "Maude, please don't put her hair up; let it hang down her back. I have something for her head."

"What is it, Tommy darling?"

There was a knock, Tommy went to answer, and one of his men brought in a box wrapped in velvet. Giving it to Maude, she smiled and he winked at her. "I will do as you ask me, Sir Tommy."

"When did you have time to get a gift?" asked Deirdre.

"My dad brought it. It was for you as a wedding gift, and I never got to give it to you."

Deirdre was wearing her green and royal blue dress with slits in the top of the sleeves, around the bodice; and around the full skirt was silver thistle. Silver acorns, oak leaves, and lots of heather, all in silver, were all around the bottom and top of the dress. Tommy asked Deirdre to close her eyes until Maude had finished her hair. Then Maude placed it on her head. Tommy asked her to look in the mirror. There was a circle of silver with a large pearl in the middle and on each side were an emerald and a sapphire.

"Shall we go to our celebration, Lady Deirdre MacDarroch MacDonald?"

Deirdre smiled up at him with all the love she had shining in her eyes, "Yes, my husband."

While they were having a great time at the celebration, the door opened. It was Laird Glen MacDonald, out of breath. "Tommy lad, you must leave—you and your brothers"

"Why, Father?"

"The Campbells are coming with the king riding at the head."

"Are you sure?" asked Deirdre.

"Yes, I am."

"Alright. Tommy, Hugh, Richard, go back into the cave, and we'll just go on as before."

"I'll not be running!"

"But you have to. Don't you see, we all are at the mercy of the king? You wait just a little longer, please."

"Alright, brothers," he said, "let's go," each giving their lassies a big hug and kiss before they left.

"Everyone, I'm going up and get MacTavish," remarked Deirdre.

"I'll get Darroch too," stated Monica, who had raised her large black wolf from a pup.

"Angus." Kimberly called her large gray Irish wolfhound mixed with wolf.

Deirdre got halfway up to her bedchamber when she thought of something. "I need to go to the cave. I'll be right back."

"Deirdre, what are you going to do?"

"Kimberly, I'm going to have the lads go to Edinburgh to the palace, to be with the queen. They would never do anything while the queen is watching; I'll tell them that we'll come later."

Kimberly smiled, "Go now, it's a good idea."

"Tommy, where are you?" Deirdre said, feeling his strong arms around her, coming from behind.

"I'm right here."

Turning around, she said, "Tommy, listen. I just had a great idea."

"Look out, brothers, here it comes," laughing, Tommy squeezed a little tighter.

"Now listen, all of you. If you go straight to the palace you will be with the queen. No one would dare to bother you. Just think about it. You know the queen, she doesn't like what the king is doing and you'll be safe at her side."

Hugh looked at Richard, and then said to Tommy, "You know, she is right."

"Yes, she is. So, what do you say, shall we get started?"

"Tommy, let's go. Deirdre, tell our darlings, our loves, not to worry."

"I will."

Tommy drew her back into his arms, and kissed her like there was no tomorrow.

"Tommy, I'll send you word through your father."

"So be it, my Kitten," kissing her hard, he then left.

Tommy and his brothers left out the secret way to the loch, and then they would find a ship that would take them to the palace. Deidre went back to Sea Oats, and the unwanted guests.

Deirdre slowly walked down the stairs. The two Campbells, Earl and Patrick, were in the front hall talking. Both of them turned around at the same time. "Well, well, look who is here, come to me, love?" Patrick said, walking over to block her way.

"No and no. Patrick, did you ever find the ones who escaped from you?"

"No, but we will."

They didn't see MacTavish coming up behind her until he made his battle growl. Patrick and Earl flew like scared birds from the hall.

"No, MacTavish, you must not do that. Come, let's greet the king," she said with a giggle. "Come on, sisters, let's go."

With MacTavish at her side, Deirdre kept her hand on his head. He knew what to do because of his training. When they came to the king, Deirdre bowed and MacTavish came up on his hind legs; he then put his front paws on the king's shoulders while he licked the king's face with his large, rough tongue. Then he got down. King William of Orange had such a look on his face you would think he was going to faint.

Deirdre bowed and walked away, greeting other guests and members of the clan. She waved at her mother. Mary Kate came over to Deirdre with her arms open. They hooked arm in arm as they walked over to her father, Laird John. He was standing straight and tall with his bright red beard and hair just shining. In his green, he looked just magnificent.

Mary Kate looked at her husband with love in her eyes; she was very proud of him. They had so much love for one another. You could see it in their faces.

Turning around, Deirdre took in all the hangings from the walls of the great hall. It was covered with the shields and banners of all the small clans who had joined the MacDarrochs, just as they had done with the MacDonalds.

There were all the crests that belonged to so many of the clans. The bright colors were most fascinating; it would hold you spellbound. They were irresistible, with the light shining upon them. Coming back to earth, she felt her father close by.

John put his arm around her and asked everyone to go in for dinner. As they sat down, the serving lads and lassies brought in platters of pheasant, tatters, wild pig, venison, greens, turnips, rabbits in wine sauce. Lamb that was nice and brown with mint sauce. Berry pies and baked apples; all kinds of cakes.

They `drank dram, sweetened wine with honey, wonderful dark wine of the very best.

Uncle Jamie always made the finest wine and mellow ale. He made very good whiskey, which was so-so smooth. Everyone ate, drank, and seemed to be enjoying themselves. When the meal was done, footmen and servants came to clear the tables. Maude brought in the biggest birthday cake you have ever seen. With tears in the old dear's eyes, she sat it down before Deirdre and her father, Laird John, for it was his birthday, as well as hers.

"Now, you both cut it and make your wish," Maude said as she wiped tears away with her apron.

Deirdre smiled at everyone, hugging her mother and her father. They both picked up the knife, and cut the first slice together. Shouts came from her clansmen, "Did you make your wish, Lassie?"

"Yes, I did."

"Laird John, did you make yours?" asked Charlie O'Neil, an Irish warrior friend of Laird John's ever since they were lads.

"That I did, Charlie."

"May it come true, then." A shout of respect came from everyone in the room.

Smiling to herself, Deirdre sliced a big piece and put it on a plate, stood up, walked up to the head of the table, bowed and sat the cake before King William. He looked around to see if MacTavish was with her. Seeing that MacTavish was in front of the fireplace eating a large leg of deer, he accepted with a smile.

As she walked back to her seat, Laird John had a big smile on his face. Deirdre thought to herself, *What's going on here?*

Laird John banged on the table and said that he had an announcement to make. Looking at Deirdre, he asked if she and her sisters would join him.

Now, what's this all about? Once again, wondering to herself.

She was standing by her father, with her godfather on the other side, and her mother in front; the front door burst open and Grandfather and his men came in. Grandfather, with his big broad shoulders and blond-gray hair down his back, had his Viking helmet on his head and was in all his armor.

"John, daughter, sorry to be late. Bad storm delayed us." He turned and looked at Deirdre, "My Warrior Lass!" Holding out his arms to her, she ran and jumped up into his big hairy strong arms, hugging with both of hers. Kimberly came into them also, "Oh Grandfather, hold me. I love you so much. I missed you!"

Deirdre thought to herself, *It looks like we had never seen him before this night.*

"And I missed you, my Golden Lady."

"And who do you think I am? A knot on a log?" Monica asked.

"My little Silkie, come here, you water baby!

She went into his arms laughing, and then asked, "When are you going to let me go to China with you?"

Deirdre thought to herself, *I'm very glad Grandfather got back here with his story.*

"Never," came from her father. Everyone started to laugh.

"Kirk, the table at the lower end is for you and your men. But first I need to get back to the business at hand. I have the need for you to stand with the family for this."

"I certainly will, John."

Then it hit Deirdre, saying softly aloud, "What was the king doing here with the Campbells. Now seems to be the time to faint." She did just that.

Standing over her was her mother, father, Kimberly, Monica, and Grandfather. All with very worried looks on their faces.

"Don't look so frightened. I just needed to know something," Deirdre said as she looked at each of them.

"You scared us to death," Mary Kate spoke up with tears in her eyes.

"Everyone in the whole castle, as a matter of fact." Her father spoke with anger in his voice.

"Kitten, I know you wouldn't have done it if you had no cause; now what is it?"

"What is the king doing here, as well as the Campbells? Who invited them, as they are our enemy?"

"I thought your mother did. Didn't you, Mary Kate?"

"No, I thought you did, John."

"Then no one knew. Doesn't it seem odd that they showed up?" Deirdre asked.

Everyone looked at each other. Godfather Glen spoke up at that time, "What do you think, Deirdre?"

Deirdre looked at her mother before answering her godfather, "Mother, remember the dream I told you about?"

"Yes, love."

"I have a strong feeling it's about to happen. Now this is what you're to do, go down and call off the party. When the king and Campbells are gone, explain to our people and yours godfather what is going on. Prepare them for battle."

"Deirdre, you're right. I'll go and tell my people you have taken ill. Then tell them the truth after the king leaves with the Campbells.

"That's good, Glen. We'll do the same with our clan as well as our neighboring clans. We'll look very worried," her father said, getting into the swing of things.

Mary Kate spoke, "Monica, you and Kimberly stay with her and we'll do the rest." When leaving the room, they were all looking very sad.

"Wait, I have something to tell all. As you know, Tommy and his brothers have gone to the king's palace. I found out from overhearing the captain of the king's army that he was heading there with his men. The lads were due at the king's castle before the raid started."

"That was good thinking, lass, to send them there."

"Monica, Kimberly, go and change your clothes. I'll do the same."

"But Deirdre, what if someone comes up to check on you?" asked Kimberly.

"I'll just cover up to my chin, that's all."

Looking at one another, the girls nodded, and then started to leave. They stopped at the door, turned and said, "We'll be back soon. Lock your door until you hear our old signal of a cock's crowing."

"I will," Deirdre said, then went and locked the door.

Shortly, Deirdre heard the cock's crow. The door opened, and the girls brought Deirdre clothes as well as her sword and other weapons. When they could not hear anything but silence, they slipped out the secret passageway. They made their way to the crofter's hut. That's when all hell broke loose. It all happened just like in Deirdre's dream. Her left leg had been ripped open. She could not find Earl Campbell. Deirdre had dropped her sword, but while she was looking for it, she heard Timmy, Molly's son, screaming. It was coming from the horse shed.

Deirdre ran through the back of the shed, and just as she got in, she saw Earl lifting his sword to plunge it into Timmy. Not thinking, Deirdre picked up the pitchfork that was covered with horse dung and ran toward Earl, screaming as she rammed it into his stomach. He looked at her, not believing she would do such thing to him. When his father came through the door, it was a bloody mess which seemed so unnecessary. But as always, the Campbells started it.

Laird Robert Campbell bent down over his son's body. As he picked Earl up into his arms, he moved to the door of the horse shed. He turned with such hate in his face and spoke, "Deirdre, you will die at my hands, so watch your back!" Then he left with a screaming Earl in his arms.

Deirdre was losing a lot of blood when Tommy found her and carried her up to her bedchamber. Molly, with Kimberly's help, sewed her up. Tommy insisted on staying with her. Much later that night, Deirdre awakened and tried to get up. The next thing she knew, Tommy's voice came to her saying in a very firm tone, "You will get up when you're told that you can; you'll not give anyone any trouble. Because, my darling, I'll be here to see you don't. Is that clear to you now?"

Deirdre tightened her lips together, biting her tongue as she did. "Yes, my darling. But what the hell are you doing back here?" she said, making sure he saw how unhappy she was.

Smiling up at everyone, he stated, "See, all she needs is to know who is boss."

"Boss!" Deirdre shouted. "You are not the boss of me! She got up even with everyone protesting. She reached over and slapped Tommy's face. With a startled look, he got up, went over, threw her over his knee, pulled up her gown, bared her ass before her family, and gave her a spanking she would never forget.

With the humiliation of everything, Deirdre began to cry. Her father started over to her when Tommy spoke, "My Laird, you don't console her when she has been rude and vindictive."

"Father, please throw him out of here, I hate him! I'll dissolve our marriage!"

"Oh no, you won't, because you know I'm right; you are spoiled. By your grandfather, mother and father, your whole family and myself. But you won't be now, my love. Now, if everyone would go out, please. I wish to talk with Deirdre alone."

Everyone left shaking their heads; even their shoulders were shaking. Deirdre thought at first they were crying for her, but then she could hear them laughing their heads off. She heard

Monica say, "Well, she'll know who the boss is, I bet." She could still hear them laugh as they walked down the hall.

Sitting up in bed, she was thinking to herself and watching Tommy pace the floor. *I hate to admit it, but Tommy is right. I'm stubborn, spoiled, and unbearable. I manipulate people to get my way. He is right, I'll stay in bed, take it slow, and then when I can, I'll go show those damn Campbells.* She was smiling to herself when she heard, "Oh, no you don't, Kitten. I see what's going on in your mind and no, you won't."

"Now Tommy, how do you know what I'm a thinking? But please explain why you came back here."

"I can tell by those cat eyes and the look on your face, love. Oh! I'll tell you, one of the king's men told us what the Campbells were up to, so I asked to come home with my brothers."

"I'm so glad you did. You're right about me, Tommy. You were right about me with what you were saying."

"Now wait one minute, Kitten," he remarked as he ran his hand through his hair, "are you saying, for once, I'm right?"

"Wait? For what? When you're right, you're right," Deirdre said as she slipped back down under the covers to have herself a nap.

"I'll have to remember this, for sure." She was smiling with a mischievous grin.

Tommy sat down in the chair by the fire, with MacTavish at his feet. He looked so handsome, with his long legs all stretched out before him. Deirdre was thinking, *What I would like to do to you, my darling.*

With his eyes closed and a smile on his face, his imagination was also racing, as if he were reading her mind. *I know what I would love to do to you, my Kitten, and as soon as you're well or maybe sooner, if it presents itself, I'll make you mine now and forever, again and again.*

Seeing the smile, Deirdre thought, *Wonder what he is thinking about. Oh, Tommy, what you do to me! My body tingles all over, my stomach aches. I just get the most thrilling feeling up between my thighs.* With a smile, she drifted off to sleep.

A sharp pain hit her leg. "Oh, what the devil!" It was just MacTavish laying between her and Tommy who had also slipped into her bed. Smiling to herself, she went back to sleep.

The next morning she looked over to see Tommy, but she was alone in bed. She rose up, trying to slip her legs out from under the covers. Deirdre made it to the side of the bed OK. "Now, let's see if I can stand." Suddenly the door burst opened and there was Grandfather in all of his glory.

"My God, lassie, what are you trying to do to yourself?" he said, running over to grab her.

"Grandfather, all I was trying to do was to get my legs out for a bit, then get back into bed. Come tell me about your trip."

He helped her back into bed. He sat beside her, bent over with a smile on his face and gave her a kiss saying, "I have been hearing things about you that are not too pleasing to my ears, lass. Now you tell me your side of it."

She told him about her dream and what really happened. About going into battle with the Campbells, plunging a pitchfork into Earl Campbell while his father looked on. Also, about the Campbells wanting to kidnap her. All of what Tommy had said about the way she was; all those bad things.

Deirdre looked up at Grandfather's face; he was smiling. "You are, as you know, all those things, love."

"Yes, I do know, but it's all the family's fault."

"You're right, my darling." He leaned over and gave her a kiss. "Now, do you want to go home with me?" he asked.

But before she could answer, they heard a deep voice say, "No." Grandfather looked up, as well as Deirdre, into Tommy's face.

"And why not, may I ask? He is my grandfather, you know."

"Yes, I know, and a good day to you, sir."

"And to you too, Tommy, my boy."

"Tommy, my boy, well if that don't beat all! You got them all snowed, haven't you? But not me!"

Looking at the stubborn look on her face, all of a sudden both men were laughing hard. "And what are laughing at? Pray tell?"

"You, my love; the look on your face."

"What look, Tommy MacDonald?"

"My darling, the look of stubbornness." They all three were laughing when the door opened and the whole family came in.

"What's so funny to all of you?" asked Kimberly.

"Oh, nothing, Kimber," Grandfather answered.

"Well, you'll have to all get out. I need to check Deirdre's leg. Out, out." Everyone, still looking shocked at all the laughter, left the chamber.

"Deirdre, what was so funny?"

"Kimberly, it was me, and my pride, stubbornness, and all."

"I'm sorry about all that was said, but honey, you are."

"I know."

"You have met your match in Tommy."

"It's for sure I have. Kimberly, I think I'm in love with him all over again. I feel he is safe now with his brothers. Did you know the queen is behind them and is against the king?"

"Are you sure that they are safe and Queen Anne is behind them?" Kimberly started to take off the bandages. She put her hands on her hips. "Deirdre, he is the main reason you came back, remember? Really, now, the queen is on their side?"

"Yes, she is that, and Kimberly you're right. What a great husband. But they are back here, now; remember?"

"Yes, you're right, I had forgotten. Now let's see if you can stand a little."

"How does it look?"

"Hum, it's coming along fine. I'll take the stitches out in another week or so and let the air get to it. Sister, how would you like to sit in the sun? I think it would do you good," Kimberly said as she started to redress the wound on her leg.

"Kimberly, could I, I know it would do me good. Help me with my robe. But how will I get out there? Oh!! Goodness sake, be careful. Man, that stings," Deirdre shouted.

"Tommy, Tommy, she's ready." Tommy came through the door smiling.

"Now, will you promise me you'll be good, lass?"

"Yes, sir, that I will."

"OK. Up you come, my Kitten, we'll go to the garden."

She thought to herself, *At last, I'm in his arms.* She looked up into his smiling eyes. She got all shaky inside as Tommy picked her up.

"Are you chilled, darling?"

"No, just the excitement."

"I see." Tommy thought to himself, *She feels something; wonder what it is.*

When they entered the garden, it felt as though eyes were watching them. But where were they? On the hill beside them, maybe. She was looking around as Tommy sat her down on the stone bench, lifting her leg up and putting it over his.

"What's the frown for, Kitten?"

217

"Tommy, I feel as if someone is watching us, but I can't see anyone. Did you or anyone else find out who gave the king or the Campbells an invite to the party?"

"No, do you want me to take you back inside, and then go have a look around?"

"No, please, just stay with me."

"I will, love," he said, holding her close to his side.

They just sat quietly for awhile listening to the birds and the sounds of the wild. Deirdre looked up at Tommy and asked, "Do you think it could have been someone in the clans who needed money? And what has happened to Uncle William and Uncle Jamie? Where are they?"

"Kitten, love, listen to me. Your Uncle William and Uncle Jamie followed at a distance from the king and Robert Campbell back to the Campbells' stronghold. Then they followed the king to Edinburgh. So it will be another week or so before they get back home."

"I see. Thank you, darling, for letting me know."

Before Tommy could say anything at all, MacTavish joined them in the garden. He had something in his mouth. Tommy got up and went over and took the fabric from him. Tommy took it over to Deirdre.

"It's a piece of Campbell cloth. I'm going to take you inside and have a look see. Just me and MacTavish."

"Please, be careful, Tommy darling." Tommy picked her up in his arms and ran to get her back into the castle. As they came into the great hall, Laird John looked up, startled.

"Tommy, lad, what's wrong?"

"MacTavish brought this to us in the garden. I'm going to see what's happened."

"I'll go with you."

"No, My Laird, please, just me and MacTavish." Tommy kissed Deirdre softly on her lips and left. "Let's go, MacTavish." MacTavish ran on the heels of Tommy out the door.

The waiting was awful. Deirdre could not pace, not even stand. She felt so helpless. Tommy was risking his life for her. But would she do the same for him? You damn better believe that she would.

Monica spoke to break the silence, "I'm going out to see."

"No you don't." John spoke, "This is what the lad wanted, just he and MacTavish. If MacTavish left anything to see," was Laird John's remark.

"Oh, Father, do you think MacTavish would do that? I mean eat a man?"

"No, Deirdre, but tear him up to where he can't be recognized. Yes."

"This waiting is killing me! Please Grandfather; help me up to my bed chamber. By the way, where is Maude?"

"She'll be back tomorrow, with Sue and Sara. They went to see her oldest lass, Millie, who just had a wee one. We wanted them to be safe, with all that has been going on."

As Grandfather took her upstairs, thoughts ran through Deirdre's head. *Maude will be very upset about things; so will Sara and Sue. But it will be so good to see them again.*

Grandfather had barely gotten her all settled when Kimberly and Monica came in. They had very worried looks on their faces.

"What's wrong?" Deirdre asked.

"It's Tommy, Deirdre, honey. He'll be alright, but he has been shot in the shoulder with an arrow. It was tipped with poison. Now Deirdre, I got the arrow out and Molly is with him trying to clean out the poison with hot garlic water presses."

As Kimberly was talking, Deirdre found herself halfway across the room dragging her leg.

"You get back here right now! Grandfather, please put her back to bed."

"Monica, no, I need to be with him. Don't you see, if not for me, this wouldn't have happened?" Deirdre was crying as she spoke.

Grandfather picked her up after she fell on the floor. He lifted her in his arms, holding her close to his chest, and put her back into bed. "What about MacTavish?"

"He's fine, very proud of himself, as a matter of fact."

Mary Kate came in about that time. "Kimberly, Monica, will you please go to help our poor Molly? She needs you both to help hold Tommy down. Go now, I need to talk with Deirdre. That means you too, Grandfather Kirk. Or shall I call you Father?" she asked, smiling up at him.

They all left, leaving Mary Kate and Deirdre together. "Mother, what is it?"

"To be honest, honey, it looks very grave for your Tommy. We have sent for his father."

"Oh, it's entirely my fault, he should not have gone!"

Deirdre started to cry so hard that she shook all over. She was getting hysterical.

"Now, now, control yourself, darling. This is not going to do Tommy any good."

"Please, leave me alone. Please, Mother!"

Mary Kate left shaking her head. Deirdre eased up and hopped over to the big chair and just sat there. "Please, Holy Mary, Mother of God, hear my prayer."

"Oh, God the Father, I offer you Tommy's illness and suffering in union with the sufferings of Your son, Jesus Christ. You willed that He should suffer for the salvation of the world. May Tommy now strengthen his resolve to do God's will and be an example to others who suffer.

If it's in Your plan, may Tommy be restored to health so he can continue to serve You in holiness and wholeness. If not, give me the understanding to accept this cross, the humility to accept the help of others, and the grace to see Your purpose in all the events of my life. Amen.

Chapter 13

Deirdre was sitting by the fire. She must have dozed off; there was a great light, and a voice that she recognized spoke, "Don't fear my child." Deirdre was now wide awake and listening to the voice, "Take care, Tommy will heal, it will take time, as you know. You will marry again, but beware, child, the Campbells still seek their revenge on you." Then the light started to fade.

"Grandmother, please don't leave, I need you so."

"I love you, things will be alright, but be careful, watch your temper; it's like your father's and grandfather's. Sleep now; remember, you must go back to make a closing."

Deirdre, with shock in her voice, asked, "What closing?"

At that point, the room grew dark. She blinked her eyes to get used to the dark. Deirdre hopped on her good leg over to the door. She needed to find Tommy. Monica came in just as she reached the door. "Where the devil do you think you're going?"

"Please, Monica, I must go and see Tommy. Please help me?" with tears running down her face.

"Oh, alright, come on. But if you tell anyone I did this, I'll deny it."

"Ok! Thanks Monica."

"You, must really love the man?"

"I do, with my whole being."

"Wow, must be nice, here we are."

Deirdre turned, looking Monica straight in the eyes, "Don't you love Richard?"

Smiling, she answered, "With all my heart and soul." Laughing, she opened the door. There was a small candle that was lit on the table beside his bed. Deirdre could only see his outline, pale, with a pained expectation on his face.

"Do you want me to pull a chair up to the bed?" asked Monica in a whisper.

"No thanks, I'm going to lie beside him."

"What!! Are ye crazy?"

"He needs to know I'm here with him."

"You can do that in a chair."

"Monica, for Christ sake, just once in your life, stop questioning and do it."

"OK...OK, don't get all steamed up."

She helped Deirdre onto the left side of the bed so her leg was up on a pillow and on the outside. Monica covered her up with the fur cover and made sure the fire was burning. Deirdre put her hand on Tommy's arm and fell asleep. Monica tip-toed out with a smile on her face; they were one.

The next morning when Deirdre awoke, she looked over at Tommy and saw him looking back at her with a weak smile, and he whispered, "I love you, Kitten." Back off to sleep they both went.

Maude had gone into Deirdre's bedchamber, and not finding her, ran to the family, which at this time included Laird Glen MacDonald and Deirdre's grandfather. They all started looking for her. They found Deirdre asleep with Tommy, her hand on his arm and a smile on Tommy's pale face. Looking at each other, they backed quietly out, and went back downstairs.

Mary Kate told Maude and Laird Glen MacDonald the story of what had happened.

Maude had tears in eyes. She wiped them so she could see her way going up the stairs. She needed to let Sara and Sue know what happened in case their charges, Kimberly and Monica, acted a little upset.

Maude tip-toed into Tommy's bedchamber, looking down at Deirdre. She leaned over and gave her a kiss on the forehead, pulled the fur cover up over her arms where the cover had slipped down, then stoked the fire.

"Maude love, is that you?" Deirdre whispered.

"Yes, love, now go back to sleep and I'll be in later in the morning."

Deirdre fell right back to sleep. She had no idea that Maude sat up all night in the big overstuffed chair by the fire, just in case Tommy, as well as she, would need something during the night. They slept for two whole days and nights.

It was daylight again. Deirdre woke up feeling something in her hair. Bolting upright, she saw that Tommy had rolled over and put his good hand in her hair. Smiling at her, "good morning my Kitten, how are you feeling today, love?" he whispered.

"Better now that you're getting better. You are, aren't you, Tommy? You do feel better?" she asked with love in her voice.

"Yes, I am. Is that dear old Maude over there in the chair?"

"Yes, I think she has been here all night, just in case we needed something."

"Oh, love you know what I need!!"

"Tommy MacDonald, shame on you!" Deirdre was smiling as she whispered, "Yes, I too, my darling."

"Now, what are you two whispering about? Would you both like your bath, then breakfast?"

"Maude, my darling, I'm as ravenous as MacTavish, when he hadn't eaten in days," answered Tommy with a smile on his face.

"Maude, I too would love to have a bite, but as you can see, I can only walk a bit and it will be hard to make it over to the little table."

"Forget that, I want you here close to me," Tommy said, grinning, as he tried to stretch.

Maude, looking at Tommy's face and the grin on it, "Tommy, I'll wash you so you can get set for Molly and Kimberly, then we'll see about your wound, then maybe your breakfast."

"Maude, you wouldn't do that to me, would you?"

"Yes, I would, Sir Tommy," Maude answered as she left the chamber with a big smile on her face.

No sooner had Maude left, when Laird MacDonald came in, "How are you two this morning?" he asked.

"I'll be fine in a few days, Father," Tommy said, trying to set up while he talked with his father.

"You'll come home so Deirdre can prepare for the wedding. The clans want to see you married here at home again," commanded Glen MacDonald.

With his head bowed down, he turned toward Deirdre, with a smirk on his lips. "Yes, Father, it will be done, sir, but if you will remember, we were married in the church before we were taken away in that cursed Black Fog."

"I remember, but you'll do it again." Laird MacDonald got up from the foot of the bed and looked at Deirdre. He smiled, saying, "I love you, child," kissing her on the forehead.

"Now, out with you Father, she is mine." Tommy laughed, but they could see the pain in his face. His wound still hurt him.

Deirdre was slipping out of bed to put on her robe. "Now where do you think you are going, Kitten?" Tommy asked.

"To my bedchamber; Godfather, could I lean on your arm please, to help guide me?" Deirdre asked.

"Of course, my dear." Taking her by the elbow, they started toward the door.

226

"Now, what about me?" asked Tommy.

"You'll be alright, son, just rest because you'll need it later," laughed Laird MacDonald.

As they started down the hall toward Deirdre's bedchamber, Maude came around the corner. "My Lord, I'll take her now, thank you, you are very kind," Maude said as she took Deirdre by the arm to help her back to her bedchamber.

When they got in the door, MacTavish jumped off the bed where he had been taking a nap, "Hello, my wonderful lad," Deirdre said as she patted him on the head, scratched him behind the ear, and gave him a big hug. You could hear purring loud and clear as he ran out the door. His nose was up in the air, he smelled food coming from the hall below.

"You'll spoil him," remarked Maude.

"I know, Maude darling, but he caught a Campbell, before he could get me."

"You are right; tell your old Maude what really happened."

She told Maude the whole story, not only about the fight, but also about the hunt, and what happened to Tommy.

Deirdre got into the tub with Maude's help; the water was nice and warm. It felt so good after not being able to take one for a few days.

"Are you sure you should take one, lassie?" asked Maude.

"Yes, Maude love. Kimberly took the stitches out and said that it would be just fine in the healing. She said I should start walking on it. So that's what I'll do today."

"I'll leave you and see to Master Tommy's bath." Maude left Deirdre daydreaming about her wedding.

"Are you sure you should be in there, darling?"

Tommy, what are you doing out of bed?" she asked, trying to cover herself up.

Laughing, Tommy said, "I'll sit on the foot of the bed. You're right, Kitten, I'm still a little weak."

Just as he got the last word out, the door opened with a bang. "So this is where I find you, laddie. Up you go; get back to your room so you can get cleaned up. My Lord, how you smell!" Holding her nose, Maude started laughing.

"But Maude, my darling, it's lonely way up there away from my Kitten."

"Oh, go on with you, don't try and wheedle your way out of this one, because it won't work. Come on now, up with you." Maude went over to help Tommy get up and out of the door, even as he protested.

Deirdre got out of the tub, rubbed her hair as dry as she could, then her body. She rubbed her long shapely legs and there she stood, her long red hair sticking to her back and all the way down to her thighs, just sticking there. Pushing it out of her way she put her robe on, when the door opened and her mother walked in.

"You got a bath; feel better my darling?"

"Weak, but I'll be fine. Mother, what about this Campbell business?"

"Well, from what we can make out, after you jabbed Earl Campbell, he died a very painful death. Patrick and his father, Laird Robert Campbell, threatened to kidnap you. Patrick said that he would make you so very sorry you took his brother's life."

"And this has gotten everyone quite upset? Did Earl die?"

"Yes, I just told you he did. He had a bad infection that did him in. You will not be able to go anywhere without guards being with you."

"But Mother, I can't live like that!"

"I know, love, but just until we figure something out. Will you get that stubborn look off of your face?" Mary Kate asked as she put her arms around Deirdre.

The door opened; Kimberly and Monica walked in, "Deirdre let me look at your leg."

Raising her leg, she said, "Kimberly, look, it's healing just fine."

"Did you have a nice bath?" asked Molly. Deirdre did not see her come up behind Kimberly.

"Yes, vey nice and how's my Tommy?"

"I just got through looking in on him; he's coming along just fine, but he shouldn't be running around so much," remarked Kimberly with a smile on her face.

Molly was laughing as she spoke. "Yes, we know that Sir Tommy has gotten up and has been in here."

"How did you know that?" Deirdre asked.

"Maude told us that he was here, at the foot of your bed, just sitting and talking to you while you were in the tub." Molly started laughing right along with Kimberly.

"You should have seen his face when we told him to stay put for another three days, then he could go home." Kimberly started to make a face like Tommy had done.

Monica came in and asked, "What's going on?"

They told her, and they all started laughing like a bunch of silly lassies. Monica broke in, "You have got to be kidding!"

"No, we're not; his jaw was set and he actually pouted, thinking that would weaken us. Then his eyes looked like two hot coals. The way his face changed, you would have died laughing." Kimberly laughed so hard she had tears in her eyes – as they all did.

Out of breath, John MacDarroch burst in, "Deirdre, can you ride, lass?"

"I guess so, why, Father?"

"The Campbells went to the king. He and his solders are on their way. They just landed on Islay and are on their way here now."

"But Father, the Campbells raided us and started this fight. I'll not run!" Deirdre stated, standing up, "No, I'll not run!" she repeated.

"But Deirdre, the Campbells have a pull with the king."

"I told you, no, I'll not run."

Everyone stood there with their mouths open. The door burst open and in came Grandfather, not saying a word. He picked Deirdre up and put her over his shoulder with a fur robe. He went through the hidden passageway and down to the caves where his boat was docked. He took Deirdre aboard, locked her up in his cabin, and left her. Not long after her grandfather left, Kimberly and Monica came in with clothes, medicine, and everything she would need for a long trip.

"No, no, I'll not run like a rabbit!"

Grandfather came in red in the face, mad as a bull, "You'll listen to me, lass, and do what you're told, whether you like it or not." Deirdre and her sisters had never heard their sweet, loveable grandfather talk to them like that before.

"But...bu...bu...Grandfather what's wrong?" Deirdre asked.

"You don't seem to realize what kind of trouble you are in, Deirdre, me lass."

She stood looking him straight in the eye and spoke, "I'll not go; I'm needed here. I'll not run away from a fight; and besides, I can take care of myself."

Grandfather's face turned much redder. It was as if Deirdre could see steam coming from his ears. "You'll do as you are told. You are stubborn, hardheaded and very willful, but you and your sisters are to go with me. That's all there is to it. Now lassies, get ready to shove off." Then, putting his hands on his hips, "Kimberly, Monica, go top side and help. As for you, my little devil, you'll stay down here and I'll lock the door."

He turned to leave when Deirdre asked, "But what about Mother and Father and poor Tommy, wounded and all? He killed a Campbell, too, you know."

"No he didn't, it was MacTavish who did that. A Campbell shot Tommy; besides, he is on his way home."

"Thank God; but Father and Mother?"

"They'll not do anything to them if you're not there."

"Oh, that's good to hear."

"Now lie down and rest; I have to go top side. Don't feel bad, lass; I love you, but this is the only way. I had to do this; besides it was your father's orders. We all know how stubborn you are." Out the door Grandfather Kirk went, smiling.

Deirdre started to pace, trying to think as she rubbed her thigh. She smiled as she thought aloud. "Just can't let the Campbells get away with this. I just can't." She looked at the window in the cabin, "I could slip through; I'm a strong swimmer. I could swim to shore and hide deep in the cave where the silkies stay. That's what I will do." She stripped down to her chemise, took her plaid with her and jumped. Little did Deirdre know Monica saw her from the crow's nest.

The water was freezing, but the harder she swam, the warmer she got. Deirdre neared the beach as the silkies came down to the water's edge for their nightly swim. Seeing her, they clapped their fins in welcome.

Deirdre started toward the cave, making sure no one was watching. She slipped inside the cave. Deirdre was halfway back when she heard voices. It was the Campbell solders. The silkies heard them, too, and started coming out of the water. She went further and further back into the cave as a big bull silkie stood guard. One of the soldiers, seeing him, spoke very softly, "No one could get past him. Let's go, no one is here. They'd have to be crazy to go past him." As he was saying this, they slipped by the cave.

Deirdre went quietly up the secret stairs that no one knew about but the family. Creeping up the stairs to one of the secret doors, she heard voices. It was the king and Robert Campbell; they were putting questions to her father and mother.

"We have searched this whole castle from the caves to the towers, Deirdre is nowhere to be found. Is she here?" asked the king.

"Your Highness, she has gone to Norway for a visit with her grandfather. I don't know when she'll be back. She and her sisters are together," explained Laird John.

"Now John, are you telling the truth?" asked the king with a smirk on his face.

"My husband does not lie, Sire. If anyone does, it's Robert Campbell," Mary Kate butted in.

"Dear Lady, your lassie, Deirdre, killed Earl Campbell, the son of Laird Robert Campbell. She must stand trial."

"Your Highness, forgive me for speaking out of turn, but Deirdre was protecting herself and little Timmy, our stable lad, from the likes of Earl Campbell. He tried to kill her and the lad," she said, looking at Robert Campbell as if she could kill him.

"There was a witness to this, Lady Mary Kate?"

"Yes, there was, the whole MacDonald Clan, with the MacLeod Clan, and also the Gordons. There were a few more; it was quite a raid the Campbells did, Sire, at our expense. We needed help and we got it. If it had not been for our neighbors, we would not have any way of knowing about the fight." Mary Kate looked Robert Campbell straight in the eye, then turned to the king.

The look of shock and dismay on both the king and Robert Campbell's face was the greatest thing Laird John had ever seen.

With a smile on his lips, the king remarked trying to change the subject. "I understand that there is to be a wedding again, your lassie Deirdre to Tommy MacDonald. When is it to be?"

Laird John looked straight into King William's eyes, then answered, "Tommy MacDonald was shot with a poisoned arrow in the shoulder by a Campbell, and we have a witness to that, Sire. There will be a small delay in the wedding."

"My word!! How is he?" asked King William.

"My lassie, Kimberly, with Molly, who are healers, saved his life. MacTavish, Deirdre's pet lynx, killed the man who did it. We have a large piece of his plaid." Laird John took it out of his belt to show the king. As the king looked at him, Robert Campbell started to leave.

"Just one moment, Robert," the king commanded. "You lied to your king and I'll not have that. You'll come to my quarters at once."

Deirdre saw her father step up to King William, "Sire, may I have the cloth back?"

"What's the matter, John, don't you trust me, your King?"

"It's not that, Your Highness, but Deirdre wishes to keep it as a reminder; so does Laird Glen MacDonald."

With a huff, the king threw it at Laird John, and left the room to go into his quarters, quite red in the face, as if he would blow any minute.

As they left the room, Mary Kate asked, "Husband, do you think our girls are safe?"

"If I know your father, they are."

"Father," Deirdre said very softly, standing in the secret passageway door, wet and cold.

As they turned with shocked looks on their faces, her father turned purple with rage. "What in the devil are you doing back here?" he asked, coming over to Deirdre, taking her by the hand and pulling her into the library.

"I jumped ship, and hid in the silkies cave," Deirdre answered, with just as stubborn a look on her face as he had on his.

Mary Kate asked softly, "Where are your sisters?"

"Still aboard ship."

"Oh, no we're not, we are right behind you, you stubborn, hard-headed sister," remarked Monica. "I saw you jump, so I slid down the pole. I told Grandfather. By the way, he's not happy."

Looking at everyone, Deirdre was so mad, she could have bitten a sword in half if she had had one. "I don't give a damn. Now you listen to me for once, this is my fight and I'll not run from it, do you all hear me? I'm not afraid of the king or Robert Campbell. I'll not run! Is that clear?"

With everyone's mouths wide open, Grandfather came in at that moment, "You had better change clothes, lass, before you catch your death." Smiling, he thought to himself, *That's my lassie, a fighter to the end.*

Deirdre slipped back into the passageway, her sisters following her up to her bedchamber. "I want to go to the king's chamber and see what those two are cooking up."

"We're right behind you, let's go," Monica said with a grin.

As they got to the door in the wall, they heard angry voices. It was Robert Campbell and the king. "Robert, do you not realize what a spot you put me in? Deirdre MacDarroch was defending herself against your son, Earl."

"She has got to pay!"

"She will, but I need proof that it was intent and it can't be done with all the clans testifying it was you and your sons who started the raid."

"It wasn't me; my lads just got a wee bit drunk and started it, but still she had no cause to kill him. Your Grace, I had to watch him die slowly from the poison from that damn pitchfork she ran him through with."

"What was she to do, let him kill her and the lad? No, Robert, like I said, you have no proof; you will have to do it some other way."

The girls heard the door slam and the king telling his manservant, "Robert Campbell is a very stubborn man. He is also a very dangerous one. I fear Deirdre MacDarroch had better watch her back. But if he ever hurts her, I'll kill him myself."

"You love her, Your Grace?" asked Paul, the king's manservant.

"Yes, I do, Paul. This is just between us."

"Yes, Your Grace."

After hearing all of that, the sisters slipped very quietly back down the passageway to Deirdre's bedchamber. Closing the door, Monica spoke, "Well, did you hear that?"

"Sisters, please calm down," Deirdre remarked, pacing the floor.

Maude came in and asked, "What are you doing here, you should be on your grandfather's boat."

"Maude, dear, take it easy, I jumped ship and the rest followed."

"That's right, sweet Maude," spoke Kimberly as Monica shook her head up and down.

"Robert Campbell is here and so is the king."

"Maude, we heard what was said, I'll think about what to do, but now I'm very tired and my leg hurts like the devil."

"Here, let me check it, Deirdre; you may have pulled it. I'm glad I took the stitches out earlier," remarked Kimberly.

"Yes. I am too. I'm thought I had bruised my leg, but here, check it anyway," she replied, taking off her plaid and what little clothes she had on so Kimberly could check out her leg.

"It looks alright, but you could have pulled the muscle a little. Please be more careful, sis, if you can."

"I will, Kimberly, I promise."

"Have you thought about what you're going to do?" asked Monica.

"No, not yet, you both should go to bed. Try to get some rest, we'll talk tomorrow."

"You're right. Come on, Kimberly, let's go."

"Alright, Monica. Deirdre get some rest, please," turning and looking at Maude, "Maude see to it please, love."

"I will, Kimber, lass, now you both do the same," Maude said.

They left as Deirdre lay back on her bed. Then Maude asked, "Ma Lady, do you want a hot bath? Might make you feel better."

"Yes, Maude, you're right. I would love one, but you sound very tired yourself."

"Never you mind about that." Maude filled the tub, and put the screen around it. With the warm water and fire, and smelling the herbs and heather, Deirdre leaned back, closed her eyes, and felt herself drift off. Maude spoke to her, "Love, here let me wash your hair to get it free from the sea smell and salt that has collected in your beautiful red locks." Maude had tears in her eyes as she thought to herself, *My little warrior, do you realize how close you came to being killed? No, I don't think so.*

Chapter 14

The next morning, after Deirdre dressed in her soft leather, she made her way down the hall. Monica and Kimberly came from their bedchamber. All three had dressed for battle. She noticed that Kimberly, as well as Monica, had their pets with them. Kimberly had an Irish wolfhound mixed with wolf; Monica's plain wolf, a very large black one, had been born wild.

"Where is MacTavish?" asked Monica.

"He went down earlier looking for food."

"Shame it couldn't be Laird Robert Campbell," remarked Kimberly.

Deirdre smiled to herself, "Ye got a point there. Let's join them, shall we, I'm starved?"

Both sisters said in unison, "Let's."

They walked slowly down the steps so they could hear what was being said in the great hall. Everyone was quiet when the king spoke. "You'll let your king and queen know when the celebration will be held, will you not, John?"

"Yes, Sire, I will."

Deirdre whispered to the girls to fellow her lead, shaking their head yes. "Well, good morning, Your Grace, family. How are you this fine morning, Laird Robert Campbell? You have the gall to be here, Sire."

"He is with me, Deirdre. I thought you were with your grandfather."

"Really now, well I was, but turned the ship around." Smiling, she looked at the king, "You don't care with whom you associate, do you, Sire?" Turning, she kissed her mother on top of her head, "Nice day, isn't it, Father?"

Monica smiled at her father as if she knew something no one else knew. Smiling back, Laird John MacDarroch thought, *Wonder what those three are up to now, dressed as if they were going to war.*

"Father, we are going to the practice field for a while. Will you have some of our men there to practice with us? We don't feel safe with the Campbells around." Deirdre had a slight grin on her face as she spoke.

The king was getting quite red in the face as he spoke, "That's not a fair assumption, Deirdre." He thought to himself with a smile, *Lassie, I would love to have you as mine, with your spirit and fighting power. But most of all, I would love to own your body. Have it as mine, all mine, not that thing I'm married to.*

"But, Your Grace! You were not the one being called a bitch as the man ran toward you yelling, and telling you he would have your head, now were you?"

The king saw her look at Robert Campbell. "Laird Campbell, let it be known that as of now, I'm not frightened of you or your clan. I'll kill anyone of them if they try anything even you, Sir." Deirdre turned on her heels, and with her sisters, left the hall, leaving everyone's jaws falling down to the floor.

"Come on, ladies, let's see what you are made of," shouted Deirdre, going out the door.

Uncle William and Uncle Jamie went to the practice field a short time later.

Uncle Jamie tried so hard not to laugh. "Deirdre lass, you really stirred up a hornet's nest this time," Uncle Jamie spoke as he handed Deirdre her staff and picked up his own as well.

"Yes, oh yes, lass, you did that," repeated Uncle William. He could not hold it back any longer, he burst out with his deep laughter, "Yes, lassies, you should have seen their faces." He laughed until tears came into his eyes.

"I wish we could have; how did they look?" asked Kimberly.

"The king even had a smirk on his lips, like he would burst out laughing any minute. But Robert Campbell made a mistake, he remarked. 'That Bitch will be sorry and will pay dearly, you all will see.' He left in a huff. As he left, the king was talking to your father, but I didn't hear what was said."

Back at Sea Oats, the King was telling Deirdre's father and mother, "John and Mary Kate, you should guard Deirdre and Monica and Kimberly, but especially Deirdre. Robert and Patrick will get their revenge."

"Yes, Your Grace," John MacDarroch said with a sad look on his face.

"You had better warn Tommy MacDonald also. He should know about what is going on."

"We will," spoke Mary Kate, with a very sad look on her face.

The king, with his Dragoons, left the Castle. Laird John had his people start putting things back in order.

"John, I'm worried about Deirdre. You know how head-strong she is."

"Yes, I do, love, but I'll have a talk with her and Tommy. The wedding must take place very soon. You go and start to prepare for it."

"I will, husband. It will be a grand wedding; you'll see."

"I know it will, my wife, the woman who has always held my heart in her hand. Now off with you," John said as he patted Mary Kate's backside.

Mary Kate ran out of the great hall laughing then she shouted, "Maude, Sue, Sara, all staff come quickly, we have a wedding to get ready for."

Everyone was busy getting ready for the big wedding celebration, while John MacDarroch sent word for Tommy and Laird Glen MacDonald and his other sons to come as soon as possible. It was about the wedding, and to be careful on the way. Watch out for the Campbells.

Deirdre and her sisters were really working up their energy, rejuvenating their bodies. They worked up a good sweat. Their muscles were getting strong, not only in their arms, but in their legs as well.

Suddenly Angus came running at them, and MacTavish as well as Darroch, jumped up knocking them down. The girls laughed and hugged them, but the pets started to pull at them, wanting them to go somewhere — but where?

"Wait a moment, MacTavish, where are you taking me?" Deirdre asked, patting him on the head as he growled.

"Looks like they want us to follow them up to the castle," remarked Monica.

"Is that where you want us to go?" Deirdre asked MacTavish.

"Looks like it. You don't think something is wrong, do you?" Kimberly asked.

"Let's go," Deirdre said on the run. As they ran, so did the men on the field, running as fast as they could. They ran through the great doors shouting, "Mother, Father, what's wrong?"

John was coming from the library asking them, "What's all the fuss about?"

"MacTavish, Darroch, and Angus came after us. We thought something was wrong," answered Deirdre, a little out of breath.

"No, my darlings, everything is fine. Maybe your mother sent for you."

"Where is she?" asked Kimberly.

"About! I would think, seeing to the wedding plans."

"The what?" Deirdre asked with a shocked look on her face.

"The wedding. Are you hard of hearing, lass?" John asked, smiling at everyone.

"That's what I thought you said. But wasn't quit sure — but didn't we already marry?" she asked.

"But it's for everyone again; it's been a long time, lass," John answered with a big smile.

"Now what's that supposed to mean?" Kimberly asked.

"Well, Kimberly, it just simply means that Deirdre and Tommy never got to consummate their vows."

"That's when we vanished? Was that it? But what happened in the cave, was that not what Father said?" asked Monica.

"Oh, my little water babe, what *did* happen in the cave?" asked Laird John with a smile.

Deirdre sat there listening as though in a dream. "Father, what if it happens again? I'm afraid this time, and nothing happened in the cave," she said, looking at her sisters with a scowl on her face.

"No, love, it will be a long while until the solar comes again."

"Long while? How long is that in years?" Monica asked.

"What's wrong, lassies?"

They looked at one another, when Deirdre spoke, "Father, what if we all were to marry and then something happened? We had to go away, but would return. How long would it take then?"

"Another five years, of course. Why, lassies? Are you to go back at that time?"

"Yes."

"I see. Well then, your husbands may wish to go back at that time with you." Laird John was trying to keep his spirit up in front of them.

"What in the world are you saying, Father?" Kimberly asked with a surprised look on her face, as well as her sisters.

"I'll let your mother explain it to you later." His head bowed, and he went looking for Mary Kate as he had other questions for her.

After a few minutes, Kimberly looked up with an expression on her face as if she felt that Hugh and his brothers came back before she and her sisters did.

Monica started to say something, but Deirdre put up her hands, "Not now, love; it's all too much to take in now. As you know, we talked about it before, and when we came back, so did the laddies, only long before us."

"You're right, Deirdre," Monica said as she left to go upstairs, with Kimberly and Deirdre right behind her.

Deirdre lay back on her bed; boy, she was really tired. They had had a hard workout. Looking up at the ceiling, she asked, "Who in either clan could have invited the Campbells, as well as the king?"

"Listen, Deirdre, could Robert Campbell have told the king that they had been invited to your celebration?"

"Kimberly? Sorry, sis, but I didn't hear you two come in. On second thought, you may have a good idea there, Kimberly.

You know Robert Campbell is sneaky enough to do just that. What is your idea on the matter, Monica?"

Monica had a deep expression on her face as she walked around playing with her dirk, then she stopped. "You know he would do that, and if he were caught in a lie, he would say he got a message and left it back at his Castle Glenlyon."

"Yes, he would," replied Kimberly.

"Deirdre, you've got to be careful; never be alone. Those Campbells are planning some good tricks, I'll wager."

"You're right, Monica, isn't she, Deirdre?" asked Kimberly, looking right at Deirdre as if she were studying her face.

"You know, lassies, you're both right. I do have to be very careful, and still try to find out what is going on."

"You'll do no such thing," Tommy remarked as he came very quietly into Deirdre's bedchamber. "How are you feeling today, my darling?" asking as he came over to her bed. "You know, I'm so tired, Kitten. Could I just lie beside you and rest awhile, ye love?"

"No."

Everyone laughed, even Mary Kate with Laird John at her side. No one had heard them as they came in. Tommy turned red as a beet in the face while his ears turned bright pink. "You're a bad one, Kitten, that you are, but I still love you with all my heart," he whispered as he kissed her and left.

"Well??" Mary Kate asked.

"Well what?" Deirdre asked, looking at her with a question in her eyes.

"Did he say anything about the wedding?"

"Oh! Mother we didn't speak of it; you were here. Maybe soon, I don't know."

"And just why not? We're ready," asked Laird John.

"It just didn't come up, that's all."

"Didn't come up? On whose part was it, pray tell?"

"Now, Father, don't get upset."

"Who's upset, Deirdre MacDarroch MacDonald? Who may I ask, it's not me who is, but maybe you should be."

"What are ye saying, Father?" she asked with a puzzled look on her face.

"Tommy seems to be losing interest in you, ye know he's been to the Royal Court. Maybe some lassie there has caught his eye."

"You know not! He doesn't act it to me," she said with a puzzled look on her face.

"Well, you keep putting him off and he is off to Edinburgh in the morning. His father was just telling me." John looked at his lassies and winked.

Deirdre sat up, putting her feet on the floor and then stood up. Her leg still cramped up on her at times and hurt like the devil, but she gritted her teeth and closed her mouth tight. Then spoke, "I would like a bath, now please."

Everyone moved fast. Maude looked at her, and smiled, she told Kimberly and Monica that they should do the same. The girls went out on a run.

"Now what dress are you wearing?

As Maude washed her hair, Deirdre started to cry, "What if he has found someone else to love? I never thought he would, or could, love anyone else but me. Was I that sure of him? Oh! Maude, why can't I tell him how much I have loved him all my life? Why do we always fight, and then make love? He was the first and will be the last as far as I am concerned."

"It's because you both are afraid to show it. Afraid you'll let your emotions go before you marry again."

"You're right, sweet Maude. I get a funny feeling in my body when he is near. It's not the kissing; it's the other I fear will not please him.

"Let him be the judge of that, love. As your sister, Monica, says, you go with the flow." Maude smiled as she went over to get linen to dry Deirdre's hair.

"Maude, what color should I wear?"

"What's Tommy's favorite color?" asked Maude.

"He loves the emerald green," Deirdre answered.

"Then that's it," Maude said, going to the room where Deirdre's clothes were kept.

Tommy came in and saw Deirdre in the tub. "It seems I keep finding you in hot water, Kitten," smiling as he looked at her trying to cover herself up with a rag, "I thought wild cats didn't like water."

"What are you doing here?"

"To see if you need anything. Didn't expect to see you in the tub. You stay there more than anyone I know."

"Well... I am, now. Would you mind if I got out too dry off?"

"No, love just go right ahead, I'll dry off your back."

"No, Tommy MacDonald, you go now, I'm sure you have things to do and people to see."

"But, Kitten, I just want to check your leg out. And by the way, what did you mean by that remark?"

"Sir, first of all, my leg is fine, thank you. See." She lifted her leg out of the water and also ignored his last question.

"Yes, it is, just as beautiful as the other, I bet."

"Oh, Tommy, please, the water is getting cold."

He blew a kiss, laughing, and then walked out the door.

Maude came in laughing so hard, "See, he does love ye."

"How would you know? We have grown up together, like brother and sister. But my feelings are not that way. I have loved him all my life, even dreamed of him. Why, I even gave myself to him when we were young. Oh, what's the use? He doesn't feel the same way. If he did, why would he be looking for someone else?"

"Now, now, you don't know that for sure, do ye?"

Maude fixed her hair and put on the emerald green silk dress that fit like another skin. The neckline was low to show off her full breasts, and then on went the shoes. A little lace stood up around the bust line, as if it would draw eyes. She would wear one strand of pearls, with earrings to match. Tommy had given them to her when she was but fourteen, as she remembered, the time he found her at their secret pool. That was where they made love for the first time. He took her that day and she let him, for she loved him then and now.

Monica, with Kimberly behind her, came into the room and spoke to her, bringing her out of her dream. There stood Kimberly in her dark rose pink and Monica in her bright blue.

"Oh!! Deirdre, you're beautiful. Now you lean on me to help you down the stairs. Is your leg still sore from cramping?"

"Somewhat, it will be ok. Thank you, Kimberly."

"I'll get on the other side of you."

"Thank you, too, Monica. Shall we go?"

"Yes." They both answered at the same time. When they went down the stairs, everyone was in the great hall. Mary Kate saw them come over.

"How are you feeling, Deirdre?"

"I'll be alright, Mother. Just a little sore, but fine."

"That's good," Mary Kate said. She turned and went to where John stood talking to their guest, Duke Edward MacDonald, who came with his daughter, from England.

Deirdre looked around the room to try to find Tommy, but could not. Then all of a sudden, she heard his laughter. He was alone with someone else. Deirdre turned around to see a lovely lady hanging on to his arm, looking up at him adoringly.

Tommy stopped suddenly and looked at Deirdre in great surprise. The lady with him stopped laughing and looked to see what he was staring at. She looked up at him then whispered, "So, that is her, she is beautiful, cousin." To Deirdre it looked like to her she was saying, "He's mine, hands off."

"Deirdre, you did get to come down. Oh, I'm so glad. How's the leg? Still cramping up with you?"

"Sometimes, thank you. How are you now, Tommy?" Deirdre asked with a smile on her lips. "I'm glad to see you. Are you ready to go to Edinburgh? Who is this lovely lady, Tommy? Is she the one you'll marry when you set me aside?"

Tommy just stared at her with a shocked look on his face. But before he could answer, Deirdre turned and walked over to the other guests, laughing. But she felt her world had come to an end.

"Deirdre, what did you say to Tommy? His chin is down to the floor," asked Monica.

Deirdre told her, but got all choked up and the tears seemed to be filling up her eyes. "Monica, please excuse me. I'll be going up now and then I'll slip out to the beach. Don't tell anyone, please."

Seeing the tears, she said, "I won't."

Turning around, Deirdre started to run out and bumped into Tommy. She knocked him down. "Excuse me," Deirdre choked.

Tommy saw the tears, but before he could speak, she was gone. Getting up, he went up to Monica. "Where is she going?"

"Where? Who is going?" asked Monica looking him in the eye with hate and hurt in hers.

"You know who. What's going on here, Monica? I love her; I'm going to marry her again. Now, where is she?" he asked with anger in his voice and in his eyes.

"Tommy, who is the lady you are with?" asked Kimberly. "No one saw her come in."

"She is my cousin from England. Now, where is Deirdre?"

"Deirdre thought you were going to marry the lady. Oh!! Tommy her heart is broken, she ran up to her bedchamber, then out the passageway to the beach. Lord, I hope she is alright," was Monica's answer and prayer.

"Where did she get the idea that I was going to marry anyone else but her?"

"I think it was from our father," Kimberly answered.

"I'll take care of him later." He ran like a bullet shot out of a gun, taking two steps at a time. As he burst into Deirdre's bedchamber, he saw her dress and the broken strand of pearls all over the floor. *Dear God, let her be safe. I just might have to kill her father for this,* he was saying to himself as he ran down the passageway.

Tommy got to the beach, but he could not find her, "Please Kitten, where are you?" All of a sudden Tommy heard her voice. In doing so, he took off his clothes behind a large bolder, where he saw Deirdre's chemise. He spread his clothes out on the sand like a bed. Then he heard her voice, "Come, my spotted friend, let's swim, so as I may forget."

Tommy didn't like the sound of her voice, and started running toward it. "Kitten I love you, Kitten. Deirdre where are you? Please answer."

Not hearing Tommy, Deirdre was in the water, cold as it was, the waves crashing against the rocks and beach. Little did she know her little spotted silkie swam up to Tommy and shoved him toward her direction. She didn't realize she was floating out to sea.

All at once, she felt a hand on her shoulder. Deirdre was startled, and went underwater to get away from whatever it was. Coming back up, she was in front of Tommy.

"What in the world are you trying to do, kill yourself? For what?"

"No," Deirdre answered. "I had to get out; the room seemed to close in around me, just seeing you and her. She is beautiful, Tommy. I wish you the best of everything in life. I'll not stand in your way," Deirdre spoke with tears choking her voice.

"Now you wait just one moment. Me, marry her!!! For God's sake, Kitten, she is my cousin. She has been talking about meeting you. You're all I talk about. I love you and want you for my wife. Now I have said it. Well, what do you have to say?"

Deirdre was trying to stay afloat, as she looked him in the face, "Are you sure, Tommy boy? Are you?"

"Yes, you silly lass, I'm sure, more sure than you'll ever know."

Tommy started for the beach when he looked around and saw Deirdre swimming with the silkies. He just stood there on the beach watching her swim, looking like a water sprite. Deirdre walked from the water, each step revealing her splendor until she stopped sensing he was around. She turned and there he was. Deirdre walked up and stopped before him. Tommy's gaze searched her features, her smoldering eyes, and she took a step farther bringing another fracture into his heart.

His hands folded into fists as he stared at her. Her pale skin was rosy, her breasts peaking hard against her wet hair. Deirdre knew what she was doing. She turned to Tommy. "I'll teach you to tease me," she said, as she reached out and took his arousal into her hand.

"You are certain of this, Kitten?" Tommy said, taking her hand away from his arousal.

"You tease me unmercifully for days and you ask me this?" Deirdre nipped at his lips and throat.

"I don't wish to rush you, Kitten."

"I plan to take you, My Laird." Her tongue snaked over his nipple as she loosed his hold, "Perhaps I didn't make myself clear?" Deirdre's hand dove down again, her fingers sliding mercilessly over his erection.

"Oh, sweet Mother of God, woman." Tommy pried her hand from him, a warning in his eyes, "Want me to slam into you and not please you?"

Tommy's excitement was Deirdre's, coating her, arousing her with the power of it. "You please me with your trembling, My Laird."

He had spread his clothes on the sand behind a large bolder. Deirdre pushed him down on the clothes, and Tommy laid there trembling with desire for her.

Without hesitation, Deirdre climbed onto his lap, her moist flesh pressing hotly to his hardness. Tommy caught her jaw in his broad palms, the threads of his restraint snapping as he kissed her, a dark plundering of lips and tongue that ignited the passion to glorious heights.

Deirdre rocked against him, her body begging for more, and Tommy's hands rode down her shoulders, her arms, sweeping around to cup her buttocks, and then ground her to his hardness.

"You know, someone could come upon us," he said, even as she hurriedly looked around. He put her arms above her head; he looked his fill of her swelling breasts, her naked belly and the red tuft that lay between her legs.

"I know." Deirdre smiled like a cat, wicked, as her hands floated to his shoulder. He cupped her breasts, kneading them, and she leaned back, offering him more. Tommy wrapped his lips around her nipple and sucked the tender tip deep into the heat of his mouth. Deirdre arched and gasped, her fingers digging over his strong arms, his mouth torturing her bosom with the heat of his kisses, his teeth scoring lightly over the soft cushiony underside.

The velvety tip of him slicked her; he growled like a beast, pushing her to her back, his hips spreading her.

Deirdre still played, "I want to taste you as you did me."

"No, Deirdre, if you don't cease your squirming I will come right now."

"Where?" Deirdre teased.

She rolled him easily onto his back and straddled him, her hair like a red veil of privacy as her mouth played over his throat, his chest. Suckling and stroking, as she was molding the carved muscles of his chest, the ridges of his stomach. Deirdre met his gaze; her eyes seemed to darken with seduction as she pushed him down to further have her way with him.

"Deirdre, Deirdre, not now, lass." Tommy pleaded, even as she bent to him, taking him into her mouth. He flinched violently, curling up to watch, feel, and absorb this magnificent woman unleashing her passion on him.

Tommy had forgotten how passionate Deirdre could be. His heart thundered so hard he swore she could hear it, his body bleeding with fiery sensations, demanding that he toss her to the sand and pound into her like the sea to the shore. But her pleasure, the feel of her flesh brushing over his, was a grand prize he would savor and cherish her surrender a step to winning her trust again.

Deirdre's mouth played. He thickened and hardened, and he called her name over and over again, begging her to cease and let him pleasure her. But Deirdre was having fun, refused, letting her tongue slide, her lips pulling until he was near to exploding. Tommy wanted her, and caught her beneath the arms, dragging her over him, thrilling at the feel of every inch of her laid bare to his touch. Deirdre's skin was on fire, pure heat against the cool air.

His broad hands mapped her contours, hands coarse with calluses, fashioned to wield a sword and crossbow, and ax and a javelin—hard, unyielding. Yet when Tommy held her, the sensations of war turned to vapor and he knew he held a woman, finely shaped, soft with skin of silk and tasting of honey.

His life had been battle, survivor, and conquer, yet she was the victor as she always had been, leaving him vanquished and weak. Tommy had always cherished her. He cherished her love, wanted more of it, a willing prisoner to her power over him.

No woman had ever touched him as she did this moment. No woman gave of herself in a single kiss, or in a tiny stroke of his flesh, and Tommy knew he would do anything to keep this woman who had always been his, close, private and in possession of his soul.

In the seclusion of this tiny spot on the beach, Deirdre abandoned the cloak of her position. Hidden beneath the shade of the large bolder, she spread her thighs, toeing herself further down with eagerness that stirred him to explosion. When Deirdre rose up, sliding, slicking him, Tommy could stand no more. He sat up sharply, looking at her startled look, his arousal pushing between her thighs, seeking the warm nest, and he reached between their bodies, his gaze never leaving hers as he guided himself deeply into her. He filled her, loving the flare of her eyes, the way her tongue passed over her lips, the breathy pants... and the feminine muscles flexing wetly around him.

"Oh . . . oh husband," she repeated over and over as she threw her head back gripping his shoulders. He shoved upward, sheathing himself to the hilt. Tommy groaned aloud, his body quaking.

Suddenly Tommy pulled her hard against him, chest to breast, taking her mouth with all the heat and raw desire grinding through him. Deirdre's arms wrapped his neck and Tommy gave her hips sweet motion; lifting her, lowering her, obliging the important whimper of his lady. He could feel her body pawing his. Tommy heard her whispers of encouragement, the telltale signs he was just beginning to know; a tuck of her hips, a fractured breath.

When Deirdre spoke, whispering how delicious he felt inside her, that she could feel him throbbing, his blood pulsating, her words were hot, bold and were meant to drive him mad. And they really did.

Tommy yanked Deirdre's legs around his hips and pushed her back on the soft sand, bracing his weight on his arms. He shoved and withdrew, his mouth whispering an apology, yet she gripped his hips and demanded more of his long torturous strokes. She dug her heels into the cushiony sand, her hips rising to greet his. The cadence buffeted, smooth motion, and Tommy gazed into her eyes, watching her rapture climb to its peak.

Deirdre's eyes never closed, looking over him, watching his body disappear into hers. And each time, she bit her lower lip to hold back a cry.

"Kitten love, let me hear you."

Deirdre did, her gasps coloring the air, her emotions cresting with the tightness peeling through her undulating body. Her delicate muscles gripped in. Tommy plunged, taking her mouth, wanting to taste her pleasure on his lips.

"My Laird!"

He laughed as she pounded his shoulders, and then cupped his buttocks and that drove him deeper. He retreated and plunged deeper, tight, hard, and spearing.

Tommy knew he conquered only here, only at times like these. Deirdre surrendered, receiving him. Bare skin to bare skin, Tommy's bronze body against her ivory silkiness.

Seeking, seeking, and hastening toward the prize, finding it, the clash shattering swelling. Tommy drove Deirdre across the earth and sea, touched her soul, and she arched, bowing, beautiful beneath him, her fingertips digging into his chest as he slammed into her, once, twice, and she cried out, scattering the sea birds and begging for more. Tommy gave, unable to contain even a shred of restraint and threw his head back, pleasure roaring through him like a caged wildcat set free.

Deirdre felt his climax slip through her, every cell breaking his throbbing arousal elongating to spill his seed into her. The hard base of him pressed and rubbed, sending exquisite convulsions down to her toes. She flinched over and over, taking all he had and finding her rapture in his release. She held his gaze, watching it; the flutter of his lashes, the softening of his creased features, and the blaze in his eyes as she held him vulnerable inside her.

He was suspended on the edge, Tommy could not move, wreaked with tremors, he was trapped in the grip of desire. He stared at Deirdre, his chest heaving for air; sweat was rolling down his temples and the center of his chest as he took in every detail of her. There was a vapor simmering over her hot skin, her red hair spread like a halo around her beautiful face. Lord above, she was exquisite. Always had been headstrong, rebellious, stubborn — oh, yes, that she was. But laying in his arms, beneath him in loving, Deirdre was a magnificent wildcat that had been caged too long.

She reached up, playing with his nipple, outlining the contour of his chest before her fingers curved his neck that brought him down to her mouth. Her kiss probing and turbulent, stirring him deeper than it had before, he groaned, and sank onto her, rolling to his side, taking her with him. Her foot rubbed over his, her fingertips drawing some kind of pattern on his wet back.

He was still lodged inside her and her hips pushed deliciously to his. "Did I hurt you? I have never pounded into a woman before with such ferocity."

"You didn't hear me complaining, did you? Nooo, you didn't!"

Tommy grinned, "So then, are you still hungry for the beast?" He smiled as he teased, while stroking her wet hair from her face as she tipped it up to look at him.

"Now would you deny me the pleasure?"

Tommy laughed, kissing her again, "I would indulge you all day and night, but we will be missed soon."

"I don't care."

"You will, Kitten, when the entire house comes looking for you, and they see you in your all together." He patted her bare ass, "I'm surprised all of Sea Oaks didn't come running when your cries were so loud, like I was killing you." He teased, but found only a tender humor.

"My cries?"

His brow was arched. She shoved at his chest, "Oh, don't look at me like that, as if you were not roaring like a lynx that had been too long in a pen."

"Kitten," he was saying as their bodies were still joined, "when you opened the cage, love, you let the wildcat out."

Her gaze lowered to where their bodies joined, "You know when one knocks long and hard enough," Deirdre said with a moan, thrusting softly against him, "one must answer the door."

Tommy rolled her on her back, plunging deeply and gazed into her eyes, "Knock, knock."

They held hands as they went into the water to cool themselves off, their naked bodies glistening in the moonlight. As they came out of the water Deirdre looked at Tommy; he was a beautiful man. She did love him, more than life.

"Kitten," he warned, "that is not way to look at me; it's dangerous. You'll find yourself on your back."

"I would prefer my knees," she said tartly and his head shot up, his eyes flying wide. "I have shocked you, I see. Forgive me."

Squatting in front of her, tipping her face up, with love in his eyes, "You could never shock me. I love you so, my Kitten."

They got up and headed for the cave, then to Deirdre's bedchamber, holding on to one another. She looked down, "Tommy!"

"What, darling?"

"Look! We forgot to put our clothes on."

Laughing, he said, "That we did."

With their arms around each other, they climbed up the stairs. Deirdre could not help but feel as though she were in heaven. He had the most beautiful body she had ever seen.

As they opened the door that led from the passageway into Deirdre's bedchamber, what they saw took their breath away. Maude had brought in the large tub that two people could fit in. It was in front of the fireplace, filled with hot water. You could smell the scent of heather with roses. Clean linen, the clothes that she had let drop to the floor were picked up, so were the pearls.

Tommy saw his fresh clothes on the chest at the foot of the bed. "How did Maude know?" Tommy asked.

"Maude is very different. She said that our trouble was that we were afraid of our feelings. That's why we fought all the time." She looked into his eyes, then took her finger and ran it over his cheek.

He picked her up, carried her over, sat her in the tub, and climbed in behind her. He put his arms around her, holding her breast in his hands.

"Don't you think I should wash your back?" Deirdre asked, leaning back against him and smiling.

"No, my Kitten, I'll do you first." Tommy picked up the cloth, then put the sweet-smelling soap on the linen rag and started to wash her back and arms, then her whole body, as well as her hair.

"You know, Kitten, I love to feel your body; you're so soft and warm," he whispered in her ear.

"Now, your turn, I'll do you."

Smiling, Tommy turned to let her wash his back, but then he leaned back against her chest. "Oh, Kitten, I love you, so does it make any sense at all that I just had you and I'm wanting you again? My darling, does that wanting ever go away?"

"Tommy, I hope not, for I feel the same way as you do."

They finished their bath, and dried each other off. "The bed looks so inviting," Deirdre said, looking up into his sweet face.

"Yes, it does, should we try it out?" Tommy asked. "Any way, love, you'll have to marry me now. I have ruined your reputation."

"I too have ruined yours." Laughing, they hopped into bed, and cuddled up together. It happened again, even better this time, which was slow and longer. After the fireworks had died down, they both fell asleep wrapped up in one another.

As they slept, Maude came in and let the bed curtains loose so they would be in their own little world of privacy—a world of love.

Chapter 15

The next morning Maude slipped quietly into the room to kindle the fire.

"Maude love, is that you?"

"Yes, it is. Would you like another bath, and a bite to eat?"

Tommy kissed Deirdre's ear then said, "Maude love, better tell everyone there will be a wedding as soon as possible. We may have started a wee one."

Laughing for joy, "I'll do that right now!"

"Maude, don't come back until about noon, please."

"That I will," laughing with joy as she waddled out of the door as fast as she could.

"Now, my darling, what do you think you are going to do between now and noon?" Deirdre asked while cuddling up to him. She ran her hand over his chest, and it kept getting lower, and lower.

"I think you had better stop, Kitten, you may get into trouble."

"Now do you really think so?"

"Yes, I do," he said, gritting his teeth as she lowered her hand then took hold of his velvet shaft. It felt hard and ready, with the dew of love on the end. "Kitten, you are not doing us any good doing this."

"Don't what, my darling?" Deirdre asked, smiling up at him with a little wicked giggle. *Oh!! It felt so good being in control,* she thought to herself.

All of a sudden he rolled over pulling her under him, with a smirk on his face, "So you want it, do you lassie? Well now I'll give it to you." With that he filled her with his stiff, wonderful shaft, hard and swollen, thick and wanting. Thinking he could outdo her, she'd showed him. She met him each time, hard thrust for thrust. Soon there were drops of sweat dripping on her. They both were hot, and sticky, loving, laughing, rolling around; him on top, then her, sliding over each other. Oh! It was a wonderful feeling. After they had both came down from the heaven and let out a big moan, they fell into a deep sleep, still wrapped in each other.

They were awakened by a knock on the door. When it opened, Maude came in saying, "Is it safe now to bring in your bath water? Laird MacDarroch wants to see you both in the library soon, so Sir Tommy can sign papers. He's there with your father."

"Alright, Maude, come on in. Is it a large tub? I'm hoping so?" asked Tommy.

"Yes, it is."

"Maude, didn't we sign papers before?" Deirdre asked.

"You did, but it needs to be updated, to make it all proper, now that you have consummated before the wedding." Maude laughed as she went out.

Tommy got out of bed. He watched Deirdre try to get up. It was a little hard for her to just spring out. "Love, are you a little sore?"

Smiling up at him, she replied, "Yes, just a little."

He went over to help her up, returning her smile. "Don't tell anyone, but so am I."

They both laughed, and got into the warm water. It felt like heaven to both of them.

They bathed, dressed, and went down to the library. Meanwhile in the library, Laird Glen MacDonald and Laird John were discussing whom to invite to the wedding.

"You know, Glen, Deirdre doesn't want the king and the Campbells. But if you invite the king, then the Campbells will come."

"You're right, John. Tommy doesn't want them here either. So who then, besides the clans and neighbors?"

Just then Deirdre and Tommy both walked in, "Is that not enough? Why the long faces, and on the eve of our wedding day?"

"What are you saying, Tommy?"

"Well, Father, my Kitten and I happened to overhear you; right, Kitten?"

"Father, Laird MacDonald, we have already consummated our wedding, so don't you think we should get married in a hurry, I could be with a baby," she said, looking at them with their mouths open, in shock.

Tommy and Deirdre started to laugh, when the others saw their point.

"You're right, we must hurry, Deirdre, call your mother," Laird John said with a big smile.

"Someone call me?" Mary Kate asked from the door.

"We must have a wedding tomorrow. Can you do it?" asked John MacDarroch.

"Why, husband, it's done. The Gordons, MacLeods, and of course all the MacDonalds, our neighbors and our own clan," Mary Kate said, laughing at the look on everyone's faces.

Maude stuck her head in the door. "My Laird, you had better get the priest. You don't have to wait for the bands to be read. It's already done. Now, Laird Tommy, you must leave until tomorrow, Deirdre has to ready herself."

Tommy went over to Deirdre at that time, put his arms around her, then whispered, "Meet me at the glen, darling, in about an hour."

Hugging him, Deirdre said aloud, "Love, I'll see you tomorrow inside the chapel." As she let him go, she winked. He knew that she would meet him in the glen by the water.

Maude started upstairs behind Deirdre, "Now, if you think you two can fool old Maude, you have another think coming."

With a look of innocence on her face, Deirdre asked, "What in the world are ye talking about, Maude love?"

"Don't you just love me, missy, I know you and Sir Tommy quite well; you can't fool me. Now, which dress will you be wearing to your wedding, lass?"

Looking at Maude, Deirdre smiled and answered, "Why not the white silk and silver one that Grandfather brought me from China?"

"It will be perfect; you have the shoes and all."

"You know, Maude, I'm quite tired. If I could have a nice hot bath then I'll go straight away to bed, big day tomorrow."

"I would think you would not be tired with sleeping all day and already having a bath," Maude said, laughed as she left the room.

Deirdre left by the passageway down to the beach and ran up the steps by the cliff. Reaching the top, she looked around then started toward the glen. She saw Tommy waiting for her and she was about to reach him when he saw Campbells come out of the woods.

"Kitten, it's the Campbells. Run fast, love, I'll try and hold them off. I love you, darling, never forget that."

Before she ran, "I love you too, my love, be careful." Deirdre ran as fast and hard as she could. She made the mistake of turning and seeing one of the Campbells hit Tommy in the head with the butt of his gun, and then draw his sword. He plunged his sword into Tommy's stomach laughing. When it happened, she heard MacTavish give his loud cry.

"Run, run, MacTavish, run and warn the others to run," Deirdre screamed.

Deirdre cried, for she thought they had killed Tommy. She saw Patrick riding hard. He grabbed her up, slinging her over his saddle like a bag of oats. "I have you now, Deirdre MacDarroch. You'll pay now, wait and see."

Laughing like a crazy man, he rode off down to the beach where boats were waiting for Patrick and his men.

MacTavish grabbed Deirdre's shoe then ran up to the Castle, through the passageway, right into the bedchamber where Maude had just discovered that Deirdre was gone.

"MacTavish, what wrong?" asked Maude. Seeing that he needed to get through the other door that led into the hall, she opened it. She followed him as he ran to the library, jumped on the door and dropped the shoe. The door opened up; Glen MacDonald looked at John MacDarroch then at Maude with the shoe in her hand.

"Something is wrong! Maude? Deirdre is in her bedchamber, is she not?" asked Laird John.

"No, Me Laird, she slipped out to meet your son, Laird MacDonald."

Looking at one another, Mary Kate burst in, saying, "Patrick has Deirdre. I feel it deep in my soul, something is wrong. MacTavish is having a fit like we should follow him."

"What are we waiting for? We need to round up everyone. Let's get on the move!" Laird Glen shouted.

As they followed MacTavish, Monica saw Tommy on the ground in a pool of blood, thinking to herself, *Funny his arm seems to be pointing toward the beach.*

"Kimberly, hurry!" shouted Monica.

As they came closer, Kimberly jumped from her horse. "Monica, go get Molly, we must get him into bed. Look, he has a large stab wound in his stomach and, my goodness, his skull has been badly battered in."

"Go and get some men to make a carrier for him. We must hurry or we'll lose him!" shouted Mary Kate.

Everyone was rushing around helping Tommy, when they heard him shout, "Kitten, look out behind you." Then he blacked out.

Monica was looking for signs, trying to find out which way the Campbells went. She looked down and found Deirdre's footprints then shouted, "Mother, come here — and hurry."

"What did you find, lass?" asked Mary Kate.

"They have her; here are her footprints, also signs of boots."

"Monica, we must hurry and follow them. Come let's get supplies, and then ride. Kimberly will have to stay with Tommy."

Kimberly had come up behind them as they were talking and overheard what was being said. "Sorry, Mother. Molly and Annie with Aunt Sue can stay and help with Tommy. My sister may need our help more than he does."

The men passed with Tommy on a carrier; he looked up all glassy-eyed at Kimberly. "Find my Kitten, Kimber, please find my love." With that, he went unconscious again as if he were dead, but still breathing.

"Molly, can you and Annie with the help of Sue...?" asked Kimberly, not able to finish her sentence because of the tears that were choking her.

Sue, with the others, came up and put their arms around her. "Now don't you worry about Tommy, we'll take good care of him. Now, you go along and find our Lady."

"Sue is right; you go find your sister. Lord knows what that Patrick Campbell will do to her. May the good Lord be with you." Molly ran to catch up with Annie and Sue.

Mary Kate looked at her husband who seemed to be in a state of shock, "John, are you going to just stand there? Get the men. We have to find her!"

Monica looked at her father and his men with a very disappointed look on her face. "Well now, Father, you and your men stay here and do women's work." Shouting as she started to ride, "COME MOTHER, KIMBERLY!"

All three had ridden to the castle and retrieved their weapons before the men knew what happened.

Mary Kate found traces of horse prints and the place where Deirdre's shoe had fallen. "If we don't find her soon, I fear for her life. Lassies, lets ride." Mary Kate rode hard as well as Kimberly and Monica. They all three were mad — madder than hell about what had happened.

On the way to the beach, they ran into their uncles, Jamie and William. "Mary Kate, sister, what's happened here?"

"Jamie, William, Patrick Campbell has taken Deirdre prisoner."

"Say not. Where are the men and our brother?" he asked, looking around.

"Back at Sea Oaks, I suppose. At least they were when we left," stated Monica with fury in her voice.

"Cowards, all of them, to let this happen. Tommy was badly wounded, maybe dying, trying to help her. But the rest just stood and did nothing about it," said Kimberly in an angry tone.

"Do you know in what direction they went?" asked Jamie.

"It looks like they went toward the beach; maybe they had boats waiting," replied Mary Kate.

Just then, Laird John MacDarroch and his men rode up, with the MacDonalds behind them. "Wife! You and the lassies go back to Sea Oaks.

"We're going to find Deirdre."

"Now, Mary Kate MacDarroch, you'll not be doing any such thing. You'll do as your husband tells you, lassies, do as you are told."

"Sorry, Father, not this time. We're going to find our sister." They turned and rode straight for the beach. There they found where the boats had been beached.

"Bet they took her to Robert Campbell's Glenlyon. If so, it will be something to get her out," Mary Kate said.

"You're right, Mother, do you know someone over in the Campbells' Glenlyon that could help?" asked Monica.

"Yes, but getting word to her is not going to be easy, but I'll try."

"Who is it, Mother, do we know her?" asked Kimberly.

"No. But she was once a beautiful woman. My father loved her very much when they were young. But her father sent her away. My father thought she was dead, but though the years I have heard about her. She is the mother of Earl Campbell and Patrick. Robert is her husband. It has been told that he treats her like a prisoner. She has been beaten and had her bones broken. Lord love her. Yes, she'll help; she hates what Robert has taught her sons."

"But how will we get word to her?" asked Monica.

"There is a maid servant of hers who does the marketing. Her name is Marie, I understand. Maybe we'll find her in the market square. I met her some years ago. Come lassies; let's go to the market place."

"What does she look like?" asked Kimberly.

"Let's see, she is about as tall as you are, Kimberly, reddish-brown curly hair. That's about all I can recall. Girls, pray we find her."

"We will, Mother," was their answer.

Finding a boat in the tall sea grass, they tied their horses to a log and put out across the sound. Landing on the other side, Monica hid the small boat. They then walked in the direction of the market place.

Kimberly and Monica entered the road to the market with Mary Kate. Marie came out of the walled courtyard of the castle and walked down the same road toward the market. Mary Kate and the girls entered at the same time as did Marie. It startled all of them. Marie looked in all directions to see if anyone was watching.

Mary Kate and the girls pulled their hoods closer to their faces, "Lassies, maybe you should stay behind the trees."

"Alright, Mother, but please be careful." They went behind the trees in a small grove.

"My Lady," Marie spoke very softly. She had recognized Mary Kate from long past when Mary Kate had helped her fight off dragons many years ago.

"Marie, I didn't think you would recognize me after all these many years. But now I need your help. Patrick Campbell has kidnapped Deirdre and I'm certain she is in the Castle somewhere. Would you please speak to Georgeanna about it?"

"My Lord!!! So that's why he is so happy, he has gone mad. He has always loved her, you know?"

"No, I didn't. Will you help us?" Mary Kate asked with a worried look on her face.

"Of course I will," Marie answered. "Let me hurry and do the marketing so they won't suspect anything."

"Thank you. Tell Georgeanna there will be a ship. It's my father's and the name on it is DEIRDRE; on the sound it will be. She'll have to get her there."

"Don't you worry; I'll help, My Lady, and go with them. For I know Patrick, he will abuse Deirdre, as well. He is just like his father. Don't worry, My Lady will help. You be here tomorrow, this same time. I had better go do shopping and get back. I shop every day for My Lady.

"Thank you, Marie, we'll be here." Looking around, they parted from each other. Mary Kate went to where Kimberly and Monica were hiding. "Mother, you were so long we thought you were caught," Monica said with a worried look on her face.

"What did Marie say?" asked Kimberly.

"She is going to speak to Georgeanna and tell her what happened. We must get word to your grandfather about the boat."

"But how?" asked Kimberly.

"One of you has to go back and let them know. Monica, can you do it, love, and be on the boat with your grandfather?"

"What about Kimberly?"

"I'll need her and her knowledge of healing for Deirdre, and if what Marie said is true, she'll need all of the healing she knows."

"What do you mean, Mother?" asked Kimberly.

"From what Marie told me, Patrick is like his father. He has no qualms about beating a woman if she won't do his bidding and you know Deirdre; she'll not summit to anything."

"You are so right. I can make it back and bring Grandfather." She turned and kissed her mother and Kimberly. "Don't worry Kimberly, I'll be alright. Mother, how long do we have?"

"I don't know. We'll have to just wait and pray."

Just then they heard a scream so loud it made cold chills go down their spines. It was just like MacTavish, when he knew something was wrong with his master.

"Mother, is it her?" asked Monica, with tears in her eyes.

"I don't know, love, you must hurry now."

Mary Kate and Kimberly knelt on the ground under a shade tree after Monica left on the run. They prayed for the good Lord to be with Deirdre.

Chapter 16

Meanwhile, in the Campbells' stronghold, Marie was telling her Ladyship, Georgeanna Campbell, what was going on. She said she had met Mary Kate MacDarroch and explained who Mary Kate's father was. They needed her help because Patrick had kidnapped Deirdre.

With tears in her eyes, she told Marie that she was going to help. The two of them would leave on the same boat to Norway. She had a softness in her eyes as she spoke of the Viking Chief Kirk.

"You go and listen, Marie, while I go to the upper tower and get my medicine box."

Deirdre did not remember how long she had been knocked out and chained up. There was a piece of metal around her neck and her arms were chained to the wall as well as her legs. She tried to look at herself, which was hard through one eye, as the other was swollen shut. There was a long mirror straight ahead. "My Lord, I'm naked and black and blue and my eye is swollen shut. My God, what will this madman do to me next?"

She looked up when she heard the door opening. There stood Patrick, with a drunken grin on his face. "Well, my beauty, how are you this day?" he asked.

"How long have I been here, you pig?"

"Now, now, you know how I get when you make me mad. You have been here about a few days to a week, I think. I'm going to put this Feileadh-Mor, the big wrap up over you, so that my men can come up and chain you to a bed. As you know, I have plans for you in bed," he said, laughing like someone totally out of control.

"There you are, my good fellows. Put the bed over next to the wall. Now, you know not to look at my darling, soon to be my wife, don't you?"

"Yes, My Laird," the men answered. They put up the bed and made it look so comfortable, nice and soft.

Patrick went to her, taking off the covers, saying, "We can't have it too easy for you now, can we?"

The men came back in and put up the rings to hook the chains in. They moved Deirdre ever so slowly; it was as if they could feel her pain, as well as her shame.

"Men, let's hurry. I wish to be alone with my love. You can understand, can't you," smirked Patrick.

Little did Patrick know that outside the door was Marie, listening to everything. But afraid someone would see her, she left and ran straight to her Ladyship Georgeanna.

With tears running down her cheeks, Georgeanna looked at Marie and spoke with a choking in her voice, "He'll rape her now, just like his father did me."

"Oh no, My Lady!" Marie said as she put her arms around her Ladyship.

Georgeanna cried until she could not cry anymore. "Marie, hand me my medicine box. I'll go and see what I can do."

As she opened the door they heard Deirdre scream out, "He has done it!"

"The devil will take him one day just like he will his father," said Lady Georgeanna, with hard hate in her voice.

Coming to after Patrick had hit her again with his fist, Deirdre said with a smile on her face, "Do what you will, I'm Tommy MacDonald's wife, now. You'll not be the first, he was."

"No, that is not so," Patrick said, his face red and his whole body shaking with fury. "I'll take you anyway so you can compare who's better," he said, laughing his insane laugh.

Looking up into his face smiling as best as she could, "My husband is the best man in all ways, you drunken sot."

Deirdre saw Patrick's fury grow. He drew back his fist and hit her square in the face, knocking her out.

Deirdre came to, very slowly, feeling as if an army of horses had trampled over her. She tried looking through the slits from her swollen eyes. She saw Patrick on the floor, passed out dead drunk, *thank heavens*, she thought to herself.

When he finally came to, he got back up to try again.

"You go ahead, your day will come. I'll kill you for this." All of a sudden she felt his hand go around her throat as if he were going to choke her, but thought better of it. Deirdre tried to twist against the metal cuffs as they cut into her wrists making them bleed, as well as her ankles. Then without a word, he left.

She was thinking to herself, *Why would Patrick do this? Of course I killed his brother, but this way, why not on the battle field of honor? Oh!!* But she said, "It's more degrading and so I would lose Tommy, that's why. He also thinks I'm a defeated warrior and will not rise and fight again. But ye are all wrong, Patrick, all wrong. I'll have your head for all of this. My day will come, you'll see!'

Trying to get a little rest was impossible. She heard Patrick coming in again. She had almost gotten used to the horrible smell, but the thought of him touching her made her want to vomit.

"Well, my darling, just look at you, laying there waiting on me — waiting for me to make mad love to you. Just can't wait, can you." Laughing, he staggered over to the bed.

"Don't you ever take a bath? What's happened to you? I know you hate me for killing your brother, but to let yourself be a pig is another thing."

"Hate you? No, Deirdre, that's not true. Earl got what he wanted. You see, he loved Kimberly so much that the thought of her belonging to Hugh MacDonald drove him mad. As for me, I have loved you all my life. But you see, I have you and Tommy MacDonald doesn't; he'll know I have you. If you ever got away, which you won't, you know he'll never touch you again. Besides, we killed him," he said, laughing more like a mad man than ever.

He then flopped on top of her and fell asleep. As Patrick slept, Deirdre started thinking. *Patrick was right, Tommy won't want me. All I ever wanted was for my clan to be safe, as well as my Tommy. Dead, no, he couldn't be, for I would feel it.*

Even with Patrick's attempted rape, her Tommy never left her thoughts and heart. Even being here for weeks, she had a deep feeling she was carrying Tommy's babe. Deirdre felt dirty, inside and out, because of Patrick. Not that he had entered her; it was just the thought of him even touching her.

She felt it was her fault all of this that had happened to her. What did it matter what Patrick did to her? She had brought all of this on herself. She should have said no to Tommy. Now he could be dead and here she was a captive. *Yes, it's all my fault.*

Patrick aroused himself from sleep and started kissing her all over, trying to make love to her in his way. Deirdre just lay there, not feeling anything. With her hands and feet chained, she felt already dead.

"What's the matter with you? Is there no feeling in you?"

"What should you care? You will just get mad and beat me again. I'm already dead."

Patrick staggered as he got up. He found his bottle and started drinking again. The more he drank, the madder he got. He stood looking down at her, his face red, his fist clinched at his side. "Tell me you love me," he demanded.

"I can't. If I did, it would be a lie."

His hand came back and hit her across the face. It was so hard that it knocked her out again. Patrick was so mad that while Deirdre was out, he took her left arm out of the cuff chain, and broke it. Deirdre did not remember screaming. But later, Lady Georgeanna said she and the whole castle did.

It was dusk and Deirdre could feel that maybe one candle was lit. Through all the pain she heard the door open. "Who's there?"

"Don't be frightened. I'm Lady Georgeanna, I came to treat your wounds and clean you up a bit. I couldn't come any sooner for I have been locked in my room, a prisoner myself"

"Sorry, but as you can see, I can't see you, for my eyes are swollen shut, Lady Georgeanna. I have heard my grandfather speak of ye. He loved my grandmother, but he had never gotten over you. He thought you were dead."

"I might as well have been," replied Lady Georgeanna.

"What are you doing here? If they find you trying to help me, they'll do bad things to you, My Lady."

"Deirdre, please, don't fret about me, just let me see to your wounds and set your arm. This will hurt."

Lady Georgeanna was tending to her wounds as she whispered to Deirdre the plans that were in the making, and she would get back to her. She was treating her eyes and the other wounds just as Patrick walked in.

"What the hell are you doing here? How did you know where to find her? Speak, you meddlesome old fool!"

"I just came in to clean her wounds, Patrick, my son."

"You did, did you?! But how did ye know she was here?"

"Why, the whole castle knows. Ye have gone around looking so happy and smug with yourself."

"Aye, I pulled it off, ye know, right under their noses. One of my men pistol-whipped Tommy MacDonald in the head, then stuck him like a pig. Ye know, he might just be dead!" Patrick started laughing. "Well, get on with it, I need a drink. And you, don't worry, love, I'll be back to give ye more loving," he said as he staggered out the door, still laughing.

Lady Georgeanna finished cleaning Deirdre up, set her arm, and dressed her wounds. She spoke very softly, "Your mother and sisters were here. There will be a lassie named Marie who will come to feed ye. She'll let ye know what's going on. I'll see to ye wounds. Now one of us will get the keys from Patrick when he has passed out drunk, so we can unlock ye. There will be three horses for us to get to the beach for the boat that your grandfather will have waiting. Ye understand?" Georgeanna asked as she bent over Deirdre and gave her a kiss on the forehead.

"I'll be ready, Me Lady. Thank ye very much for all you are doing."

"I know what ye are going through. Patrick's father did the same to me."

"My Lady, I am so sorry for ye." Deirdre choked, with tears running down her cheeks and eyes so full.

"I pray your young man will understand and loves ye enough to help ye through this."

"I don't think he'll be able. He was stabbed in the stomach. The last I remember, I saw him being hit in the head with the butt of a gun, but I pray he is still alive."

The door opened and in walked Patrick, dead drunk, smelling like he had not taken a bath in a month of Sundays. "Out ye go, Me Lady. I wish to make love with my soon-to-be wife," staggering with a big smile on his face, he made his way over to the bed.

Lady Georgeanna turned and walked out of the chamber with a frightened look on her face. She walked down the stairs as she heard Deirdre scream from pain. Crying, she ran into Marie. "Marie, we have to get her out of here."

"A thought came over me, Me Lady. What if she is with a baby? Ye know she is Laird Tommy MacDonald's wife? That is what her mother told me."

"I pray not, but if she is, I pray she'll not carry it."

"My Lady, that be a sin."

"Maybe, Marie, but God forgive me, I still pray it. With the beatings she has had, it will not be right in the head," Lady Georgeanna remarked as they went into her chamber.

"Now, tomorrow, ye go to the Market Place and see if ye can find Lady Mary Kate MacDarroch. Tell her about our plans and to pray we can pull it off. We'll be on horseback as far as the beach and we'll need a row boat to get to the ship."

"Yes, Me Lady, I will." As Marie was leaving the chamber, she ran into Laird Robert Campbell. He looked at her with his cold blue eyes and his red hair sticking out from under his bonnet.

"Well, Marie, me gal. What are ye up too?"

"Helping My Lady, My Laird."

"Well, be gone with ye, then."

Robert turned with his cold steel-blue eyes, stared at Georgeanna, then said, "I understand ye went up to clean and dress Deirdre MacDarroch's wounds?"

"Yes."

"You'll not do it again, do ye understand, Lady, or you'll get the same as she."

"Yes, My Laird."

"Well, see ye don't."

"As ye say, Me Laird, but with the infection and all, she could die; what then?"

"What do ye mean infection?"

"Yes, she has a bad infection. But I'll not treat her, we'll just let her die and Patrick will lose, as well as the king."

"What do ye mean, so will the king? What does the king have to do with it?"

"Why Deirdre is Laird Glen MacDonald's godchild and Tommy MacDonald's wife. He'll go straight to the other clans, tell them that Patrick took Deirdre, then shot Tommy. He's badly wounded, ye know, or maybe even dead. He may even take it to Parliament, then there could be war against the king. In turn, the king will blame ye and Patrick."

"Ye are out of ye mind! The king wouldn't." He stopped as he looked at his wife, nodding her head yes.

Turning around, Robert Campbell went out of the door and up the hall, taking the steps two at a time to where Deirdre was being kept prisoner. Opening the door, he saw a sight that even turned *his* stomach. The smell was so bad that he almost vomited. Going over, with a linen over his nose, he leaned over and shook Patrick until he woke him up.

"What? Oh, Dad. What's the matter?" asked Patrick.

"I want Deirdre cleaned up and this room cleaned, fresh linen; her washed good, the room aired. Do I make myself clear? Do ye understand?"

"Yes, I do, but I don't want to; she'll expect to be treated good all the time."

"You'll do as you're told." With a slap to the face, Patrick grew red. His dad left, shouting orders.

Patrick was madder than hell, staggering off after his dad, shouting, "I'll not have it. You'll not interfere with my life, do you hear me old mon. Answer me, ye tyrant, answer me."

Patrick started down the long, steep stairs, staggering, when he lost his footing, slipped and fell to the bottom. Marie saw him land there, out cold. She ran over and searched his pockets for the keys. She found them hooked on a piece of rope around his waist. Turning him back the way he was, she noticed that his neck was broken. Running as fast as she could back to Lady Georgeanna's chamber with the keys, she said, "Me Lady, come quick. Master Patrick has fallen doon the steep stairs."

"Marie! What are ye sayin'?"

"Me Lady, Master Patrick fell doon the steep stairs and I found his keys. But it looks like his neck is broken."

"Marie, bless ye. Noo we must hurry. This is the opportunity we hae been lookin' for. Hurry noo." Thinking to herself, *'Tis funny that I feel nothin' for me own son as I did for Earl. Is it because, at last, I feel free o' all the hate and fear?*

They came up to where Deirdre was kept. She heard them coming through the door as Lady Georgeanna spoke, "Deirdre, we must hurry. Do ye think ye may be able tae walk?"

"I dunnae knoo, but I'll try." They unlocked Deirdre's chains, trying to be careful while putting on her clothes due to her broken arm. The insertions of old-style words were becoming more frequent, as they were the natural order of speech in the Campbell Stronghold.

"Hurry noo, we must leave 'afore we are discovered missin'."

"Ma Lady, I'm afeard that I cannae see. Ye'll hae tae guie me."

"Dunnae ye worrit, ma darlin'. We weel help ye. Come Marie, let's ga. Take her other arm."

They left the chamber, hurried down the stairs, and stepped over Patrick's body. They almost ran as they got outside and down to the stables where they helped Deirdre mount a horse. Marie took hold of the reins. Marie walked the horses at first, then gave them their heads, moving towards the beach where a ship would be waiting for them, or at least they prayed it would be.

"Do ye see ma mathair and sisters, Lady Georgeanna?" Deirdre asked.

"Nay, ma dear. I dunnae, but pray the ship is there. I fear that I hear Robert's army behind us."

"Ma Lady, are ye alright?" asked Marie.

"Aye, Marie, thank ye. 'Tis Deirdre I'm worrit aboot."

"Lady Georgeanna, I'll be alright, just keep ridin'."

"Are ye sure, ma dear?"

"Aye, I'd rather die as tae be back there. 'Tis seems years instead o'few days, or was it a week?"

"Deirdre, Marie tells me ye dinnae hae ye woman's day!"

"Nay and aye, I hae no' had one in quite a while, ye see I'm hae'in' a wee bairn." The flow of the ancient Scottish accent seemed natural now to Deirdre, as it would for them all until they set sail.

"Ma Lord, nay."

"Aye, Me Lady."

"Are ye sure, Deirdre? What weel ye young mon say?"

"He does no' knoo, I was ga'in' tae tell him when I was captured. Tommy, he does no' knoo that 'tis his babe."

"Aye ye sure, dear?"

With tears flowing down her face, Deirdre could not answer, but nodded her head yes. They came to the beach and there was a row boat with two of her "gran'faither's" men in it. When they saw Deirdre, they were shocked, but mostly very mad.

"Ma Lady, when the Captain sees what Patrick Campbell has done tae ye, there weel be war."

"Nay. Who 'tis it? Is that ye, Robbie?"

"Aye, me Lady," Robbie answered with tears in his eyes and his voice choked up.

"Who else is aboard?"

"The Lady, Mary Kate, yer sisters, and the Captain, yer Godshire Clan."

"Och! Nay one else?"

"Nay, me Lady Deirdre. Sir Tommy is still in a verra bad way. His stomach wound is healin' but 'tis his head they are worrit aboot," Robbie answered.

They drew along side of the "Deirdre", which Grandfather had named after her. His other ships named after her sisters. His men along with Lady Georgeanna and Marie helped Deirdre aboard. "Dhia, please help me, I cannae see them and please, dunnae let them show me pity."

She heard the hurt and anger in her grandfather's voice. "I'll be back and kill e'ery last one o' ye Campbell." Pulling her into his arms very gently and she could feel the wet tears on his face.

"Dunnae, Gran'faither luve, please, I'll be alright."

"I'm sorry, ma warrior. Come, ye mathair and sisters wait for ye," Kirk picking his way down to the Captain's cabin. When he turned, he looked into the eyes of the only woman he had ever loved all these years. He thought she was dead. "Georgeanna? Och! Ma Dhia, 'tis it really ye, darlin'?"

"Aye, but take Deirdre doon tae bed sae I may tend tae her, then we can talk."

He kicked open the door. "Here, ma dears, take care o' her. We need tae be on the way. Monica, please, I need ye top side."

Planting a kiss on Deirdre's cheek, Monica went topside to help get on the way.

After being cleaned up and her wounds treated, Deirdre asked, "Is Lady Georgeanna here?"

"Aye, ma dear, I'm here. What is it you need? We are all here wi' ye."

"Please... all o' ye, dunnae feel sorry for me. Robbie told me aboot Tommy, me darlin'. Georgeanna is the swellin' ga'in' doon? Kimberly, are ye here?"

"Aye, sweet sister, ye'll see soon. We're on oor way tae Gran'faither's."

"Och!! Mathair, are the mon oot?"

"Aye," she answered with a puzzled look on her face.

"Mathair, Georgeanna knoos and soon ye weel. I'm wi' child, 'tis Tommy's."

"Ma Lord," Mary Kate said wi' tears in her eyes. Thinking to herself, *She would no' tell anyone else, until the time came and she had tae.* "Are ye sure, Deirdre?"

"Aye, that I am, Mathair. Please dunna tell Da or the MacDonald's, no' e'en Gran'faither until it has tae be."

"I weel no', luve, dunnae ye worrit," she affirmed, kissing Deirdre on the forehead.

"Hae ye seen Tommy?" Deirdre asked again.

"Aye, when ye were bein' taken by the Campbells, the mon picked him up on a litter tae carry him up tae Sea Oats. He woke long enough tae ask us tae find his Kitten."

"If ye see him, tell him I'm sorry, but it cannae e'er be."

"What do ye mean by that?" asked Mary Kate.

"Mathair... wi' all that has happened, I feel unclean. Then there was the attempted rape of Patrick, or let's just say he tried. But I still feel unclean just from his touch.

"Darlin', ye are ga'in' tae ye Gran'faither's. There ye weel be treated and ye'll gea weel. We'll just talk aboot it later. Noo, gea some sleep." Mary Kate kissed her and left with tears in her eyes.

Rest and sleep, Deirdre wished that it would come. But instead, thinking of the pain of her Tommy lying there, as well as her being in agony and all that has happened, she said, "Dhia, would life e'er be the same again?"

After much tossing and turning, Deirdre finally drifted off to sleep. The rocking of the boat made it easier to rest. But all of a sudden, she was feeling very hot. Hot, as though she were on fire.

Deirdre woke herself up screaming like she was in a hot fire. Then through the fog and heat came a voice, "She is burnin' up wi' fever. We need tae just keep wipin' her doon in cold water."

"Nay, please dunnae beat me again, please," she cried out loud in her sleep.

She woke up with someone's cool hand on her forehead. It was Mary Kate's, and she was looking into her face. There were tears running down her cheeks. "Dunna cry, Mathair, I'll be me old stubborn sel' soon again."

"Aye, that ye weel, ma luve, that ye weel."

The door opened softly and in walked Grandfather. "How is she, Mary Kate?"

"I'm ga'in' tae be just fine, ma sweet Gran'faither, dunnae ye worrit. How long hae we been at sea?"

"Who's worrit, I ask ye. 'Tis no' me and we hae been oot three weeks, aboot a half a day and weel be tome. How's that, ma gel?" standing with a grin on his face.

Deirdre saw her mother look at her grandfather, then spoke, "O' course no'! Ye dinnae worrit at all o'er ye first born, gran'lassie, yer favorite," she said, looking him in the eye, smiling.

"She is a fighter, I taught her tae be. But is she ga'in' tae be alright?"

"Aye, I'm, would ye both please quit talkin' like I'm no' in the room," Deirdre stated.

Turning, Mary Kate asked, "Da, is Sister Ellen at yer stronghold?"

"Aye, that she is, why?" he asked.

"Does she knoo where the healer is, maybe?"

"Mary Kate, I dunnae knoo!"

"Mathair, why do ye need tae knoo where the healer is? Kimberly is takin' guid care o' me, is she no'?"

"Ye hae a fever inside ye and there is a special herb for that, we dunnae hae on board. Kimberly has looked for it, but we canna find it anywhere."

Deirdre looked at Kimberly. "Kimberly, why this special herb?" feeling sluggishly as she asked. Then all of a sudden Deirdre was completely out of it.

"Deirdre..... Deirdre.... Do ye hear me? Henny, do ye hear me?" Kimberly was shaking Deirdre hard to get her to respond.

"Aye," Deirdre said, and then went unconscious.

It was a long time when it felt as if the ship was rocking her. But there was a breeze on her face and it was cold while the rest of her body was hot as she would imagine hell would be like.

Later, Deirdre found out the rocking was Grandfather's men carrying her up to the stronghold that was her grandfather's home. The heat she felt was fever.

Deirdre was carried into a bedchamber where there was a hot fire in the fireplace. Clean linen was on the large bed with piles of furs to cover her.

Kimberly, with Monica at her side, kept vigil over her all night. Sometime up in the wee hours of the morning Deirdre looked up from swollen eyes and asked, "Kimberly, Monica, come close luves. Noo the truth, how bad am I?"

"Ye want the truth, do ye?" asked Monica.

"Aye, that I do," she answered.

"I'll tell her." Kimberly looked at Monica and stated, "Weel ma dear sister, ye are comin' back slowly from the dead, and yer no' oot o' the woods yet. Och!! How dare ye do this tae us," Kimberly said with a choking in her voice.

Lying there looking at the both of them, Deirdre said softly, "I dinnae mean tae."

"Och!! Hush. We know it wasna yer fault. I just wish thin's could hae been better," Kimberly remarked.

"That's right. We sent word tae Da and the MacDonald brothers. Mathair sent a letter tae Tommy tellin' him ye canna marry him again. Just in yer own words, henny," Monica told her with a sad look on her face.

"I wonder what' he'll do noo?" asked Kimberly.

"Feel sorry for himsel' o' course. No' thinkin' o' anyone but himsel' as always," was Monica's answer.

"Please gels, dunnae be sae hard on him," Deirdre said before going back to sleep. She thought she felt herself begin to shake and then her body felt as if it were on fire. She could hear voices, but could not make them out.

"I luve ye, Tommy, I'll always luve ye," Deirdre was saying before she passed out.

Georgeanna came to her side, then screamed as she ran to the heavy door. "Come, come quick. I fear she is dead."

Everyone ran into the bedchamber. Mary Kate came over to where Deirdre had slumped over. Mary Kate touched her forehead, "She's burnin' up wi' fever; somethin' is wrong. I feel the brain is dead wi' in her. Aft' all, the beatin's could hae done it."

Aunt Ellen walked over to the door and called Karen. "Ga and get the midwife, then the old womon on the mountain."

"Bu-but? She is a witch, Ma Lady."

"Do as I say. She is the only one who can save ma niece. Noo ga."

Karen looked at her Ladyship, turned and ran out the door. She ran as fast as she could. It had seemed hours before Karen came back with the old woman and midwife.

After looking at Deirdre, the old woman, who everyone called a witch, spoke to Karen. "Gea hot water and brin' clean linen. Alsae gea the mon tae scrub the large table in the great hall." Looking at Ellen, she continued, "We hae tae work fast, I'm afeared we may lose her. Hurry noo."

Bonnie, the midwife, worked with the old woman to get things ready. Ellen spoke to her father, "Da, please carry Deirdre doon stairs and lay her on the table."

"That weel be done, Ellen. E'eryone oot o' ma way." With tears in his eyes, Grandfather Kirk lifted her ever so gently, then carried her downstairs as he put her on the table and kissed her forehead.

"Ellen, would ye please gea me some Cistus Landaiferus. "Tis the rock rose tae make laburnum tea for Deirdre tae drink? Child, 'tis a cluster of yellow low flowers. If ye canna find the flowers, then get the rock rose. Ye'll find it a plenty."

"Aye, but is nae that poison?"

"Nay, if we use it in a way tae help her wi' pain and help her sleep. She weel need that noo," spoke the old witch softly.

Aunt Ellen went out and did as she was told. The old witch, whose name was Maggie, got Deirdre undressed and covered her with a clean linen. Mary Kate saw the old woman lay out a very sharp knife, needle, thread, herbs, some old black salve and an old yellow green salve. She laid out a pile of clean white linen. Maggie put the salve all down Deirdre's swollen stomach, saying the words of the ancient healers. No one could understand what she was saying, as she cut down Deirdre's stomach. She just repeated the words over and over again.

"Spirits o' life and health, I ask renew this body for its task. Make her strong and full o' glee. Oor hearty thanks, we gi' tae thee."

Aunt Ellen helped the midwife and Maggie with cleaning up the blood. Just at that moment, Mary Kate asked, "What is that awful smell?"

"'Tis the poison in Deirdre from the dead bairn."

"How long had it been dead, Maggie," asked Ellen.

"I couldnae really say, Me Lady. But with all the beatin' that ye say she received, the shock alone could hae done it aft' the first blow. She was aboot six weeks along."

Grandfather came in looking very pale. "Weel she be able tae hae more bairns?"

"Aye, that she weel, but we hae tae watch her. She'll hae a high fever for awhile until the poison gea's oot o' her body. Noo leave sae that Bonnie and I can finish here."

The family left and went into the chapel to pray. Kimberly met them at the door of the chapel. "Gran'faither, weel she live?"

"Aye, me darlin', that she weel."

Hugging one another, "Where is Monica, Kimberly?" asked Mary Kate.

"Weel she was here; bet she went ootside tae pray. I'll ga and find her," Kimberly said, going out the chapel door.

Finding Monica, "Hinny, Deirdre weel be fine, but it weel take a long, long time."

Grandfather Kirk came out just at that time. Monica looked up into his face. "Och! Gran'faither, what is ga'in' tae happen noo 'atween Deirdre and Tommy? They luve one another sae much."

Grandfather put his arms around Monica and she around his neck, then started to cry hard. "Luve, I dinnae knoo, but we need tae gea word tae yer Da."

Monica was about to answer when they heard a loud scream that put chills up their backs. They all ran up the stairs then into the room where Deirdre still lay on the table. "Maggie, what's wrong?" asked Mary Kate.

"She came tae as Bonnie and I were talkin' aboot the wee bairn. Her fever is verra high. If we dunnae gea it doon, we'll alsae lose her." Maggie spoke as she put her hands in water that had herbs in it.

"Nay, nay, och... She'll no' be doin' that. Let me hae her. I'll take her back tae her bedchamber."

Grandfather Kirk carried her up the stairs, holding her like he did when she was a "wee bairn," with tears in his eyes. "Ma little luve, ye'll gea weel and then we'll ga sailin' like we used tae."

Lying Deirdre down on the bed, he turned, looking at his daughters, Ellen and Mary Kate. He stood up and then ran downstairs, bellowing like a mad bull, shouting for his men to get ready to set sail for Scotland.

Chapter 17

A few weeks later, Laird John MacDarroch saw his father-in-law, Chief Kirk, coming through the gate at high speed. Hearing a loud shout, "John, get packed to leave," it made John jump.

"Kirk, what are you shouting about?" He asked, coming out of the library on a run. Kirk told him about what happened to Deirdre. "My God, Kirk, will she live?"

"Not good when I left, John. We must go to Tommy and explain to him what happened was not Deirdre's fault."

"Kirk, we tried. But as you know, he almost died, and is still not well."

"You're right. The lassies told me the story. I'm so worried about Deirdre," he said, running his hands through his hair and beard. "You see, John, she lost their baby and he needs to know that."

"You're right. The lad should know about this." Turning, he left the room shouting, "Men, we must ride." Then, after giving orders to the household where they were going, he ran into William and told him what happening. "You take care of things for my bother. We are bringing her home." With tears running down his face, William gave the war cry, "Darroch", as he ran into Sea Oaks.

As they rode up to the MacDonald's, they heard a loud scream, "Run, Kitten, run!" It sounded like the words of a man that had lost his reason for living.

When they entered the library, they saw Tommy sitting in a chair near the fire, all bundled up in a fur coverlet. Just staring into the fire, he cried to himself.

With Kirk and Tommy's brother behind him, John knelt down in front of him. "Tommy, my lad, Deirdre is alive, but very sick. She needs you, lad. She lost your baby and could die." He laid his hand on Tommy's arm, but did not get a reply from him.

He only said, "Look out, Kitten, God, take care of her, she is my life."

Hugh spoke in a soft voice, "Laird John, he has been this way ever since he came to and we told him she was very ill. It's like he doesn't want to live."

Back in Norway, Deirdre stayed in bed with a very high fever. Her family was all around her, bathing her body with snow to try and bring it the fever down.

In Deirdre's feverish state, she called Tommy's name over and over again. When she quieted down, her family left to go to the great hall and get a bite to eat.

Georgeanna and Marie stayed with her. They were sitting in a couple of chairs near the fire doing needlework, when all of a sudden, a great light filled the room. Georgeanna and Marie sat very still, while they watched and listened.

Deirdre sat straight up in bed, and looked directly ahead into the light. Her grandmother was there in the mist, "My darling child, you'll not die. It's not your time yet." The voice in the mist repeated itself, "Love, it's not your time. You must go back to the twentieth century and make your closing as well as your sisters; also the MacDonald lads who came before you.

This is what you must do when you are strong enough. You must go to the Highlands and stay for a long while. There your strength will come back to you. It will return as well as the warrior you are. When you come back you will be stronger than ever.

Before the light went out, Deirdre heard, "Send Glen MacDonald and his family to the new world. That is where they will be safe from the king and Campbells who wish to kill them. Bless you, little love." Then all went dark in the bedchamber.

All through the night, she rolled and tossed, talking in her sleep; but by morning, her fever had broken. Georgeanna left, with tears in her eyes, to let all of them know that Deirdre's fever had broken. Marie stayed in the bedchamber to look after her.

Cheers went up and everyone was in a joyous mood. Mary Kate came up with a tray of dark bread and beef broth and a large cup of hot mead.

Georgeanna went over to the bed. "You had me so frightened."

Georgeanna, you need not ever worry. You'll always be safe and warm with us, no one will harm you. You'll have a home with my family as long as you live."

"Oh... it's not that, My Lady. It was when your grandmother came to you when you were so sick."

"I must do all of what she said I must do."

Patting Deirdre's arm, she said, "That I know, you will, My Lady."

"Georgeanna... we'll be going back to Scotland and the Highlands as soon as I'm able to travel."

"I know, My Lady, but right now you must get some sleep," covering her with a nice white fox cover, she fell asleep. It was then that Marie helped her Ladyship straighten up the bedchamber.

Everyone had gathered in the great hall to rejoice that Deirdre was out of danger. They all felt a cold breeze come through the great door. Mary Kate looked up, and crying, she ran over to her husband, "John, my dear."

"How is she, love?" he asked with tears running down his cheeks.

Mary Kate wiped the tears away from her husband's eyes. "She is going to be fine."

Monica saw Richard, and gave him a big hug. "Love, thank heaven you're here. Where is Tommy?"

"Monica, love, he was not able to travel"

"But, why? Does he not love her anymore?"

"Love, look at me." Taking her face in his hands, he said, "He still is very ill. Yes, he loves her, but feels it was his fault."

"Hugh, darling, what's going on?" Kimberly asked, holding out her arms to him.

"Kimberly, darling." Hugh came to her, kissed and hugged her like he would not let her go. He looked into her bright green eyes. "Love, we don't know what to do about Tommy. When we left, no one could get him to eat or drink anything. Funny though, we don't know how he got it, but he was holding the medal she gave him when he was but fifteen summers. Your Grandfather told him she had lost their baby, I'm sure he heard him, because there were tears running down his face."

Richard came over holding Monica around the waist, and said, "We all believe that he feels like it was his fault."

"Yes, Richard, it's like he feels guilty for asking her to meet him. But those two have always loved more deeply all their whole life than anyone I have ever known." Hugh spoke with a very sad look on his face.

"That's what I just said, brother."

John got red in his face, "He could have gotten off his ass and saved her from Patrick."

"No, John, he couldn't, for he was badly wounded himself, remember? But you all could have saved our lassie. You sat and argued among yourselves about who was to start first. Not any man here can blame anyone but your own self. As for Tommy, he pointed the way for us to follow."

Mary Kate left the main hall. Everyone looked at her as she left, with their mouths open.

"Mother is right," the lassies said, as they turned and looked at all the men in the hall. Everyone had their heads bowed. "All of you, we feel shame for you." Kimberly left crying right behind Monica. When Hugh stepped out to grab her arm, she shook it off.

As the days passed, Deirdre became stronger, with help of everyone, including Marie, Georgeanna's maid. The stronger she got, the more she began to travel back in her mind.   She remembered what her grandmother had said. She made plans to go into the Highlands, then back to the twentieth century.

A very strange feeling came over her. It was like a dream, or maybe a flashback, of how her sisters, along with her, went into the twentieth century years ago. Smiling to herself, it all came back to her now. Yes, she and Tommy had just gotten married and her sisters had gotten betrothed to the MacDonald brothers, Kimberly to Hugh and Monica to Richard, the younger. Tommy or Thomas Edward, the older, would be Laird of the Clan when his father Laird Glen MacDonald retired or stepped down.

Deirdre and her sisters grew up knowing about the Black Fog, and that many of their kin had vanished from sight and had never been heard from again. That is what had happened to her and her sisters, Great-grandfather and his family; as told to them a long time ago by their father, Laird John MacDarroch.

It was the time of the Solar Moon that she and Tommy had gotten married and they were all celebrating their marriage on the cliff overlooking the sea. All at once, the Black Fog had engulfed them all as they were hugging each other. They were pulled apart from the laddies, but held on to one another. Each group was taken and passed through time into the twentieth century.

I'll never forget that day, she was thinking to herself. *That was the day they were thrown on to the MacDarroch Mountain in Marshall, N.C., all frightened and cold and very wet. There he was. It was like he knew they were coming.*

"Well now, lassies don't be frightened. I'm your Great-grandfather Oliver. The Black Fog got you. Am I right?"

They all three just looked at him. They were hungry, and frightened, and their clothes were rags, but somehow they knew that they were safe. Looking at each other, they shook their heads yes. They looked at one another with an expression on their faces of shock, not knowing where they were or even how they really got there. Deirdre thought to herself, *Was it really the BLACK FOG that they had always heard about?*

Smiling to herself, Deirdre remembered how Great-grandfather Oliver trained her and her sisters to ride and fight bareback on the horses — even joust. Deirdre, at that moment, wiped the tears away from her eyes. She missed the old dear. *The mountain, wonder how it is. Wonder if we will ever see him again. Lord, how I miss him and all his wisdom of the ages. The papers that we found in the old clock told us what to do.*

With a mystified look on her face, Deirdre looked down at her hands which were clinched together very tightly. She thought of the letters from him telling them about being seers and how they knew when things were wrong. How special, if he knew about the thing that I have been through with Patrick Campbell. She looked down at the ring of heavy gold on her finger. The setting held an oval-shaped blue-green stone surrounded by small pearls. The image of a heather bouquet had been painstakingly carved into the stone. Tommy had put it there and it had never been off her finger and never would.

Smiling as she slid down under the fur covers, she immediately fell asleep. Deirdre drifted off into a dream. There was the living room with its polished log walls and hardwood floors. She and her sisters were setting on large cushions in front of the very large stone fireplace and how she and her sister reminisced about their past and coming back home to Jura. The old home in Marshall had been in the family for three centuries before they came back.

They were astonished greatly to find out how many generations the house, land and large mountain behind the house had been rerecorded. *Wonder how it will all look when we go back from this time? The land and all, was left to them by one of their ancestors. I just can't remember his name, right now. I remember someone talking about it being handed down from Great-great-great-grandfather Donal to Great-great-grandfather Oliver, then to his son Grandfather George to Deirdre, Kimberly and Monica. Then when they had children, it would be handed down to them.*

Smiling in her sleep, she could see the mist rising in the corner where Great-grandfather sat in his rocking chair. *They both are still there guarding all that is ours with his Indian Chiefs. You old darling, you trained us right and things will be fine. One day we'll all be together.*

Dreaming that Great-grandfather Oliver took them by their hands and led them down mountain, a little afraid to really say anything, she thought, *You'll be safe now and soon you'll be warm and have supper. My sons are, George, Jim and Bryan, oh yes; I have one lassie, Julia. She is a good cook, she'll look after you.*

After resting for about two days, Deirdre heard the door open and Mary Kate came rushing in with Aunt Ellen, Monica and Kimberly and Georgeanna behind her. Marie stood up, looking at their eyes, which were shinning, for they had been waiting for this day.

"Now, what do we have here?" asked Marie. When the door opened, Grandfather's men came in with box after box. Their arms were loaded down with boxes and chests which they sat down in front of Deirdre.

Deirdre got out of bed and put her robe on, then smiling, said, "Everyone, open them up."

As they opened the boxes, their eyes got very big. Oooh and ah were the sighs as they saw the bright silks, lace, and thread; everything to make great gowns. Even Mary Kate and

Auntie Ellen, Marie and Georgeanna were like little lassies at Christmas time. It made Deirdre's heart sing.

"Oh!!! My," Kimberly said with a big smile. "Which is mine?"

As Georgeanna and Annie looked at the fine fabrics and sighed, Deirdre said, "We are going to make the most elegant grown ever! Georgeanna, you and Marie will have one too. We'll all have beautiful gowns when I come back from the Highlands and then take another trip. We'll have a great ball, which all of Scotland will talk about for years to come."

Now sister, back up a bit. Highlands, yes, but what about the other trip?" asked Monica.

Kimberly looked Deirdre straight in the eye, "No, no. Deirdre, NO ! ! Please say it's not what I'm thinking about?"

"No, Kimberly."

"Then what are you talking about?" asked Mary Kate.

"Lady Mary Kate, I think I know what this is about."

"How could you know, Georgeanna?" Deirdre asked.

"Lady Deirdre, when you were so ill, I to saw the light and the spirit of your grandmother. I heard what she told you to do. My dear, remember it was when I told you about seeing her."

"I, too, saw my mother. She came to me also. I was just waiting for you to come and tell me."

"Oh, Mother, so you know where we have to go?" Kimberly asked with tears in her eyes.

"Yes, I do. You have nothing to fear," Mary Kate answered.

"But Father and Grandfather Godshire? Deirdre asked.

"Don't worry about them, Deirdre, I'll explain after." Mary Kate then bowed her head so the tears would not show and started to sew.

After a brief silence, Deirdre said, "Alright. Let's get to work on the gowns. But first I think I should dress."

"That would be a good thing," smiled Monica.

Georgeanna and Marie started getting everything out of the boxes. The colors were so bright and soft. Just as everyone was looking at all the wonderful fabric, the door opened. There, in the door was Grandfather with another large chest.

"This one is for you, my fighting warrior." He put down the other chest in front of Deirdre. As she opened it, everyone's mouths opened wide as they saw the most beautiful silk of gold and green.

Deirdre looked up into the face of her grandfather. There were tears in his eyes and running down his face. He looked down at her with all the love that heaven would allow. Deirdre got up off her knees and went to him, lifted her arms, put them around his neck and kissed the tears away.

She remembered that ever since she was born, he had carried her, even when she started to walk. She would follow him everywhere he would go. He taught her how to defend herself, use a sword like the great warrior he said that she would be one day. He taught her how to hunt, and make clothes from the skins. Oh! Yes, she really loved her grandfather.

When Deirdre was small, her father, head of the clan, turned her training over to Grandfather and Mother, as well as her sisters. But her father taught her what to do when she would take over the clan and what they needed.

"With your ginger hair and your golden cat eyes, you'll, make a beautiful bride for the second time when you and Tommy renew your vows."

"I don't know if there will be a wedding, for Tommy is still very ill. But we will see, my darling, we'll see. But with what Patrick had done to me, Tommy may change his mind." Looking up at this sweet, wonderful grandfather, Deirdre said, "I'll wear it to another special day, Grandfather. But don't you worry, love, I'll wear it."

Deirdre saw her grandfather turn and walk slowly out the door. She sat back down and started sewing again, looking at her sweet sisters under her lowered eyes. Smiling to herself, she could just hear their questions unasked. "How does she know that Tommy won't be up to the wedding? We know he loves her."

Monica got up and danced over to where her cloak was, then shipped out of the cabin in hopes she would run into Richard. *Who does she think she was fooling?* Deirdre smiled, thinking to herself.

Deirdre saw her mother smile to herself. Mary Kate lifted her head, looking at Kimberly, taking her time sewing the beautiful green silk into a gown. They all knew that she would look beautiful in a green silk gown, with her green eyes and long blonde hair.

"Kimberly, is Hugh on deck?"

"I don't know, Mother."

"Alright, I know you wish to speak with Deirdre alone." She smiled at her mother and Deirdre as she put her cloak on, then slipped out and up on deck she went.

"My darling Deirdre, may I ask you a question?"

"But of course, Mother, ask me anything."

"How do you know Tommy doesn't love you? And how do you know he'll not be able to wed you?"

"First of all, I know Tommy. The idea of another man touching me, let alone a Campbell trying to take me, even have me in his bed naked while he looked upon me, would make him raving mad."

"But, he could change!!"

"My dear Mother, not Tommy." I know now his love has always been very deep. But his jealously is something else again. I could forgive him anything, but when he finds out Patrick made me lose our baby, I don't know how I'll tell him or if he'll ever listen or forgive me."

"My love, I see what you mean, but his actions... he has a bad temper, but it wasn't your fault. I fear one day life will deal him a hard blow. He will not know what to do."

"I feel the same way. He is always in my prayers. But, Mother, is something else that is brothering you?"

"Deirdre," looking at Georgeanna and Marie she said, "Would you please leave us for a moment?"

"Yes, My Lady," they replied, smiling at each other as they went out the door of the cabin.

"Daughter, have you seen how my father looks at Georgeanna?"

"Yes, I have, with great love in his eyes."

"No, Deirdre. It can't be. He is too old."

"Too old? Oh!! Mother, he is just sixty-five summers and that's not old. Georgeanna is the same age Grandmother would have been around sixty summers.

"Do you really think?"

"I hope so; they need each other so bad."

"Yes, they do." Just then, Mary Kate started to giggle. "Let's finish her dress so it will be a surprise."

"Mother, will you give them your blessing? Oh! How will Aunt Ellen take this?" asked Deirdre.

"With open arms," Mary Kate said as she came over and they hugged one another.

While on deck, Kimberly found Hugh. With their arms around one another, they walked the deck coming up on Monica and Richard.

"Hugh, Deirdre said something back in the cabin that bothers Monica and me."

"What is it, my darling?" Hugh asked.

"That she and Tommy will never marry. Do you and Richard feel that's true?"

"If Tommy doesn't come completely out of these black-outs and moods he is in, I would say so."

"Come on, Hugh, Tommy had gone through a lot. And another thing, the thought of Patrick even looking at Deirdre, let along touching her, would drive him mad," Richard stated.

"He's gone through a lot, but how about Deirdre? Raped, beaten, losing their baby and then almost dying herself. Was that not something?" Hugh stated with anger in his voice.

"You must remember, Tommy was almost killed, too; he feels he killed Deirdre. That was not his fault that this happened. He is on a guilt trip," remarked Richard, with a look toward Hugh as if he could just sock him in the jaw.

"We know. How is Deirdre taking all of this?" asked Hugh, looking at the girls.

"Kimberly can tell you better than I. What do ye mean a guilt trip?" asked Monica with tears in her eyes and her throat seeming to close up.

"When we get home, she will ready herself to go up into the Highlands to build up her strength and prepare for the long journey back."

"BACK where? My God, Kimberly not from where we all came?" asked Monica.

"I'm afraid so. It's what she has to do.   Back at Grandfather's she had a vision. Grandmother came to her and she must go back to a closing of the twentieth century. We all must do that. It will be the biggest test of all and will prove our love for one another."

"Do you mean Tommy, Hugh, and I will have to go the also?"

"Yes," answered Kimberly.

"What about Tommy's guilt trip?   I'm asking again, please?" Monica asked, getting red in the face.

Hugh ran his hand through his hair, and looked at Richard. Both of them smiled and knew their love was strong enough to endure anything, but Tommy was the big QUESTION.

"Sorry, love, he blames himself because he asked Deirdre to meet him, and feels it's his fault," answered Richard.

"But it wasn't, it was both of them just loving each other too much," stated Monica as she put her arms around Richard.

Chapter 18

No one on board was watching Grandfather and Georgeanna as they walked around and talked about when they first met, and fell in love with one another.

"Remember, lass, when I was a young man sailing up and down the Scottish coast raiding the villages, one night I came into your village looking for food for my men, but most of all for fresh water. I looked up and saw your castle overlooking the small village. I thought to myself, *Wonder what is up there.*

They were standing on the bow of the ship. "Georgeanna, love, you still have a body on you like I have never seen. How could I ever forget you, with your deep dark red hair, still long and silky to the touch? Your eyes bright and dark as midnight blue. Your full breast that heaved up and down when you got a little bit excited, like now. Your waist so small, I could put my one hand around it. Remember when I caught you running across the field and pulled you into my arms. You said they felt like steel bonds around you."

Georgeanna had looked into his sea-green eyes and his long blond hair and fainted, "You know what I thought, Kirk, my darling."

Smiling, he answered, "I said to myself, 'what will I do now,' but you came to while I still held you."

"I was a bold one, remember? I put my arms around your neck, like this and kissed you on the mouth just like this." She did it again.

"I almost dropped you and then I asked, "Now, My Lady, why did you do that?"

"Remember, I told you that you had a kissable mouth, and I would like to kiss you again.

"I remember, but as you were talking, I was looking at your lips also, then I wondered what the rest of your body would feel like, let alone what it would taste like."

"Well!! So, was that was what you thinking, my darling?" asked Georgeanna.

"Yes, it was, My Lady. I would like to kiss those lovely lips of yours." Putting his arms around her, he kissed her as if it were the last time. His mouth came down on Georgeanna's; his tongue opened her mouth to him like a rosebud opening up to the morning dew. A moan came from both of them. His hand began to roam.

"No, please don't," Georgeanna pleaded with a smile.

"That's what you said the last time," Kirk stated. Smiling, he continued remembering, "My name is Kirk, and I won't hurt you. I'll be very gentle with you, dear Lady. You started this; didn't you know where this might lead? And why me? Why not one of my men?"

"You remember what I said? You had raided my village more than once. You never killed anyone, but just took food and water. I just wanted to see for myself what kind of man you were. And a handsome man you were and are, Kirk, the Viking of the sea," Georgeanna said, smiling as the words brought back memories. Memories that seemed so real, it could have been yesterday. . .

"And how do you know, lovely lass?"

"I have seen you bathe in the cold stream," she answered with a giggle.

"Oh! I see." With a smile, he put his arms around her, and then lifted her up in his arms. He carried her to the stream, laid her down on the soft moss and began to kiss her sweet mouth. Georgeanna started to respond to his kisses. Kissing her eyes, nibbling her ears, as well as her neck, he took his hand and cupped her breast. He worked his tongue down to her stomach, then back up, sucking on one breast, then the other.

Georgeanna was so high, she felt as though she was in the heavens. Then she felt his finger enter her soft red vee, between her thighs; she had never known such joy. As he withdrew his finger, he placed his lips there and blew on her. She thought she would die right then and there. All of a sudden, she felt his hard rod of steel as he began to insert it. Kirk spoke, "Honey, it will hurt, but just for a little while. It will be easy."

"What?"

Kirk repeated himself. He held off and with a thrust, he entered her. With tears in her eyes, she moaned under his mouth. But like he said, it just hurt for a little while. Their bodies blended together; they were in total ecstasy. . . .

"What joy, Kirk, my Viking. Thank you for being the one who took me to the greatest joy I have ever known."

Looking at her in the moonlight with tears in his eyes, he asked, "You remember, Georgeanna?"

"That I do," she said as she put her head on Kirk's shoulder. "Do you remember smiling at me, Kirk? You then rolled off onto the ground beside me. You got up on your elbow, looked down at me smiling and said, 'I must see your father, to ask for your hand.' "

"Then, if you recall, I said, 'No, my love. This must be our secret.' You looked so sad when you asked 'Why? I wish to marry you; I want you with me forever.' "

Grandfather Kirk replied to Georgeanna, "I recall, you answered me, but not with the words I wanted to hear."

"I had to tell you the truth. I told you it was because I had to marry the one man I hated. And that you were my love, and I would never forget you. I begged you to go and never say anything. I had fallen in love with you, but I had to send you away, for my father would have killed you then and there. I hoped I would see you again one day!"

"Then we heard the horses and soldiers, and I got up, put my clothes on and left."

"I slipped into the stream and was swimming when I saw my father and his men coming.

"He asked me, 'Isn't the water too cold for a swim?'

"And I answered, 'No Father, it just fine.' I looked around to make sure you were gone, I could then breathe easier."

"But did he say anything else?"

Georgeanna laid her head on his shoulder, then spoke, "I haven't told you, Kirk, what else he said. He always spoke in an overbearing way, 'You seem happy, even with the treat of the Vikings so near.'

"I knew you and your men would protect me. I had answered him with a big smile on my face."

"I bet he got mad at you, love, with the smile you gave him."

"Yes, he did, but he said, 'Huh!!!'

"He asked me why I had such big a smile on my face. I said, 'Why!! You are running the Vikings from our shores, Father.'"

"Of course, my Darling."

They stood there with their arms around each other, with longing in their eyes. Georgeanna spoke softly, "You know, love, I often wondered if I would ever see you again. I felt in my heart we would someday meet, but was never sure."

After they talked about the early years, when they had met and fallen in love, they stood by the railing, holding each other. A voice came through the mist. "Captain Kirk, we are entering Scottish waters."

"Thank you, Robert." Kirk turned to Georgeanna with a smile and love in his eyes; he grabbed her up by her waist and swung her around. He held her over his head and asked, "Love, will you marry me?

"Oh!! Yes, yes. I have waited for so long, my darling."

Grandfather Kirk slid her down his body, kissing her eyes, nose, and mouth until they both were breathless.

Little did they know that Monica, Kimberly, Hugh and Richard had overheard the lovers. They smiled while they watched the lovers looking at each other with so much love on their faces.

Monica went down to the cabin; she just had to tell all what she had seen and heard. Also, that they were in Scottish waters, almost to Jura and Islay. Everyone needed to start getting packed.

Everyone had such a big smile on their faces when Georgeanna came in and saw that her gown was finished. She thanked them all, with tears in her eyes.

"You are welcome. Shall I call you Mother?" asked Mary Kate.

With a look of surprise, "You all know?" Georgeanna asked.

"Yes, my dear. We know and are so happy for both of you, but please, may I go and talk with my grandfather?" asked Deirdre, as she hugged Georgeanna and gave her a kiss on the cheek.

"My dear child, of course."

Deirdre left to go on deck. She saw him at the helm, "Grandfather, may I speak with you, please?"

"Peter, take the helm."

"Aye, aye, Captain," Peter replied.

Talking Deirdre by the arm, Grandfather led her to the back of the ship where they could talk in private. Deirdre put her arms around him and kissed his cheek.

"Now, what was that for?" Grandfather asked.

"Oh... For a lot of things, the love you have shown me all these years, how to protect myself in a fight, how to become a great warrior and a great leader of my people one day."

"So, that's it. But, love, there is one thing I couldn't protect you from and that is a broken heart," Grandfather said with his head bowed.

"Grandfather, no one can do that, but ones own self. Look how all these years you have looked for Georgeanna?"

"What are you saying, lass?"

With a big smile on her face, Deirdre looked into his eyes and saw the truth there. "Dear heart, you know what I'm saying. We all know and are very happy for you."

"What does Mary Kate say about it?"

"She asked Georgeanna if she could call her Mother."

"She what?"

"You heard me."

"Oh!! My dear, I'm the happiest man in the world." Grandfather grabbed Deirdre and they danced on deck. His men looked at them like they had gone mad.

"What's going on here?" Grandfather and Deirdre stopped dead still. There stood John MacDarroch, smiling at them. He had come up on deck after a long bout of sea sickness. "For someone who is Captain of his own fleet of ships, you get seasick a lot. Poor darling." Deidre teased.

"John, old lad, my son, the children have made me very happy."

"Well, that's nice, but what about?"   John looked bewildered.

"Please, Grandfather. May I tell him?" Deirdre asked.

"Yes, dear."

"Well, Father, Grandfather and Georgeanna have known each other for a long time, many years before Grandmother.

Still looking bewildered, he mumbled, "That's nice."

"Oh!! Love."   John turned to see his Mary Kate coming toward him with her arms open.

Smiling, John ran over, grabbed his wife with his hands around her waist, and then lifted her up high into the air. As he lifted her, he smiled real big. He let her body slide down his body and then gave her a long hard kiss.

"John, no love, everyone is watching."

"Let them look. No one could be happier than I am at this very moment."

"Well now, son, I wouldn't say that," Grandfather looked at Georgeanna, smiling.

"What are you saying, Kirk?"

Georgeanna walked over to Grandfather and they put their arms around each other. They both just looked at John, smiling.

"You don't mean?"

"Yes, son. You see, we have loved one another for many years, but lost each other. Now that I have found her, she will not get away again. She'll be my wife."

"Well, I'll be," was all John could say, with his mouth wide open, and everyone laughing and cheering.

Everyone was dancing and celebrating over the good news. Deirdre went to the front of the wheel and looked far out to sea.

"Are you alright, Lady Deirdre?" the young man standing at the wheel asked.

"Yes, thank you. It's just that I felt like being alone for awhile."

"I understand, My Lady." He smiled, and went back to the wheel.

Deirdre stood looking out to sea. With everyone so happy, tears filled her eyes. Yes, she was thrilled for everyone, but she was also very sad in her heart. Deirdre knew what was ahead of her. She had to get stronger again to be the best warrior, so that one day she would be a great leader of her clan. It would take a great deal of courage getting her strength back, and not knowing if she would ever have Tommy in her life again or not.

Deirdre, not wanting to spoil things for the others, turned and went back to the dance, smiling. Everyone had worn themselves out and started going to their cabins. Deirdre said, "Goodnight," and went to the cabin that she shared with her sisters.

Georgeanna and Marie came running in to help her undress and get ready for bed. "No, no, Grandmother, go to Grandfather. No, go now."

"My dear, please, let me help."

"No, dear Grandmother, Georgeanna." Deirdre said it with so much love in her voice that Georgeanna let her tears roll down her face.

"Now, go please. Take Marie with you."

"Thank you. I'm praying for you." Georgeanna took Marie by the hand and left the cabin.

Monica, and Kimberly, looked around as they came into the cabin. Together they said, "How are we going to get ready for bed?"

"By helping one another," Deirdre answered.

"Sure, Deirdre, we could do that," Monica said, with her eyes very large.

They then helped each other get ready for bed. They were all very tired and were thinking about tomorrow.

Kimberly and Monica lay in the dark thinking of the day's events – of what had happened. They heard a soft crying coming from Deirdre's side of the room. "Deirdre, honey, are you alright?"

"Yes, Kimberly. I'm so overcome with happiness for everyone that it just spills over."

"I know, honey. You still love Tommy and miss him so," stated Monica.

"You are so right, Monica. I'll never stop loving him." It was almost dawn when she drifted off to sleep with tears stains on her face.

"Hurry up, sleepy head. We'll be landing in an hour. Deirdre, honey, wake up." Kimberly was trying to shake her awake.

"What? Where are we?" Deirdre asked, trying to open her eyes.

"Almost home, darling," answered Monica.

"Oh... my, I had best hurry." Jumping up, she splashed cold water on her face. She put on her deep green wool dress with red fox fur trim on the bottom and around her dress as well as on her cloak. She wore her hair loose, and as Deirdre looked down she could see that she was a lot thinner and paler than before. She just shook her head at how her clothes fit so loosely. *That will change soon; when I get home and eat some of Grace's cooking,* she thought, smiling to herself.

Deirdre could hear everyone up on deck greeting folks on shore, welcoming her sisters, father, and mother home. All at once, everyone called her name. She went up on deck smiling, and everyone made a path for her to walk up to the railing. Deirdre stood smiling, as great cheers of WELCOME HOME, MY LAIRD, rose from the crowd.

Deirdre raised her hand for them to quiet down. "My family and friends, I have a great announcement to make. My Grandfather Kirk and Georgeanna are getting married. I know she was with Robert Campbell, but it was never approved by the Church."

With that, cheers and shouts of joy rose from the crowd. Kimberly and Monica with Hugh and Richard came next and started to depart, but were stopped by shouts and cheers from the crowd calling for Laird Deirdre. Deirdre started down the gangplank with the rest of the family behind.

Seeing Thunder waiting for her, Deirdre went up to put her arms around his huge neck when her hood fell back. As she turned to pull it back up, she felt eyes on her. She looked into the crowd and saw a man in a black cloak with the hood pulled over his face, apparently trying to hide. He was on the outskirts of the crowd. It was as if he did not want to be seen.

Deirdre got up on Thunder. As he pranced, she held her head up high, with her hair blowing around her face.

Tommy watched Deirdre. She looked paler and thinner; but to him, she was still the most beautiful woman in the world. How his heart ached for her. Tommy thought to himself, *How can I ever face the only woman on God's green earth I have ever loved or will ever love, after what I did to her.* His head bowed low as he rode away.

The moon was very bright that night. Much brighter than it had been in many nights. She could see everywhere. "Old moon above, are you trying to tell me something?" She asked to herself, out loud.

Out of the darkness came a horse with a dark rider, she felt his hand cover her mouth. He said in a muffled voice, "Don't scream and you won't get hurt."

Deirdre tried to place the voice, but she could not.

"Shake you head, yes or no. Will you be quite?"

Deirdre nodded, yes.

"That's good, now just set here and listen."

Deirdre asked in a whisper, "Could I go over and sit by the fire?"

He answered, "Yes."

Deirdre went to the fire, picking up her robe as she went. The light from the fire shadowed her long legs and the rest of her body through her gown.

Oh, my God, what you do to me, was the thought that ran through Tommy's head.

"What do you feel for this man of yours?" he asked.

"I have no man." was her answer."

"Don't tell me that, I know you do. Where is the baby you had of his?"

Deirdre had a deep feeling that this was Tommy, so she asked, "I will tell you the whole story, if you wish to hear?"

"I don't wish to hear."

"But, you are the one who asked, so I shall tell you. Are you afraid to hear the truth?"

"No, I'm not afraid of anything."

So she settled in her chair by the fire and looked as if it happened years ago, instead of a few months. "You see, I had a man, whom I loved very much. It was after I was made to be next in line to be Laird, one day when and if my father stepped down. We were very much in love, he and I. He was my first, you see. It seemed we just couldn't get enough of one another. But he was a very jealous man, always had been, ever sense we were children. He told me I couldn't have a life without him. And, it's true, I can't. But on the night that we went to sign papers, he whispered to me to meet him in the glen, a special place for us. That's when Patrick Campbell came from out of the woods with his men. I would have tried to fight him off, but I had no weapon."

"Tommy tried to hold them off, but one of the heathens stabbed him in the stomach. Then another one clubbed him in the head so bad it left him unconscious. That's how I was captured."

Deirdre sat back and looked at the dark man. He asked, "Would you please continue?"

"I was taken to the Campbells' stronghold, tied and gagged, and was taken up to a tower where Patrick thought no one could hear me. He knocked me out. When I came to, there was an iron collar around my neck, arms and legs, and I was also naked. I could see this in a long mirror that had been placed in front of me. I was also chained to the wall. I had one eye closed shut from when he had hit me. Shall I continue?"

With Tommy's hands balled up into a fist and through gritted teeth, he answered, "Please do."

"Patrick had his men put a bed in the room. He still had me chained to the wall, as well as the bed. I told him he wouldn't be the first, my husband, Tommy, was. Also, that Tommy was a better man in all things than he was or ever could be. Patrick stayed drunk, beat me, starved me, and raped me as well as a drunken pig could. His mother, Georgeanna found me. She and her maid, Marie, treated my wounds, set my arm that had been broken, and fed me. Patrick's father gave his orders to clean things up — the room, himself and also me. Patrick was really mad at his father. He went to the door, and came back and hit me again, which closed the other eye and opened up the cut on the first one. Patrick was so drunk that he fell down the steps and broke his neck, and he died on those steps. Georgeanna and Marie rescued me and took me to a waiting ship. I was beaten so that I lost Tommy's and my baby, I almost died. So that's the end of the story, but my Tommy, I'll always love him."

With a choked voice, the dark man said, "I'm sorry, but do you feel better now?" Tommy wanted so to take her in his arms. He needed to be held, and his sorrow was just as great as hers; his baby was lost. *God, what she must have gone through and I wasn't there to help her! Love, please forgive me,* he said to himself.

"Sir, please tell me. Who are you?"

"I can't say; I don't know who I am." The man in black left, and disappeared into the dawn.

Deirdre watched him leave. "Oh, my Tommy, I love you so. I know you hurt for our baby. It wasn't your fault."

Chapter 19

Two weeks after Deirdre returned home, the whole clan got ready for Grandfather Kirk's and Georgeanna's wedding.

Everyone was in such a festive mood; there was singing from all the servants. They worked so hard on getting the castle in shinning order, with torches, greenery from the trees, and large white candles. A very large tree in the corner of the great room was decorated with bright candles and bows. The huge doors were taken down between the rooms so all the clan could fit in and dance.

You could smell the wonderful food, bread, sweets, and meats of all kinds coming from the kitchen. The smokehouse out back held the tempting smoked salmon until ready to eat.

The band at the far end of the room was getting in tune as were the dancers. All the clans started to arrive, and were excited about the wedding. The ladies were dressed in their finest silk dresses, beautiful jewelry, and fur cloaks, their hair beautifully done. It was getting very cold, although it was just late autumn. Everyone was enjoying themselves while preparing for the wedding to begin.

Monica was dressed in her bright green gown, trimmed in white fox fur. Her black hair was up, with curls hanging down, adorned with gold and green ribbons.

Kimberly wore her deep royal blue gown with the white ermine trim. She had her long blonde hair braided with royal blue ribbon and wrapped on top of her head like a crown. Wispy curls hung down around her face.

Deirdre and Mary Kate were helping Georgeanna get dressed. Mary Kate was already in her bright red velvet, with the green tartan, and its large brooch of deep emeralds and pearls. Aunt Ellen was in her bright pink velvet gown. Everyone looked so grand. "Deirdre love, you must get ready. Go now, we'll finish here."

"Alright, Aunt Ellen." Deirdre ran over and kissed Georgeanna as she left the room. When she got to her bedchamber, she stopped short as she saw it there on the bed. It was the white dress with the gold threads. "Maude, love," she called out.

"Yes, darling," Maude answered, as she came through the door with all the bath oils, brushes, and herbs. "Let's get your bath, first. What in the world are you wanting me for, darling?"

"Maude, I'll not wear the white one. I'll be wearing the gold with gold lace and green leaves, and the soft green leather shoes."

"Bu-bu-but, your Grandfather wants you to wear it," Maude said as she looked at Deirdre with a sad look on her face.

"That one is for the ball later," Deirdre replied.

"Love, whatever you say." Maude turned and left the room, shaking her head.

"Besides, I told Grandfather I would wear the gold one for his wedding."

While trying to get her bath, someone knocked on the door. "Oh... come in," Deirdre said in a sharp tone. Kimberly and Monica rushed into the room.

"Well, aren't we the snappy one," remarked Monica.

"I'm trying so hard to get ready, and you two aren't helping one bit."

"But, there is something we need to tell you and tell you now!" said Kimberly.

"OK, what is it, get it out?"

"Tommy is here; he looks like death."

"Tommy! Kimberly, honey, don't worry. It's alright, I will handle it."

"But what if he wants to dance?" asked Monica.

"Well, Monica, I'll dance," she came back, getting out of the tub and putting on her robe. "Sisters, come and sit here beside me, here on the bed. I must tell you both something," she said, patting the bed.

The girls went over, huddling together, one on each side of her. She continued, "One night after we had just gotten home, I had a male visitor, all in black with a hooded cloak. I didn't see his face and his voice was muffled."

"But, did you know him?" Monica wanted to know in a hurry. You could tell it in her voice from the sound of eagerness.

"No."

"What did he want?" asked Kimberly.

"To know what had happened to me. I felt, sisters, it was my Tommy. I told him the whole story."

"All of it!!!?" asked Monica with eyes so large.

"Yes, Monica, all of it."

"Oh, boy. I bet he felt really bad and sad after he left," remarked Kimberly.

"Kimberly, can you not just look at him and see what my Tommy is going through?"

"Yes, but it serves him right," Monica remarked.

"Why, Monica? It was as much my fault as it was his. Now, both of you leave so I may finish getting dressed."

The girls left and went down the stairs like ladies. Grandfather was waiting in the great hall, pacing up and down like a man waiting for his sentencing to the gallows. The men were ragging him about it. He just smiled.

Chief Kirk looked great with his hair pulled back with a gold string, his ermine vest with a shirt of black silk, and black leather breeches with white ermine tails down the sides. His boots were black fox.

Georgeanna and the wedding party were about ready to go into the great hall, but were waiting on Deirdre. Mary Kate with Ellen looked at each other and let out a loud sigh. They looked up to see Deirdre coming down the stairs wearing all of her gold and bright green, as well as her tartan. Her hair was down in waves, pulled back with gold combs that had green leaves on them. The neckline was cut low to show the tops of her white full bust. The waist was tight enough to show how small it was. Around the bottom, green emeralds were sewn in shapes of oak leaves.

"Oh, my, you look like a dream of loveliness. But why not the white and gold one?" Aunt Ellen asked.

"I'll wear that one, at the Great Ball, when we come back, Aunt Ellen." Turning, Deirdre looked straight into Grandfather's eyes. "Love, look at your beautiful Georgeanna. See what she is wearing. Isn't she lovely in her pink? Besides, love, I told you I would wear this one to your wedding."

"Mary Kate whispered, "I'll tell you later. Come, let's make merry for our father," hugging her sister.

Deirdre's Grandfather Kirk looked at Georgeanna. "I know she is like a soft pink cloud. See the pearls I gave her. My only love, come make me the happiest man in the world and be my wife."

Deirdre, with all the rest, went in and took their places. With Georgeanna on his arm, Kirk smiled down at her. He then looked straight ahead, smiling as if he would burst.

Seeing how happy her Grandfather was, Deirdre and the rest of the family smiled.

With the wedding taking place, Tommy watched Deirdre. He thought, *Ma love, how beautiful you are. My arms want to hold you close to my heart. To kiss those sweet lips of yours, just to hold you forever.* As he heard the vows he just stood watching his Kitten.

Deirdre felt eyes on her and looked around. She caught Tommy's eyes and they locked with hers. She smiled as if to say, "I know, me too."

Sir Alex was also watching Deirdre with a smirk grin on his face. After the wedding was over, he walked over to where Deirdre was talking to another guest. They had a great old time talking and laughing. The dancers seemed to come out of the blue, as they started entertaining with their dancing. Deirdre smiled as she ate from a plate that Monica handed her.

"Would you care to dance?" Sir Alex asked.

Deirdre sat her plate down on the table and smiled at the voice that spoke. "Well yes, thank you most kindly, sir. Deirdre curtsied quite low. "We have not seen you in a long time, Sir Alex? King keeping you busy?"

"Slow down. Yes, he is, but I must say how you have grown. And what a beauty you are," holding Deirdre out to have a look at her.

Tommy saw how Sir Alex's eyes lingered on Deirdre's bust line as he slipped his hand around her waist.

"Why thank you, kind sir," Deirdre said with a big smile on her face as she went on the dance floor with him.

Tommy was watching as he clenched his fist to his side. "If he makes one move toward her, I'll kill him," saying this as he clenched his teeth together.

"Look everyone, it's snowing out side. And I thought it was just autumn," Monica shouted as she danced past the large window in the great room.

"It can snow anytime here in the Isles," shouted Sir Charles O'Neil.

"Yes, it can." Looking down in Deirdre's golden green eyes, he smiled. "As I remembered, you enjoyed walking in the snow, Deirdre, and wasn't that just a few years ago? Do ye still enjoy it?" asked Sir Alex.

"You know, I haven't done that in a long time," she answered, "let's go and walk in the snow," smiling up at Sir Alex in a flirty, little way.

"I'll get our cloaks." Sir Alex left her side. She looked around to see if Tommy was watching, but couldn't find him anywhere.

Smiling to herself, she thought, *I feel that Tommy will be outside hiding to see the actions of Sir Alex. He never liked him anyway.*

"Here we are," Sir Alex said as he helped Deirdre on with her deep green cloak. She noticed how his hands lingered a little longer on her shoulder than she liked. She started moving out of his way. "Come, let's walk."

They walked outside. The snow was still falling and the moon was as bright as day. Slowly, Sir Alex took her by the arm, to make sure that she didn't fall.

"When are you going to think about getting married yourself and having babies of your own?" Sir Alex asked.

"I haven't thought about it, Sir Alex, but I have been so busy with clan business."

"Please call me Alex; we have known each other a long time."

"All right, Alex. Why have you not gotten married?" she asked as they walked further down the path where they stopped at a bench. Alex brushed the snow off and suggested they rest a little while.

They sat down and Alex reached over and pulled her close to him and kissed her hard on the mouth. Deirdre struggled trying to fight him off, when all of a sudden, a black-caped man came from nowhere. He picked up Sir Alex, and hit him hard on the jaw, knocking him out cold.

"Tommy, what are you doing here?"

"What, what are you saying, do you or do you not want to be saved? Where you just going to let him have his way with you?" He stood with his hands on his hips.

"No, but I can take care of myself," Deirdre answered, throwing her head back in defiance, as well as it was in her voice.

"Oh!! I see. Just like last time, I reckon." Tommy knew when that statement came out of his mouth that it had hurt her. "I didn't mean it. I know it was not your fault; it was mine," he said in a choked voice, with his back to her.

Deirdre had tears in her eyes as she touched his arm. "No, my love, it wasn't anyone's fault. It was just one of those things that happen in life. I love you, Tommy. I would have jumped into fire if you had asked me to."

Turning, he took her in his arms, and kissed her eyes and mouth. He held her so close to him and cried like a baby. When he had control of himself, he turned Deirdre loose, and then asked, "Can you get back by yourself, Kitten?"

"Yes, but what are you going to do with Sir Alex?"

"I'll take care of him. Please send my brothers to me"

"I'll do just that, but Tommy, don't do anything rash," Deirdre said with a smile on her face.

"Don't worry." Tommy then propped Sir Alex up against the tree. "I don't think he'll remember much."

Deirdre went back inside. Seeing Hugh and Richard, she went over to them and whispered in their ear, telling them what happened. They were laughing as they went outside to help Tommy.

Deirdre smiled to herself. Her father came up and asked where she had been. "You have a cat look about you. Like one who has a lot of cream on its face."

"Have I? Oh well, it's a happy night."

"But, lassie, it's not that kind of a smile."

"Father, I couldn't be happier." Kissing him on the cheek, she ran over to Kimberly and Monica and told them what had happened. They started giggling and Monica said, "Poor Sir Alex. That will teach him not to mess with Tommy MacDonald's wife."

"But Deirdre, what if he doesn't take this lying down?" asked Kimberly.

"You're right, Kimberly, what if he doesn't? You know he has a very bad temper. My, oh my, do you think that he'll call Tommy out?" asked Monica, looking around as she spoke.

"Deirdre, Monica is right. He may want satisfaction."

"You're right, Kimberly, he may just do that," spoke Deirdre with a concerned look on her face.

"What is going on in this corner?" asked Mary Kate and Aunt Ellen as they came closer to the girls. When they told them the whole story, they laughed, and then Mary Kate went straight over to her husband and relayed the incident to him.

John MacDarroch turned and looked at his daughters with anger on his face, not paying any attention to his wife as she tried to tell him the rest of the story. He walked over to his daughters, and then said to each of them, "You three know what will happen, don't you? The king will hear of this. Oh!! Lassies, can't you stay out of trouble, even now at your age?"

"But Father, it wasn't us." said Kimberly.

"It was I, Father. If I hadn't walked out in the snow with Sir Alex, Tommy wouldn't have knocked him out," Deirdre told him.

"But why did he? His... him? What I mean to say is why did Tommy hit Sir Alex?"

"Didn't Mother tell you, Father?" Deirdre asked.

"Yes, but you tell me, I lose my temper too soon," John said, smiling.

As Deirdre told him what happened, he got a big smile on his face—so broad. "He did? You mean Tommy? Why, lassie, that lad loves you. But honey, you need to leave for the old coffer's cottage up in the Highland tomorrow. Are you able to travel?"

"Yes, Father. I'll leave and prepare for the trip." Deirdre said goodnight to all her guests, then went to her bedchamber.

"Father, Kimberly and I will see to her food and weapons," stated Monica.

"Tim, lad, get Thunder ready," John spoke to the young lad who helped in the stables. He was Molly's son.

"On my way, My Laird."

"That's a good lad, Tim. Kimberly, lass do you and Monica think Deirdre is really ready to go?" Laird John asked his daughters.

"We don't really know, Father, but she has to be strong for the next one," replied Kimberly.

"What next one, lass?" John asked with a surprised look on his face.

"Father, we'll let Mother explain that one to you," stated Monica with a smile on her face as she walked off.

John walked over to his wife and father, Kirk. "What is this I hear about another trip Deirdre is to make? No one told me of this." The ladies looked at one another, all knowing that even Kirk did not know.

"Shall we go into the chapel?" Georgeanna asked as she led the way.

"Why the chapel, Georgeanna?" Kirk asked, as he followed behind her into the chapel.

"Mary Kate, tell me right now, do you hear me!" John said, running after his wife.

"Hush, John, everyone can hear you. I will as soon as we get into the chapel and please quiet down."

"Wait, is it!? Quiet down, is it!?"

"John, do you remember when the lassies came home we talked about it."

"Georgeanna!" Kirk was getting red in the face.

"Tell me now, what's all this that John is shouting about?"

"Now, Kirk, when we get into the chapel, we will tell you, so calm down."

They all entered the chapel. "Alright, we are here now; please tell us, lasssies!" John was still shouting when he saw Father Ira, his brother.

"Sorry, Father Ira," John spoke softly.

"All is well, and it's easy to see that you're very upset, brother." Father Ira left the chapel so they could be alone.

"Georgeanna, will you please tell them what you saw at my father's stronghold when Deirdre was so near death?"

Kirk and John both looked at Mary Kate, then back to Georgeanna.

Georgeanna started telling them what she had seen and heard. "When Deirdre was so ill and we almost lost her, she was propped up in bed, calling for Tommy, when all of a sudden, a bright light came into the room. There stood her grandmother right in front of her. She put her hand on Deirdre, and spoke these words. 'My love, you will be strong and will also go on your first trip up to the Highlands. It will make you much stronger. For you will need that strength on your last trip, back to the twentieth century.'"

"Deirdre was weak at the time and answered, 'Yes, Grandmother,'" spoke Georgeanna.

"John, my mother came to me." Looking at her father and then at John, "Father, it was the same night Mother told me all about Georgeanna. Yes, my dear, she knew, and she was very happy."

Georgeanna had tears in her eyes as she spoke. "For Deirdre to return back to us from whence she goes she will have to want to bad enough."

"You mean she may not want to return?" asked John, with tears in his eyes.

"Yes, my husband."

John, along with Kirk, fell on their knees in front of the altar. The two of them had not taken time to pray in a long time, until now, both of them staying in the chapel long after everyone else had left.

When they came out, Georgeanna spoke, "My husband, Deirdre must not realize that we know about all this, for it would upset her a great deal."

"You are so right."

"John, husband, do you hear?"

"Yes, Mary Kate, are we going to lose her again?"

"No, she will return to us. I feel it very strongly."

"And how about the others? Will they do the same later on?"

"Yes, when the time is right."

"Oh, Father in Heaven, will it be like we lost them before?" John then sat down on the edge of the bench, put his face in his hands and cried.

"My husband, you remember, it was the Black Fog that took them. Now don't be so sad. I know they will all return and have many grandchildren for us."

"Do you really believe this?" John asked as he put his arms around Mary Kate, drawing her close.

"Yes, love, I really do. We'll not lose them. They will return to us and be with us in our old age, and with a house full of children."

"For us to spoil rotten," John said, holding Mary Kate as they both left the chapel behind Kirk and Georgeanna.

Chapter 20

Grandfather Kirk rose early and went to the stables to check on the horses and things that Deirdre was to take with her. He made sure she had more traps, knives and plenty of furs to keep her warm.

As he was working to get things together, he heard a voice. "Kirk, Kirk, love." It was Georgeanna bringing food, and extra furs to be packed for the trip.

"Wife! What are you doing out in this weather?"

"Mary Kate and I wanted to make sure Deirdre had enough to eat and to stay warm. And, also to make sure she didn't see that sad look on your face."

"Does it show that much?"

"Yes, it does."

Charles, the stable boy, was sent to the cottage a few days before to store lots of supplies. He needed to take enough food for the livestock, and clean the cottage. It had been closed up for a long time.

"Where is Charles?" Kirk asked.

"I have no idea. I thought he was getting things ready for the trip, and was supposed to escort Deirdre up to the Highlands. I'm sure he is back by now," answered Georgeanna.

"I hear someone." Kirk went over to the stable door and peered out. "Is that you, Charles?"

"No, Grandfather, it's your lassies." They were all laughing together as they came into the stable. "I met these sisters of mine outside," Deirdre stated, as she came in, dressed in her warrior robes of fur, her chakram hanging at her side. Her sword was on her shoulders.

"You look quite like the fighting warrior that you are. Are you sure that what you have on is not too heavy for you at this time?"

"No, Grandfather, but thanks for caring." Looking around, "Is everything ready? Where is Charles, Grandfather?"

"Right here, My Lady. Sorry to be late, but I had another chore to do."

"That's alright, are you ready to get started?"

"Yes, Lady Deirdre," answered Charles.

Thunder stood still as his master got up on his broad back and patted his large neck. MacTavish sat in front of his master in his leather harness and fur. Thunder was trained to carry MacTavish. They were like partners where their master's life was concerned. Charles mounted his horse and took the reins of the other horses, and they rode off.

"Do you think she'll be alright, Grandfather?" asked Kimberly as she watched them ride off down the hill. "Why did she let MacTavish go?"

"You know, wee one, I feel sure she will be fine, and as for taking MacTavish, that was for safety." Grandfather Kirk hugged Kimberly and Monica as they went up to the castle.

They all walked into the great room. Kirk spoke to John, "It's a good thing you had Charles go up to get things ready for Deirdre at the cottage, John."

"What are you talking about, Kirk? I didn't."

"Charles just said you did, Father," Monica butted in.

"Kirk, didn't you see his horse? It was all wet and covered with lather from riding hard. He even had to change horses before they left to go up to the Highlands," explained Georgeanna.

"Monica and Kimberly, you remember all he said was he had to do another chore," remarked Kirk.

Nothing would do but for Laird John to ask Mary Kate when she came into the great hall. "Mary Kate, love, did you?"

"Did I do what, husband'?"

"Have Charles go up to get the cottage ready for Deirdre?"

"No, she didn't want anyone to do it for her; it was part of her training."

"Then who?" asked Kimberly.

"Oh!!! I know a young lad who is in trouble when our wildcat gets through with him," laughed Grandfather Kirk.

"Who is that, Father Kirk?

"You know him, John!"

John stopped, and put his hand to his head. "Yes, I do." Both men started laughing and the rest joined in, for they all knew then that it was Tommy.

"Poor laddie," Mary Kate said with a giggle in her voice and a smile on her beautiful face.

After traveling to Ardussa, where Grandfather had one of his ships in port to take them over across the sound of Jura, they went out to the Firth of Lora, which ran into Loch Linnhe. They went around MacLean land, then home to MacDonald land. As they got off the boat, leading the horses, Charles asked a silly question. "My Lady, are you sure you are strong enough for the journey?"

"Yes, I am. Why do you ask?"

"Well, I was just wondering," was his answer.

They got on the horses and started to ride up the mountain toward the cottage. It was tough going through all the snow. As they neared the cottage, Deirdre wanted to move faster.

"Let's hurry before it gets dark. There are things to be done and it has taken us three days on the trail because you wanted to make sure I didn't get weak on you, Charles."

"You still haven't gotten all your strength back."

"I know, and thank you for caring,"

"My Lady."

"Yes, Charles."

"Would you be too upset if you found out a lot of things have been done for you?"

"Why do you ask, Charles?"

"Well, I was asked to come up here and do a few things for you. I was paid good money for it, too."

"Really, and who might have done that? And what did you do?" She was already getting a little angry.

"My Lady, now don't go and get like the wildcat we all know you can be. By the way, where is MacTavish?" Charles asked, as he looked around with a frightened look on his face.

"MacTavish is running about somewhere. Now, really, what did you go and do, Charles?"

"I just cut wood, cleaned the cottage, and put in clean bedding. Then made sure you had enough candles and plenty of grain for the livestock."

"Well, thank you very much. But it was to be part of my training to do all of that. Charles, who had you to do all of this?"

"Well, My Lady, I was asked not to tell."

"I see, but if I guessed, you wouldn't be telling, would you? So here is my guess. If I'm right, they will be in deep trouble with me."

Charles' eyes got as big as the moon. "Who do you think it was, My Lady?"

"Well, let's see now." Not wanting to say too soon and spoil it for him, "Would it, by any chance be my grandfather, or my Godfather Glen?" She looked at Charles as if in deep thought, just like the cat which had eaten a bird. "Now would it be Tommy, by any chance? What do you say, Charles, am I right?"

Just as Deirdre said the name, Charles' face fell. At that moment, she knew that she was right.   When they got to the cottage, Charles started unpacking. Deirdre thought to herself, *Tommy, just wait until I see you. You'll be sorry.* Charles was busy getting things put away and straightened out.

The cottage was nice and clean, with a fire Charles had just built. It slowly started to get warm and cozy, as the wind was howling outside. She made a nice pot of lamb stew, oatcakes and hot mead. Charles went out to finish putting things away in the shed, and to feed and water the livestock. MacTavish lay in the far corner eating a large leg off a deer that Deirdre had killed that afternoon. She took the meat that Charles had dressed and salted it, and put it in the stable — up high so no animal could get to it.

After Charles had eaten a big meal, he went over and lay on a pallet in the corner, falling asleep instantly.

Deirdre knew that he must have been worn out. *After all the work he had done, making two trips, no wonder he went to sleep so fast*, she thought to herself.

As she lay in bed, the thought of Tommy and how sweet it was of him to do this, but he knew it had been up to her, as a warrior of the MacDarrochs, to clean up. But still, smiling to herself, *Oh! What she would love to do to that man.*

Charles left early the next morning. He started down the mountain in the crisp, cold morning, with the snow still falling and the wind blowing. Deirdre called out to him, "Charles, don't forget to tell them I'll be down when the snow melts in the early spring."

"Yes, My Lady, I will." He kept on riding.

Deirdre started to go back inside when MacTavish came running up in the snow. He, like his master, was ready for the warmth of the cottage.

The next morning Deirdre got up and dressed in her furs and boots. She stirred the deer stew, stoked the fire, and went outside to practice her moves with the sword. But first, she needed to set her traps and snares.

Deirdre was feeling a bit uneasy, just like someone was watching her. After looking around to see, she started setting her traps and snares. When she had finished, she went higher on the hill. The wind was blowing her hair. She stood in a warrior's stance, legs apart, and started swinging her sword from side to side, holding it overhead. *Boy, am I weak*, she was thinking to herself. *I'll do a little at a time until I regain my strength.*

She worked out for about two hours, climbing up and down the mountain to regain strength in her legs. She fed Thunder and the other livestock, and milked the cow. By lifting the feed it helped to make her arms grow stronger, and milking the cow helped make her fingers stronger. She would be able to hold her weapons longer.

Taking the milk inside, as well as to warm up, she stirred the stew on the fire. She started stretching to work out the stiffness in her body and started playing around with MacTavish. "Guess we had better stop, old boy, and have a bite to eat. After we eat, I must start meditation so that I can keep my eyes on one thing at a time. Now, you get over to your corner and be quiet." MacTavish did as he was told, as always.

After some of the stew, Deirdre started her meditation and a smile came over her face. "I'm quite happy with my first day's work out," she said as she smiled at MacTavish. She hung the dead rabbit that she caught in one of the traps up by a rope and pushed it to where it would swing. She sat watching it, moving nothing but her eyes. After doing that for a while, she became very tired, and was ready for bed. She just fell into bed without even taking her clothes off.

Deirdre started dreaming of Tommy and the feeling of his hands roaming over her body. His lips on hers, and the feeling she got as they went down her body. What a sensation that went over her. When she awoke, her blood, and her body, was very hot.

On the other side of the cottage, down a small hill in a wooded area, was Sir Tommy, thinking about her and those long legs of hers, *I can feel them wrapped about my waist, lifting that beautiful red nest up to me. Tommy, lad, you have got to stop this. If you don't, you'll go mad.* Tommy was talking to himself at that point, which he had been doing ever since he had gotten there.

As he tried not to think of Deirdre, his root rose to a great height, swollen and tight. He got up, went out and dove into a snow bank. *Everything's alright now,* Tommy thought as he got back into his little dugout.

Little did he know, MacTavish knew he was there, and had showed Deirdre where the dugout was located. "Well love, you're in for the sight of your life."

The next morning Deirdre took off her wool pants, put on just her fur boots and her vest and set out to get wood for the fire. As Deirdre picked up the wood for the fire, she bent over, showing her bare bottom. Running back inside, almost frozen, she laughed to herself knowing full well he saw her. She went to the fire to get warm, and hopefully stop her teeth from chattering, while putting her wool pants back on. The fur jacket she had on felt good after being out in the cold.

Deirdre banked the fire, and went out to do her running and climbing. She could feel the strength slowly coming back into the muscles of her legs. They seemed to get stronger each day, as well as her arms.

A week had gone by quickly. One day while she was out checking her traps and snares, Tommy walked to the cottage and went in. He was building up the fire and stirring the rabbit stew when he heard the whinny of horses. He knew someone was outside.

Deirdre could see someone was there because of the extra horse tied up in the shed.

"Well, hello," Deirdre said when she came through the door.

Tommy stood up. "Hello yourself. Hope you don't mind me dropping by?"

"No, just make yourself at home." Seeing more wood by the fireplace, she said, "Thank you for bringing in more wood." She smiled to herself as she took off her fur jacket and boots, along with her vest. Looking at him under her eyelashes, "Hope you don't mind me taking these wet clothes off and putting on something dry? Would you please turn around?"

"No, no, not at all." As he turned his back to her, she knew he could see her shadow on the cottage wall, and hoped it would drive him crazy. All he could see was her high full breast, rounded hips, and her long beautiful legs. As he looked, the thought came to him, *She is doing this on purpose.* "I don't see why I have to turn around, Kitten. We have seen each other bare-assed before and done much more. I have even given you a bath."

Deirdre smiled to herself as she put her warm robe on, with nothing on underneath. "Now, you can turn around. I'll fix us something to eat. I know we use to, but it's different now."

Tommy saw the look on her face. Smiling to himself, he thought about changing the subject. "How are you feeling and what do you mean it's different now?" He was still smiling.

"I'm getting stronger everyday with the workouts and feeling a lot better, too. You know things have just changed."

"That's good, are you going to be up here long? And by the way, what do you mean things have changed?" He asked as she handed him a bowl of rabbit stew, black bread, and a cup of hot mead.

"For about five weeks and the snow has started melting."

"I see," he said as he continued eating, watching her face to see if there were any changes.

"Tommy, may I ask you something?"

"Anything."

"Good, why did you pay Charlie to come up here, and clean things up when you knew it was my job?" As she was talking, her anger was coming up to the surface.

Tommy could see how her eyes were getting the gold specks dancing and felt a good fight coming on. They had not had one in a long time. "Yes, I did; with you being in such a weak and run down state, I just thought it would be nice to help you."

"Oh!! You did, did you? Well, let me tell you something, Tommy MacDonald. You know good and well that I could have done it myself." Her face was getting red and, at that moment, Tommy started smiling, then he burst out laughing.

"You're laughing at me, aren't you? Well, you're in for it now!" Getting up and moving over to the other side, she got a hold of MacTavish and put him outside while she did battle with Tommy boy.

"Now, love, can't you see I meant no harm, my little wild-cat?"

"Wildcat, am I? I'll show you wildcat." Deirdre jumped, swinging with her fist, hitting Tommy in his face, back and chest. He tripped, and fell to the cottage floor, hitting his head on the foot of the bed. Thank God MacTavish was outside. She looked down at Tommy. He wasn't moving.

"Oh!!! What have I done? Tommy, my darling, speak to me, please."

Tommy just lay there. Deirdre got up and went outside to get some snow to wipe his face. As she went out, Tommy opened his eyes and saw how upset she was. He saw tears in her eyes as she came back in. "Tommy, Tommy, my darling, please wake up. I'm so sorry, love."

Deirdre started to go back for more snow. She had gotten up on her knees when Tommy grabbed her by the waist, pulling her down to him. "Over, is it? Not in this lifetime or any other."

"You are bad," Deirdre said as they both started laughing together, rolling on the floor. Tommy started kissing her, and holding her close – so close, in fact, she could hardly breathe. She could feel his hardness between her thighs.

He held her face with both hands as he lay on top of her. "My love, I'm so sorry for putting you through all that you have been through. Losing our baby, and all the beatings – it was my fault. Please forgive me for wanting you so bad and asking you to meet me in the glen."

"Tommy, it wasn't your fault, it was both of us. We didn't know that Patrick Campbell would do what he did. As for wanting me so bad, why are you afraid, love? I have dreamed of being with you, it seems forever."

"You have?"

"Don't you know how much I loved you? Do you still want me after what Patrick Campbell did to me?"

"Oh yes, my darling," saying it as he held her tight, he kissed both of her eyes and mouth, and then nibbled at her ears. He went back to her mouth with his tongue and opened her mouth. A groan came from deep down inside of both of them.

His hands roamed, talking his thumb, rubbing on each nipple, to get them hard. He smiled as he started sucking on each one like a baby. His tongue went down to her stomach, and that was when he saw the scar. He stopped, "Oh!! My love, why didn't I come to get you?" Tommy was so hot for her he started kissing her stomach, going straight down to her love nest.

When his finger entered her, he felt her quaver, and she arched her back. As he removed it, she cried for more. He then entered her with his magnificent manhood, moving very slowly at first, putting her legs around his waist. She moved with him in unison. Being consumed with fire for him, she raised her body to meet his every thrust. They blended as if they were made as one. Faster, faster, they went to the heavens. They called out each other's name as they came back down to earth.

He kissed her, and rolled off; keeping her in his arms, "Look at you. You're all sweaty. I wonder why, Kitten?"

Deirdre snuggled up to Tommy. "As if you didn't know! You know you're not so dry yourself."

Both of them, holding onto each other, rolled around, when all of a sudden, she was on top. "Oh... you must want a ride, do you?"

"Yes, My Laird. I would like to ride my beautiful stallion."

Smiling, he held her, saying, "Well, hang on, my darling, your stallion will give you the ride of your life."

They made love like there would be no tomorrow. Her hair was soaking wet as was Tommy's, but they held on to each other. She knew she would have to tell him about the next trip. Deep down, she was not looking forward to it. She would do it later, or maybe not at all. *I'll think about it*, she was saying to herself as she lay in his arms.

They made love all through the night, up into the morning. Tommy held her like it was for the last time. He couldn't explain it, but it was just a feeling he had.

"You need to get up to start your run before you kill me," he said, laughing as he got up to build up the fire and put his clothes on.

"No, I want to lay here and just gaze on your body. It's the most beautiful body I have ever seen."

"Now come on, do you really think so?" he asked with a silly smile on his face.

"Yes, I do."

Moving toward the fire, he built it up and started to make oat cakes for their breakfast. "Now, what are you doing?" asked Deirdre.

"I'm making us something to eat to build up our strength," he answered, laughing.

He brought the oat cakes with butter and honey, with a large bowl of porridge to the bed. As they ate their breakfast he asked her, "Does the wanting ever go away?"

"I pray not. You asked that before, remember?"

Tommy got up and put everything away and cleaned up, then he came back into bed and pulled Deirdre back into his arms. "Am I holding you too tight?

"Are you trying to take the breath right out of me?"

"Maybe just a little, my darling."

Deirdre put her head on his shoulder, cuddling up to him. "The wanting will never go away. We won't let it. I just had you and I already want you again," she said, smiling down into his face.

As Deirdre's hand started roaming lower on his body, he replied with laugher in his voice, "Now darling, don't start anything."

"Who, me!? I wouldn't dream of it!"

Tommy started laughing. He pinned her down and kissed her until she couldn't breathe. Then he raised her legs, and drawing them over his shoulders, buried his face between them. His tongue found her honey pot and he used her furiously until she came, his mouth forcing her to climax.

"Look at me, my hot, little bitch."

Deirdre squeezed her eyes tightly closed, "No."

"Look at me, Kitten." At the cruel sharp note in his voice, she opened her cat eyes and looked into his violet blue ones. "I've fallen in love with you all over again, you bitch, and now I'll take you like a whore." Tommy rubbed his big blue-veined organ against her belly. "This is what you want, isn't it?"

"Yes, oh yes."

"You'll have it in good time, in fact... I'll give it to you now." Tommy spread her wide, "All of it, sweet love!" He drove deeply into her, enjoying her gasp and the look of satisfaction on her face.

Tommy was huge and filled her to overflowing, pushing upward to touch her very womb as he moved his great shaft skillfully, drawing it nearly all the way out, then thrusting it home again. For a moment, Deirdre thought she would be torn apart, but her body stretched to receive him, almost devouring him in her desperate hunger. She clawed at his back and he caught her arms and pinioned them above her head. She bit into his shoulder, drawing blood, and then licked furiously at the wound. He slapped her very lightly, cursing softly at her sharp little teeth.

The pleasure and the pain mingled about within her. She had forgotten such passion. It consumed her, leaving room for nothing else. Onward Tommy drove her as she reached peak after peak, believing each time that it was not possible to go any further, yet cresting higher and higher. Behind her closed eyelids, the world exploded into a rainbow of shattered glass. Deirdre felt the contractions of the orgasm so great that she believed death was about to overtake her. Over and over again her body shuddered with the force of her passion.

Tommy joined her in her ecstasy of climax, and then rolled off of her body. For a moment Tommy could only but stare at her. Deirdre was white and could barely breathe. Sitting up, he tenderly gathered her into his arms. She was cold and he strove to warm her. "Love, you and only you could ever drive me as far as you have done. You are the only one who could ever satisfy me and no other woman ever will. Don't ever leave me, Kitten."

"I won't, Tommy."

"Kitten, sweetheart, I have to tell you something."

Turning in his arms, she said softly, "What is it, love?"

"I just don't know how to start, but I must go back to the twentieth century, to make a closing."

"Oh!! Tommy, so do I! I just didn't know how to tell you either."

Tommy took her face in s hands and kissed her tenderly. "God, you've got the sweetest mouth."

Deirdre felt herself growing liquid again and leaned back, sighing happily, and her cat eyes grew warm. "Damn you, Tommy. What is it you do to me that one kiss renders me weak and wanton."

"What do you think you do to me, Kitten, which renders me insatiable?"

Quickly they were in each other's arms again, their mouths and tongues and hands devouring each other. Bodies entwined, they kissed until their mouths were bruised and both were breathless. Already aroused, his wonderful root beat against her thigh. Reaching down, she caressed him with teasing fingers, reaching out to cup the soft pouch beneath his shaft, running a sure finger firmly beneath it, hearing his gasp of surprised pleasure.

There was no waiting this time. Deirdre parted her thighs easily and he slid into her warmth. Confident now, she tightened her muscles about him. "Jesus!" He cried out softly as the wave of pleasure overpowered him. He drew back to thrust deeper yet, and again she tightened around him. "Stop witch!!" Tommy begged, "It's the most delightful torture I've endured, but stop before I die. I want to pleasure you, too!"

Her arms were tight about him and as she loosened her grip on him he began to murmur softly to her. "Little witch, I knew that beneath the war-like demeanor there was the passionate wanton. Open yourself to me, my Kitten. God, how warm and sweet you are!

Tommy moved rhythmically with long smooth strokes, each thrust seeming to go deeper than the one before. She could feel herself opening wider to receive him, taking him all in, wanting even more. *Oh, God, I wanted more!* Sobbing, she felt herself climax, bearing down on her like a great wind, slamming into her with such force that she fainted, hearing as she slid away into the dark warmth Tommy's cry of pleasure.

Chapter 21

Deirdre's first awareness was of Tommy's kisses covering her face. *Dear God,* Deirdre thought, *he can still rouse me to such heights.* Opening her eyes and smiling tremulously at him, her eyes were brilliant with tears.

Tommy smiled back and ran his finger tenderly down her nose. "You have bewitched me all over again. You know we must go back to Sea Oaks soon. But now you must rest so that you'll get stronger."

"I will, I promise." They snuggled up together and went back to a wonderful sleep.

It was getting to be early spring. The snow had melted when Tommy and Deirdre started down the mountain, making their way to the boat. It took almost a week for them to make it down to the bottom with all the stopping and lovemaking they did. Just a little farther; it shouldn't take long for them to get home.

Everyone was so happy to see them. "Tommy, come join us. Have something to eat, it will be dark soon. Why not stay over until morning, or longer if you like." Laid John gave the invitation with a big smile.

"Thank you. I am hungry, and it would be a pleasure to dine with you."

Tommy sat with everyone, ate, drank, and caught up on the news. But noticing that Deirdre had left the table, he excused himself to follow her. He found her as he was passing the chapel, at the altar praying, and joined her. Very quietly Tommy got up and left Deirdre still praying. With his head bowed, he slowly went down to the great hall. "Sir, I know about the trip that Deirdre will be taking."

"You do?" asked Lady Mary Kate.

"Yes, My Lady. You see I, too, have to go back; I also have to make a closing. But I will be back, for you see, I wish to remarry my Kitten in the church, proper like, the way we planned and never got to, because of the Black Fog. You do understand, don't you?"

"Tommy, of course we understand. So while you both are gone, we'll prepare for a big wedding." Laird John smiled at his wife, Mary Kate, who was also smiling.

"Tommy, my husband is right. Don't you worry about anything; we'll take care of everything for a grand wedding."

"My Laird, may I see her alone when she comes from the chapel?"

"Why yes, Tommy, but why don't you go in as well?" asked Laird John.

"I was, but she was still praying when I left her kneeling at the altar."

"Why not go in again and wait until she is finished?" asked Mary Kate.

"I think I will." Tommy left and walked silently back to the chapel. Seeing that Deirdre was still there, he knelt beside her.

When Deirdre started to rise, she saw Tommy by her side. Smiling to herself, she sat down near him. She said quietly to herself, *My darling Tommy, loving you is the greatest thing that has ever happened to me.*

Deirdre was in another world. She did not see or hear Tommy rise. He came closer to her until his arm went around her waist. Whispering in her ear, "My darling, please, this one last night, together."

"Yes, Tommy darling, yes." They left the chapel arm in arm with her head on his shoulder. She was smiling to herself like she knew something no one else knew.

They entered the bedchamber where a fire was burning brightly and warm. Tommy knew in his heart this would be the last time they would be together until they both returned. But he would not speak of that just now.

Deirdre called to Maude to please bring the largest tub with lots of hot water and the herb-scented soap. It seemed like only seconds when the footman brought in the tub, water and linen to dry with. Maude looked around and smiled to herself, knowing Tommy would be hiding out of sight.

When everyone had left the chamber, Deirdre locked the door. Tommy then came into the room from the shadows smiling. He laughed as he took her in his arms, placing his lips to hers.

"We need to bathe before the water gets cold."

"Hum-hum."

"Now, Tommy. Please, love, come on."

Tommy smiled as he came closer, putting out his hands, and started to undress Deirdre very slowly, caressing each part of her body. Her hands were also working, undoing Tommy's breeches, lifting off his linen shirt with her fingers going over his chest. With their clothes off, they moved over and stepped into the tub of warm water with the sweet smell of the soap and herbs. At the same time, both of them picked up the linen rags to wash with. Tommy smiled as he started scrubbing her back. He turned so that she could do his. "Now, sweet, watch what you're doing or we will not make it to bed."

"Really now, Tommy." Laughing, they got out, each of them grabbing a large linen, and started drying each other. Out of the blue, Tommy picked Deirdre up and placed her in the middle of the bed.

The next thing Deirdre knew, Tommy slid his body over hers, kissing her mouth then sliding his tongue inside it. Deep moaning came from both of them. Tommy stopped and cupped her face into his hands, then started kissing her all over. He raised his head and looked into her eyes. "Oh!!! How I love you."

He slid his tongue all the way down her body. Deirdre's blood started to boil to overflowing. Lifting herself up to meet him, she thought she would burn and explode at any moment. But when he reached the vee between her thighs and placed his lips to the center, she went wild.

Tommy came up smiling then placed his hard, large velvet shaft inside. Their bodies blended, Deirdre met his thrust for thrust, taking them to new heights. They shook, then quavered holding on to each other until almost dawn.

There was a light knock on the door and a soft voice, "Sister, time for breakfast."

Raising her head up from Tommy's shoulder, Deirdre answered, "Alright, Kimberly, be right there." As she looked down at Tommy, "Darling, we must get up. They expect us down to breakfast."

He held on to her much tighter. "I know, but I don't want to let you go just yet."

"I feel the same."

With tears in his eyes, Tommy said, "Kitten, you will come back to me?"

"I will, because your love will bring me back."

"As yours will help me back, my love, like I told you up on the mountain."

They dressed and went downstairs to breakfast. Everyone was eating and laughing when Tommy stood up. "Thank you for everything, My Laird, but it is time for me to leave for home."

"Why, Tommy, are you alright?" asked Laird John.

Tommy was leaving, but all of the family saw the tears in his eyes. When he got to the doors, he turned and looked at Deirdre. "You remember, I love you with my heart and soul. You come back to me, my wife. Come back home to me." Tommy left, not even noticing that his father, Laird Glen MacDonald, was there. Laird Glen looked after his son, seeing him leave with tears in his eyes and running down his face. He felt very sad for him.

Deirdre looked at her family, "I need to talk with all of you," she said, walking to the head of the table. "Father, Grandfather, and especially you, Godfather. Mother, you and Aunt Ellen, and Grandmother Georgeanna, also. While I'm gone you must do this. Grandfather, your ships must get ready for sailing to the new world. You will take Godfather's family, all one hundred and forty-three of them, men, women and children, all."

"But lass, it can't be done!" Laird Glen stated with a surprised look on his face.

"Grandfather Kirk, can it be done?" asked Deirdre.

"Yes, it can be done, my darling."

Looking at her Godfather, "So! What's the problem? You want to have your whole family slaughtered by the king's order to Robert Campbell?"

With a surprised look on his face, "No, but how would we slip aboard with the Campbells looking on?"

"Well, you see, Grandmother told me how when I was so sick. Your men and women will dress as deckhands on the ship. You will put the babies in the barrels, with the older children in crates. Food and supplies will already be aboard. That's how it must be. I'll be gone and no one will know. When King William and the Campbells ask Father where you are, they can truthfully say they don't know. Also, Grandfather left for Norway with his new bride and daughter, Ellen."

"You're right, Deirdre, it might work after all, I'll leave now to get things ready. I know I'll never see you again." Laird Glen hugged her crying, then hugged Kimberly and Monica.

"Now don't do that! Head for Jamaica, then to the coast of the Carolinas. But the mountains are the best; you'll have great fishing and game. Make friends with the red man." Giving him a hug, "God be with you and yours." Deirdre turned to leave, and then said to the others in the great room, "I believe I changed history just now, but I don't care. She turned and fled the room on a run. Everyone knew that she would be gone tomorrow.

As she was getting ready for bed, a knock came at the door. "Who is it?"

"It's your Uncle Jamie and Molly."

Deirdre put on her robe as she started for the door. "Well, look at you both. Come in. What's the smiles for, as if I didn't know. When's the wedding?"

"When you get back," answered her Uncle Jamie.

"Why wait that long? Why not now?" she asked her Uncle.

"But we want you here," answered Molly.

"Well, let's see, how about a morning wedding, like right now! Come on, let's get Father Ira up as well as all the others. Molly, you stay here. Uncle Jamie, you go get ready. Well, don't just stand there with your mouth open. Move, move. Maude! Maude! Come and dress Molly for her wedding." Molly sat on the side of the bed, with her mouth agape. As Deirdre pushed her Uncle Jamie out of the door, she turned to Molly and asked, "Do ye remember how we met?"

"Yes, I do. You were so kind to Timmy, giving him a job in your stables. He was so happy. Then you gave me a job helping as a healer, then in the sewing room. You moved us inside the walls for safety and into a very nice home. How did you know that Jamie and I loved one another?"

"By the way you looked at each other. You watched each other, but tried not to let the others know. You were just like children. Both of you take care of one another, love each other forever. But now, we have a wedding to see to." Giving Molly a big hug, Deirdre left so Maude could help Molly get ready for her wedding.

"Maude, look in my clothes and see what is there for Molly to wear."

"My Lady Deirdre, one moment please, when is the baby due?"

"How did you know, Molly?" Deirdre asked with a surprised look.

"You have a glow about you. Does Sir Tommy know?"

Deirdre answered with sadness in her voice, "No, he left before I could tell him."

"What will you do now?"

"I really don't know, but the good Lord will help me. Now I must go; please don't tell anyone. I would like to do that."

"You know I won't. I love you, niece."

They didn't realize that Maude had heard everything that was said. Closing the door, Deirdre ran down the hall knocking on all doors. "Wake up everyone, there is going to be a wedding! Wake up!"

All the doors swung open and the girls came out. "What was that? Wedding? Whose?" asked Monica.

"Uncle Jamie and Molly. Come on, get dressed, all of you. Go into the chapel." Shouting loudly, "Father, go and get Father Ira."

Deirdre went to wake the cooks so they could get started fixing a wedding breakfast. Deirdre never saw the kitchen help work so fast. They even started to sing as they worked because they were so happy for Uncle Jamie and Molly.

With everything done and the wedding party already at the chapel, Deirdre quietly entered and sat down. She saw her Uncle Jamie look at his Molly walking down the aisle to him. He had the biggest smile on his face with tears shinning in his eyes.

Laird John stood beside him then spoke softly to his younger brother, Jamie. "Look at Timmy's face."

Timmy was holding his mother's arm like he was holding on for dear life. They both had big smiles on their faces. Molly wore a big smile only for Jamie as she looked at him with love in her eyes. She wore a pale blue dress with wide lace on the bodice, sleeves and around the bottom. Deirdre's soft blue shoes even fit her as well. Molly wore a wreath of white heather on her head. Around her neck she wore a string of fresh-water pearls that Uncle Jamie had given her. Molly looked like an angel—Uncle Jamie's angel.

They all listened to them saying their vows. After the wedding was over, everyone went into the great hall for the big wedding breakfast. The crofter's children laid flowers in the hallway for the wedding couple to walk on. Everyone was laughing and talking, happy for the couple.

Jamie got up from his chair, holding his cup up high to make a toast. "To you, My Lady and wonderful niece," he said with tears in his eyes and running down his cheeks. "May God be with you, keep you safe, and bring you back to us soon." He sat down holding onto Molly's hand very tightly.

Deirdre stood up, smiling, and raised her cup. "May God be with you and your new family and may you add to it as well."

Everyone laughed and cheered. "That's right, My Lady."

"My friends and family, as you know, tomorrow — actually it is today, I will be on a journey that has to be done. When I return, there will be another wedding, mine to Sir Thomas Edward MacDonald, again."

"My Lady, does Sir Tommy know this?" asked Uncle William as he held his wife's hand.

"Yes, he does, Uncle."

Hoorays and shouts went up all over the place. All of a sudden Deirdre's sisters got up and went over and stood beside her. Kimberly spoke, "My friends and family, this will come as a surprise to you all, but Monica and I have decided to go with Deirdre, because we feel she will need us."

Everyone looked at one another as if they were going into battle. Monica saw what was happening, and how they just stared at Laid John, expecting him to say something.

"My friends and family, please listen to me. It's not what you think; it's not a battle or anything like that. It's just that we wish to be like a guard to her. You should understand after what she has been through with the Campbells," stated Monica.

They all shook their heads in agreement, then started smiling and talking again.

Because time was drawing close, Deirdre got up to say her goodbyes. Hugging her father and mother, she walked up to her Uncle Jamie and his new bride. "Please look after Mother and Father. Uncle Jamie, they'll need you now more than ever before. I'll be back as soon as the time change will let me." Turning, she went over to her Uncle William. "Uncle William, take care of my land and family and most of all, look after each other."

Sue was hugging Deirdre. "Don't worry, niece, we'll look after everything here. You take care of yourself." Then Sue and William kissed her cheek.

Deirdre ran out of the great hall, not looking back. Kimberly and Monica were right behind her. Deirdre asked them, "Why?"

"Because we both had the same dream — that you'll need us — and sister, that's that," Kimberly stated. Both turned so they could go and get ready.

When they were properly dressed, they slipped out the secret passageway and down the beach, walking up to where the otters and silkies were. Their hearts were heavy and eyes filled with tears. They made their way up the cliff side and stood where they were taken many years before.

Deirdre smiled when she spoke, "Sisters, I'm so glad you came with me, for you see, I feel very strongly that I'm going to have a baby."

"Deirdre, are you sure?" asked Monica.

Well, as sure as anyone can be. What's wrong, Kimberly? You have a sour look on your face."

"We almost lost you last time."

"I know, but this time it won't happen."

"Are you really so sure?" they both asked together.

"Yes, I am," Deirdre answered, with surprise in her voice. "Molly knew the morning of her wedding."

"Well, I'll be," Monica said, sitting down on the edge of the cliff.

Kimberly sat up and spoke, "I don't think you should go back. You've made your closing and we can take care of everything for you. It will be too risky for you. Isn't that true, Monica?"

"You're right, Kimberly. We'll, tell Mr. and Mrs. D. and the rest. We can call your lawyer. We'll even go to the top of MacDarroch Mountain and make our pilgrimage and make our report there. Everything will be fine and we'll be alright, so don't worry."

"Are you sure?"

"Yes, we are, sister. Now go, here comes the fog. We'll see you later. We love you. Now go, please," smiled Kimberly as she took Monica's hand.

Deirdre got up and left to go to Sea Oaks on the run. Looking back, she saw them holding on to each other's hand really tight. As the Big Black Fog lifted, they were gone.

They had a strange look on their faces as they tumbled down. They found themselves, all of a sudden, sitting under the same large tree they sat under years ago. Monica looked around and she saw Mr. Angus Gordon coming up the hill. "Well, well, are you ready to go? But where is Lady Deirdre?"

"Mr. Gordon, she'll not be going with us. You see, she is going to have a baby, and we were afraid for her to make the trip. She has already made her closure before she came. But we'll be going back," stated Kimberly.

"But as I said, you'll be back, and don't worry about your sister, she'll be just fine. Does Sir Tommy know about the baby?"

"No," answered Monica.

"We'll try and find him in the States and tell him," said Kimberly.

"Well, I have his address in my office. If you will come to the office, I'll give it to you."

"Thank you so much, Mr. Gordon. He should know about this baby. They lost one. But things will be fine now. We sure could use a change of clothes."

"It will, lassies, and my niece will be glad to help with the clothes," commented Mr. Gordon.

As they put on the new dresses, they said to Mr. Gordon's niece, "Thank you for the clothes, and we'll see you soon, we hope." They smiled at Mr. Gordon who was standing by his niece.

Boarding the plane, Kimberly and Monica waved goodbye as they took off, knowing things would be just fine.

Chapter 22

Slowly, Deirdre walked back through the passageway on the steps that led into her bedchamber. She went in wiping the tears away that were rolling down her cheek.

As Deirdre entered, she saw Maude trying to clean up. She smiled at herself as Maude wiped a tear from her own face.

In a small, weak voice Deirdre spoke. "Maude."

"Why, lass, you didn't go! And why are you cryin'?"

"Because, you see, I'll miss my sisters very much." She took a deep breath and said, "Maude, will you please come with me down to see Mother and Father? I have something to tell them and the clan.

Taking Maude by her arm, Deirdre led her down to the great hall. As they entered, everyone looked up with great surprise on their faces.

Mary Kate stood up and ran over to her. "Deirdre, what is wrong? You didn't go?"

"Family, I must speak to you all. It's happy news I bring you."

Everyone was very quiet. Uncle Jamie and Molly smiled at her like the cat that had a large bowl of cream.

Deirdre beamed as she spoke, "I'm going to have a baby."

The shouts and cheers were deafening to the ears. Mary Kate came over to her and put her hands on Deirdre's stomach. As she smiled really big, she said, "No, not just one, but two babies. There are twins, my darling, twins. Mary Kate had big tears running down her cheeks.

John came over, put his arms around Deirdre and just cried with joy. "I'll have to get word to Glen MacDonald about the babies."

After everyone had left, Deirdre went to her room to rest. A knock came at the door.

"Come in."

"Deirdre, you must rest and take care of yourself."

"I will, Father. Will you stay awhile with me?"

"Yes, of course I will. I have sent word to my friend, Laird Glen MacDonald."

"That's good. By the way, Father, why did you move to Jura from Sterling?"

"Well, let's see. I was a roamer. I loved the sea, even though I always got seasick." Laughing, he continued his story. "I didn't like farming, like my father. He was a good Laird; his people never went hungry. Their needs were always taken care of. But most of all, they loved him and my mother very much. When I told him what I wanted to do, he sent me to Uncle Ross', who lived here on Jura, in this very castle, Sea Oaks, as a matter fact. So, that's how I came to live with Uncle Ross, who taught me about ships, trading, and how to fight off the Vikings. When he died, he left me the title of Laird. He had always tried to be a good one. He never had any children of his own, so he left all this to me."

"How about his wife?"

"He never married. The lass he loved died when they were very young. Just couldn't bring himself to marry. Said he couldn't marry anyone. So that is the story of it."

"It's a shame, but I'm glad that he didn't or then where would you have gone?"

"Back to Sterling, I think, but I wouldn't have met your mother."

"Oh! Father, I love you and Mother so much, I'm glad you didn't go anywhere but here."

"Deirdre, you are something else again." He pulled her in his arms and whispered in her ear, "Oh, lass. You're going to have your babies. You bring me much happiness." He wiped tears that were rolling down his cheeks as he spoke.

"What is this?" Mary Kate asked as she came through the door. "John, husband, you go up to our chambers. I need to talk to Deirdre."

"Girl talk, I see," he said, laughing as he left the chamber.

"Love, come here and sit by me. I need to talk to you."

"Mother, what is wrong? You have worry in your voice."

Mary Kate held out her hand. Deirdre held onto her mother as she sat down beside her on the bed.

As Deirdre sat down, Mary Kate touched her stomach again. "Just as I feared, Deirdre, you must go back to the future like your sisters. Honey there is something wrong with one of the babies."

"What are you saying? That can't be!"

"Honey, I feel that one is weaker than the other. Now, there is a sacred circle of stones I will tell you about."

"What?"

"There are about eight of them on the Isle. The one in our forest is just across from your secret pool."

"You mean I can go back into the twentieth century and then come back?"

"No, not just like that. You need to go and see if you hear a humming like the bees in a hive."

"I see, but Mother, will it hurt the babies?"

"Not now, but if you wait much longer you could lose both of them."

"My Lord, then I must go, and soon," she said, setting down again, since she had been pacing the floor."

"As soon as you can."

"Mother, will it be safe for me to return so that they can be born here at home?

"All will be fine, and I feel strongly you'll be coming back with your sisters before All Hollow's Eve."

"Why then?"

"Why, my darling, that's when they will be born and the door will close forever."

"Alright, Mother, but what about my babies?"

"Love, don't be worried; everything will be fine. You must go, and soon. I'll go with you to the Sacred Circle of Stones."

"Oh! Mother, I love you and thank you for going with me. I can't help but worry about my babies."

"Deirdre, don't worry, they will be fine. But you should go back. You said there were good healers where you came from, but here I will be worried."

The next morning, Mary Kate held Deirdre's hand as they walked to the stable where their horses were ready.

As they rode, Deirdre noticed her mother had her head bowed. When Deirdre looked on the other side of her, she saw Queen Megotta, Queen of the Fairies. Queen Megotta smiled as she spoke, "You will have a safe trip and come back safely with your babies, don't worry. You know you will have them on All Hallows Eve. That is when the door closes, as you already know."

"I thank you, Your Grace." They rode in silence until they came to the pool. They turned to the left and rode about a couple of miles longer. Mary Kate heard the loud humming, like a swarm of honey bees.

Mary Kate pointed to the Sacred Circle of Stones. "There, you see it?"

"Yes, I do, Mother. My word, it's large and the others just lying up against the tall one."

"Yes, it's the tallest of them all," remarked the Queen of the Fairies.

Getting down from the horses, Deirdre grabbed her mother and gave her a hug and a kiss.

Wiping tears from her eyes, she turned to look at Queen Megotta. She smiled, giving Deirdre a hug. "Go now and don't worry. You will be fine and you are not to worry, we will be here waiting for your safe return. Things will remain the same. You go now." The Queen pushed Deirdre toward the humming stone. Deirdre ran to it, then stopped, turned and gave her mother one last big hug and kiss.

Deirdre went between the large humming stones. The next thing she knew she was sitting on the ground outside the office of Mr. Angus Gordon. Mr. Gordon came out of his office when he saw Deirdre. "My word, lass, I thought you were staying."

"I was, until some things changed."

"I know, your sisters told me about you carrying a baby."

"No, Mr. Gordon, it's two."

"My word, what glorious news." Giving her a hug, he continued, "But how did you get here?"

"My mother showed me the Sacred Circle of Stones. That was the way I came. I needed to come back for a while."

"Well, we'll see you later then.   But now let's get you cleaned up and you will need to rest for the trip to the States."

They went to the inn where the girls had stayed before. That was the inn where Mr. Gordon's niece worked. He spoke to her about helping Deirdre to get some clothes and a room so she could rest until she had to board the plane back to America.

After a nice steaming bath and hot food, Deirdre fell into bed. It was like she had just fallen asleep and it was time to get up. There was a knock on the door.

"Are you awake, lass?"

"Yes, just one moment."

"Take your time. Tell you what; I'll meet you down in the pub for a bite to eat."

"That sounds fine, Mr. Gordon.   I'll meet you there in about fifteen minutes."

"I'll see to a table for us"

She dressed in the outfit that Mr. Gordon's niece helped her find. It was a nice green sweater and tan jeans, with leather boots. Deirdre went down to meet Mr. Gordon.

There he was, sitting at the corner table with a big smile on his face. "Are you all ready to go, lass?"

"Yes, I am, when does the shuttle plane leave?"

"In about two hours. You have a little while yet; I'll take you when it's time. By the way, I have something for you," he said, handing her a large box.

Deirdre opened it and could not believe her eyes. There, in front of her, was a beautiful soft leather jacket. "Oh! Mr. Gordon, thank you so much. But why?"

"Oh! Lass, it's not from me but from your Tommy. He said just in case you changed your mind and came later."

"But how did he know I would?" Deidre got up and tried it on. It fit like it was made for her. Sitting down, "Thank you so much, but you know I didn't dream how much time had gone. Was there a shuttle when we came the first time?"

"Don't, you remember? There *was* one, as I recall. Are you feeling alright? You look a little green around your eyes. Last time you came, you were early, remember? As for the jacket, that I can't tell you. It's like he knew you would be coming."

"You're right; we always felt each other like we had one cord between us. I seem to get just a little queasy lately."

"Maybe you should eat some porridge. It would help you."

"You know, I think I will. Sounds like it would help. Thanks, Mr. Gordon." As Deirdre ate her porridge, she smiled, and then rubbed her tummy.

"I hope you didn't mind, but I gave your sisters the address and phone number of Tommy's lawyer, so they would let him know about the baby. Oh! They don't know about the other one."

"No, they don't. Bless you, bless you, I thank you."

"Oh! That eased my mind. I was afraid you would be upset with me."

"No, my friend, but we must go now to catch my plane."

"That we must."

As they rode in Mr. Gordon's car to a small airport, Deirdre remembered how the airport had looked.

"Your plane has just landed, lass."

"Mr. Gordon, you have been a dear, dear friend. Would you give me a hug now? Until next time, friend."

With a broad grin on his face, he said, "I would be delighted."

After giving her a hug, she asked him a surprising question. "Mr. Gordon, Angus, would you be the godfather of our babies?"

Deirdre thought the man would expire right then and there. With tears running down his face, he got so choked up he could hardly speak. "Yes, of course. It is such an honor that you bestow on me to be godfather to your babies. I would love to."

"Then, it's settled! You are the godfather. Now you stay safe and I'll see you when we come back in a few months."

"No, it will be in two months, My Lady."

"So be it then; farewell until then," Angus said with a smile.

The flight seemed to go on forever. At last she arrived at the Asheville-Henderson Airport. Asking where the nearest outside phone was, Deirdre called home collect. "Hello, operator, I would like to make a collect call to Marshall, North Carolina. The number is 919-555-1212. I'm Deirdre MacDarroch."

As the operator rang the number, Deirdre started having sweaty palms. The phone rang about six times before someone answered. It was Mrs. D's voice that Deirdre heard. As the operator asked if she would take the call, Deirdre started to cry when she heard her say with a choked voice, "Yes."

"Mrs. D, I'm at the airport."

"Do you want me to pick you up there, my dear?"

"No, Mrs. D. I'll just get a taxi. Is there any money—like about two hundred dollars—on hand at the house?"

"Just one moment, please honey."

Deirdre could hear her ask Mr. D. Then she came back on the line, "Yes, we do. What is it for?"

"For the cab, it will be worth it to me. Are my sisters there?"

"Yes, they are, but they went to the bank. I'll tell them that you are on your way home from the airport."

"Alright, Mrs. D. could you fix me something to eat? I'm starving. See you soon. Bye"

Deirdre hung up the phone and went outside to flag down a taxi. One stopped in front, and the cabbie jumped out with a big smile. "Looking for a taxi, lady?"

"Yes, I am. Would you take me to Marshall?"

"That would cost you."

"How much?"

"Well, let's see, about fifty bucks," he said.

"Tell you what, my friend. How about a one hundred dollar tip?"

"Lady, are you serious?"

"That I am."

As he came around to open the door, he spoke. "Well lady, if you would just hop in, we'll be on our way." He closed the door and started whistling.

The cabbie looked into his rearview mirror as he drove down the highway, thinking to himself. *What a looker. Man alive, what I would give to have her on my arm when I go to the Taxi man dance. Man alive, her hair alone, gosh, it looks like a red sunset. Those eyes are like a wildcat's and I bet she would be a wildcat in bed. Stop this, Roger, she is a lady.*

"Excuse me. What is your name? I can't just call you cabbie?"

He was laughing out loud. "No, Miss, don't think so; my name is Roger Whitman. And yours, Miss, if you don't mind?"

"Why, of course not, it's Deirdre MacDarroch."

"The author?"

"Yes."

"Well, I'll be, right here in my taxi. Miss MacDarroch, I have read all your books. Have you been away? I detect a little Scottish accent in your speech?"

"I guess you do. I have been away now, let's see, for about one year now."

"Where in Scotland, if you don't mind me asking?"

"Of course not. I have been on the Isle of Islay and Jura."

"Bet it was nice."

"Oh, yes, it was heaven," she answered with a dreamy look in her eyes and voice.

"Well, we are almost to Marshall. Where do we go from town?"

"As you go through town, there's a road called Bull Creek. It's on the right side, and then go for about five miles. On your left is a sign that says MacDarroch. You go a very short way up to a private side road, across a small branch, then up to the house."

"Alright, there we go. By the way, may I ask a personal question?"

"Why, yes. What is it?" Smiling to herself.

"Are you married?"

"Yes."

"Oh, I see. Is he from Scotland?"

"He is from there and here."

"Are you happy and in love? Never mind, it's none of my business."

"Roger, you are very kind. Yes, I'm happy and we are very much in love. And you see, you're the first to know here in this country, I'm going to have twin babies."

With a big smile, he replied, "Well, I'll be." Just as it came out of his mouth, he stopped right in front of the house.

Chapter 23

Monica heard the taxi pull up and was down the front steps in a leap. With a slight angry look, she handed Deirdre money for the taxi driver. In turn, Deirdre handed Roger the fare for the trip and his tip. She heard a slamming of the screen door when she looked up. "Thank you again, Roger, for your help."

"No problem, hope you have a safe trip back."

"Thank you again." Deirdre watched him drive off.

She turned when she heard, "What the hell are you doing here?" It was Kimberly.

"Well, what a greeting this is," she said, smiling to all of them as she looked up.

"Well, answer me!" demanded Kimberly.

"When I come inside and have something to eat. No sooner, not later, sister."

Sputtering, "Well! Oh, alright."

Deirdre entered the long hall, looking around. "Nothing has changed one bit."

"We tried to keep it the same," smiled Mrs. D. "Now, for something to eat and a nice hot bath."

"Now you're talking, Mrs. D. By the way, how are Duke and Major?"

"They are at the house. We didn't think it would be right for them to come."

"You're so right, and thank you for remembering that," she said, giving Mrs. D. a big hug. "Now when I'm through eating and having a nice hot shower, I have a lot to tell all of you."

"Would you like a shower now?" asked Mrs. D.

"Yes, thank you. By the way, Mrs. D., how long have you lived on the mountain? And are you a Native American, and of that tribe?"

Monica looked surprised at Deirdre and then asked, "What business is that of yours?"

"I'm sorry, Mrs. D., but I'm very curious. You see, our Great-great-grandfather Donald was given this mountain by the Cherokee Nation."

Mrs. D. smiled as she spoke, "It was my great-great-great-grandfather who gave this land to yours. We were sworn through the centuries to guard this mountain when no one was here."

Deirdre went over and gave Mrs. D. a big hug while her sisters just stood there with their mouths open.

Deirdre turned and smiled at them. "See, I just knew that was it. I have done a lot of thinking while flying back home. So you and Mr. D. will take care of it when we are gone, and so will your children and theirs until we make the circle again."

"That is what we are instructed to do. We will have the house all fixed up and things will be here when you make the circle again."

"Thank you so much," smiled Kimberly as she kissed Mrs. D. on her cheek.

"Mrs. D., is Mr. D. also Cherokee?" asked Monica.

"No."

The girls looked at her with a shocked look on their faces. Then Deirdre spoke as she looked deep into Mrs. D.'s eyes, "Were you in collage when you met him? He is from another tribe, is he not?"

"Yes, he is, we met at collage. He was studying to be a doctor. In his tribe, he was the son of a Holy Man, next in turn to follow in his father's footsteps. He is Sioux, the sweetest man you could ever wish to know."

"How did your people feel about you marrying someone from another tribe?" asked Monica.

"They were not happy, of course, until the Holy Man of our tribe told them another had done the same thing many centuries ago. She had married the man with flaming red hair and he was from the tribe of Scotland."

"Well, I'll be a monkey's uncle." Kimberly looked at Deirdre. "Is that why you asked her that question?"

"Yes. I found out that our Great-great-great- grandfather Donald was a widower with two sons and when he met Sunset, he fell in love and married her. She raised his sons like they were her own."

"How wonderful," Monica spoke with a dreamy look in her eyes.

Mrs. D. smiled, "You see, Mr. D.'s real name is Deer Running. That is why we call him Mr. D. He took the name Douglas to fit in around here."

"That sounds right. Thank you, Mrs. D. and forgive me for being so nosey."

"You needed to know the truth about all of us. You see, the second mountain from here was given to us as the caretakers of this mountain."

"How wonderful."

"Yes, Kimberly, it is."

"OK! Please, when are you going to tell me what's going on? Your sisters look like they could kill you," smiled Mrs. D.

"Yes, Mrs. D., we could. But we'll see if she will tell you all, and I mean *all* of the story," spoke Kimberly with worry in her voice.

After her nice warm shower, Deirdre sat at the kitchen table, wrapped in her terry robe. She started telling them the story right up until she left, and why."

Monica spoke up. "You didn't tell us that, and neither did mother."

"She didn't discover it until later. So now I need to find a good obstetrician."

"Deirdre, my niece works for a very good one.

"Mrs. D., could you call her and have her make me an appointment?"

"Yes, I'll do that first thing in the morning, but you need to rest now."

Early the next morning, at the Asheville-Hendersonville Airport, Tommy came through the gate and heard his foreman's voice, "Edward, hey man!"

"Hey, yourself. Harry, I need to talk to you. I need to go on to Chicago to see about my other businesses."

"OK, let's go to the office. Boy, do we have a lot of work started. You were gone a year; didn't know you would be gone so long."

"Well, old man, I got married in Scotland," Tommy stated as he walked into his office.

"You what? Well, where is she?"

"She is taking care of her business in Marshall. Her name is Deirdre MacDarroch, the writer."

"You mean to tell me you married THE Deirdre MacDarroch?"

"That's what I just got through telling you, man."

"Well, I'll be! You really got yourself a prize there."

"You can say that again. Look, Harry, I need to ask you a very important question."

"OK, shoot."

"Would you like to have this construction company?"

"What!! Man, are you crazy? What man wouldn't? Are you serious? The look on your face tells me you are. But, why?"

"I'm going back to Scotland to spend the rest of my days there."

"Is your wife going back too?"

"Yes, of course. That's why she is here, to take care of some of her business and check with the doctors. You see, we are expecting a baby."

"My goodness, you're going to be a father?"

"Yes, her sisters told me so."

"Her sisters? Why didn't she?"

"I left before she did, and they felt I needed to know."

"Ed, are you serious then about selling?"

"Yes, I am. Now, would you like the business? I need to get to Chicago."

"You know damn good and well I would love it. How much are we talking about, first?"

"OK, I'll have my lawyer draw up the papers this afternoon. All you have to do is go see him and sign them."

"That's fine, but, for God sake Ed, how much?"

"Harry, it is my gift to you for being such a good friend and foreman."

"No way, how much?"

"OK, OK, two million."

"Now, that's better. Hey, is that all? You know it's worth much more than that! I would say around four million or more. You go all over the country."

"I know, but that is all I want. I'll have my lawyer do the rest." He went over to give Harry his hand, and then he gave him a hug. Leaving the office, Tommy told everyone goodbye and to stick with Harry. He had their promise to do so, and Tommy left. Everyone was so happy for Harry and knew he would make a great boss because he had learned a lot from Ed, and how to treat his employees. Harry went into the office and put his head down on his desk and cried like a baby. Not only for getting the business, but that his best friend would be gone.

Tommy caught his plane for Chicago after he left his lawyer, Robert Peterson's office. Landing at O'Hare Airport, Tommy got off his plane and started to go get a taxi, when he heard his name being called by a sweet voice. "Tommy, darling, over here."

"Well, hello. Barbara, how are things? What are you doing here?"

"Is that all you have to say? I'm fine." Looking around, she asked, "Where are your brothers?"

"They are taking care of their business back in North Carolina, and then they will come here."

"I see. So what are your plans?"

Tommy had a funny look on his face. "Barbara, how did you know I would be on this plane?"

"I didn't. I was just seeing some friends off and happened to see you, darling." She smiled up at him like honey would drip from her lips.

He looked down, "Look, could we talk later? I need to get out of here. You see, I have business to talk over with my lawyer."

"Oh! Of course, my car is across the street. I'll take you home."

Tommy thanked Barbara for the lift, then she asked, "Darling, we need to talk about our future?"

"OUR WHAT? Look, Barbara, I'm going back to Scotland and so are my brothers. That's why I came home to sell all of my businesses."

"What? Have you gone mad? What about us?"

"Barbara, could you just start the car, please. We'll talk about it at the apartment, but not here at the airport."

"Well, *excuse me*. I'm so sorry," she said in a very sarcastic tone of voice.

On the way to his apartment, Barbara kept talking, while Tommy was back in Scotland holding the woman he loved. Even now he could feel her mouth on his.

"Tommy, don't you agree?"

"Agree to what?" he asked, coming out of his daze.

"Haven't you been listening?"

"Sorry, but I'm so tired. I haven't been listening to anything. Must be jet lag."

"I can't make it tonight, so I'll drop you off and you get some rest, then we can talk tomorrow."

"Sorry, but no can do, I have a business meeting tomorrow, but how about dinner?"

"Oh! Alright, see you then at the Moonlight Room, say about six?"

"Yes, yes, see you then." Stopping the car, Tommy hopped out with his suitcase, said hello to his doorman as he went into the building. Tommy got inside of his apartment, dropped his suitcase and fixed himself a Scotch on the rocks. *I have gotten used to drinking it with ice. I'll unpack tomorrow,* he thought as he went straight into his bedroom and dropped his clothes. *I'll take a shower tomorrow.*

After a good night's sleep, if he wanted to call it that, Tommy got up, turned, and looked at his bed. What a mess. *Oh, well,* he thought.

While in the shower, he smiled as his memories went back in time. He thought about the falls where his Kitten had taken him. How they both jumped in and made love on the moss. Then just lay there, wrapped in each other's arms and bodies. *My love, how I miss you. Hope you miss me as well,* he was thinking to himself.

It was like a voice coming from afar, *Tommy, my love, I miss you so.*

He cooked himself a good breakfast, and as he ate, he checked the time. He picked up the phone and made his call to his lawyer. When Tommy finally got through to Mr. Greenburg's office, he asked if he could see him as soon as possible, that it was very urgent.

Mr. Greenburg said to come over after lunch because he would be in court all that morning.

Tommy waited, then called his two brothers. He asked both to them when they were coming and if they had finished their business. He listened to Hugh, who said that he and Richard were just finishing up and would be in Chicago soon.

Tommy waited to go to the lawyer's office. He sat back and thought about the bank in Asheville that had been there ever since the seventeenth century. That's where he wanted all his money to be put.

Thinking to himself, *Things are falling into place. My brothers and I were smart enough not to have married anyone in the twentieth century. Now they would forever be with the right ones.* He looked at his watch, "Boy, I've got to hurry. Don't want to be late."

Tommy got into the elevator in the Greenburg building where his lawyer had his office. Tommy thought, *I wonder what my love is doing?* Just the thought of his Kitten got him very hot around his groin. Looking down, he closed his jacket in front of him. *Got to stop this, but God, that woman has me crazy.*

The elevator stopped, and he got out on Mr. Greenburg's floor. Going through the door, there was a secretary who was a very attractive lady. She smiled up at him and motioned for him to go on in.

Mr. Greenburg got up from behind his desk. "Did you have a good trip, Mr. MacDonald?"

"Yes, I did, thanks for asking."

"Now tell me, what can I do for you?"

"Well, I guess I had better start from the beginning."

As Tommy told Mr. Greenburg his story, the man was speechless, just staring at Tommy like he had lost his mind.

When Tommy finished, he asked, "Well, can you draw up the legal papers to have everything sold and the proceeds to be put in my account in the Asheville Bank?" Looking at the lawyer, "Mr. Greenburg, did you hear me?"

Mr. Greenburg came out of shock, "Why, yes, I think I did. Are you sure this is what you want?"

"Please, Mr. Greenburg, snap out of it. Please, sir, I need this done. I have to be back in Scotland in two months. My brothers are in North Carolina taking care of their business there, and then they are coming here to finish up. All of us need to be back in Scotland in two months."

"Yes. Now Tommy, are you sure?"

"Yes, I am. I have never been so sure of anything in all my life."

"Then it shall be done. You're selling everything — everything including your stocks and bonds and your art gallery?"

"That is right."

"How are you going to live in Scotland without money?"

"Sell all the stock and bonds; deposit the money in the bank of North Carolina. I'll leave the name with you. My brothers will be here to sign the papers on the art gallery. You sell it and put the money in the same bank. Besides, I have a job in Scotland and it starts in two months."

"But aren't you ever coming back?"

"No."

"Well then, you come back day after tomorrow. Bring your brother to sign the papers."

"I'll do just that."

Tommy left his lawyer's office in time to go and meet Barbara for dinner. Walking into the restaurant, Tommy saw her. *There she is in all her glory, waiting for me. You poor girl. You were OK until I found my own true love again. She is my soul mate. The one girl I have dreamed about all my life.*

Walking to the table, he spoke. "Hello Barbara, how nice you look this evening."

"Thank you, but it's about time you got here. I almost gave you up. What kept you?"

"It took longer than I thought at my lawyer's office."

 "Your lawyer?"

"Yes, just some very important matters concerning my businesses."

"I see. Well now, let's talk about us, Tommy. When shall we set the date?"

"Set the date for what?"

"Why, love, our wedding, of course!"

"Wedding? Barbara, we never spoke of marriage."

"But I thought that after all these years."

"How many? Three? We went into this relationship with no strings. You could have gone anytime."

"But! But! But."

"No buts."

Barbara sat there with tears in her eyes. Then asked, "Tommy is there someone else?"

"Yes, Barbara."

"Is she beautiful?"

"Yes, she takes my breath away."

"Then I can't say anything to keep you here?"

"There is nothing anyone could say or do to change my mind."

"Not even your business friends?"

"No! Not even them. As much as I like you, and them, no. You see, Barbara, she is my wife."

"Your wife?" Tears were running down her cheeks. "Tommy, would you mind if I went home? I don't feel like eating now."

"I'll take you."

"No, please, I have my car. I wish you the best of everything and the greatest happiness." Barbara turned and did not look back as she left the restaurant.

Tommy went to the bar and had a few whiskeys. Then he went home. Lying awake in bed, he turned over and pulled the extra pillow into his arms. *Kitten, my love, how you torture me with the thought of you. Where are you? What are you doing? Are you with anyone? If only my jealousy would leave.*

Tommy felt Deirdre in his arms, holding her, feeling her long silk ginger-red hair go though his fingers, her gold-green cat eyes looking into his. He could hear her voice. 'My darling, you are my life, breath, sun and stars, my whole being.'

Tommy could feel her body under his with her long, strong legs wrapped around his waist, pulling her warm, hot body up to his, "Oh, my God, woman, I can't help but want you all the time." Tommy had to get up and run into the bathroom to take a very, very cold shower.

After his shower, he put on his terry robe, and sat on the couch. *If I were back home in Scotland, I would jump into the cold lake.* Laughing, he got up and got a very cold glass of orange juice. He went back into the living room and sat down on the couch. He read the paper, turned on the TV, and heard the news. He felt so tired at that moment he just fell asleep on the couch.

Tommy woke with a sound of knocking. "Just one minute." As he opened the door, there stood his two brothers.

"What time is it?"

"It is seven at night," answered Richard, his youngest brother.

"What's the matter?" asked Hugh.

"I must have slept around the clock. Couldn't sleep in bed, so I took a very cold shower, and fell asleep on the couch. I read the paper and saw the news on TV."

"So you could not sleep in bed? Richard asked as he meandered over to his brother's bedroom. "My word, Hugh, will you look at his bed? He was laughing as he saw the look on Tommy's face.

"Oh! No you don't," Tommy said as he got hold of Hugh's arm.

Shaking his brother's hand loose, he ran to see what Richard was laughing at. "Lord have mercy, Tommy, what were you doing?"

"Never mind, never mind. Now you two pain in the asses come over here. I need to talk to you before we go to the lawyer's office."

"Why are we going?" asked Hugh.

"That's what I am trying to tell you, if you both will take those smirks off your faces."

"OK, OK! Don't get upset, we'll behave," Richard said with laughter in his voice. "What did you want to see us about?"

"Richard, this just had to do with just you two. I need your advice on what I'm doing."

"Where do you want to eat?" asked Richard.

Tommy was getting dressed when he spoke. "Well, I thought we would eat here. I got steaks, wine, and the rest of the fixings. What I have to say is just between us."

"OK by me," laughed Hugh.

"Tommy, now what's going on?"

"Hugh, get the potatoes washed, and Richard, you chill the wine."

Both said together, "OK."

As the three cooked, laughed, and drank the wine, Tommy got tears in his eyes, knowing this would be the last time they would be eating together in this century and maybe not in any other. Looking at Hugh, he had a very strange feeling—but didn't know why.

"Boys, I have some news."

"Question here, when did you leave? And did you both finish your business matters?"

"Yes, at least, I did," answered Hugh.

"So did I. Even put our money in the bank you suggested in Asheville, North Carolina."

Tommy smiled at each of them. "Good boys, first have another glass of wine to celebrate." Tommy poured the wine and continued. "I have a story to tell you. But first, I sold the construction company to my foreman, Harry. Now we all sold our companies and put our money in a bank that has been in business ever since 1702."

"What in the world are you talking about? The wine has gone to your head, Tommy."

"No! Now listen very carefully. I'm going to tell you a story. But first you remember me telling you about when Deirdre spoke of the bank. I have a feeling we all will be coming back in or around that time. Our money will be there collecting interest."

"Are you sure?" Both saying at the same time.

"Yes."

"You really mean we will? Live and live well at the time?"

"Yes, Hugh, that is what I mean."

"Well, brother, that is enough for me," remarked Richard.

"And me, said Hugh.

The next day they all three left to go to the lawyer's office. The boys had to sign off on the art gallery that they were equal partners in.

"Mr. MacDonald, are you sure you want to do this?"

The three responded at the same time. "Yes."

Mr. Greenburg got on the phone to put a call to the bank. "May I speak to Mr. Walter MacKenzie?"

As Mr. Greenburg talked to Mr. MacKenzie about what was going on, he had a smile on his face, turned and smiled at the three MacDonald brothers, then hung up. "Well, you are all set. Everything is set up and you have nothing to worry about. Plus he thinks he has a buyer for the art gallery."

All three shouted, and then danced around the office. They then left and headed straight to the nearest pub for a drink. It was after midnight when they got back to Tommy's apartment.

Chapter 24

The next morning, Tommy thought he was up early. "Come on you sleepy heads. Coffee is ready."

"OK, smart brother. We have already had our shower." Hugh smiled as he came into the kitchen with Richard behind him.

Just as they all carried their coffee cups into the living room, the doorbell rang. Sitting his cup down, Tommy said, "Wonder who in the world that is at this hour?" He went to answer the door and his brothers heard, "Barbara! What in the world are you doing with that gun?"

Barbara looked at Tommy with a crazy smirk on her face as she pointed the gun. "If I can't have you, no one else will."

Hugh and Richard got up when they heard her voice. Racing to the door, they heard two shots and Barbara's crazy laughter.

"My God, you shot Tommy! Woman, have you gone crazy? Richard, call the hospital for an ambulance, NOW! Lady, you come with me. You'll stay by my side until the police come," stated Hugh, as he took hold of Barbara's arms.

Richard called the hospital, then the police. "The police and ambulance are on their way, Hugh."

"Barbara, why, in God's name did you do it? Why did you?"

"He led me to believe that he would marry me."

"Oh no, I did not."

"Don't talk, Tommy, just lay still." Richard spoke with a worried look on his face.

Just then the medics came through the door, then the police. Taking care of Tommy's wounds, the medics put him in the ambulance, and then took him to the hospital.

Meanwhile, Captain Lewis took Barbara to jail to book her for attempted murder.

The boys started to leave when Richard said, "Hugh, go to the hospital and I'll call the girls."

"Do you think you need to?"

"Yes, this will delay Tommy's return awhile. I think Deirdre should know."

"NO!! You can't tell Monica and Kimberly. We can't talk to either of them."

"But, why not?"

"If we speak to them, we can't go back, you dummy."

"OK! Hugh, you're right, but who?"

"Tommy can tell them, that's who, but first we'll have to find out about his condition."

"Let's hurry."

By the time Richard and Hugh got to the hospital, the doctors were coming out of the operating room. "Doctor, how is he?"

Doctor Morgan answered, "He'll be alright if he does as he is told, but I don't think he likes taking orders."

"You have that right, Doc." remarked Hugh. "He hates it. The only one who can order him about is his wife, and then it's in a loving way. He thinks everything is his idea."

"You mean a turn-around?"

"Yep, Doctor, that is what he means," smiled Richard.

"Who did this to your brother?"

"Her name is Barbara Miller. She told him if she couldn't have him, no one else could," answered Hugh.

"We heard her, then she shot twice," remarked Richard.

"She must have lost it, slipped a screw loose."

"You better believe it, Doc," Hugh agreed.

"Can we see him now, Doctor Morgan? Richard asked.

"Give us fifteen more minutes. Oh, yes! Who is Deirdre?"

Hugh answered with a worried look, "She is his wife, why?"

"It's just that he keeps calling for her."

"We'll explain later, Doctor, but where was he shot?" asked Hugh.

"He was shot twice in the abdomen, but he'll be alright in due time, like I said, if he does as he is told." Dr. Morgan looked at both young men with a puzzled look. "There were scars near the same spot. Was he shot or stabbed before?"

"Yes, it's been a long time and a long story, Doctor, but we'll see he does as he is told. And thanks a million, Doctor Morgan," Richard said as he was shaking the doctor's hand.

"But you must get her here as soon as you can."

"But, but!!" stammered Hugh.

"No buts to it. Just do it. Hugh, is it?"

"Yes, Doctor."

Both stood still with their mouths open, and looked at one another. "Richard! Deirdre said if we ever needed her to call and ask for a Mrs. D., the caretakers and dear friends.

"You're right, Hugh. Now is the time. You are the one to call, Hugh, you know. You're the second son.

"What a cop-out, Richard. OK, I'll do it."

Hugh went back to Tommy's apartment. He looked about in the hall where Tommy was shot. The blood was still on the floor. Hugh had a cold chill. *Bitch could have killed me*, thinking to himself.

Hugh sat down, and reached for the phone. He shook his head as he dialed Deirdre's number. On the other end, he heard it ringing when a man's voice came on the line. "Hello, this is the MacDarroch residence. Jake Mull speaking."

"Hello, Mr. Mull, this is Hugh MacDonald, Thomas Edward MacDonald's brother. May I speak to a Mrs. D.? Please, it's very important."

I understand, very well, sir. Just one moment please."

"Jake, wait. What I have to tell her is about my brother, Tommy. You may need to stand by with something for Deirdre when she tells her."

"I see, is it very bad news, sir?"

"Yes, Jake, it is very bad news, I'm sorry to say."

"I'll get Mrs. D. and stand by, Mr. Hugh."

Hugh waited. It seemed like hours. But it accurately was just a few minutes. "Hello! Hugh, what is it?"

"Mrs. D.?"

"Yes, it is. Sorry, but when Jake said it was you and that it was urgent… What in the world has happened?"

"Is Deirdre around?"

"No, she's down at the stream fishing. But Hugh, it's Tommy, isn't it?"

"Yes, how did you know?"

"This morning, Deirdre screamed out loud and it was around eight o'clock."

"My God, that's the time it happened."

"*What* happened?"

"Mrs. D., Tommy was shot twice in the abdomen. By the way, why is she fishing?"

"What? She sometimes goes fishing when she is upset."

"Do you want me to repeat it?"

"No, no. That's when she screamed and held onto her abdomen."

"My Lord, she feels his pain."

"I believe so. Tell me the whole story."

Hugh told her everything and that Tommy kept calling for her. But knew they could not see one another because if they spoke, they could not go back.

"I see. OK, then what if I come out to Chicago and talk to him, and tell him what's going on with Deirdre?"

"Would you please? Oh, Mrs. D., God bless you. Yes, that would do him worlds of good. But how will you tell Deirdre?"

"Hugh! She knows, were you not listening to me?"

"Yes, you're right, Mrs. D. Look, I'll make the arrangements for your ticket and call you right back. Stay by the phone."

"I'll do just that. Hugh, Deirdre and her sisters leave tomorrow for Scotland."

"Tell Kimberly and Monica not to tell her until after the baby comes or at their own discretion."

"OK, but when will you ever learn, she already knows."

"I know, I know. But I'm not thinking too straight and I need to get back to the hospital."

"Hugh, you do what needs to be done and I'll wait for your call. I'll pack and be ready to leave. Jake Mull will be on alert."

"Gotcha, stand by," then he hung up.

Kimberly and Monica came in the door. "Who was that on the phone, Mrs. D.?" asked Monica.

Mrs. D. told both the girls what had happened. "My God, is he still alive? asked Kimberly.

"Yes, but he keeps calling for Deirdre."

"That's why she screamed and clutched her abdomen," remarked Monica.

"Yes, and I'm going out to see what I can do."

"Bless you, Mrs. D. We would go, but you know we can't."

"I understand, Monica. I understand. Look, I may not ever see you girls again. You take damn good care of your sister. You'll find things all boarded up well and tight as a drum when you come again."

The phone rang at that moment. "Hello? Yes, Hugh, I'm leaving right now. Yes, you were real lucky to get me a ticket just like that, as you say." She hung up the phone when she heard...

"What's all the commotion about?" Deirdre asked as she came through the door.

"My word, you are as quiet as a mouse."

"Oh, it's nothing," answered Kimberly.

"Nothing? Then why the suitcase? Mrs. D. getting in the car?"

"Alright, Deirdre, I'll tell you," Monica interrupted Deirdre before she could say anything else. "Tommy was shot and Mrs. D is going to Chicago to talk with him. Hugh just called, Tommy is calling for you. Now, any messages?"

She ran down to the car. "Ho, Mrs. D." Deirdre looked back and spoke to Monica. "Monica, I knew before you told me."

Deirdre got to the car just in time. She stuck her head into the window, as Jake turned off the motor. "Mrs. D. will you tell him his babies need him and so do I. I'll keep the door open as long as I can. But when it closes, that is when the babies will be born. That is on All Hollow's Eve. Please tell him to be with us; we need him. I love him more than life itself."

Giving her a hug, and saying, "I'll do that. You girls take care of her or, by golly, I'll haunt you in your grave," Mrs. D. turned and left with tears in her eyes.

Deirdre stood by the stream thinking out loud, "Tommy, my darling, you get well and come to us. Your babies and I need you. I'll always be with you, my darling."

413

The next morning, Monica, Kimberly and Deirdre left for Scotland, while Mrs. D. landed in Chicago. "Mrs. D., it's me, Hugh, over here."

"Hugh MacDonald?"

"Yes."

"How did you know it was me?"

"Why Mrs. D., by your name tag."

"Oh, yes. The airline made me put it on. Let's go; time is wasting."

"You know, Mrs. D., if Kimberly was here her herbs could heal Tommy."

"Yes, I know, but she isn't, is she? They all left this morning for Scotland."

Arriving at the hospital, the doctor met them as they came up the corridor. "Did you get in touch with Deirdre?"

"No, Doctor, they did not. I'm Mrs. D., Deirdre MacDonald is a very dear friend of mine. Now, if you will please move aside, I'll take over." With that, she walked into Tommy's room.

"Who are you" Tommy asked in a weak voice.

Taking her jacket off, Mrs. D. went to sit down by Tommy's bed. "I'm a very dear friend of your wife's, Tommy. You must get well for Deirdre. She needs you right now, very badly."

Tommy answered softly, "Is she alright?"

"Yes, for now, she is. When you were shot, she grabbed her abdomen. She knew what had happened."

Tommy sat straight up in bed. "The baby?"

"They are alright, but it's you they need. Deirdre told me to tell you she would keep the way open until the babies are born, and then it will close."

"Wait, did you say THEY?"

"Yes, I did. You are going to have twins!"

"Oh, thank you for coming, Mrs. D. I will get well. I heard her, you know, last night. I will get well enough to go back, you will see. I'll be home in time to help with the birthing of my babies.

"Yes, and I know you will, Tommy." Mrs. D. looked down at him, then touched his wound in a healing way. Take good care of yourself, my friend. Maybe one day we'll meet again."

Tommy took Mrs. D. by the hand. "I will, dear friend."

Mrs. D. left for the airport. She felt things would be just fine, although she felt a pain of sadness.

When Deirdre and her sisters arrived at the airport in Scotland, they had a message waiting for them. Deirdre knew what it said before she opened it. But she read it anyway as she walked, to send a spoken reply. "All will be alright, do not worry."

Over the loud speaker system, they heard the call that the Islay shutter plane was taking on passengers. They ran to get on board just in time.

"Kimberly, do you have your herbs, seeds and plants?"

"I have the seeds, Deirdre, but we were not allowed to bring the plants."

"Oh, you're right, I forgot."

"We're home. Can you believe it?"

"Deirdre."

"Yes, Kimberly."

"I'm worried about you. Are you sure you're alright?"

"Yes, I am, and don't worry, everything will work out in God's own good time."

They landed at Islay's small airport. As they descended from the small plane, there stood Angus Gordon. He had a big smile on his face. "Well, you made it. I knew you would.

All three gave him a hug. "It's good to be home, dear friend."

"How are you feeling, Lady Deirdre?"

Patting her nice small round stomach, Deirdre said, "just fine, carrying this load," then she laughed with Angus.

"You take good care of my godchildren. Now we must go and you must eat, and then get some rest."

"You mean we can't go home today?"

"No."

"And why not?" asked Kimberly.

Monica spoke up before Angus Gordon could answer Kimberly's question. "Deirdre needs to get home soon."

"No, no, lassies. I understand that, but she will need her rest before she goes on. The trip alone will put a huge strain on her body, let alone the babies."

"Sorry, we never thought of that." Looking at Deirdre, "He's right, you know."

Mr. Angus Gordon smiled at them. "Then let's get going so she can rest. You know, lassies, it will take a lot out of you, too."

They arrived at the Broken Wave Inn and Pub. The landlord showed them upstairs to their room. "When you have rested, My Lady, I'll bring you something to eat."

"Thank you very much, but could you have someone bring us hot water so we can freshen up?"

"Yes, I'll have it here in no time." He stood in the doorway a few moments.

"Is there anything else, Mr. MacGee?" Deirdre asked.

"I just wanted to say welcome home to you and your sisters."

"Thank you so much, it's good to be home! By the way, Mr. MacGee, we'll come down to eat."

He backed out of the doorway with a big smile on his face, "Thank you. I'll have things ready for you."

When the door closed, they all three just fell back on the bed, laughing their silly heads off. Deirdre didn't know how long they had lain there, when a knock came on the door. Sitting up, Monica said, "Come in." A young lass came in with water for them to wash in.

Thanking her, she smiled, and then said, "My Lady Deirdre, It is so good to have you home. If I can help in any way, please let me know."

"Thank you and I will. What's you name, lass?"

"It's Mariote."

She went over and gave the young women a hug. "Thank you for being so kind."

"It's no trouble at all. It's just an honor to wait on you and your sisters. I must go now and get your supper ready." Mariote ran out the door with a little dance step on her feet.

Later, all three went down and had a wonderful meal fit for a king. They dragged themselves back up the stairs for a good night's sleep after that great, hearty meal.

Bright and early the next morning, they were up early, dressed, had their porridge with buttered sconces by the time Mr.

Gordon got there. Angus Gordon was at the base of the stairs waiting on them. "Good morning."

"To you, too."

"Did you rest? I certainly hope so."

"We did, and they fed us very well," answered Kimberly.

"My Lady, you still look tired. Is something wrong?"

"No."

"Now Deirdre, Mr. Gordon should know." Kimberly looked at Mr. Gordon. "Sir, would you please sit down, we need to tell you what happened."

"Alright."

Mr. Gordon sat down with a worried look on his face. "Now, Kimberly, tell me."

"Sir Thomas Edward MacDonald was shot twice in the abdomen and that is why Deirdre is so worried. She is worried that he will not be here before the babies come. If he isn't, the door will close."

Angus looked up into Deirdre's face with tears in his own eyes. "Now please don't worry so much. Sir Thomas would not like that, you must think of the babies."

"I know! I thank you for your concern and I will be careful and take it easy. Now we must go and see about the humming of the Sacred Stones."

"The what?" asked Kimberly.

"You heard her," replied Monica.

"But we did not come that way. It was the fog." Kimberly spoke to Deirdre with fear in her voice.

"Kimberly, listen to me. We will go back through the Sacred Stone. It's not bad; I came forward that way," replied Deirdre.

"But Deirdre, what about the babies?" asked Monica.

"I know, but it's the only way. Mother will be waiting for us there."

"If you say so. But the babies? I am worried about them." Kimberly spoke with worry on her brow.

"If it's the Lord's will for them and me to make it home, then we will make it."

"She is right. Come on, Kimberly, we need to go home."

They said their goodbyes and left with Mr. Gordon. He helped them get into a small motor boat that would take them across the channel to Jura.

As they landed, it started to cloud over like a large thunderstorm was rolling in. "We must hurry, it looks like we might get caught in a big storm."

"No, we won't. It's just telling me it's time. Come on, it's not far from here. It is just over the rise there."

Pointing to a small hill, the closer they got, the louder the thunder and lightering got.

"Deirdre, do you hear that?"

"What are you saying, Kimberly?" asked Monica, with a frightened look on her face.

"She is saying that she can hear the loud humming of the stones. Now when we are there, you hold on to one another," shouted Deirdre over the noise.

"But, Deirdre, what about you?"

"Kimberly, I'll hold on to my babies. You will get there before me, so just be ready to catch me."

"We will. Are you sure?" asked Monica.

"I am."

The closer they got to the humming, the more deafening it was. Deirdre stood there and watched her sisters go through, praying that they would land by the pool in the forest. Now it was her turn, holding her abdomen with both hands really tight. She prayed, "God above, be with me and my babies," as she walked in.

Chapter 25

Deirdre landed on the other side, but did not see her sisters. They were not at the pool.

All of a sudden she heard, "Look oot below." It was Kimberly laughing. Kimberly landed next to Deirdre, and Monica right on top of her.

"What?"

"Ough dear! Sorry Deirdre, did I hurt ye?" asked Kimberly, a bit of the old way of speech returning.

"Nay. What is that smell?"

Kimberly started to laugh again. "Ocuch! Hush," spoke Monica with anger and hurt in her voice. As she got up to brush herself off, "Hinny, how did ye get that smell?" Deirdre asked.

'Tis a long story. I'll tell ye later."

"Nay, ye'll tell me noo or aft ye wash in the stream below the pool."

"Alright, Deirdre, I'll tell ye while I'm washin'."

Monica told Deirdre that she heard music and put her foot out just to see if the stones would drop her there. All she got was splattered. As she put her foot out, it hit a nice fresh pile of horse dung.

Everyone laughed, even Monica. Now that it was over it was funny. But when it happened, it was not. Just as Monica had put her wet clothes back on, they heard a wagon and horse coming at a fast gallop.

"Hide quickly," Deirdre said to her sisters.

"Who do ye think 'tis?" Kimberly whispered.

"I pray that it be Mathair and Queen Megotta instead o' the Campbells."

The noise and whinny of the horses came closer. All of a sudden, it stopped. "Deirdre, Kimberly, Monica, are ye there?"

Mathair, 'tis ye? Deirdre asked.

"Aye, lassies, 'tis me and Queen Megotta. Come oot noo 'tis safe."

Queen Megotta saw them first coming from under the bank of the pool. Smiling, "Weel there ye are." Going over to Deirdre with her hands stretched out toward Deirdre's stomach, "Ye see, I told ye tha' ye would be fine and sae are the bairns." She turned to Lady Mary Kate, "Aye. E'er thin' 'tis jus' fine; they are growing." She said a questioned look on her face, "Are ye sure the be twa?"

"Aye that 'tis what the healer said and he is verra guid at what he does, yor grace," Deirdre smiled as she hugged herself.

She, with her sisters, climbed into the wagon. They lay in a deep pile of straw and closed their eyes, not realizing how tired they were. Lady Mary Kate looked back at her daughters and smiled. *Go dream, ma luves,* she was thinking to herself.

Queen Megotta had a startling expression on her face as she turned to look back at Deirdre. The look on Deirdre's face was quite frightening to queen Megotta. Little did she know Deirdre was dreaming of Tommy and what had been done to him.

All of a sudden, Lady Mary Kate heard and saw her eldest thrashing about, muttering out loud in her sleep. Turning back to the front, she had a worried look on her face.

"Tommy luve, look out. She weel try again. Hide. Make yer pillows intae body, please, ma luve." Deirdre shouted out into the night.

Tommy sat straight up in his hospital bed as it seemed he heard Deirdre's voice coming through the window on the night breeze. He struggled to rise up from his bed. He was still very weak as he reached out for the bell, hoping the night nurse would hasten to his aid. Nurse Jane came in and saw Tommy in the chair beside his bed. "My goodness, what in the world are you doing out of bed? You know that you shouldn't move just now."

Tommy looked at her name tag that read Jane. "Jane, listen please, very carefully." Jane bent very closely to hear what he had to say. Tommy told her what happened to him and he had word that she had escaped and would try again.

"Jane, will you please help me?"

"Why, yes, of course. What would you have me do?"

"First, call the police, then my brothers. Third, would you help me make a body out of my pillows?"

"I'll do all those things, but you just sit still. I'll put a chair in the bathroom and fix it so you'll be very comfortable while we wait."

"But Jane, I can't risk your life.   Barbara had lost her mind."

"Mr. Thomas Edward MacDonald, she almost killed you, and besides, your wife would be very mad if I let anything happen to you."

"Yes," he said, "she would," smiling as he could see Deirdre with an angry look.

"Indeed, she would and her in Scotland getting ready to have your twins," she said, shaking her head.

Jane went around fixing the pillows into the shape of a man after she called the police as well as Mr. Thomas Edward's brothers.

They waited what seemed like hours when they heard the door open into the room. Through the crack in the door, Jane and Tommy saw a dark figure move slowly to the bed. The hood fell off and they saw Barbara raise a gun, then as she fired three times, the police burst in and grabbed her.

Barbara, knowing she had been caught, said, "You're too late, I have killed him."

"No, Barbara, you did not."

Turning, she looked into Tommy's eyes.

"Bu-bu-but. It can't be, I just shot you."

"No, you missed again."

"But how?"

"Barbara, my wife saved me both times. The first time, making me want to live. This time I heard her voice coming through the night warning me."

"You are the one who is mad, not me."

"No, Barbara, you are."

As Barbara turned away, the policeman put the handcuffs on her. She started laughing like a madwoman.

Tommy could hear her all the way down the hall.

Hugh came in, with Richard right behind him. "Well, late as usual," smiled Tommy.

"What's this all about?" asked Hugh.

Tommy told them about hearing Deirdre's voice giving him a warning. So he had Jane call the police, then them.

"You mean you heard Deirdre? asked Richard.

"Yep, and I felt the need to get out of here so we can go home."

"But are you able?" asked Hugh.

Tommy got up and stood, "Yes, I'll be ready."

"Well, we hope so. When do you get out of here?" Richard asked. Just as he got the question out of his mouth, Doctor Morgan came through the door. "So you think you're ready to leave, do you?"

"Yes, Doctor, I do. Look. See, I can stand. Yes, I know that I'm still weak, but by walking, it will build up my strength."

Doctor Morgan put his hand up to his chin and started pulling at it. Then he said in a harsh tone, "You may be right. Let's see you walk."

Tommy started ambling slowly toward Doctor Morgan. The doctor smiled. "Well, you know, you may be right."

"How about travel, Doctor?" Hugh asked.

"Now maybe about a week at home, then have him come to see me next Friday and we'll see."

Tommy smiled, "Thank you, Doctor Morgan, I'll do that. You'll see. I'll be a lot better and can travel to Scotland."

"What!! Travel to Scotland? Man, are you crazy?"

"Doctor, my wife is going to have twins and I need to be there in the worst way."

"But Tommy, I understand; but that far?"

"Yes, Doctor, that far. You'll see. I will be well enough."

"I certainly will think hard on this," Doctor Morgan said as he left the room.

Back in Scotland

Deirdre sat in the garden as she had ever since she had returned. Even though she had gotten bigger as her time drew near.

She prayed on a shooting star as it shot across the night sky. Deirdre smiled, then made a wish.

" Deirdre, Deirdre, are you here?" called Monica.

"Aye, here I..."

"Where?"

"Oh, Monica, over here, by the roses."

Coming over Monica smiled. "Roses, you mean the ones that are sleeping until spring?"

Deirdre smiled as she held out her hand to show Monica a yellow rosebud she had picked from one of the bushes Tommy had planted.

"What does it mean, sister?"

"It means that Tommy will be back soon."

It was almost All Hallow's Eve. Deirdre was at her same place in the garden praying.

"Ma Lady, ye shouldna' be oot here." It was young Timmy.

"Timmy, I'm, fine. Thank you for warning." As she spoke Deirdre felt a sharp pain. "Timmy, ga sae help; hurry, please. The bairns are in a hurry tae say hello."

Chapter 26

Timmy ran to the big doors at the castle, shouting as he entered. "My Lady, My Laird, Lady Deirdre is having the babies in the garden."

"My word, summon the guards to get a litter, blankets, Kimberly," shouted Lady Mary Kate. "Everyone, get the birthing room ready. We are on our way to get her!"

Everyone was running around when Queen Megotta came smiling. "My Lady, I have news that will please Lady Deirdre."

Lady Mary Kate turned, "My Queen, what is it?"

"Let Lady Deirdre know that her husband, Tommy, is on his way. He should be here soon."

"I will, and thank you. She'll be so happy. This will make it easier on her to have the babies."

The Queen turned to leave, and then stopped, walking over to where they had lifted Deirdre onto the litter.

"My Lady, there are not just two, but three you will have," she said with a big smile.

Deirdre looked up, "Are you serious?"

"Yes, I am."

"Mother, did you hear that?"

Smiling, Lady Mary Kate answered, "I did, love."

"Mother, did you do what I ask? The birthing room should be cold, not hot because of germs."

"Yes, I did and when the babies are born, clean them up in a warm room. Clean their eyes, their noses, and mouths first and thump their feet."

"Ouch! You got it, Mother!"

"Everything is ready."

Holding the sides of the cot on the litter, she screamed loudly, "Oh, God, they are in a hurry to say hello." As the last word was spoken, Deirdre's water broke.

"Hurry, we must get her to the birthing room," shouted Lady Mary Kate.

While everyone was running to get things started, it seemed Tommy heard Deirdre scream his name.

His plane landed on Islay. Tommy looked around as he got off the plane with his brothers. He saw Mr. Gordon waiting for them.

"There you are, Tommy, we must hurry now." He walked fast, expecting the lads to follow.

"Wait up, old man," shouted Hugh. "My brother can't run; he still is weak"

"Sorry lad, but Lady Deirdre is having her babies. There are three, so Queen Megotta says. Lady Deirdre is having a very hard time."

"We must hurry, brothers."

"Come, Mr. Angus, do you know how we can get to her?"

"Tommy, I do. Follow me. Help your brother."

"We will, just go." Hugh on one side with Richard on the other helped Tommy into the boat which would take them to Jura. Mr. Gordon had a carriage waiting for them that would take them straight to the Sacred Stones.

They helped Tommy out of the boat and into the carriage. Hugh could see that Tommy was in great pain. "I knew you should have waited."

"But Hugh, she needs me and so do the babies. Hurry Angus. Oh, God, be with my loved ones. Let my Kitten know that I'm coming."

"Tommy, she knows, she knows," Mr. Gordon spoke softly.

"There they are, the Sacred Stones," shouted Richard.

"Listen, do you hear it?" asked Hugh.

"Hear what?" asked Richard.

"The humming, like bees in a swarm," smiled Tommy.

Mr. Gordon helped Tommy out of the carriage with the assistance of his brothers.

"This is where I leave you. But I'll see you later."

"Thank you, kind sir," spoke Tommy as he grabbed Angus' hand. Angus was quite surprised as Tommy kissed it with tears streaming down his face.

"Remember, you walk between the stones," Angus said as he patted Tommy on the arm.

"Tommy, I feel you need to hurry. I feel that something is wrong."

"I feel it too. Brothers, let's go."

They said their goodbyes and ran toward the stones. As Tommy entered, it was as though he could hear Deirdre's screams. It was like he had no sooner gotten the sound out of his head that he was by the pool. He had gotten up just in time, when out came his brothers.

"Wow, what a ride," remarked Hugh.

"You got that right," laughed Richard.

"Come, let's go. I feel my Kitten needs me in a hurry."

"Tommy, take it easy. Remember you're not well yet." Hugh grabbed at his arm, trying his best to slow Tommy down.

"Can't you hear her screams?" asked Tommy.

"It's all in your head," was Richard's remark.

All of a sudden, they heard horses. Out of the mist Tommy saw Uncle William leading a horse and Jamie leading two.

"Thank God, you're here. She needs you bad. Tommy, lad, we all thought there'd be only two, but there seems to be one more, and that one is waiting for you, we think. It just won't be born. We're all afraid we could lose Deirdre."

"The hell, you say? Not my Kitten! I'll go and get my wee one out; you'll see." Tommy jumped on the horse, holding his abdomen. If you looked closely you could see a small bit of blood seeping through.

He rode like mad. When he finally came to the big doors, they opened up for him. He shouted out, "I'm here and I'll help with this one."

Out of breath, he climbed the stairs. As he got halfway up, he heard a chilling scream and his name called.

Tommy opened the door, telling everyone to leave. "Out, out, all of you. I'll handle this." He fell to the floor in front of Deirdre.

"Sir Tommy, you're bloody," remarked Maude."

"I'm alright, Maude, tell her I'm here and things will be alright."

"Yes, sir."

Maude went to Deirdre's ear and whispered, "Love, your Tommy is here. He'll help you now. You do what he asks."

Tommy, Tommy love, are you really here"

"Yes, Kitten, I am. Now listen to me. When you feel a pain coming on, you need to push as hard as you can, alright?"

With a smile and a large pain coming, she shouted, "Your father is here, little one, please come and meet him."

"Yes, your father is here." Tommy had soft linen in his large hands.

All of a sudden, out came Alura, with a red tuff of hair, crying with all she was worth.

The other babies heard her and started crying too. When they cleaned Alura up, they laid her beside her sister. But that didn't stop her crying, so Maude put her in the middle and all went quiet. You could hear them all sucking on their fists.

"My darling, you are here," cried Deirdre.

"Yes, love. Look, three little darlings. We'll need maids for Jesse and one for Jessica. But you'll nurse Alura. Deirdre saw Tommy clutch at his abdomen in pain. "Maude, Kimberly, help Tommy. He is all bloody and is not well."

Everyone helped with Tommy. They put him to bed and attended to his wounds.

Deirdre raised up speaking in a commanding voice, "Put him in our bedchamber." Then she added, "Please."

Everyone smiled, "We will, My Lady."

Chapter 27

It was a beautiful warm day with a breeze flowing down from the mountains. At other times the breeze came from the sea.

Deirdre looked out toward the laughter of the children playing with their father, smiling. Tommy was well again — strong, healthy and loving his children. She laughed to herself.

Tommy was running with Alura on his shoulder as they chased the others. Alura held on tightly to her father's ears. You could hear her say between giggles, "Hurry Father, get them."

Jesse, waving his small sword, called to his mother. "Look Mother, see what Great-grandfather taught me with the sword he made for me." He tried to stand off his father. "Father, stand still."

"I see your stance; it's good."

Jessica, not to be outdone, showed her mother what Grandmother Mary Kate had taught her.

"My goodness, you're good."

"You bet I am. One day I'll take on the whole clan of Campbells. You'll see," Jessica said with a big smile.

"But not too soon, my darling," her father said with a grin on his face as he and Alura sat down on the blanket beside Deirdre.

"Are you tired?" she asked Tommy.

435

"No, Kitten, but this one is like her mother. She never gets tired," he spoke as he put Alura down between them. Alura wiggled down, smiled, and went to sleep on the blanket beside her parents, while the others played on for a while longer.

That is where the messenger found them. Tommy woke with a start. "What is it, lad?"

"There is trouble, Laird Tommy. You must come at once. Your brothers need you, sir. It's the Campbells."

Tommy jumped up, waking Deirdre and the children. "Kitten, I'm needed at the stronghold. My brothers sent word; it's the Campbells. I feel the king is also mixed up in this."

"I'll get the children to the castle and come with you."

"No, you stay here."

"But you may need me."

"Kitten, I need you here. What if they make their way down here and you are gone? What would happen then?" He took her chin with his finger and pulled her head back to look into his eyes. "Now, tell me, am I right?"

With tears in her eyes, "Yes," she said, "you are. But please be careful."

"I will."

Tommy kissed all of his loves goodbye. He also had tears in his eyes when they shouted, "Godspeed." All except Alura, who ran after him. "Father, please, may I go? Crying hard, she sat down.

Deirdre picked her up in her arms and held her tight.

The children's nurse came to help get them back into the castle.

At the next clan meeting, Deirdre found out that the king, along with the Campbells, were taking the jeweled altar goblets, crosses and all the altar sacraments.

"But why are they doing that?" asked Deirdre, just as her Uncle Ira came into the great hall.

"Why?" he shouted, his face red with anger. "He is mad, that's why."

"I'll tell you, lass. The reason is, the Spanish, with Portugal ships, are taking all the gold, spices, and fine silks from King William."

"Are you sure about this, Uncle?"

"Yes, I know it is true."

"How do you know?" she asked, looking her Uncle straight in the eye.

Wiping his brow, not liking to be put to question by his niece or anyone, he said, "By my own sources."

As she looked over her people, she thought about how soon the king, as well as the Campbells, would be raiding their land. The king did not care if they starved, just as long as his fat belly was full.

That night, she paced the floor. Just as she passed her window, she saw a small light on Colonsay. It looked like a light on a small boat. *What's going on over there?* she thought to herself. *Maybe I should row over there one day. Yes, that is what I should do.* She continued to pace. *I should let Monica and Kimberly know what I'm up to. I'll just go now.*

Deirdre left the bedchamber and ran head-on with Monica. "What are you doing up at this hour?" asked Monica.

"Coming to see you."

Monica started walking back towards Deirdre's bed-chamber. "I need for you to see something and we can see it better from your chamber."

"What are you saying, Monica?"

Monica opened Deirdre's bedchamber door and walked straight to the window.

"There is something going on over there. Come, look, see."

"I know, I saw the light. What could it be?"

"I bet its Doug O'Brian. You remember his father and our father were good friends."

"Ye don't mean he has gone into pirating?"

"Have you seen him lately, Deirdre? He has grown into a giant of a man."

"How would you know, little sister?"

"Well, you know, I see him once in a while. You know, he asked about you each time," smiling at Deirdre as she talked.

"Now, how would I know that, pray tell, and me not there?"

Monica laughed as she looked out the window. "I wonder," she stated.

"You wonder what?" Deirdre asked, just as her door opened.

"What's going on." Kimberly answered.

"We thought you were asleep."

"No, Deirdre, how could I sleep when I felt you and Monica were up to no good?" Kimberly smiled as she put her arm around Deirdre's shoulder.

"Come look. Hurry!"

"Monica, what is it?" asked Kimberly.

"We'll explain in a moment," stated Deirdre as she went over to the window.

All three saw more lights going in and out an opening in the rocks.

"I must see what is going on."

"No, Deirdre, don't you think I should be the one?" asked Monica.

"I know Doug O'Brian better than you do."

Kimberly was looking at both of them with anger in her eyes and in her voice. "Would you both tell me what is going on?"

Monica told Kimberly all about it.

"My word," was all Kimberly could say.

"And that is not all. Deirdre wants to go over and talk to Doug."

"What in the world would Tommy say? No, Deirdre, you know you can't." Kimberly looked at Deirdre with fire in her eyes.

"I know you both are right. But stop and think what the king and Campbells are doing. They are robbing, stealing cattle, everything from our people. I can't just stand by and let that happen, now can I?"

Both girls looked at one another and Kimberly spoke, "No, we can't. Deirdre, we are going with you, to help." Seeing the look on Deirdre's face, "Now, you'll not argue. We're all in this together or it's called off."

Deirdre knew when she was beaten, so she just smiled and hugged both of her sisters.

"Should we get our uncles involved or not?"

"No," spoke Monica. "I'll have my Captain Robert help; he'll not say a word."

"Monica, that's great. We'll take wine aboard. Have Robert ask if Doug will meet with me and talk."

"What will you talk about?" asked Kimberly.

"I don't know just yet. But we have to do something about the king."

"Deirdre, what about taking back all he has stolen from our people?"

"Monica, you're right. We could use different flags on our ships. With a little planning we can do just that," Smiling, she started dancing around the room.

Chapter 28

Captain Robert, with his aid, docked their small craft at the end of a stone pier. After tying it up, they walked to the pier to an opening.

"Who comes?" shouted a loud voice.

"Captain Robert, from the ship, Deirdre."

"State your business."

"I want to see O'Brian."

"Everyone does."

"He'll see me. I'm from Laird John Macdonald."

"I'll go ask," said the red-headed man, walking off.

Robert looked around him. The walls were damp with green mold. The boards on the floor had seen their better days. They were all matted down and mixed with old bones. Several scrawny dogs that were there, snarled. The few tables were none too clean and both the fireplaces and the tallow torches smoked.

The man returned. "He says for you to follow me."

Before Robert knew what was happening, a beautiful maiden led him to O'Brian. *Not bad,* Robert thought to himself with a smile.

"I'm here, Captain." Robert pushed through into the room and his jaw dropped in surprise. He could not believe what his eyes told him. The room was positively opulent, the most splendid the Scotsman had every seen. The walls were hung with silk and velvet tapestries. The stone floors were covered with magnificent, thick sheepskin. On the wall was a huge fireplace, burning with sweet-scented apple wood on this late-summer's eve. He also noticed a long oak table with two large golden, twisted candelabras, burning tapers.

At the end was a very large chair which held a comparably large man. Even though he was seated, Robert could see that he must stand at least six-feet, seven-inches tall. His hair was as black as night, as well as his full, well-barbered beard. His eyes were as green as the sea. He sported a gold earring in his left ear. His doublet was of fine soft leather, and his green silk shirt was open, revealing a thick mat of hair growing upward from his navel. His high brown leather boots rose well over his knees.

In his lap sat two pretty young girls, both naked from the waist up. They were feeding dainties from silver platters to the Lord of Colonsay Caves.

"Sit down, man!" came a booming command. "Mary!" Doug O'Brian dumped one of the girls from his lap. "Serve my guest."

The girl good-naturedly picked herself up off the floor, rubbing her lovely rounded posterior. As she did so, she poured a goblet of wine for Robert. He swallowed hard at the close proximity of her large breasts. The nipples were as large as a plump sweet French grape.

"She's yours for the night." Doug O'Brian laughed. The lass grinned, with delight.

"I like your style of hospitality, by God, I do, My Laird! If the Deirdre doesn't sail tonight, I will gladly accept your gift."

He raised his gobbet to his host. "To your health, sir!"

"I'll see your master as soon as he comes ashore. This will be a busy night, with many celebrations. Would Laird John MacDarroch and his men like to join us?"

Robert hid a smile. "I'll go immediately and take the MacDarroch your invitation."

Doug O'Brian was bored this night. As the Scot left the room, O'Brian wondered what MacDarroch had up his sleeve.

O'Brian looked up to see a shadowy figure in a dark green cloak.

"My Laird, this is the MacDarroch of Sea Oaks."

At that moment, Deirdre dropped her cloak.

"Christ's sacred bones!" He swore. "A woman? What the hell kind of joke is this, Robert?"

"My Laird, this is MacDarroch of Sea Oaks."

"The Laird is John MacDarroch, I don't do business with women," came the flat reply.

"Are you afraid?" Drawled Deirdre softly.

With a roar of outrage, the tall man stood, dumping the remaining girl from his lap. She got up and ran over to Mary while Doug O'Brian stomped over to Deirdre. He towered over her in his most intimidating manner. Robert got a sick feeling in the pit of his stomach. Robert was a brave man, but he was old and didn't have a chance against this giant.

O'Brian stared fiercely down. The woman, instead of trembling like all of the other females, stared boldly up at him. He began to cool down a little and realized she looked familiar. He asked, "Are you Deirdre MacDarroch, Laird John's eldest?"

"Yes, I am. But my father stepped down and now I'm Laird." Taking a deep breath, "Doug, I need your help."

Doug thought to himself, 'She's a brave one, and is a beauty as well."

"I own", Deirdre began abruptly, "close to two dozen ships of various sizes. One of my fleets has just finished a successful three-year voyage to the East Indies. My sister, Monica, is the skipper of that fleet. I'm a rich woman. I have a quarrel with someone in a high place. To avenge myself against this person, I'll need assurance that Colonsay Isle is open to my ships. You will be paid well, Doug."

`So, you remember me, do you?"

"Is it a deal, then?" she said, holding out her hand.

"Not so fast, lass. How high a place?" he asked.

"William of Orange," came her cold reply.

Chapter 29

"The king?" he whistled. "Are you serious, or merely out of your head?" He looked down into Deirdre's face. "By God, you're serious!" He began to laugh, which grew into a great roar of mirth that shook the entire room.

Deirdre stood her ground, unrelenting. "Well, Doug O'Brian, do we do business or do we not?"

"How much?" A crafty look narrowed his eyes.

"Name your own price, within reason," she answered.

"We'll discuss this alone, Deirdre," said O'Brian. "Robert, why don't you take Mary and her sister downstairs."

"My Laird?" The Scot looked at Deirdre."

"Go, Robert, dear friend. I'd spend a full year feeling guilty if I denied you such choice company. Also, tell the men that they may come for the celebration. Alternate the watch so they can all have a bit of fun."

Robert hesitated and Deirdre laughed. "Oh, man, you're such an old woman! O'Brian, give my men your word you'll not harm me, or we'll never get down to business."

"You've got it. Good God, Captain, do I look like a violator of helpless women?"

Robert reluctantly withdrew and O'Brian motioned to the chair the Scotsman had recently vacated. Pouring her some wine, he shoved the ornate silver goblet at her. She sipped at the ruby liquid smiling at the excellent vintage. Doug eyed her closely again, and then re-opened the discussion.

"So, I can name my own price—within reason, of course?"

"That is correct."

"Deirdre, as you can see, I don't need money. There's precious little to spend it on here and I've more than enough at any rate. So, what's within reason?" He drank a bit of wine.

"What have you been doing with your life?"

"As you know, I'm married to Tommy MacDonald?"

"I do. What does he say about your coming here to me and asking for me help?"

"He doesn't know, and I want it that way." Her eyes flashed.

Doug smiled. "You tell me that you wish to wage war on the King of England? Before I risk my small standing, I'd like to know why I should join your personal war."

"O'Brian, we knew each other growing up; our fathers were great friends."

"I remember. You don't remember that I told you that I would love you forever."

"You did?"

Yes, I did; you did say name my price! And that you wish to wage war on the King of England. Before I risk my small standing, I'd like to know why I should join your personal war."

She considered a moment, and then nodded. "As you know, the king, with the Campbells, is robbing all the people around us of all they have. He is taxing them until they have to sell their land, only to fill his fat belly."

"You're right there."

"My pirates can be safe here, and no one will be the wiser. You're not trying to tell me that all the goods that go through his island are legal trade, now are you?"

Doug O'Brian laughed pleasantly. "It would seem, Deirdre MacDarroch, that you need me a hell of a lot more then I need you. Nevertheless, I'm not adverse to a bit of piracy. So, I'll make you a proposition. You can have my aid and sanctuary on my Isle for your ships in exchange for one percent of the goods you take." He paused a moment, then finished quickly. "And if you will spend this night in my bed."

She went white. Recovering quickly, she said, "Two percent of the goods taken, and not a penny more."

"One percent, and this night," he repeated, with a mischievous smile crossing his handsome face.

"Why?" she burst out.

"Because you are beautiful and a lady and I know of no other way for someone like me to possess something as fabulously rare as someone like you." Deirdre seemed genuinely troubled, as he continued. "Come, Deirdre MacDarroch, if you really desire vengeance on your enemy, then no price is too high. It's only one night."

Deirdre was torn. She knew her plan was flawless, but it could succeed only if she had the use of Doug, and she thought of William of Orange calmly in his own way using her. She thought of King William of Orange calmly admitting to her the he had love for her and if she would not submit to him, he would make it very degrading for her.

Now, Doug O'Brian wished to possess her also, but he at least offered a fair return.

"You know I'm the wife of Laird Thomas Edward MacDonald?"

"Yes, I do."

"What choice do I really have?"

"Not much, if you want your plan to work, I would say."

"Doug, if Tommy found out, he would kill the both of us. Besides, I'm in my first stage of pregnancy."

A shocked looked appeared on O'Brian's face.

"How far along are you?"

"About two months, I would say."

"Does he know?"

"No, nor does anyone else. I want it to stay that way, if you don't mind."

"No one will hear it from me."

"Thank you, O'Brian. Do we still have a deal?".

"Yes, but you be back here by midnight."

"Damn it, man, I'm not a whore to perform for you!"

"Precisely, Deirdre MacDarroch. You're a beautiful, and I suspect, passionate woman. I want nothing from you but to gaze on your body."

She blushed furiously, and his laughter rumbled about the room like a distant thunder. "It's agreed then?" He held out his hand. She hesitated, and then grasped the great hand with her own. "It's agreed on," she answered him.

Chapter 30

Late summer had been unusually lovely. In the autumn, Deirdre looked back on the last several months with deep satisfaction. At least half a dozen treasure ships had been taken, robbing William of Orange's coffers of his much-needed revenue. Only two had been her ships. The others had been funded by wealthy courtiers, including Alex, and Deirdre felt no guilt about robbing them. The monies from the ships, other than Deirdre's family's, found their way into the church's boxes to help aid delinquent taxes for the poor and hardworking farmers, the sick, the old; and the hungry were astonished when they began receiving gifts of medicine, firewood, food, clothing, and small bags of coins.

With winter coming, however, the parade of ships would be slowing down. The sudden increase in piracy off the Devon coast had only just begun to attract royal attention. Now Deirdre would have her pirates lie low, and if the royal curiosity had been piqued it would be forced to remain unsatisfied. She chuckled. It had all been so unbelievably easy. Suspecting nothing, the trading ships had been like fat white ducks that had waddled, by mistake, into a fox's den.

Each time they attacked, it had gone smoothly. Amazingly, no one was hurt and no lives were lost in this venture.

The cargo that was taken was transferred quickly and quietly by silent, well-trained seamen who, responding to whistles and hand signals, gave no hint of their nationality.

The pirates disappeared with their booty as quickly as they appeared. The whole great affair was eerily well-done. The royal commission sent to investigate returned to London at a loss. No one had the slightest idea of who was behind this genteel pillage. The pirates had to be Spanish with English spies. How else would they know when ships were due and the courses the ships would take? Since the piracy stopped as suddenly as it had begun, the royal commission had concluded the incidents were isolated. So the king was informed. Deirdre knew somewhere along the way she would have to stop going to Colonsay to see Doug, her dear friend. Timmy, a fifteen year old, the son of Maggie and her friend, had been assigned to clean out the cave, to keep torches always burning and to see that Deirdre's small boat was constantly in readiness.

Deirdre always knew she and her sisters could pull this off, even when she first told them of her plan. They both stood beside her through all of her decisions. *Yes,* she thought, *we well beat you, King William.*

Doug O'Brian told her that if she ever needed him, to put a light in the tower window. If it was war, then put two lights in the window. Deirdre tested him one evening with two lights.

He was there within minutes. As Doug got to the entrance of the cave, he turned, taking two steps toward Deirdre. "Little Lady, I'll always love you. If you ever need me, light the lamps. I'll be here. Do you hear me, lass?"

"Yes, I do, dear friend, and I will." He left, his big frame getting into his boat.

The very next day, it was cold out, but she needed to go to see Doug. She did love him, but only as a dear friend, and she needed to tell him so.

Deirdre hesitated on that cold late February afternoon. But the day was so beautiful it just beckoned her. She needed to get away from all the chatter. She longed to laugh and sing.

"Deirdre!" Doug greeted her, delighted to see her. "My beautiful warrior! I've been thinking about you, didn't mean to rush off like I did."

"I understand, Doug."

"Do you. I wish you could love me, Deirdre MacDarroch," he said quietly.

"But Doug, I do," she protested. "You're one of my best friends."

"I hope Tommy knows how lucky he is to have you."

Reaching up, she put her arms around him, and then planted her lips to his. Doug pulled back. "Don't do that! You belong to a fine man."

"I know I do, dear friend." She turned to go, as she spoke. "The weather is turning nasty. I should be going now."

"You be careful. Put a lamp in the window so I will know you are safe."

"I will."

"The wind is from the west, you'll be home in no time."

The fresh winds sent the little sailboat skidding swiftly across the tops of the waves. It was dark by the time she reached her mooring.

It was very still. Deirdre was sure it was the fastest she'd ever made it from Colonsay.   Securing the boat tightly, she then took a torch from inside the cave and lit the ledge beacons.   If ever Doug needed to make his way here, he would be safe.

She flipped the hidden lock and entered her bedchamber, then drew the tapestry back into place. She could hear definite sounds of merrymaking below in the main hall.   Puzzled, she moved toward the door the led to the main hall, but the door opened suddenly and Maude flew in, slamming it behind her.

"Oh! My Lady! Thank God you're back!"

"What in the world is going on down there?" demanded Deirdre.

"Right after you left, the king's soldiers came. The captain was furious to learn you weren't here. Then he just took over, ordering a feast, and sending to the village for some lasses."

"What?"

"Maids," he said.   "They had to be maids," Maude explained, tearfully.

"My God!" said Deirdre. "Are the lassies all right, Maude? I'll send them home immediately. They're probably frightened to death. The king hasn't allowed this sort of abuse in years. Trust King William, the fiend, to revive such an appalling custom!"

"It's too late, My Lady. The lassies have already been ruined," Maude said.

"Are they all OK, though?" asked Deirdre.

"All except little Betty Brown. She bled quite heavily."

454

"Christ's bones! Betty Brown is but eleven! Damn! Damn! The king will pay for this. I'll raise such hell with the king that he'll be forced to punish these men!" I shall have to pay a bounty to the families involved. Were any of the lassies walking out yet?"

"About four."

"Where are my sisters?"

"They just slipped in the back and are headed this way."

"Good, who is the captain, Maude? Do you know?"

"Yes, I do. It's Captain Gavin. He is a big man with a loud, rough voice."

The door opened quietly so as not to let the king's men hear.

"What are your orders, Deirdre? Just tell us and you know we'll obey. These slimy men can't get away with this."

"I'll go down and see just what is going on. You watch, and please, both of you, be very careful.

"You're the one that needs to be careful."

Little did anyone know that Timmy had heard every word. He left in a hurry, but was very careful not to be seen. Up the steps he ran to the tower, and lit two lamps in the window. He knew help would come.

Help did come. Doug, with his men, beat the captain and his men to a pulp. The king's men left, leaving Deirdre's men to clean up.

Deirdre saw Doug. Before she could get to him, he had left with his men.

Clan MacDarroch cleaned up, and put things back in order.

Deirdre sat in her bedchamber, thinking of the day's events. She couldn't get her friend out of her mind, or how he was helping her and her people. She must go and see for herself how he was.

Deirdre had no way of knowing that Tommy was on his way home, having taken care of his clan and driven off the Campbells with the king's men.

Not finding Deirdre, he started asking questions of Maude and others on what had happened. No one realized that Timmy had left the room. He ran hard up the tower to light the three lanterns, hoping that Deirdre would see that he was trying to let her know that Tommy had come home.

Timmy did not know Tommy had followed him up to the tower as well as down to the cave. Tommy watched Timmy light all the torches for Deirdre.

"Timmy, lad." Timmy heard his name and jumped.

"Yes, My Laird."

"Lad, could you please tell me why you are lighting all torches as well as three lanterns? You are not in trouble with me."

"It's for Laird Deirdre."

"Why?"

Timmy bowed his head in shame.

"Now, now, you only did what any good warrior would do. Your only concern was your Laird, wasn't it?

Timmy looked up with a huge smile. "Yes, that was it."

Tommy ruffled Timmy's hair, saying "Go on, now. I'll wait on my wife."

"Thank you, sir," he said as he ran out of the cave.

Tommy could hear the oars splashing in the water, which told him she was in an all-fired hurry.

As Deirdre tied up the boat, she called out in a whisper, "Timmy, lad, what's wrong?" When there was no answer, she called again. Deirdre put her hand up to her ear—nothing. She started to walk away when she heard a very angry voice. "Wife, where in the hell have you been!"

"What, where are you and who are you?"

"Don't you know your own husband?"

"Tommy, you're home," reaching out to him. Tommy held her as she told him what had happened. All except the lying with Doug.

"My word, Kitten, are you alright?"

"I am fine."

As Tommy looked at his wife, he noticed that she was with child. "You did all of that and you with my child?"

"Yes, I did," she answered with a big grin on her face.

"How far are ye?"

"Close to seven months."

"Now you listen to me." That's as far as he had gotten when Timmy and Maude came up.

"My Lairds, you must come in a hurry. Sir Alex is here with his men, and he wants to take you before the king."

"What do you mean, before the king?"

Timmy spoke up. "To arrest you, by the king's orders."

Deirdre almost ran up the steps to her bedchamber. When she got there, she turned to Maude, What did you tell him?"

"I said you were lying down."

"That's great."

Tommy looked at his beautiful wife. "I'm going down and find out what this is about."

"That's fine, darling. I'll be down shortly, after I change. Maude, help me please."

Maude got out her warm gray dress as Deirdre changed her shoes. "Maude, I need a little help with my hair."

Maude stood back to look, after they had finished. "You look wonderful."

Deirdre went down to the great room. As soon as Sir Alex saw her, he said, with a sad look on his face, "My God, you're with child."

"Yes, she is," remarked Tommy, with a big smile.

"How far along are you, Deirdre?"

"Good day, to you, sir."

Tommy went over and put his arms around Deirdre's shoulder saying, "It will be alright."

Deirdre looked Sir Alex in the eyes. "Why are you here?"

"I have orders from the king, along with his cabinet, to arrest you for treason on the high seas."

Just at that time, Kimberly came in, with Monica right on her heels. "What pray tell would a woman, in her sixth month of caring a child, be doing on the high seas?" shouted Kimberly.

Deirdre slowly put her hand on Kimberly's arm. "It's alright, sweet sister."

Monica put her hand on the head of her sword, as if to draw it.

"No, sister," spoke Deirdre in a firm voice.

Tommy put his arm around Deirdre. "You go upstairs and have your supper with our children."

"I will." She looked up into her husband's eyes full of love, and then reached up to give him a sweet kiss on his cheek.

Deirdre left the room to go upstairs. As she did, she heard Tommy shout, "Elias, have a chamber opened up for Sir Alex. He will be spending the night."

"But, sir, we should be starting back tonight."

"No, Sir Alex, my wife needs to rest. This has been a shock to her, knowing she has been arrested by the king for something she doesn't know about."

Tommy left the room, leaving Sir Alex looking at him. He mumbled to himself, "How dare him."

Elias entered the room and saw how outraged Sir Alex was. He smiled, "Sir, would you care to take your supper here or in your chamber?"

"I'll take it in my chamber, thank you, Elias."

"Just as you say, sir. I'll show you to your chamber now."

Tommy went to the tower to signal Doug to come. He needed to speak with him about what was going on. He also felt that he may need his help.

Chapter 31

It wasn't long before Doug arrived and Timmy led him into the underground room where he found Laird Thomas MacDonald waiting for him.

"My Laird."

"Doug, my friend, there is no need for you to address me in such manner. We are friends, are we not?"

"Yes, we are."

"Come, friend, let's talk. I need to know all that has happened. You see, Sir Alex, with the king's men, are here to arrest Deirdre."

"For what?"

"He says piracy. Doug, tell me, friend, what has my wife been up to?"

Doug told him everything, all except him lying with her. Even though nothing happened, he felt Tommy would not understand, and that he would not have.

"Thank you, Doug, for telling me. Now I know what to do."

"Listen, My Laird, I mean, Tommy. She wants so much to have one more haul. We found out that there will be another ship to set out."

"Wait one minute, Doug. If the ship is taken while she is under arrest, that would be good, would it not?"

"Yes, it would!"

"Well, will you and your men do it?"

"We will do just that. You had better get back now."

"I love your wife, Laird Tommy."

"That I know, Doug."

Doug left the cave room, and Tommy went up to Deirdre. He had to tell her everything. Tommy knew Doug would let him know when the job was done.

He walked in as Deirdre was sobbing. She had managed to bring herself under control, and sniffing noisily, sought for her handkerchief. Tommy handed her his, and she wiped her eyes and blew her nose.

"Should I be jealous?" he asked. She began to wonder how long he'd been standing there, watching her. Blushing, she peeped up at him with big green eyes.

"What are you talking about?"

"I talked with Doug, love. I know everything."

`Deirdre sneezed, and then sneezed twice again. Tommy shook his head and picking her up, said, "You can tell me after you are tucked warmly into bed."

"I believe your mistress has caught a chill," he told Maude.

"I'll have a hot tub ready for her," she said. "Don't worry; I'll take care of her."

"No need, Maude. I will. You go on to bed."

Deirdre nodded at Maude that it was alright.

"Kitten, Doug told me everything."

"Everything?"

"Yes, unless you have something else to say."

"No," she answered as she turned for him to unfasten her gown. Then he undid her petticoat and under blouse and pulled them off too. Kneeling, he took her garters off and unrolled her stocking. When she was naked, he picked her up and laid her ever so gently in the hot tub. She sighed deeply and closed her eyes. "I know it must be the boat ride, and the dampness of the cave, he said. She murmured agreement and came close to purring when he began soaping her back.

Tommy's mouth turned up again in a small smile. Less then half as hour ago he stood in the mist hearing her row to shore and after talking to Doug, knew that Doug loved her. A few months ago he might have acted irrationally. Now, however, he knew better. She loved him. He knew it. He rinsed her back off with a sponge and moved on to the more interesting portions of her anatomy.

He felt his desire mounting, but pushed his hunger down. First, he wanted to hear her explanation. Lifting her from the tub, he wrapped her in a large towel and placed her on the settle by the fireplace. He took a smaller towel and rubbed her dry. Ignoring the pale-blue silken gown Maude had laid out, he tucked Deirdre between the down feather bed and a fur coverlet.

He undressed and washed himself lightly, then dried off and climbed into bed beside her. Turning to look at her, he said quietly, "Now, madam."

"Doug is my friend," she said.

"Doug O'Brian is in love with you," he returned bluntly.

"But Tommy, you should know you are the only one I have ever and will ever love."

"He told me that you are the only one in the world for me."

"Oh, Love! He told me and I know you love me and will forever."

"You know?" she said, then started to cry again. "You can't beat me," she said, anticipating him. "I am going to have a baby."

"Good God, woman!" He burst out, and she began to cry. Then Tommy started to laugh. "Kitten, you're the most impossible female God ever created. Deirdre, you wage war on King William of Orange of England, and still retain all your possessions. Did it never occur to you that you could have been caught?"

"No."

"Indeed and why not?" He couldn't wait for her answer.

"There is nothing to connect me, O'Brian or the MacDarrochs with any acts of piracy."

"You're sure?"

"Yes. My ships fly no flags. My people do not speak; they communicate with whistles and hand signals. The cargo has been carefully disposed of, and I even pirated two of my own ships last summer to keep suspicion away from me.

"But William has obviously sent Alex to capture the pirates. You can't take the bait. Besides, Doug and I have a plan. And this, my Kitten, is the last venture against the king. My dear, I swear it."

"It will be."

He pulled her into his arms and brushed her lips with his. "When is the child due?"

"It will be born in less than three months."

"There will be no more adventures, Kitten," he said sternly. "I want your promise."

"I'll sleep on it," she said mischievously.

"Madam, your word!" he thundered.

"Alright, you have it, My Laird," she lisped meekly.

"Let's go up on the battlements to look at the sunset."

"It should be beautiful from there."

As they left their bedchamber, Sir Alex caught them in the hallway.

"My Laird, we should start to London."

"But my wife hasn't rested for such a long trip."

"What has she been doing?"

"Saying goodbye to her children, Sir Alex," Tommy said in a stern voice.

"Have her ready to leave in the morning." Sir Alex turned, with anger on his face and stomped down the steps.

With arms around one another, they went up to the battlements which looked over the channel to Colonsay.

"I love you, Tommy." With a glad cry, he swept her into his arms and kissed her passionately.

There was great joy in Scotland, mostly on Jura. But in London, William of Orange fumed with important rage. The King of Spain's treasure ship had been boldly pirated from under Robert Madeira's nose. The king was both outraged at the incident and scornful of King William's ability to keep order in his own land. This piqued William more than the loss of all the treasure. He would have to borrow heavily from the goldsmiths to finance his household, anticipating the wealth of the treasure ship. Now he was heavily in debt and several of his creditors had already shown they were not intimidated by the royal office.

"Is there no evidence to connect Laird Deirdre MacDarroch with the piracy, Percy? Surely there is something we can use. Percy Peak had finally confided his suspicions to King William.

"Sir, there is nothing. All the MacDarroch ships are where they should be and there is no evidence of the treasure ship's cargo anywhere.   We searched both Innisfarea and Colonsay.

"I want her arrested, Percy."

"On what charges, sir?"

William whirled to face him and he saw the angry red patches on his cheeks. "I am the king, Percy! I do not need formal charges! Laird MacDarroch has offended me, and I want her in the Tower!"

"Sir!" Percy was shocked. "This is not like you."

"Damn it, Percy, we know she is guilty!"

"We suspect, My King." He had not spoken to him so familiarly, so gently, since he had become king. "We only suspect, and since the Spanish ship was taken, no other ships have been pirated, despite that, this is the busiest season for shipping."

The king remained adamant. "I want her in the Tower," he said. "Perhaps, if we frighten her, we can force her to confess. I need that gold, Percy! My creditors are pressing me."

Percy sighed. If Laird MacDarroch hated King William before, she would hate him far more very soon. The Scottish people were so damned emotionally! Offending both the MacDarrochs and the MacDonalds could roust all of Scots. The hatred of the king would spread. *We don't need a war in Scotland now,* Percy thought wearily.

"What of Laird MacDonald?" he asked.

"He is to remain on Jura," said William. "He is forbidden to come to London. Let him look after that she-wolf's whelps."

"The Laird Deirdre has many admirers, sir. They will not be happy to see her imprisoned unjustly, and talk will be detrimental to Your Majesty."

"Then do it secretly, Percy, send Sir Alex. Since he lost me my ship, let him see if he can redeem himself by delivering the Laird safely and secretly to the Tower. Tell the governor there is to be no official record of Laird Deirdre. If no one knows she is in London, and her husband is confined to Jura, then there will be no court gossip."

"I do not approve of this," he said, looking very displeased at his king.

"But you will obey me nevertheless," returned William.

He nodded. "You are, My King, and you've always learned from your mistakes. I expect you will in this instance, too." He couldn't resist making his opinion clear.

The king's head shot up. Percy's face was quite impassive, but there was a hint of a twinkle in his eyes.

The advent of spring offered promise of a new and fruitful season. The final snow had barely melted, and the terrain was still wet. Along the roadside, newly-budding wild roses fought a territorial war. The workers were preparing to plant new crops, and winter wheat lay stacked in the fields. The apple trees were beginning to blossom. The apple presses each year would turn out many barrels of Jamie MacDarroch's famous cider.

Into this peaceful setting rode Robert Madria, a troupe of the king's own men at his back. Madria was horrified, getting orders from Percy he did not understand. He had been incredulous when he received those orders. He was to turn them over to Sir Alex. He remembered his meeting with Percy. "And you have been known to be loose-lipped when in your cups."

At that remark, Madria flushed guiltily. "It would be most unwise to babble this news, for the king wishes total secrecy." Madria had nodded.

Madria remembered the look on Sir Alex's face, when he gave him the message of what he had to do about Laird Deirdre. He and his men waited outside all night, until it was getting light.

Sir Alex rose early, dressed and called Elias to have his laird ready for the trip to London. Laird Tommy came into the room while Sir Alex was eating his morning meal.

"Now, tell me Sir Alex, what is this really all about?"

Deirdre came into the room. Just as she came up beside her husband, Sir Alex spoke in a very cold voice. "As I told you last night, My Laird, you are under arrest in the name of the king."

The smile on her face died away. "But I thought you were jesting, Sir Alex."

"It is no jest, My Laird."

"The charges, sir?" asked Laird Thomas MacDonald.

"Again, as I told you last night, here is a list of charges, My Laird. My orders are to escort Laird Deirdre MacDarroch to London as quickly as possible."

"And when we arrive in London?"

""The Tower, My Laird," said Sir Alex, softly.

Deirdre cried out. The children heard their mother and came to cluster around her knees, frightened. "I will not allow you to remove my wife in her condition. She carries the MacDonald's heir.

"Unless you are prepared to battle the king's guards, My Laird, I intend on taking her today."

Thomas wore no weapon, but he towered over Sir Alex. "Over my dead body, Englishman!"

Sir Alex drew his sword and Deirdre shrieked. "My Lairds! No!" She awkwardly got to her feet. "Sir Alex, for pity's sake, what is this all about?"

"God as my witness, Deirdre, I do not know. My orders are to bring you secretly to London where you are to be lodged in the Tower. Laird MacDonald, you are forbidden to leave Jura. That is all I was told to say, and it is truly all I know, and all of us feel the king is going mad."

Tommy was getting very red in the face as he spoke. You can not transport a woman who is more than six months gone with child all the way to London. Man, have you gone mad, too?"

"I have my orders, My Laird." Deirdre put her hand on her husband's arm. "I can use the traveling coach," she said softly. Everyone in the room turned to stare at her. "If we go slowly and carefully there shouldn't be any danger to the baby. I don't know why the king is doing this, but if I have go to London to straighten this out, then I will. Will you give me time to prepare, Alex?"

"You have had all night, now you better be ready by noon." He left the room in a huff.

470

Calling out, Deirdre spoke with anger in her voice. "My servants and I will be ready."

Alex yelled back. "You can only take one."

Kimberly, at that moment, stopped Sir Alex in the hall. "Sir, I and my sister, Monica, will attend her and that's that." She left Sir Alex with his mouth open.

Tommy escorted his wife from the room. In their chamber, Deirdre hugged her children as she spoke to them. "I'll be gone for a while, but there is nothing to worry about. Now go and get yourselves ready to eat."

Giving their mother a hug and lots of kisses, they left the chamber, all except Jesse. He turned and looked at his father with lots of questions in his eyes, then left.

"Deirdre, the king is suspicious. They know nothing for sure," she said in a positive tone. "If they did, Sir Alex would know the charges."

"But they're suspicious," he said. "Suspicious enough to arrest you."

"They can't prove anything!" argued Deirdre firmly. "They will try to frighten me, but they will not succeed. If they had any evidence at all, Tommy, wouldn't they be tearing the place apart?" They have nothing. The king is trying to out bluff me, but remember, love, I'm a better opponent than he's used to dealing with."

"He can keep you imprisoned for as long as he chooses, Kitten."

"I know. You must not disobey him, Tommy. You must stay on Jura and watch out for all those here.

"But how can I help you if I remain here?"

"Doug!" She said quietly. "Set two lights in the topmost window of the west tower, one high and one low. You got that? He'll come."

He put his arms about his wife and buried his face in her beautiful red hair and soft neck. "Kitten." There was such anguish in his voice.

"I know love, we have talked, please don't worry."

Helplessly, he held her, knowing full well he had no real part in this war. She had begun it without him, and now it seemed she would end it without him. All he could give her was his love to carry with her into imprisonment. After she had lunch, Deirdre told the children again, "You must mind your father and don't be afraid for me. I will be back."

She dressed warmly, pulling on her long knitted wool stocking, following with first a silk, and then two lightly-spun wool petticoats. Her gown was of heavy dark-blue silk with pearl buttons, long sleeves, and a high neck. Her hooded cloak was lined in silk and edged in fur. Her short boots were fur-lined. Maude arranged her thick red hair in a low chignon.

Hearing the door to her bedchamber open, she heard her son, Jesse's voice. "Why is the king arresting you, Mother?"

"I don't know, my love," she answered. It's just a misunderstanding. Don't be afraid for me."

"If you say so, Mother. I'll help look after the lassies."

Hugging her son close and trying so hard not to weep, she pulled back, and then smiled. "I know you will, my big lad."

Tommy was waiting for her in the family hall. Seeing the look on her face, he quickly caught her to him and kissed the hot tears that slid down her cheeks.

"It must be my condition," she muttered.

"I know," he soothed. "It must be, for you, forever, and never give the king a victory over you. I know that."

"I certainly will not, ever," she sniffed, fumbling for her handkerchief.

He laughed. "That's my Kitten!"

She wiped her eyes. "I must not keep Sir Alex waiting." She stuffed the handkerchief away in an inner pocket of her cloak and started for the door.

"I will miss you!"

"There's still time to flee, my love. Just claim you're in early labor, and then it's off to MacDonald country."

"No, I can't do that!" she said sharply. "I mean to beat King William, and keep it all!"

"You are a stubborn lass, Laird Deirdre MacDarroch, MacDonald, but I believe you will win."

"I will, Tommy! I will!"

He took her small hand in his and kissed it slowly, first the back and then the palm. "Farewell, madam, I'll look after everything here."

She felt a catch in her throat as he stepped out of the coach and shut the door firmly behind him. She watched him stride over to Sir Alex and speak with him, his face grim.

"I want you to travel carefully, Alex. I'm holding you personally responsible for the safety of my wife and unborn baby. Do you understand that? If anything happens to either of them, I will personally slay your wife and family and burn your bloody house to the ground!"

"I'll be careful, My Laird," said Sir Alex, "I'd not take Laird Deirdre at all in her current condition were I not under direct orders from the king."

"I understand," said Tommy quietly. "Will you keep me informed of any news? And if she may have visitors, go to see her so she won't be lonely."

Sir Alex nodded. "Remember, Laird Thomas, she'll have her sisters, which I may add, will not set too well with the king." He shook hands with Laird Thomas, and with a smile, he mounted his horse. He led the procession of soldiers, coach and baggage wagon from the courthouse of Sea Oaks Castle, across the drawbridge and out to the road. To his vast surprise, the road was crowded with people for one or two miles. Tenant farmers, villagers, merchants and fishermen, gamekeepers and castle servants, young and old, stood lining both sides of the road, all quietly supporting their Laird. Here and there Sir Alex heard a voice call out, "God, keep our Laird and bring her safely home to us!"

What the hell is King William about? Sir Alex wondered. What had Deirdre done that no one knows about, yet had offended the King so terribly? Everyone knows he loves her beyond reason.

Chapter 32

The trip, which should have taken only a few days, took well over a week. The coaches moved at a sedate pace, stopping frequently so the lovely Laird might stretch her legs or refresh. They asked if they might move a little faster. Deirdre took to her bed, thus delaying them an additional day. Thereafter, Sir Alex gritted his teeth and kept his peace.

They finally arrived in London. Sir Alex transferred Deirdre to a closed water barge so her coach, with the Sea Oaks arms emblazed on the doors, would not be recognized. The coach and its drivers were to return back to Jura immediately.

Watching her drivers depart, Deirdre felt some of her courage ebb away. No one would have known it from the serene look on her face. She had learned long ago that to show fear only encourages one's enemies. Being very careful, Sir Alex handed her down to her sisters, Kimberly and Monica.

"I always wanted to take you out on the river in my barge," he said in a lighthearted attempt at conversation.

"I'm sure, Sir Alex, that cruising on your barge would be far preferable than the cruise we are about to take on this one."

Sir Alex turned to Deirdre, "Damn, Deirdre what is going on between you and the king?"

"I really have no idea, Sir Alex," she replied, and turned her face away from him to gaze out on the river.

Sir Alex shook his head, but made no further attempt.

Deirdre breathed slowly, concentrating hard on the small act of drawing air into her lungs and expelling it. With each turn of the oars they brought her closer to imprisonment and God only knew what else. But she kept silently to herself, she would admit to nothing! She would beat the king at this game if it was the last thing she would do on this earth. Deirdre felt the soft rain on her face, in the twilight. It was quiet on the river, and there seemed to be no other boats on the water. Deirdre caught her breath as she saw the Tower of London looming tall, dark and menacing in the early evening. The barge turned shoreward, and the child in her womb kicked as the craft bumped the stone quay.

Monica saw her sister place a protective hand over her belly.

Fear not, my baby. I will protect you. She shivered.

Sir Alex leaped from the boat to help Deirdre out. She stood for a minute savoring her last moment of freedom, and turned to mount the stairs. The tower steps were smooth with age, and slick with the rain, to Deirdre's annoyance. She slipped once, but Sir Alex caught her beneath the elbow and steadied her. She stopped to regain her balance, the pulled away from him. "I'm not afraid, Sir Alex."

"It was only the steps, Deirdre, I know," he answered, all the while thinking how brave the laird really was.

The wife of the governor saw her enter the tower. "Husband! She is here."

The tower governor met her at the entry, looking extremely distressed as he noted her condition.

"Laird Deirdre," the governor's wife spoke first, "would you like to dine with us before you go to your room?"

"Thank you, My Lady, I would. Could my sisters join us? You can see they will be here to assist in the birthing."

"Yes, My Laird, they are welcome."

The governor spoke again before his wife could say another word. "I'll have my own people carry up your baggage and see that the fires are lit."

"Thank you."   Turning, she said, "Farewell, Sir Alex. Please tell His Majesty that if I had really wanted to come to London, I would have done it before this. I wish a complete listing of the charges against me, and if there are none, then tell the king he holds me illegally." She turned again, "Sir Jimmie, your arm, please. I'm so ungainly these days."

Sir Alex made his way to Chancellor Percy, the king's head councilor and advisor and asked to see him immediately. The young secretary to Percy made haste and was surprised when Percy told him to send in Sir Alex at once. When the door had closed behind him, Percy motioned for him to take a chair and asked, "What took you so long, sir? Was there difficulty at Sea Oaks?"

"No, My Laird, none at all. Although Laird Thomas is very angry and Laird Deirdre is confused about why the king would have her arrested. There is one more complication, and that was what delayed us."

Percy looked inquiringly at Sir Alex as he started explaining. "Laird Deirdre will be having a child within about three months. It was necessary, therefore, to travel slowly."

"Damn, Damn!" shouted Percy. "I warned the king and now... " He stopped himself.

"My Lord," Sir Alex plunged in, "why has Laird Deirdre been arrested? What in the world has she done?"

"Done? Why she has done nothing that we know of, Sir Alex. She is merely under suspicion."

As Sir Alex got to the door, turning around he spoke softly, "Oh, yes. Laird Deirdre's two sisters came along with her to help her."

Sir Alex noticed that Sir Percy was getting quite red in the face as he shouted, "Who gave them permission?" as he went out the door.

Deirdre was resting when a knock came on the door. She said, "You, on the other side have the keys, come on in."

The governor's wife stuck her head in. "I'm sorry, My Laird, but Head Councilor Percy wants to see your sisters right away."

"But why?"

"I don't know! He just sent word for them to come right away."

Kimberly stood up. "Don't worry, Deirdre. It will be alright; come on, Monica."

"Right behind you. We'll handle him, don't worry."

"Please do be careful, and above all, don't make him mad."

They both smiled at her as they left the room.

As they walked in to see Percy, Kimberly spoke. "We have come to attend our sister in her traveling," she said in a soft, but firm voice.

Percy pretended ignorance. "Madam," he answered coldly, "I have no idea to what you refer."

Monica, along with Kimberly, just flashed him a hauntingly familiar mocking smile. "My Lord, let's not waste time. Your signature was on our sister's arrest warrant," Monica spoke softly. "We mean to be with our sister and unless you let us do so, we shall find some means of getting in to see the king and making this whole affair public. The MacDonalds have held their peace thus far, for Laird Tommy. The other clans assure us this is but a misunderstanding."

"Why?" demanded Percy, now becoming very irritated. "Why should I allow the both of you to be with your sister, madam? I will not allow her husband. Why her sisters?"

"Our brother-in-law is a great fellow to be sure, sir, but I'm a healer and Monica is here to help.

"But the keeper of the tower's wife is there."

"We will stay, and you don't to say anymore."

"Good God, woman!" snapped Percy. "We wish no harm to Laird Deirdre. We would have sent someone to help her when her time came."

"I can well imagine," rejoined Monica scornfully. "You would get some ancient crone, with dirty fingernails, who would undoubtedly infect both Deirdre and the baby. What do you know, My Lord Percy, of midwifery?"

The king's closest advisor felt his temper rising higher. The ladies were insufferable.

"Madams," he thundered, "getting into the tower is easy; the getting out is much harder."

Again the girls smiled. "We are not afraid," they both answered him, and he acknowledged that they were not. *These over-proud Scots*, he again thought.

"Go then, madam. My secretary will issue the necessary papers," he said.

"I trust we shall be free to come and go, My Lord? There will be necessities we must get when my sister's time comes."

"No, said Percy. "It would be too simple for Laird Deirdre to escape the tower. What you need, you must either take in with you or have the servants fetch from the markets. You both may enter the tower; but once you leave it, you will not be allowed back inside. Those are the conditions."

Kimberly, with Monica at her side, smiled. "We will abide by your conditions." They bowed faintly to him and turning, said together regally, "Farewell, My Lord. Our thanks."

Several hours later, clutching the precious parchment in her slender hands, Kimberly, with Monica, entered the Tower of London and were escorted to their sister's apartment, high in one of the several towers. As they mounted the stairs, they were pleased to see that the soldier who escorted them was respectful.

Deirdre was sleeping when they arrived. They tried so hard to be quiet, but she woke up. "You're back. What happened?"

They told her everything and also their worry. "I'm so glad they let you come back to me. Come, let's go to bed."

Later, the three sisters bundled together in the large bed that took up almost the entire bedchamber. It was hung with Deirdre's own deep green colored velvet hangings; the sheets, feather bed, goose down pillows and fur coverlets. The fire blazed in the corner fireplace, warming the room and scenting it with the fragrance of apple wood. Because it was at the top of one of the towers, they had total privacy. It was the one place they felt free of being overheard.

"Deirdre, are you sure they have no proof?"

"The king can't do anything without proof and he has nothing."

"But he can; he needs no proof to keep you here."

They kept taking Deirdre down to the court where Sir Percy questioned her day after day. She stuck to her story. They tried to break her, but could not.

At the end of one of the sessions Deirdre got up from her chair looking hollow-eyed and her skin gray. She was tired, and little did anyone know she was in labor.

It was one of her guards who saw the trail of water and blood. "My Laird, may I help you?" the young man asked.

"No, but thank you, young man."

When they got to the steps going up to the tower, Deirdre walked up very slowly. The young guard shouted, "We need help down here."

Deirdre closed her eyes and called her sisters. To the guard's surprise, Laird Deirdre's sisters were there immediately, helping her up to the tower room.

"Would you please tell the tower governor that Laird Deirdre has gone into premature labor?" Kimberly lowered her voice to a whisper easily audible to both Deirdre and Monica. "I hope we don't lose them both. All this nonsense of arresting our poor sister. And what are the charges, Captain? There are none! Well, thank you for your aid. You're a good Christian lad, and I'll pray for you." Then she shut the door firmly between them and the guard.

"Oh, Kimberly!" Deirdre was laughing between contractions "You're the most wicked healer I've ever met! You terrified that poor nice young guardsman. He'll run all the way to the governor and tell him I'm at death's door."

Chapter 33

"Monica! Quick, drag the table in front of the fireplace."

"Kimberly! Help her, I can stand alone."

Together the two women swung the oak board around before the blazing stone fireplace. Though spring bloomed about them, the tower still held the winter chill. Monica ran upstairs to Deirdre's bedchamber and came back down with the goose-down pillows, a pad, and a sheet that she and Kimberly placed on the table. They then helped Deirdre up onto the table, and she half sat with her legs spread, the pillow propping her shoulders as she labored. Kimberly washed her slender, strangely elegant hand in the basin that Monica provided.

Kimberly leaned down to examine her patient. "Holy Mary! The child is half-born, "she exclaimed. Reaching out, she carefully turned the slippery infant.

"I – told – you," gasped Deirdre as a contraction passed. "Is – he – alright? All his fingers – and toes?"

Kimberly swiftly wiped the baby off and gazed down at the tiny face. "She's fine, Deirdre! All her fingers and toes!" She smiled at Monica and winked.

She? Oh, damn!" Deirdre laughed weakly. "Alura will love having in a little sister.

"Sister, I'm sorry, it's a little boy. I was teasing you."

"Why you!" she started laughing," I love you both."
Deirdre reached for her sister with love.

Percy walked into the king's chamber.

"Yes, Percy, any news?"

"The news, sir, is Laird Deirdre is having a hard time in having her child. It is feared both could be lost."

"Both? Is there nothing that can be done?"

"This comes from the governor's wife."

"What!!" The king's eyes got quite large. I'm just concerned about Laird Deirdre. Did you hear me? Will Laird Deirdre live?"

"The babe is still living, but Laird Deirdre is very weak. That is all I know for now.

"Alright. You let me know if anything changes"

He turned away from the window. "When can you start interrogating her again? We need to break her."

"Your Highness, she has just had her child and both are very weak."

"I do not care. You get back and break her, do you hear me?" He paced around the room like a mad man, his eyes ablaze.

Percy bowed, and then left the room. "He must be mad.

War will come from this. What is it really that he wants from her?"

Laird Thomas had spies all over London. He got word about what happened to his Kitten. "Timmy!" he shouted. "Put a light in the tower, I must speak with Doug. Hurry, lad."

"Going, sir."

Before Timmy could light the lanterns, Doug came through the large doors, out of breath."

"Tommy, I know how to save our lassie."

Tommy jumped out of his chair; you could see tears running down his face. "Doug, how, my friend?"

Doug picked up a large dram of peat whiskey and put it into Tommy's hand. "Drink up, man. I know how to bring her home, safe."

"How?" Laird Thomas gulped the smoky amber liquid down, reveling in the burning sensation that spread upward from his belly and into his veins.

"Well, me buckaroo, there's a well-hidden cove down by my lighthouse and in that cove right now is a ship — a ship of dead men. The tidal currents around the end of the island are erratic and they drove the vessel ashore. My men found it two days ago, floating half-beached in that cove. I've already given orders that no one is to go near the ship. I've placed my share of the booty back into the hole. The men who carried the cargo of gold for me are a family of mutes. I have always taken care of them. I've seen to their welfare and, as they are grateful for that, they will never give me away. They wouldn't even if they could talk.

"This ship is of English design, yet bodies aboard her appear to be Arab or Moorish. I will wager you that they be Barbary pirates. How they were killed, I don't know, but if we take the ship in tow and take it to London, I believe Percy could be convinced that these unfortunate dead men are part of whoever was responsible for the recent piracy. Especially considering what they'll find in the hold. That should free Deirdre!"

Tommy's face began to relax itself as he digested Doug's idea. "It's possible!" He thought for a moment. "Did you happen to find a log on board?"

"We did, but it's a funny kind of scrawl that bears no resemblance to anything I've ever seen, the writing, I mean."

Laird Tommy's face lit up, crinkling the corners of his violet blue eyes. "It's probably Arabic; you're probably right, Doug! They're Barbary pirates! We do have one problem, though. We can't board. But if Percy finds someone who can read Arabic, the log might prove it's not a pirate ship. We must have that log read."

"Who the hell do you know who reads Arabic?" demanded Doug. He was beginning to lose confidence.

Tommy leaned back laughing. "Deirdre does."

"Damn! Is there nothing that woman can't do?"

The men were getting ready for their big adventure.

Your Highness, there is some disturbing news of a strange ship named Santa Maris being sighted."

"I'm not the least bit concerned about that ship"

"But, Your Highness, don't you think we should investigate?"

We'll worry about that ship when it gets closer and not before!"

At Sea Oaks plans were being made. "Robert, old friend, you saw the log from the Santa Maris?"

"Yes, I did. Sir Doug let me read it. It is in Arabic. The ship is out of Algiers, and she has been pirating."

"Robert, are you sure?"

"Yes, sir. Sir Doug's men picked up some men in a longboat several months ago. I was excited when he told me that, and then the log."

"Go on, Robert. Soon we may get Deirdre home. Go on, please."

"I will. Shortly after that, their crew began to get sick and start dying. The men in the longboat perished almost immediately. This last entry was made a few weeks ago. It says simply, "Allah have mercy."

Robert looked up. "Poor devils." Suddenly his old weathered face split into a smile. "There was a piece of luck! An entry made early last spring says, 'Took a cursed Spaniard today, and we're heading to the Atlantic, off the coast of Scotland!'

"They were on their way out then. They were primarily Spaniard hunters, which is greatly to our good. If Percy is suspicious enough, and can find someone who reads Arabic, this should confirm Deirdre's story. We'll have to wait until she reaches London tonight. We want her to arrive before we get there; otherwise we lose the element of surprise."

It was difficult for them to wait, but wait they did. The time was getting near; they knew that and would be ready.

Deirdre could not believe her baby was five months old.

"Kimberly, Monica my baby is five months. The king is still trying to break me. Will he never give up?"

"Sister, I feel something is working all around us and the king will release us soon."

"I hope you are right."

Deirdre looked up as her son nursed. "He's a little pig, listen to him suckle."

"What is working?" asked Kimberly.

"I don't know, but I feel them."

The ship was at the dock. They had stopped at Robert's favorite inn. The men revived a bit with hot mulled wine. "The horses will be ready to go at dawn. What's for dinner?"

"Meat pies," said Robert.

"Filling," answered Thomas, and Doug grunted his agreement. They are with very little conversation, shoving pieces of the hot flaky pies into their mouths. They washed it down with the mulled wine, and were finishing off the meal with a wedge of cheddar and some crisp apples. The innkeeper then showed them a dormitory-style room beneath the eaves where the three men fell asleep instantly upon husk mattresses.

The next day they dressed and went to Percy's office. As the three men entered the office, Thomas said, "I wish to see Chancellor Percy."

The young secretary failed to recognize any of the three. When the chancellor arrived in his long, furred black velvet robe, he was immediately surrounded by the three men and taken to his private rooms.

Unafraid, Lord Percy settled himself comfortably at his desk and said to the anxious secretary, "I am not to be disturbed, Master White." The secretary bowed out, and Percy turned to his three visitors. He eyed them dispassionately, and then spoke. "My Laird MacDonald, I distinctly remember forbidding you to enter London."

"I have come to take my wife and child home, My Lord. You have had Laird Deirdre here for eight months and I've not yet been informed of the charges against her?"

"She is under suspicion, My Laird."

"For eight months? And for what?"

"Piracy," was the cool reply.

"What! You're mad, man!"

"Thomas, Thomas!" Robert spoke. "Percy, my friend, be reasonable. Laird Deirdre is a beautiful woman who, I've no doubt, has stolen many hearts. But ships? I think not. Proof?"

Laird Macdonald stood up. "Chancellor Percy, may I ask where is the motive? Where is Laird Deirdre's motive? My wife is the wealthiest women in Scotland and possibly the wealthiest in most of England. Everyone knows her to be generous and charitable. She is not a seeker of thrills. So why would she risk her children's inheritance, and her own position, by breaking the king's law? And above all things, my dear Percy, Deirdre is a good mother."

"No... there are no grounds for your suspicions, nor justification for holding her. None besides William of Orange's jealous spite and you know it, Percy." Robert peered deep into Percy's steel eyes.

Percy looked both annoyed and uncomfortable. "The piracy ceased with Laird Deirdre's arrest," he said.

Laird Thomas' look was as black as a storm cloud, but Robert put a steady hand on him. "The piracy stopped over a year ago, more than six months before you arrested Laird Deirdre."

"The Santa Maris was taken off Ireland late last spring!"

"But not by Laird Deirdre," replied Robert, "for she was but newly married and on her second honeymoon. The Spaniard was taken by Arabic pirates and we have the proof. Percy, this giant who's accompanied Laird Thomas and me, is Doug O'Brian."

Percy began to look interested.

"Well, over a month ago, O'Brian found a ghost ship floating off his island. Naturally he claimed it for salvage."

"Oh, naturally," murmured Percy.

Everyone ignored the sarcasm and he continued with his story. "When O'Brian opened the hold of the ship and saw the treasure, he realized the implications at once. He went immediately to Laird Thomas, and Thomas sent for me. The ship's log is in Arabic, of which I have some small knowledge. There is a list of all the items." He pulled a velvet bag from his doublet and opening it, poured a stream of uncut green emeralds on Percy's desk.

The chancellor gaped open mouthed at the flashing blue-green fire that lay before him. For a moment, the silence was thick, and then Percy found his voice. "Where is the crew of his ship, My Lord O'Brian? You can hardly expect me to believe this fairy tale of an empty ship floating conveniently off your island."

"The crew of the Santa Maris is still aboard her — in various stages of decomposition," replied Doug. "I would have buried the poor bastards, but Robert said you would not believe us unless you saw them, and I can see that he was right." He shook his head, disappointed in human nature.

"Where is this ship?" Percy croaked.

"The Santa Maris, it's out in the Pool. She has been towed in from the outer waters.

"The log says nothing on how the crew died."

Percy was incredulous. "Do you mean there's a ship of dead men in the Pool? Christ's bones! They might be caring the plague! Are you mad?"

"They didn't die of the plague," stated Robert calmly. "More likely a passing sickness brought aboard by some shipwreck victims they rescued."

"A ship of rotting bodies? Here in London?"

"You were ready to disbelieve me without the bodies, Percy. I've brought the log along, too. You may be able to find someone here in London who can speak Arabic and read it, and thus collaborate our story."

Percy looked sourly at the three men, determined to find someone who could read Arabic. Yet, he knew that if Robert, the old sea captain, seemed this confident, he must be sure of his story. Percy still did not trust these men. But it seemed too convenient of a tale.

"We'll take you to the Pool ourselves, Percy," said Laird Thomas. "Now, perhaps you'll give me back my wife and my child. By the way, do I have a son or a daughter?"

"A son, I believe," said Percy abruptly. "I'll have to inform the king about this new turn of interesting events. We'll go aboard the Santa Maris to inspect her. Where are you staying?"

"A son!" Thomas exulted, feeling no disappointment at all. "I have a son, a little laddie!"

"We are at Shady Oaks," said Robert. "Deirdre's small residence next to the Gram House," said the old white-haired Robert. "Deirdre's small residence, we felt was a bit more discreet."

Percy nodded, glad they had considered that.

"I wish to see my wife and my son," said Thomas.

"In time, My Laird, in time. In the king's own good time."

"For God's sake, Percy have you no pity in you?"

"My Laird! You're forbidden in London, and yet you are here. You're in no position to ask me for anything. Wait on my word on this matter at Shady Oaks and be thankful that I haven't ordered your arrest. And, please, avoid being seen. Master White!"

The secretary nearly fell through the door.

"Master White, show these gentlemen out through my private entrance."

They were dismissed and Percy was once more in control of the situation.

Robert could see that Thomas wanted to argue. He looked to O'Brian, and Doug clamped a firm hand on Laird Thomas' shoulder. "Come on, man," said Doug gently, Thomas sighed. It was an angry, frustrated sigh, but he nodded and followed Robert out of Percy's closet.

In the west tower, Deirdre had awaked with a sense of hopeless futility. She relieved herself in the chamber pot which was behind a screen, and then picked up little Robert, and changed his wet napkin. Climbing back into bed with her son, Deirdre put him to her breast. They would question her again today as they had done for months now and she would fight them again, and would again ask for a list of the charges against her. Robert sucked noisily, smacking his little lips with pleasure, and Deirdre smiled down at the baby. Gently she rubbed the little head with its silky red curls. It was just yesterday they had threatened to take the baby away from her. No one really knew how frightened she was except her wonderful sisters. *God bless them giving up their freedom to be with me,* she thought.

She was the king's prisoner, and helpless if William of Orange chose to assault her. The baby hiccupped, Deirdre patted his small back. *I will not be beaten*, she thought. *I won't!*

At Shady Oaks, Laird Thomas paced helplessly. Outside, the rain drizzled softly, and wind blew while the pale gray dripped into the darker gray river. Along the river banks the blanched yellow willows had begun to send forth their green leaves, but the rain showed no sign of letting up. The rain and trees reminded Thomas of his three wonderful children asking, "Will you bring our mother home, Father? Promise us you will!" And he had looked down into their little faces, and he had promised.

Down river in the Pool, Laird Percy learned weakly over the Santa Maris's rail, vomiting the entire content of his belly into the rolling dark green waters. Next to him, and just as sick, was the Spanish ambassador's second secretary, a Christian from Algiers. He had corroborated the story told Percy by Thomas, O'Brian, and the old sea captain, Robert. It was all in the log and on board the ship. The sight greeting the men had been hideous, a vision none would ever be able to forget. Bodies were rotting, scraps of cloth and flesh still clinging to the skeletons. The smell alone would kill you!

Chapter 34

A sympathetic Captain Robert Brown handed Percy a basin to spit in. "Percy, take another sip of this good wine. I can assure you, it will stay down, eventually." Percy swallowed again, and although his stomach rolled rebelliously, the wine remained where it was. Heat began to seep back into his body.

"Well," said Captain Brown. "You have seen the evidence with your own eyes, Me Lord, and the Spaniard confirmed the log entry. Will you release Laird Deirdre?

"Yes," said Percy weakly. "It would appear that we have made . . . an unfortunate mistake."

"When?" Captain's Brown's voice was quite sharp.

"In a few days, Captain. I must tell the king and then, of course, His Majesty must sign the release for Laird Deirdre."

"You'll let Laird Thomas Macdonald see his wife and child?"

The wine had given Percy courage enough to decline. "No," he said firmly. "Laird MacDonald was forbidden to leave Sea Oaks. The king is not to know he's even been here, for it would anger him to learn the he disobeyed him. I will tell him that I have sent for him to come up to London and escort his family home, knowing His Majesty would want it so. That way, when we release Laird Deirdre, her husband's appearance will not offend the king."

In the king's chamber, he had dismissed his man servants and waited for the queen's head lady in waiting. He opened his robe to admire his manly figure. A soft knock came upon the door. "Come," King William spoke, closing his robe.

"Your Majesty sent for me?" Lady Jane spoke with fright in her eyes.

"Yes, but don't look so frightened, My Lady. I'm not going to eat you. . . yet!!"

The King of England caught her by the hand, and then kissed it, as he pulled her toward him. Angrily he bent her backward and kissed her. It was a brutal kiss — a cruel kiss of such intense love-hate that Jane shivered with fright. "I want you, Deirdre," the king muttered furiously, "and I mean to have you!" He yanked Jane beneath him and straddling her, pushed her shirts up, exposing her long, slender legs with their black silk stockings, gold lace garters and milk-white thighs.

"Your Majesty, please!" she protested, as he fumbled with his own robe. "I'm not Laird Deirdre, are you going to rape me?"

"Yes, Jane, I'm going rape you! You've played your teasing game with me once too often."

"You said Laird Deirdre's name, may I ask why? You called out her name."

Just then, there was a knock on the door. "Majesty, its High Chancellor Percy. He says it is urgent."

"We will receive him!" The king cried out, laughing at the frightened look on Lady Jane's face.

The door opened, and the king's man servant said, "Chancellor Percy, Your Majesty."

"Majesty," Percy bowed as he looked in the corner where Lady Jane stood, wrapped in torn clothing. "I regret disturbing your leisure, but I have received important information in the matter of Laird Deirdre."

"She has confessed?" William looked eager.

"No, Sir. It would appear that she is not guilty at all. The evidence presented to me is irrefutable. Captain Robert Brown, Doug O'Brian, and the Laird of Sea Oaks, came from Jura to present it."

"And what is this evidence?"

His chancellor told the story simply but thoroughly. "Their story would appear to be a logical explanation of the pirating of King Phillip's treasure ship, especially since much of the treasure was on this ship. Since no evidence can be found against Laird Deirdre, and believing that you will want to release her now, I have sent for Laird Thomas MacDonald."

"You take a great deal upon yourself, Percy. You think I should release her, don't you, Percy?"

"Yes, Majesty, I do. It is only just, and you have always been justice's champion."

"Do you truly not think she is guilty?"

"No, Sir. I did once, but no longer. How can I, in the face of such overwhelming evidence? Captain Robert said he could understand my suspicion given the circumstance and the MacDarroch history, but Laird MacDonald could not see my point at all." Percy shrugged, "These Scots and Irish are such volatile children."

"Very well, Percy. Write the order for Laird Deirdre's release into the custody of her husband. She is not to be freed until he arrives to claim her. You may tell her today, though."

"Sir, once again your generous nature has served you well. I am proud of you," the king bridled with pleasure.

"I am feeling gay, once again," he said. "Come Jane, Percy will take you to your room. I feel like riding now." He smiled at his old friend who knew him so well.

Late that afternoon, Deirdre was startled with surprise when Chancellor Percy was ushered into her room. He was enchanted by the sight before him. Laird Deirdre, her hair loose about her shoulders, sat on the floor playing with her son. The little lad lay on his back, kicking his little feet and legs, cooing softly. "Good afternoon, My Laird," said Percy. "I bring good news."

Deirdre scrambled to her feet. "Kimberly, take the baby." Kimberly picked up little Robert and hurried from the room. Deirdre smoothed her shirts. Pouring two goblets of wine, she offered one to Percy. "Sit down, My Lord," she motioned him to a seat, "and tell me your good news."

"You're free, My Laird."

Her beautiful cat-green eyes grew with surprise, then dark with suspicion. "Just like that, My Lord? 'You're free'?" She could feel her temper rising. They had snatched her from her husband and family, endangered her unborn child, imprisoned her without charges, and now they calmly said, 'You're free.' Deirdre fixed her gaze steadily on Percy. "I'm free to go home?"

"In a few days. The release is now being drawn up, and the king will sign it tomorrow. Your husband will be allowed into London to escort you home to Sea Oaks."

"Perhaps you will tell me why I have spent the best part of eight months here? Asked Deirdre.

A wry smile touched Percy's lips, and his eyes twinkled for a moment. "Deirdre MacDonald," he said quietly. "We both know the truth of why you are here, though you'd not admit to it and I don't have the evidence I need to prove it. Over the last two years you have cost William of Orange considerable revenues with your piracy. When we set out to trap you with the Santa Maris, I thought we would be in time to catch you with the booty. I was wrong. You are well organized and a frighteningly intelligent and bold woman."

"Your husband, Captain Robert, and the Lord of Colonsay Isle have gone to enormous length to present me with evidence supporting your innocence. I am accepting their story and freeing you, but hear me well, My Lady. You have seen that a royal whim can imprison you without explanation. Should there be further trouble in the king's land, we shall know where to find you. The next time, nothing will free you. I think the king has paid dearly for his appalling error in judgment.

Not a muscle in Deirdre's face moved during his speech, nor did her eyes betray her. Percy was very much impressed. She was truly a worthy and impressive adversary. "Well, madam, what have you to say to me?" he demanded.

"That I'm glad to be going home, Master Percy," Deirdre answered calmly. "That I will be happy to see my husband. And that," she added mischievously, "if you can find no proof of my alleged crimes, then I must be judged the innocent that I am."

Percy drained his goblet. "I suppose you must," he answered thoughtfully. He rose and moved to the door. "It was a good revenge, madam, well organized, well thought out, and very well-executed. I salute you, My Laird."

Deirdre flashed him an impudent smile, silently acknowledging the praise. But she said, "Sir! I don't know what you mean."

The door closed behind Percy and, for a brief moment, Deirdre stood very still, listening to his footsteps retreating down the stairs. Elation began to build. She has won! She had beaten the King of England! Then she began to shudder, the tension of the last few months started to release in the tears that poured down her face.

The door from the bedchamber opened and Kimberly and Monica both hurried in. "Deirdre!" Kimberly flew to her sister's side. "Deirdre, my love, what is it? What did Percy want? Are you alright? Damn the English anyhow!"

Monica was shocked by Kimberly's cursing. The look on Monica's face moved Deirdre from tears to laughter. "We're free," she laughed. "Sisters, we're going home! I've beaten the king!"

"Is it's a trick?" asked Kimberly.

"No, there is no evidence against me, and Robert and Doug with Tommy had somehow managed to convince Percy that I'm not guilty.

"I'd be interested in knowing just what it was," said Kimberly.

"So would I, my sister," returned Deirdre, now much calmer and more thoughtful. They did not have long to wait.

The following day, Sir Alex brought Deirdre the signed order for her release. Sir Alex handed it to her. "You are to pack and go tonight, Laird Deirdre. You are not to be seen leaving the tower."

"I don't wish to take anything but my sisters and baby."

"You'll go by river barge to your home under the cover of darkness. Your husband is waiting there for you. You are ordered to be out of London by tomorrow night."

"Thank you, Governor, and my thanks to you and your wonderful wife for making my journey as pleasant as it could be."

The tower governor smiled good-naturedly. "I'm not often thanked for my hospitality," he said humorously. Then he took her hand and raised it to his lips. "Godspeed, Laird Deirdre."

In the dark of a misty evening, three robed muffled figures made their way from the dark tower through the river's gate and onto a waiting barge. A guard on the walls thought he heard a baby's cry in the darkness. Deirdre and Kimberly breathed deeply of the saturated air which carried a scent of the sea and then, laughing softly smiled at one another. Monica felt the barge cut smoothly through the black water. Peeping through the curtains which were as black as the dark water to ascertain their position, they spied a quick glimpse of the city of London.

Soon the elegant palaces and houses of the Oak bend were visible. Deirdre felt her heart quicken as the barge swept by them all and swung around the bend to make for Oaks landing. The house stood dark next door, only a few lights shone at Oakwood.

The barge bumped the landing, and the guardsman accompanying them leaped out to secure the craft. Then he helped the passengers to the dock, starting with Kimberly, to whom Monica handed the baby. Deirdre and lastly the faithful serving women stepped out. The guardsmen jumped back down into the barge, lassoed its rope and the boat swung back into the current and headed down river.

They just stood in the windy night, looking around. "There is no one here to meet us." whispered Monica. "I wonder why!"

"I have no idea," replied Deirdre, "but the lights are on in the house." Deirdre moved determinedly up the steps from the boat quarry toward the house. Kimberly, with Robert cradled in her arms, followed her sister. Monica struggled behind with little Robert. The glass doors of the library glowed with the reflections of firelight as she put her hand on the door handles and pushed them open.

Laird Tommy turned, startled, as the wet night wind rushed into the room. Tommy just stared at her as though he could not believe she was before him. He found his voice and gasped, "Kitten!"

"Aye, My Laird. I'm home, and a poor welcome it is with no one to meet us at the dock."

"We didn't know you were coming! Doug! Robert! Deirdre is home!"

The library door crashed open, and Doug and Captain Robert rushed into the room. The Laird of Colonsay stopped just short of kissing her, his smoky eyes meeting her car green graze, saying all the things he dared not say aloud.

"I don't know how you did it, Doug, but thank you," she said softly. Doug O'Brian nodded mutely, and Deirdre turned quickly to Captain Robert Brown.

"My dear, thank you also. I am certainly blessed in my friends."

The little white-haired captain wiped tears from his eyes. "No more of your mischievous ways, lass. We may not be so lucky next time."

"So Percy told me," she said drily. Monica, give me little Robert." Gently taking the sleeping infant, Deirdre walked across the room to where Tommy stood. "My Laird, may I present you with your son, Robert. He is five months old." She turned and looked at her old friend. "Captain Robert, you may come and meet your namesake."

Robert had a smile on his face as he walked over to look the happy little lad. "Young lad, I hope you get more hair!"

Everyone laughed at the remark. Captain Robert tried not to cry, but when the baby grabbed hold of his finger, the tears rolled down his cheeks. Captain Robert smiled as he gave Tommy the bundle of joy. Wondering, Tommy lifted the blanket and gazed for the first time on his sleeping son. "God, he said softly, "he's so big! And he's so handsome."

"Big?" snapped Kimberly. "He's most certainly not big! He was little when he was born. He's just right and we bless him growing every day." She snatched the baby back from Tommy. "I trust there's a cradle in the house, sir?"

"Maude is here, Kimberly, she will show you."

Kimberly looked to the two men. "Come along, you two great buffoons," she snapped. "Laird Tommy will not kiss her until we've gone," and she rushed them out of the room.

Laird Tommy looked down at his wife. "Oh, my Kitten," he said softly, his voice trembling. "I have missed you so much. I never thought it possible to miss you again. This makes three times you have been taken from me, Kitten."

"Never again, Tommy. Only God can part us now. I promise you!"

"No, that's a promise we will have to keep, my love," he said and then took her in his arms kissing her passionately. Their lips explored the familiar so long denied. It was like an explosive wave of fire that all of London could see. Deirdre clung to him. His fingers tenderly caressed her unturned face. He gently brushed away tears that were slipping slowly down her cheeks.

"You will never again go away from me," he said again. "I will give you your head in many things, but not in all matters, Kitten. You're too headstrong for your own good. You could have lost your head, but for a little of luck and Doug O'Brian's clever thinking. He loves you a great deal, my love. It's almost too painful to behold. And the Captain, you're the lass he has never had, Deirdre, and you hurt him terribly. He thought we had lost you. I don't think he would have survived you by very long."

"It's over, Tommy. I swear it!"

He held out his hand to her and she eagerly took it, delighting as his warm fingers closed around hers in the lovely and familiar sensation. Together they ran upstairs to Deirdre's old bedchamber overlooking the river. As they removed their clothing, memories started crowding around them. As the two lovers met, the hot flames from the past were once again ignited.

Deirdre heard horse hooves below. "Who is that?"

"It looks like Hugh and Richard, with the carriage and horses."

"You mean he brought Thunder?"

"Yes."

"You are a darling, thank you." Deirdre hugged him close.

"That's not safe," he laughed as he kissed her madly and hugged her close to him.

The next morning the luggage was packed in the coach, along with Maude and baby. Wine bottles were filled and secured. An open large woven wicker basket was carefully fitted into an iron rack attached just three inches above the seat in the center. Lined in silk with a small down mattress, it would shortly hold Sir Robert MacDonald. Betty, a maid Deirdre liked, decided she would love to live in Scotland.

"Should we draw the curtains?" asked Betty.

"Please do," Maude answered. "I want no more of London."

Deirdre saw Hugh hug Kimberly and whisper something in her ear. Kimberly shouted in glee. She hugged Hugh in such a loving way.

"You two, what's going on?" Deirdre smiled lovingly at them.

Everyone was riding their horses instead of riding in the coach. Thunder pranced along, happy to have his master on his back.

"Did you hear me?" she shouted.

"Yes, we did, we're going to China," shouted Kimberly back.

"What?"

"Didn't you hear me? China!"

"No, I couldn't hear," she said, riding hard to try to catch them, "China... did you say China?!!"

When they arrived home they were overjoyed at the sheer thought. They were home at last. All of them were safe and sound. All of them got a well-deserved rest after their journey. All the family was once again together. For now, that is.

Kimberly and Hugh were laying goods on the ship that would take them to China. It was time for them to leave.

Deirdre took her children to the big oak tree to have a picnic. Maude, with her sister, came down to care for the baby. They carried a basket of food and a blanket for all of them to sit on. Deirdre fed the baby and watched the other three as they played with their father. She smiled, life was good.

She looked past the entire happy scene and at the ships as they were loading up for the trip to China. She started to cry softly. Everyone had said goodbyes earlier in the day. Kimberly and Hugh were now on the ship that would take them to China and away from the family... and her.

Deirdre stood up, as tall as she could, and waved goodbye. "Godspeed, be safe, watch yourself, but most of all, watch the Emperor.